ALSO BY JAIMA FIXSEN

The Specimen

PRAISE FOR *DON'T LOOK CLOSE*

"Dark, atmospheric, and edged with menace, *Don't Look Close* is unsettlingly intimate. Its simmering tensions and richly drawn characters create suspense that's absorbing and inescapable, while the twists land with quiet, chilling force. I read it with the dread of watching a friend walk into a trap. This is a smart, deeply unnerving thriller I won't soon forget."

—**Rebecca Zanetti,** *New York Times* bestselling author of *You Can Run*

"This intricately woven, superbly plotted suspense will keep you on your toes... Exploring medical ethics, prejudice, and the power imbalance between men and women, *Don't Look Close* is a riveting read with serpentine twists that strike when you least expect them."

—**Samantha M. Bailey,** *USA Today* and #1 international bestselling author of *Hello, Juliet*

"A chilling, atmospheric masterclass in historical suspense... *Don't Look Close* pulls readers into a suffocating web of secrets and betrayal where the shadows are as dangerous as the mountains themselves. A sharp, propulsive thriller that proves the past is never truly buried."

—**Rea Frey,** #1 bestselling author of *When She's Gone*

"*Don't Look Close* takes a pair of unlikely protagonists and drops them into the dark valley of a small town, where friendliness is the norm until a shadow of danger envelops them all."

—**Lisa Black,** *New York Times* bestselling author of the Gardiner & Renner series

"*Don't Look Close* is a well-drawn story of a brother's determination to save his sister and to stop a killer!"

—**Debra Webb,** *USA Today* bestselling author

"I was completely hooked from the start. Fixsen crafts unforgettable characters and puts them in situations that are frighteningly real."

—**Jonathan Whitelaw,** author of *The Bingo Hall Detectives*

"A gripping and very well-crafted mystery... Believable characters and a nicely twisted plot make for terrific entertainment."

—**Martin Edwards,** author of *Miss Winter in the Library with a Knife*

"A roller-coaster ride of a mystery... Fixsen's well-drawn characters had me invested until the very end. A knockout read!"

—**Terri Parlato,** author of *She Thought She Was Safe*

PRAISE FOR *THE SPECIMEN*

"An absorbing and expanding mystery...ripe for a book club discussion."

—*First Clue*

"Propulsive and lush, Fixsen weaves an exquisitely gothic tale."

—**Jess Armstrong,** *USA Today* bestselling author of *The Curse of Penryth Hall*

"*The Specimen* is a fantastic read! Tense, gripping, and full of fabulous characters you grow to love or hate! I devoured it in two sittings."

—**Gareth Brown,** bestselling author of *The Book of Doors*

"A haunting tale of secrets, sacrifice, and obsession. This is a brilliant story that delves into the darkest corners of the human soul, where the quest for knowledge collides with the primal instinct to protect what matters most."

—**Kim Taylor Blakemore,** author of *After Alice Fell* and *The Companion*

"A dark delight! Jaima Fixsen has crafted a dynamic cast of characters with real heart and set them against a riveting backdrop of science, witchcraft, and scandal. I couldn't put this book down!"

—**Emily Ruth Verona,** author of *Midnight on Beacon Street*

"*The Specimen* offers a fascinating glimpse into the shadowy world of nineteenth-century medicine, full of historical detail. A vivid and atmospheric read!"

—**Ritu Mukerji,** author of *Murder by Degrees*

"Part gothic horror, part detective tale, Fixsen's smart narrative peels back the surface of respectable doctors seeking knowledge from anatomical studies to reveal an underbelly of theft, murder, and questionable medical collections, sending the reader along the path of the woman at its center, Isobel Tait, who determined to reveal the truth and seek vengeance, both for herself and for the innocent victims... A compelling gem of a novel!"

—**Amiee Gibbs,** author of *The Carnivale of Curiosities*

"Fixsen's ghost story is the most haunting of all: a tale of the real-life evil that shapes our world and the heroines who dare name these men monsters. With a meticulous hand, Fixsen conjures Edinburgh and its history of music, immigration, murder, ghosts, and above all, love."

—**J.R. Dawson,** author of *The First Bright Thing*

DON'T LOOK CLOSE

A NOVEL

JAIMA FIXSEN

Poisoned Pen
PRESS

Published by Poisoned Pen Press, an imprint of Sourcebooks
1935 Brookdale RD, Naperville, IL 60563-2773
(630) 9613900
sourcebooks.com

Cataloging-in-Publication Data is on file with the Library of Congress.

Printed and bound in the United States of America
VP 10 9 8 7 6 5 4 3 2 1

For Blake

CHAPTER ONE

SATURDAY, JANUARY 22, 1955

EDIE TURNED UP THE RADIO, HUMMING ALONG, URGING THE DAY'S accumulated tension to slide off her shoulders. She turned on the tap and swirled a squirt of acid-yellow Palmolive through the water until the sink filled with suds. She needed her pills. And a bottle of beer. Couldn't have both though.

Single girl, single girl, she's going dressed fine, the woman on the radio crooned.

Edie decided on the tranquilizer, because it would put her to sleep fastest. By the time she was done with the dishes, she'd feel drowsy enough for bed.

Still humming, she two-stepped her way to the bathroom, swallowed a single tablet, drained the glass of water, then unzipped her dress as she moved farther down the hall. The full skirt and stiff crinoline would wrinkle, just dropped on the floor, so she hung both in the closet, resenting the necessity of being responsible.

Sighing, she reached for her pajamas. The worn cotton felt good on her bare skin.

Comfortably clad, free of the constrictions of bra and garters, her hair bundled off her shoulders in a ponytail, Edie returned to the kitchen and snapped on a pair of yellow gloves. She swung her hips twice in time with the music and pushed her hands into the sink full of suds. Scrub brush in hand, she attacked the lone dinner plate hiding in the hot water.

As she rinsed the plate, the back door rattled. Edie jumped, dropping the plate with a splash and a clatter. She spun away from the sink, one hand flying instinctively to her chest, while the other brandished the long-handled scrubber like a sword, dripping lather onto the floor.

A barrage of percussive taps assaulted the back door. "Edie? I know you're in there."

The voice was familiar, and the hand at her chest tightened.

What the hell is Jack doing here?

Edie swallowed and lowered the scrubber, but the death grip on the front of her pajamas didn't loosen. "I don't have to answer," she called. Why wouldn't he just go away?

"I rang at the front. You didn't hear. Turn off the radio," he demanded.

"Why are you here?"

A pause. She could almost see him collecting his patience by closing his eyes. "Can't I just come inside?"

He said it so reasonably.

"I'm not dressed."

"Edie."

Goaded by a growing feeling of ridiculousness, she shuffled out of the kitchen, flicked on another light, and unlocked the back door.

"You scared the life out of me," she muttered.

His eyes took in the wet spots on her pajamas, the scrub brush still in her hand.

"Not quite," Jack said, edging his thick wool overcoat and cashmere scarf away from the sudsy bristles.

Annoyed, Edie jabbed the brush at his lapel. "Get it dry-cleaned." Turning on her heel, she stomped back to the kitchen. He followed, brushing his wool tweed, but not saying anything, so Edie returned to the sink, tossing her next words over her shoulder. "We're divorced. You shouldn't come here."

"Why do you automatically think I'm here for you?"

She glared at him over her shoulder.

"I could have clients out here," he shrugged.

She snorted. Biting the inside of her lip, she rinsed her plate, her fork, her glass, and set them on a dish towel to dry. She did not offer water or coffee, though it felt like Jack was waiting for it.

Instead, she unplugged the sink drain and reached across the counter to switch off the radio, strangling the singer mid-syllable. The tunes weren't easing the weight in her arms anymore. And she was tired...probably the tranquilizer kicking in.

"I came by earlier, but you weren't home," Jack said in the silence. "I even tried your office."

"Clinic," she corrected, heart thudding. *It's fine,* she told herself. *Nothing to see. We were closed today.*

She turned to face him, folding her arms across her chest. "I had the day off," she told him. "Visited my brother in the hospital."

No way to tell from his expression if he believed her.

"How is he?"

Edie shrugged, her throat tightening. "About the same."

"I only stopped by to ask if you had my grandmother's crystal," Jack said quietly. "The brandy decanter. You remember it?"

Edie remembered the set. Art Deco, gifted from Jack's grandmother to his mother and passed to her on her first wedding anniversary. "I don't have it."

She'd hardly taken anything from their house. Hadn't wanted to. Having their things here would be like having him here, and the sight of him, annoyed, in her kitchen, was giving her chills.

"Check the attic," she said.

"Already did."

She turned her back to him again, pretending a calm she didn't feel as she wiped the sink dry. "Unless there's anything else..."

She heard his chair scrape against the lino. No footsteps, but she sensed him moving close behind her, not toward the door, though there was no other sound, no stirring in the air. And she'd have felt the slightest tremor, what with every hair prickling on the back of her neck.

"Edie."

He was closer than she'd thought, his breath sliding over her shoulder.

She stiffened. "Don't—"

He pressed a thumb to her skin on the slope where neck met shoulder, just above her pajama collar.

"You lied to me."

Her hands tightened on the dish cloth. Resolutely, she lifted it and wrung it out. "I don't have your damn decanter. Go ahead and look."

"I'm not talking about that—now," he said calmly and lifted his thumb away, leaving behind a patch of burning skin. "You said, when we divorced, that you couldn't imagine yourself with anyone else."

"I don't," Edie said reflexively, tensing again.

"I wonder," Jack said.

She heard his shoes moving away, and the trip wire tied around her heart loosened enough for her to turn around and follow him through the front hall, where he stopped, pausing at the door.

She hadn't switched on the light in the hall, so it was too dim to read his face. Jack had so many different kinds of smiles, and in these shadows, she couldn't classify his expression or predict what might be coming next. But then, she'd never really known, had she? He always kept her guessing.

Jack put on his hat, then unbolted the front door. "Have a good evening, Edie."

Unbidden words floated past her lips before she could stop them.

Polite nothings, passed without thinking, day after day between husband and wife. "Good night, Jack."

The door closed behind him. Edie bolted it, then collapsed on the couch, reminding herself for the hundredth—or even the thousandth—time that Jack Gainsford wasn't her husband. Not anymore.

She shouldn't have let him in, but it was always more difficult, not letting him have his way. Heat suffused her throat, pushing tears out the corners of her eyes. The game was supposed to be over, now that they were divorced, now that she'd moved out here.

Have a good evening? What did he mean?

And that touch.

Edie stalked to the bathroom and tugged away the pajama top, twisting before the mirror, trying for a glimpse of the spot.

Her eyes widened. There was a mark, resting low on the back of her neck. A love bite, one she must have gotten two days ago, and though she remembered the kiss that must have left it there, she couldn't feel it now.

Not like Jack's thumbprint, which might as well have been stamped onto her skin in corrosive ink.

Edie bit her lip. Her marriage to Jack hadn't been long, not really. Five years, but that was ample time to know she was in trouble.

CHAPTER TWO

WEDNESDAY, SEPTEMBER 21, 1955
EIGHT MONTHS LATER

"It's a terrible idea, son. Be sensible."

Peter stared at the leg braces hanging on the opposite wall, visible over his father's left shoulder and impossible to ignore.

"I've decided, Dad. The doctor can't keep me." Not when he didn't want to stay. Because in spite of their protests and the invincible cheeriness of the physiotherapists, one thing was plain—he was never walking out of this hospital. The best he could hope for was leaving on his own terms.

"The doctors out there—" Walt Simmons glanced toward the nursing station and lowered his voice, something he seldom troubled to do. "Well, you know my thoughts about small towns, that one in particular. You aren't thinking it through. How will you manage?"

"I'm staying with Edie."

"Stay with us, if you want someone to take care of you. Your sister's too far away."

"Dad—"

"Or get yourself a high-rise apartment with a doorman, no stairs. In a city, there's plenty of places to enjoy from a wheelchair. Half the streets in Clairbeck are gravel."

Peter swallowed a frown. Dad was probably right.

He'd deal with the gravel when he got there. Couldn't be worse than relearning stairs.

"Your mom and I looked at nearby apartments," Dad said. "There's a nice unit not too far away. You'll have a view of the river, and the building has a pool, which will help you keep up with your exercises..."

Walt was used to convincing people, and today he'd prepared quite the list. Peter stifled a sigh.

Of course, there was another place he could go, but Dad knew better than to bring that one up. Peter was not staying in the cute little bungalow he'd purchased two years ago, before he got polio. The house still had the curtains he'd picked out with Ginny. Yesterday, he'd spoken to a realtor about selling it.

"How was the wedding?" Peter made himself ask.

Walt patted his jacket pockets, searching for his pipe. "Your mother and I didn't go."

"I thought Mom—"

"Yeah, I thought so too. Ginny did try to persuade her, but with you still here..." Walt gave up the search and leaned back in the chair, hands empty. "Well, you weren't going, so why the hell would I? I hate those things."

"I don't know." Peter rubbed circles into his right temple. Didn't help much. "Mom just kept telling me it was important to make the best of a bad situation." According to her, not going to the wedding was more awkward than showing up with a brave face. Besides, Steven was a good man, and Ginny had every right to be happy.

Peter dropped his hand, resting it on the arm of his wheelchair. Yes, Ginny deserved happiness, but it was hard to give up the idea that, if not for his illness, she might have been happy with him.

"So why didn't Mom go?" Peter asked. "You'd think after all the pep talks she gave me—" He broke off. No point going over that again. "She didn't want to at least get her money's worth from the new dress?"

She'd bought one for Ginny's wedding, back when Peter was the groom.

Walt snorted. "Probably won't wear it until you find someone else."

"Jesus, Dad." Peter looked away. The sun was too bright outside. Usually by now, one of the nurses adjusted the blinds to keep the room from overheating.

Walt rearranged his limbs, uncomfortable in the hospital's narrow bedside chair. "Dumb idea. Sorry. There's probably some rule against that. Bad manners to reuse 'em."

"I think that only applies to engagement rings. Mom's wardrobe should be exempt," Peter said dryly. "Tell her to wear it. Don't wait for me."

Walt lit his pipe carefully. "You don't know what's in your future."

"Not a wedding," Peter retorted and pressed his lips together. This morning he'd stared at his body before concealing it with socks and trousers, a brown camp shirt, and the sweater vest Edie'd knitted while visiting him in hospital.

It took hope and confidence to bother knitting clothes for someone in an iron lung, and he could use some of that confidence right about now. Also, the sweater she'd made gave him more bulk on top, and loose trousers made him look less wasted, though baggy khakis could only do so much.

Time to accept that. He should be grateful to be alive, to have regained the use of his arms and enough leg movement to be able to manage, some of the time, on crutches and braces. Not everyone did. Most of the time though, he didn't feel so lucky.

"I worry about you." Walt stood up and adjusted the blinds, peering down to the courtyard. At this time of the morning, it would be filled with other polio patients taking in the sunshine and getting used to new braces or forearm crutches. "You sure about this?"

Dad wasn't talking about some eventual bride now, but he was still probably talking about a hypothetical future, where the impact of his son's polio was exercised into submission. A nice picture, but an impossible one.

Peter pasted on a smile and looked his dad square in the eyes. "I'm sure. Staying in Calgary won't help me recover any faster. I'll do better away from here for a while. Close to the mountains."

His father's mouth softened. "Always loved them, haven't you? Maybe they're what you need."

Peter nodded. "I think so." For Dad's sake, it didn't hurt to pretend.

Walt left the hospital soon after, with injunctions that Peter let his parents pack for him tomorrow, before driving him the hour or so west, to Clairbeck, the mountain town where his sister Edie lived.

Peter smiled, but never actually agreed. His clothes were packed, the cupboard assigned to him emptied, his camera and typewriter strapped inside his suitcase.

Edie'd brought both from his unwanted, unusable house months ago, and though the nurses had encouraged Peter with both, the work he'd attempted was utterly dispiriting. Poorly composed snaps of hospital corridors and therapy pools were so unlike his usual subject matter he hadn't dared show the hospital staff his previous work.

So, Edie'd brought some of that in, after they pinned his snaps onto the ward's bulletin board with chirpy, extravagant praise.

"Peter's a serious photographer," she told them, holding out a folder with pictures of dizzying peaks, of a fellow climber grappling a cliff face, halfway up a grade VI ascent. After the hospital staff finished looking, Peter told her to chuck them. Probably hadn't, but at least she took them away.

Time to get moving. Peter stared at his crutches, grimaced, and decided not to chance them today, even though he preferred them to the wheelchair.

Not that there was anything wrong with it. He didn't lose control on ramps or get stuck in doors anymore, and he'd listened to plenty of encouraging testimonials from chairbound war veterans claiming to be happy, successful, and fulfilled after wheeling themselves around for ten or more years.

Peter had been in his teens when the war ended, had never imagined a future as a cripple. When he was climbing mountains, death was always more likely than any kind of broken survival.

And that's what this was. Not only was he helpless without a chair or crutches, he needed to conserve energy, because he woke each day with only so much, and it was much, much less than he'd been used to.

Grimacing, Peter maneuvered his wheelchair out the door and down the long hallway. He was sick of antiseptic smells, and a world done up in gray and salmon pink.

The nurse's station wasn't far, but he'd have to get in and out of Edie's car today, manage the six stairs to get inside her bungalow, negotiate her kitchen and the poky little bathroom...

By the time he went to bed tonight, he'd be exhausted.

"Hiya, handsome."

"Morning, Jean." Peter's frown melted into a grin for the nurse peering at him over the desk.

"It's afternoon now, though only just."

Peter glanced at his watch and saw she was right—the time showed ten past twelve—and passed the mistake off with a laugh. "Time stands still when my dad's here."

She huffed. "You haven't told him, have you?"

"Are you kidding? They'd nab me as soon as I put a foot outside the door."

"There's worse things," she said, tapping her pencil against pink-tinted lips. As usual, her nails were painted to match. "I'm sorry to see you go. Not all our guys are so pleasant."

"I'll miss you too," he said, with smitten eyes and a hand on his heart. Jean laughed, but it was true. He really would. He'd lived in this hospital for ages, and this particular ward since he'd come out of the iron lung twenty-one months ago.

"You want me to ring Edie for you?" Jean asked.

"You betcha."

"What's the magic word?" Jean gave him her best teasing smile. A kindness, one he enjoyed but never mistook, always aware of the blindingly bright diamond flashing on her ring finger since Christmas.

"Pretty please?"

"Here you go." She passed him the telephone. "I'll give you some privacy." Picking up a clipboard, she sashayed away from the desk.

Peter watched her progress, and the much slower, halting steps of another patient in newly fitted leg braces and a contraption to support his spine.

At least he'd recovered enough to lose that one. Flashing the patient a thumbs-up, he tucked the phone against his shoulder and listened to its trill.

Finally, the line connected. "Edie?"

"Oh my God. Peter."

"What's wrong?" His hand tightened on the receiver. There was panic in her voice and the pressure of unshed tears. Edie'd been fine since her divorce, since moving to Clairbeck, but… "What's happened?" he demanded.

"It's Jack."

"What's he done?" At the mention of her ex-husband, Peter forgot he was stuck in his chair and tried to surge to his feet. Then he remembered. And just how would he help, anyway?

"It's not—" She choked on a sob. "Jack's dead, Peter. The police found him this morning."

His chest eased, but only a little. "Here in Calgary?"

"No." Edie's uneven breaths filtered down the line. "No, he's in Clairbeck, and—" Her voice broke. "And I can't get you. The police are here and—"

"Don't worry about me," Peter said. "I'll be fine. I'll be there soon."

"Really?" For the first time, the weight in her voice lifted. "That would be—"

"Don't worry. I'm coming."

"I'll leave you a key."

"You aren't going to wait for me?" No, it would be better for her to sit with a friend, instead of being alone. "Just tell me—"

"I have to go." He could almost see her forcing down a swallow, blinking back tears. Before he could ask… "The police want me down at the station. They—you see, Jack was in my car. And—and they say someone's killed him."

Peter adjusted his grip on the phone. "Did they say who?" Surely the police didn't think… He shook his head, but the question persisted. Was Edie a *suspect*?

"I don't know anything, but I guess—they just want to talk to me."

Shit. He knew enough about his sister's marriage to understand this wasn't good. "I'll be there as fast as I can." He peered down the hallway. No sign of Jean. If he explained, would she help him with a taxi?

"Edie?"

"Yes?"

"Go with them." It didn't sound like she was being offered the choice. "But you don't have to tell them anything."

"I'm sorry. You can't do that."

Edie stopped, hand poised above the bathroom sink. "But I—" She gestured at the toilet.

Her throat was on fire. She wanted to cry. She wanted to be alone, even if just for a second.

The unsmiling woman, crowded in the bathroom with her, had just watched her pee. According to the detective in the living room, this level of supervision was standard procedure. Edie didn't believe him.

This was how you treated criminals.

The woman in the bathroom with her wasn't even a real policewoman, just the wife of one. Out here, in a town too small to have its own police force, the wife of a Mountie was what you got.

"My hands aren't clean," Edie protested.

"They'll take fingerprints at the station. And photograph your hands," the woman said.

Edie swallowed hard, like closing her throat would stop her heart from galloping out of her chest. "Am I being arrested?" Her voice cracked.

"Just questions." The woman sounded completely indifferent.

Edie blinked her eyes clear, swiped her stinging palms against her nightgown, and tied up her hair in a ponytail. Ignoring the woman, she marched into her bedroom, stripped and threw on the first clothes she saw.

Apparently, the detective was in a hurry.

"Late in the day to be getting dressed," the woman said.

"It's my day off." Edie grabbed her purse and her jacket. She always slept late after taking a sleeping pill.

Trailing her watchdog, she returned to the living room. The detective was waiting.

"Are we going now?" Edie asked.

Maybe they weren't going to bring her home again. She should have said more to Peter. Asked him to call Dad. Or a lawyer. But if this was serious, wouldn't they have to offer her one? Or give her another phone call?

Jack's dead. Of course this is serious.

Her fingers curled up, clutching the cuffs of her sweater, tugging the sleeves down over her unwashed hands. What did they think they would find on them? "Can I make another phone call?"

"No, we better get to the station." He was too tall and more interested in staring at the magazine rack by her feet than at her face.

She licked her lips. "I think I want to change my sweater." It was comfortable, but sloppy looking. And she'd been in her robe and nightgown when he arrived, still nursing her first cup of coffee. This guy wasn't going to take her seriously, not dressed like this.

"Not necessary." His smile, when it came, felt fake and cold. "No need to look nice on my account." He held out a hand, indicating she should precede him out the door.

Tell him you won't. Not before another phone call! The voice inside her rose to a shriek, but she swallowed it back. Her feet were already moving because that broad male hand was pointing her to the door.

Edie climbed into the back of the police car, throat tight, trying without visibly trying to see if any of her neighbors were watching, but she couldn't make out anything behind their windows.

The engine started, sending a tremor up her spine. Peter said to go—not that she'd been offered any choice. But just what did he think the police would do if she did as he said?

Jack came to Clairbeck far too often, to her house, to the clinic, to simply say nothing. And she'd never reported anything, not during her marriage or afterward.

There'd been nothing to report. Jack was too careful for that.

Except now he was dead. And that wasn't like the careful Jack she knew at all.

CHAPTER THREE

"You sure about this guy?" Jean asked.

The car pulling into the hospital parking lot was older than she was, with rust-spotted fenders. "Sounds like the engine has bronchitis," she said.

"I'm sure," Peter said. But he wasn't. He'd met his ride, Leo Martin, only in passing. Twice last summer, Leo had come into Calgary with Edie on her usual visiting day at the hospital. Back then, Leo had a friend on another ward, recovering from lung surgery.

Peter didn't really know Leo Martin at all, but of the forty or so phone calls to various friends and cab companies, Leo, Edie's next door neighbor, was the only one who'd said yes. In fact, he claimed he didn't mind making the drive at all, leaving Peter equally grateful and uncomfortable.

The drive was an hour each way, and it wasn't like he could ever repay the favor—he was about as useful as an unclaimed parcel. Lacking any other choices, the only thing Peter could do was take the help he'd already accepted and try not to be too much trouble.

His grip tightened on the handrims of the wheelchair. *No trouble? Yeah right.*

The car braked, coughed, and came to a stop. Peter rolled to the edge of the curb. "Hi, Leo. I really can't thank you enough for helping me out."

Leo, emerging from the driver's seat, silenced him with a wave. "Don't be silly. I'm happy to help."

He was thinner than Peter remembered, leaner than most people would imagine for a retired miner, about fiftyish, with a weathered face and untrimmed gray hair.

"Just these?" Leo asked, picking up Peter's two suitcases.

"And my wheelchair. And the crutches." Inside the braces that propped him up, he felt himself shrink.

"No problem." Leo grinned. "Get yourself comfortable, then I'll fold up the chair and stow it in the trunk."

"Careful, Peter," Jean cautioned, as he opened the car door. "I'm not letting you come back."

"Much as I enjoy your company, I don't plan to." He glanced at the hospital walls. Two years here was more than enough.

Jean grinned. "You lot have no gratitude."

She'd often watched him practice the complicated process of transferring from a wheelchair to the low seat of a car, and she stayed behind him, stretching out a hand when he wobbled.

"I got it," he said, hoping this was true. He levered into the seat—no safety belts in this car—and pulled his legs after him, glad his arms held steady.

"I'll miss you, Jean," he said. "Thanks."

"Take care of yourself. Good luck." Jean nodded approvingly at Leo's handling of the wheelchair—he knew without asking how to swing the footrests out of the way and fold it together—and added, "Looks like you should make it all right."

But as Leo stepped into the car, she called out, "Drive safely, Leo. I like this guy, and he didn't work his way out of the hospital just to end up in a ditch."

"You bet," Leo said, with a mock salute.

He restarted the engine, flicking Peter a smile. "Ready?"

Peter nodded. "I know you don't want to hear it, but I really appreciate..."

"Ah, don't worry, Peter. I'm glad of the chance to talk to you. Was hoping you could tell me what's up."

"Oh?" Peter turned so he could see Leo better, but his eyes were on the road, watching the passing cars, waiting to turn left out of the hospital parking lot.

"Yeah. Been pretty worried, actually, 'cause I know Edie meant to get you, but I saw the police come to her house this morning."

Since his sister's phone call, Peter had been preparing to back her against the police. He hadn't considered that she might have been spotted, that he'd have to contend with local curiosity too.

He shifted in his seat. "I'm not sure I should say anything."

"Saw her go away with them—oh, not in handcuffs or anything, but I figured it was for something important. And then my friend Garrett said..."

Peter licked his lips. Catching a ride with Leo had been awkward enough without the questions, and they were on their way now. He was stuck. With his crutches shut in the trunk, he was actually—not to put too fine a point on it—trapped with Leo in the car, a thought that set his palms sweating.

Which was ridiculous. The curiosity might be a tad off-putting, but Leo was a nice guy.

Still. Peter decided to keep his crutches close next time, just for his own peace of mind.

"Wait, sorry, what did you say?" He frowned, sure he hadn't heard Leo's last words right.

"Garrett says they found some dead guy in her car?"

Peter held back a grimace, startled this was common knowledge so quickly. "No, after that."

"Police think he was poisoned."

"How do they figure that?" Peter asked, ignoring the tautness of his neck muscles.

Leo shrugged. "I thought maybe you'd know."

Now just why would you think that?

Peter shook his head. "Edie was really upset. I only got a few seconds on the phone with her. I don't know anything about it." All he really knew was that he ought to be in Clairbeck with Edie.

"Is it true the dead guy's her ex-husband?" Leo asked, glancing sideways at Peter, even though the car was flying down the road.

Peter moved his head noncommittally, more alarmed at the extent of Leo's information than the speed of the car or the noise of the engine. "Edie said that's why they wanted her. Identification, maybe?"

Hopefully, this would put an end to the questions. It was a decent enough reason, and innocuous words felt necessary, a palliative against the fears that were turning him cold.

He'd been worrying about the state of affairs between Edie and her ex-husband for months—no, longer. Since before the divorce.

He'd come home because of her marriage, giving up a climbing expedition in India. One of the reasons he wanted to go to Clairbeck now was so that she wouldn't be alone.

"Guess it comes as a real shock to her," Leo said, shaking his head.

"Yeah."

When Peter didn't elaborate, Leo reached into his pocket, holding the steering wheel steady with his knees while he unwrapped a stick of gum.

"Want one?"

Peter shook his head. "Mind if I turn on the radio?"

"Oh, sure. Go right ahead."

Static, news, country music...why was he fiddling the dial, searching for a different station? Peter didn't care what was playing. He only wanted space to think, hiding behind some noise.

Outside of Calgary, the road pointed straight west, rolling over a series of gradually rising hills to the Rocky Mountains. Clairbeck sat at the base of a wide valley that climbed ever higher, twisting through the Continental Divide and west, into British Columbia.

The song on the radio changed, and Leo stopped tapping his fingers in time on the steering wheel. "You ever been married?" he asked.

"No," Peter said.

"Didn't figure you had," Leo said.

Peter wasn't sure how to interpret that. Did Leo know about Ginny? Edie wouldn't have mentioned his broken engagement. At least, Peter didn't think so. She'd barely spoken of it to him. No doubt she had thoughts on the matter, but so far she'd kept them to herself.

"So how long were you in hospital?"

"Went in at the height of the epidemic," Peter said. "Summer of '53."

"Jeez." Leo shook his head. "Well, it's good you're coming to stay with Edie. She'll look after you good."

"That's the plan," Peter said. At least it had been. He thought of Edie, sitting across from a desk in a police station, a paper cup of coffee cooling in front of her, and all the things policemen might ask.

He glanced at the speedometer.

Leo was driving five miles over the limit, but Peter wasn't going to say anything.

Three miles from Clairbeck, rain began speckling the windshield.

"Gonna storm tonight." Leo nodded at a bank of clouds, rolling off the nearby mountains. "Good thing we're almost home."

Peter nodded. If his weak legs weren't encased in metal braces, his knees would have been bouncing with impatience. They'd lost radio signal ten minutes ago, and the silence stretching between them was oppressive. He glanced around the car.

"What are those?" he motioned to a six-inch stack of files, piled on the backseat.

"Research," Leo said.

"Oh?"

"Suspected industrial illnesses. Local miners," Leo elaborated.

"You're a miner, right?" Peter wasn't actually sure, but in Clairbeck, it was a safe bet.

"Was. Been out for ten years now." Leo signaled, and they slowed to turn off the highway.

They drove into town through a curtain of storm. Within seconds, the spatters on the windshield swelled to a flood, sloshing against the beating wipers. Leo hunched over the steering wheel, trying to see through the rain. The car slowed to a crawl, and at last Leo pulled to a stop, squinting at a shape that must have been Edie's house. "No lights on. Maybe she's not back? S'pose I could carry your things up to the porch, then drive you to the police station. Can't think where else she'd be."

Peter chewed his lip. He had no alternative guesses. "That would be great, thanks." He'd hoped, in the hours since speaking with Edie on the phone, that the police would have finished. If she was still at the station, that wasn't good.

Earlier today, while waiting for Leo, Peter had called up a friend. A former classmate, now a criminal lawyer, who liked Peter well enough to field a lengthy list of anxious questions.

"Don't worry about her too much," Sam had said. "We both know she's...she's not..."

"Involved," Peter put in.

"Yeah." Sam cleared his throat. "But in a sudden death, even one that's not patently suspicious, the spouse, or former spouse, comes under scrutiny. So, I'm afraid Edie's in for some amount of questioning, at least until the police confirm her ex-husband's death was natural or—or something that makes more sense. It can take a while."

Chest tight, Peter had listened as Sam casually explained how they'd question Edie, search her car and probably her house. That they'd send Jack's body to the medical examiner.

How long does that take? And why has Leo heard rumors of poison already?

Peter squinted through the rain at Edie's darkened windows. "Hey, Leo—"

Too late. Leo couldn't hear over the rain, and was already carrying Peter's crutches out of reach, up to the front porch.

Peter sat back. He still had the chair. No way was he going to ask Leo to go back for the crutches in this weather. He just sat in the car, watching Leo trot down the front walk with enviable ease.

Don't be bitter, he told himself, as Leo got back in the car, pushed the dripping hair off his forehead, and shifted the car into gear.

They rumbled around the corner. Close to the end of Main Street, just a few blocks away, Leo stopped again.

The wipers groaned and sped up, and for brief intervals it was possible to make out the slender steel letters mounted on the building's brown brick walls. *Clairbeck District RCMP.*

"I don't like that she's still here," Peter muttered.

"Cops are probably just flirting with her," Leo suggested. "Maybe they wanted to wait for you. It's a hard time for her to be alone."

Bullshit.

Edie ought to be home, with him or a friend. Not with the police.

"You want me to fetch her?" Leo asked.

That would be easiest, but...Peter shook his head. He wanted to find out why they were keeping her, and he wouldn't learn that sitting in the car.

"I'll help you inside," Leo offered.

"That would be great. We'll need a lift home, too, if that's okay?" Peter said. Though the police must have taken Jack's body out of Edie's car by now, Sam predicted they wouldn't relinquish the vehicle. They'd want to photograph it, maybe sweep for fingerprints and stray hairs.

"No problem. Let me get your wheelchair," Leo climbed out of the car and walked to the back, disappearing from view when he opened the trunk.

Peter chewed the inside of his cheek, remembering what Sam had told him when they were talking about crimes in general, not ones in any way connected with his sister.

With domestic murders, you know, the killer's nearly always the victim's husband or wife. Husbands mostly. It's simple statistics really but can make for a real tough case on my end. I shoulda been a prosecutor.

The thing was, if Edie had killed Jack, Peter wouldn't blame her.

By the time Peter was situated in his wheelchair, he was damp with rain, and Leo was soaked. He didn't complain though, just smiled as he grabbed the handles to push Peter up the sidewalk. "You okay if I let go of you to hold the door?"

Peter nodded. There was a lip, but he'd practiced those and approached with enough speed that the front casters bumped right over.

"Nice," Leo said.

Peter rolled himself forward, wet wheels squeaking, his gaze colliding with the receptionist's.

She peered at him over the cherry red cat's eyeglasses perched low on her nose, then glanced pointedly at the tracks he'd left on the floor. "And you are?"

"Peter. Peter Simmons. I'm here for my sister."

"Ah. Mrs. Simmons-Gainsford."

"Ms. Simmons," Peter corrected. He didn't like this woman's arch tone.

Maybe she sensed it, because instead of replying, she sniffed and fed a clean sheet into her typewriter.

Peter rolled a yard or so closer, unwilling to be put off after coming this far. "She's here, isn't she?"

"Hmm-hm." She looked past him. "How are you, Leo?"

Peter waited while they talked, reminding himself this wasn't uncommon. Brusqueness wasn't just for guys in wheelchairs. This late in the day, she probably treated everyone she didn't know curtly.

The receptionist—Miss Clark, according to the brass plate on her desk—fussed with her typewriter a moment longer, then stood. "I'll fetch her. She's waiting for you down the hall." She marched away, nylons swishing, heels tapping.

"That's good news, right?" Leo said. "That they're done?"

Peter shrugged and adjusted his left leg—it wasn't sitting quite right on the footrest—and stared at the floor. It was speckled with shades of blue and gray and silver, not that different from the floors at the hospital. Good for wheeling around on. Not that he wanted to stay for a tour.

A door opened, followed by the sound of hurried footsteps. "Peter. I'm so sorry."

Edie stumbled toward him, fumbling in her handbag. She wasn't wearing a coat, just a too-big sweater, and her hair was mussed, her lips naked and pale. Each marker of distress scraped another layer from his rapidly hollowing stomach. She shouldn't have faced this alone.

He stretched out his hands; it was hard, in his chair, to offer the hug he wanted to give, the one she clearly needed. Edie took both his hands, squeezing hard.

"Gosh, I'm a mess."

"You've had quite a day." His thick throat made it hard to speak.

Edie had gripped his hands just this way all through his worst days in hospital, whispering sternly, *"I'm with you, Peter. Don't you dare give up."*

"I came as fast as I could," he said roughly.

"I know." She released him and wiped at her cheeks. "Thanks."

She turned to Leo. "Did you bring him?"

"Of course." Leo stuffed his hands in his pockets. "No big deal."

"I'm r-really..." She swallowed, glanced at Miss Clark, and began rifling again though her purse. "I can't think what I've done with my keys."

"It's okay," Peter told her, but she didn't seem to hear.

He wasn't talking about the keys, though. Judging from her face and the jerky fumbling of her hands, no one had told her this all day.

Peter smoothed his face. He wasn't angry at *her*. "It's okay," he repeated.

"I'm so sorry to keep you waiting."

"We don't mind," Leo said. "Come on, let's get you home."

CHAPTER FOUR

"You sure you're all right?" Leo called from the car.

"I've got him. Thanks so much, Leo," Edie said, and Leo rolled up the car window and turned into his garage.

Rain blocked the view, hiding the shapes of the surrounding mountains, but Peter could feel the peaks around him, as plainly as someone standing at his shoulder when he was trying to type. He'd climbed most of them and felt as much affection for their familiar trails and rugged slopes as he'd feel for an old friend.

If he saw an old friend now, would they recognize him? The mountains definitely wouldn't—not in a wheelchair, struggling though this rain. And he hadn't heard from his climbing friends in months, not even postcards. Of course, sending news of their climbs had to be awkward.

"I'm sorry," Edie said, fighting to push Peter up the sidewalk. The pavers were too narrow for his wheelchair, so one wheel dragged in the wet grass.

"*I'm* sorry," Peter said.

"Maybe we should get a ramp put in."

A ramp would be nice, but building it would be expensive, and Edie's house would keep its curb appeal only if they put it at the back. Peter shook his head. "If I keep on with my exercises—"

"I've listened to you too often to think you're buying that story," Edie said.

Many of the children in hospital were walking unaided now, but Peter hadn't achieved any significant improvement in a while.

"I think you're right to focus on what you've got," Edie said quietly.

"What I've got *left*, you mean."

"You fought hard for it," she pointed out.

Yes, but it's not enough, he thought, as Edie climbed onto the porch and retrieved his crutches, so he could tackle the steps.

"How was it?" he asked. "At the station?"

She just shook her head. "I'll tell you inside."

By the time he made it through the door, Edie had the wheelchair wiped down and ready for him in the hall. She'd removed the rugs and about half her furniture, so it wasn't hard to follow her, rolling into the kitchen.

"Beans and toast, I think you said? We should be able to manage that."

He'd turned down her offer of supper at the local diner because he wanted to hear her story, and she was in no state to enjoy eating out. But when Edie reached into the breadbox, all she pulled out was the heel of a loaf. Her face fell. "Um..."

Peter rolled closer. "Edie, it's fine."

She brushed at her cheek and laughed shakily. "Looks like we should've gone to the diner after all."

"I'm not that hungry. There's enough."

Edie looked at him, in a way that said she knew he was lying. He hadn't eaten since breakfast, and felt hungry enough to eat a horse, but didn't want her worrying about feeding him. "You know me." He shrugged. "I'm happy with peanut butter scooped right out of the jar."

"True." Edie reached into the cabinet. "Well, I can grant that wish."

"Do I need more than a spoon?"

"Nah." She motioned to a drawer below the counter and set about slicing the last of the bread while he located a spoon, a tin of beans and the can opener.

Two tablespoons of peanut butter perked him right up, but Edie looked as faded as ever, even with the beans bubbling on the stove. She'd had a hell of a day. Maybe he shouldn't pry at her tonight. She'd fielded enough questions at the station.

"You look tired, Peter."

"Not as tired as you." He laid two plates on the table. "How are you?" He wasn't sure if anyone had even asked yet, so this question at least was necessary.

Edie shrugged. "Tired, I guess. Like you said. Beer?"

"Please."

Edie looked less pinched after a helping of cheesy beans and a bottle of lager. Still, Peter debated for another five minutes before finally floating a question to her, and he had to wet his throat first.

If she doesn't want to talk tonight, we won't, he told himself.

"So, what did they tell you about Jack?"

"Hold on. I need another," Edie said, and got up to grab another beer from the fridge. "You want one?"

"No thanks." They were both eating like they'd never seen food before: sliced apples, spoonfuls of peanut butter, slabs of cheese, anything that didn't take thought or preparation. Edie uncapped her bottle with a quick tap against the counter, and slouched back into her chair, cradling the drink in her hands. She'd been chewing her fingernails again, but that was a good sign, in his mind. All through her marriage, Edie kept her hands perfectly manicured, chewing on pencils instead. Pencils she'd hide from Jack, who thought both habits, chewing nails and pencils, disgusting.

She was a healthy weight again too. She'd been scarily thin before. Even after the divorce, it had been hard to separate herself from Jack, but the move to Clairbeck had helped her be herself again.

"Well?" Peter prompted. "What'd the police say?"

"They wouldn't tell me much. They were trying to see what I knew, but I was as surprised as they were."

"You didn't know he was in Clairbeck? I mean, I assume that's where your car was found?" He wanted to know if what Leo had heard about poison could be true. But maybe the police wouldn't have revealed that to Edie. She'd know soon enough though, judging by how quickly Leo had heard the rumor—and how easily he'd passed it on.

She nodded. "On the Spray Highway, not too far past the dam. There's a trail up there. Cutting through the woods, it's only a mile's walk from here. Jack came out from Calgary again yesterday."

Peter frowned. "Did you know he was coming?" During her marriage, one of Jack's favorite tricks was surprising her, coming home early or stopping by the house in the middle of the afternoon. Always checking up on her.

"He's showed up a few times," Edie admitted.

Peter set down his bottle carefully. "Here?" He pointed at the table, so she'd know he meant her house, not the town.

"A few times," she repeated. "These last few months. Twice, I think, in August."

It was more often than he'd supposed. Than she'd let on, before. "Is that all?"

She paused before shaking her head. "Some phone calls. Usually late at night. No big deal." She took a long swig. "Now I take the phone off the hook before I go to bed."

"Did you know he was coming yesterday?"

"No, but I wasn't completely surprised. You see, I met with Jill. The new girl he's been seeing. Someone told me they're engaged—"

"Already?" Peter's eyebrows shot up—along with the last bit of bread in the toaster.

She shrugged, and stood up from the table, retrieving the toast with the tips of her fingers. When she returned to her seat, she gave all her attention to applying even layers of butter and strawberry jam.

"Why did you go see her?" Peter asked.

Edie balanced the knife on the side of her plate and took a bite of toast. "Well, I figured I had to tell her. Maybe he's different with her, but if not..." More chewing. "Jack wasn't happy about it. I'm sure he told her I was lying about everything."

Peter exhaled. "You don't owe that woman anything. She's capable of making her own decisions."

Edie shook her head. "He's too good at pretending. She'll never see what's coming, just like I never did. Hell, even when I was in it, I didn't understand—"

Peter stared at the smears on his plate. "He's sick. What's there to understand about that?" The worst thing was, in four years, he'd never spotted how bad it was. Yeah, he'd been out of the country a lot, and he'd noticed Edie had changed. But he hadn't realized how bad it was until her desperate letter reached him in Hong Kong, and he left the expedition and came home, so that someone was nearby to help her leave him.

"For the longest time, I thought the problem was me." She shook her head and took a pull from her bottle. "It's not the kind of thing that makes sense to people. The police wanted to know why we divorced. They asked if he was violent. A drinker. A womanizer." Her shoulders curled defensively. "They just kept asking things, and when I tried to explain—"

This was what he'd feared. People judged her for leaving Jack. Her in-laws called her histrionic. One of Mom's friends had told Edie that divorced women were a threat to society.

It made him crazy; he could only imagine the effect it had on Edie. "You didn't have to explain anything," he said stiffly.

Edie snorted. "Yeah, well, they looked at me like I was ludicrous. Maybe I am. Who gets divorced because they aren't allowed to add chocolate chips to the grocery list?"

"He's not normal," Peter said. "He's not a good man."

"He's not anything." Edie laughed bitterly. "Not anymore."

Peter turned his bottle. Condensation had soaked through the label, and it was puckering away from the glass.

"And it's not like I *actually* couldn't buy them—the chocolate chips," she continued, her words coming faster. "He wouldn't hit me or shout if he saw them in the cupboard. He'd just stop talking, except for arch comments about playing enough tennis to keep my figure."

She shook her head. "Even now, hearing myself, it doesn't sound like a real problem."

Peter kept his face smooth. It wasn't easy. Edie knew what he thought. "So, what happened?"

"I don't know. The police wouldn't tell me. But they had a lot of questions. Did I give him my keys? How come he was in my car? Why had he come here and what did we talk about? Did we eat together?"

Questions about food, so maybe the rumor Leo had heard about poison was right. "Did you tell them?"

Edie nodded, mildly defiant. "I know what you said, but I didn't kill him, so I don't need to worry."

Peter swallowed his growing misgivings with a gulp of beer. Hearing her denial was a relief, even if he'd never admit it. And he liked her logic, but Sam's advice didn't support it.

She picked up her fork and put it back down again. "They asked if he took drugs."

"And?"

"I told them no, not when we were married. Which is the truth. If he had back then, I think I would have known."

Edie was a nurse.

"So why was he out here?"

Her shoulders hitched a little higher. "I knew something would happen after I talked to—to his fiancée. Jill. You know how he is. Strolled into the clinic half an hour before we closed. Leaned on the counter and started chatting up the receptionist. I've told her before—I've told everyone at the office—I don't want to speak to him, but Brenda gets silly any time a man smirks at her. She came to tell me right off. And I was in the middle of inoculating twins."

Peter grimaced.

"So, I dawdled a bit. But he was still there in the waiting room by the time Brenda was closing up," Edie continued. "Acted like I was expecting him. He had flowers for me…from his mother, he said. I couldn't very well storm out of there."

"Why not?"

"In front of Brenda? And Dr. Irwin? Making a fuss would have drawn him out of his office."

"You don't have to care what they think of you."

"Yes, I do. And Jack was acting so reasonable, there was nothing to stop him from sweeping me off."

Peter grunted. He could think of plenty of reasons.

"We walked down the street to the Drake."

"The diner?"

Edie shook her head. "No, the pub on the corner. I didn't even think to look for his car, which annoyed the detectives. I guess they're still looking for it? Or testing my story, probably. This place is too small to hide anything for long."

She picked up her toast, then put it down again.

"What did he do?" Peter asked, alarmed by her silence.

"It was fine, Peter."

He arched an eyebrow.

"You know what he's like. He ordered drinks, sat us in a booth."

"Of course he did. Can't pull off Mr. Genial Everyman if the barman sees your face." Jack had always decided everything. He ordered her meals, he chose where they sat, how long she wore her hair. He hadn't liked her in trousers. Or a ponytail.

"Okay," Edie conceded. "He was doing his thing. But I don't have to live with it." She swallowed. "Not anymore." She pushed away her plate. "Do you want this?"

Peter shook his head.

Edie sighed. "Anyway, I told myself he couldn't do anything and just sat back in the booth and waited for him to say his piece."

"Which was?"

"He'd given me every chance. He'd been as forgiving as he could be. That I'd had no reason to divorce him and embarrass him in front of everyone. And—" She picked at a brutally short thumbnail—"if I talked to Jill again, I'd regret it."

Peter picked up his bottle. "I hope you didn't tell the police that."

This earned him a glare. "I'm not stupid, Peter."

"Good. Because he'd just threatened you, and we both know—"

"I told them he wanted some heirlooms and thought I still had them—but that was just an excuse. His excuse, from the first time he came out here. He actually has a client in town, you know. I figure it's the mine. I told that to the police too, said he didn't tell me who it was—attorney-client privilege, you know—but that he could have driven out here for work."

She swallowed. "The police said they'd check in at his office, see if they can verify it. I'm not sure if the office has to tell them, though."

Peter frowned.

"I told the police our divorce was amicable—" Peter snorted, but Edie carried on, still picking her thumbnail. "Though of course they wanted to know why we split. They kept pressing, like there had to be something else. Felt like I was explaining myself to Mom and Dad all over again."

Her chin drooped, and Peter felt the same heaviness settle on his lungs. "I'm sorry."

She shrugged. "Jack talked at me for a half hour or so, and when I left the pub, he just stuck to me. Paid the bill and followed me out. Said he wasn't finished. I told him I was, and since I didn't want him following me home, I went back to the clinic. Told Jack I needed to do some charting. It's on the same street as the pub, you know, just on the next block."

"Was anyone there?"

Edie shook her head. "Some of the shops were still open though. And the diner across the street. I locked the door behind me and paced around until I ran out of curses."

She smiled feebly, and though Peter had plenty to say, he didn't want to interrupt, now that she was talking.

She studied her hands. "It's silly, but I just didn't want to see him. To hear any more. I turned on a light in one of the back rooms, so it would look like I was working, then slipped out through the back door of the clinic."

"Was he still waiting outside?"

She shrugged. "Might have been. Probably not, but I...I just didn't want to think about it. My car was parked out front, so I figured if I left by the back and walked home, he'd think I was still there. There's a trail, not far from where the alley lets out at the end of the block. Goes along the river most of the way to my place. I'd make it home before he realized I was gone, and eventually, he'd just give up." She swallowed. "If he was watching."

"You told the police this?"

"Yeah. They looked at me like I was paranoid. Said it explained why I left my car, but they wanted to know how Jack could have gotten my keys. Told them I owned that car when we were married, so Jack could easily have had a key made. But then they showed me the keys they found in the car—"

"Were they yours?" Peter asked. His sister's face had taken on a grayish tinge.

She nodded. "My extra set. So, I said he might have taken them from my purse when we were at the pub."

Peter gave her a look.

"It's possible," she insisted. "I left it at the table when I used the washroom."

"Do you keep the extra set in your bag?"

"Sometimes," she said, in the harassed voice she always used when lying. "I might have had them there for a while without realizing it. It's not like I use them regularly or anything."

He relaxed his jaw, but his hands were still tight around his knees. "That makes sense." He let out a breath. "Glad you made it home."

"Tripped in the dark, of course. Bruised my knee." She raised her skirt enough to show him. "The police wanted to know how I'd gotten it. They took pictures. And my fingerprints."

Because she'd walked home through the woods, it was unlikely anyone had seen her. Unfortunately. "What did you do when you got home?" Peter asked. Maybe she'd phoned someone.

"I cleaned my knee. Made myself a grilled cheese, tried to do the crossword, but I was going to pieces a bit, so I took a tranquilizer and went to bed."

"Shit. You didn't talk to anyone?"

Edie shook her head. But even if she'd been awake, she wouldn't have gotten any phone calls, not when she routinely left the phone off the hook.

Sam's advice, which was all Peter had to go on, was that the best way to fix this problem was to present the police with an alibi. Peter wasn't a cop or a lawyer, but even he understood a sleeping pill wasn't a great one.

"Do the police believe you?" He would have questions, in their shoes.

"They should. It's the truth. I know the police think it's strange he was found in my car, but I think so too. It makes no sense. I didn't see him after I left him outside the clinic, and I don't know how he got my keys."

"I suppose there's that." But it seemed a slim defense.

She straightened and let out a long breath. "This…this mess about Jack isn't what I expected, but"—she smiled thinly—"maybe my life just got way easier?"

Easier? Maybe, Peter thought. *Let's hope.*

CHAPTER FIVE

I PULL UP MY HOOD AND PUSH MY HANDS DEEPER INTO MY POCKETS. My jacket is damp from the rain. I should have waterproofed it weeks ago.

No matter. A little rain never hurt anyone.

This weather reminds me of Jack. It was a night like this that I spotted him, standing on the street, forlorn as a stray dog. I ducked my head and moved aside, so that there'd be plenty of space when I passed. My footsteps must have alerted him though, because he looked up when I was a few paces away.

"What's wrong?" I asked. An uncomfortable question to lob at a stranger, but his expression was so transparent, and there was no one else about.

It must have surprised him into answering. I don't think he would have under ordinary circumstances. "I'm an idiot," he said, brushing at the wet on his coat.

"If you say so," I shrugged, because he must have been standing there for a while. "I don't mind this weather."

He took in my heavy raincoat, and glanced up at the blanket of heavy clouds, exposing his face to the drizzle.

"It's the best kind of weather for fishing," I told him.

He rocked back on his heels and dug his hands into his pockets. "Huh. Maybe I should give that a try."

I nodded a goodbye, and resumed walking, but the conversation lingered in my ears. I wasn't used to exchanging words on my walks, but we had, so the next time I saw him, we exchanged a few more.

Back then, he was often out in the evenings, after dark.

I sigh, watching my breath curl like white smoke around my face. Dusk comes earlier, now that the days are creeping toward fall. I'll be alone, tonight. No Jack, and anyone else who might be tempted by a late evening stroll is kept inside by the rain. Tonight, I haven't even seen any passing cars.

All day today, there's been talk about the man found dead in Nurse Simmons's car. My chest tightens, but I control my face carefully, trying on the puzzled expressions I've used all day.

I don't understand it. No one does. What was he doing out on that road? In her car?

They say Nurse Simmons spent the whole day at the police station, but she's home again now. The porch light is on, and there's a glow coming from deep within the house. Maybe the kitchen? I could walk around to the back of the house, looking into the windows if I wanted to be sure, but the ground is soft. I don't want to leave any footprints, so I stick to the pavement.

Jack should never have picked up the habit of coming here. He should have stayed at home.

CHAPTER SIX

PETER WOKE BEFORE IT WAS LIGHT, AND THOUGH HE TRIED TO GO back to sleep, it was hard with the sounds of Edie moving around the house. He heard the front door open and wondered if she was smoking.

He dozed a little, but once meal-making sounds emerged from the kitchen, he was glad to give up.

"Couldn't sleep either?" he called from his bedroom, while buttoning his shirt.

"Nope." Something heavy dragged across the floor.

Peter paused. Why in God's name was she messing with the furniture?

He grasped his crutches and went to take a look, shirttail untucked and flapping at his waist. He stopped dead in the hall, just outside the living room.

"There." Edie straightened, dusting her palms. She'd unpacked his typewriter and set it on a card table by the window. There was a stack of fresh paper beside it, and the heavy leather desk chair, waiting for him. "You can work here."

Peter stared at the floor, rubbing the back of his neck like the pressure would counteract the stinging in his eyes. "I can't—"

"Why not?" she countered. "It's one of the reasons I thought this was the best place for you. You can still finish your book." She walked past him, into the kitchen, and though he smelled coffee, he didn't follow right away.

He'd never recapture the angles that had earned his mountain shots so much attention, not from crutches. Not from a wheelchair. And though he had enough photographs for the book he'd envisioned—probably—he had no stomach to write it. Those pictures had been taken by somebody else. They didn't feel like his anymore.

Edie should know that. She'd seen how hard it was even to look at them.

He'd remind her. Over a cup of coffee.

Unfortunately, the view in the kitchen was worse. Oh, she had a cup poured for him, but there was no way he could swallow anything, looking at what she'd done. "I cleared out the pantry," Edie explained, gesturing through the open door at the equipment she'd installed there. "See? You can use it as a dark room. The wheelchair won't fit, but I put a stool in there, and if you use your crutches..." She broke off. "Shouldn't I have done that?"

"It's fine," he said through a tight throat.

"Peter." She crossed the room and touched the back of his hand. "You've got to keep taking pictures."

He turned his head, fixing his eyes on the geometric patterns in the wallpaper, not sure if he was agreeing or conceding or just unable to meet her eyes.

She was right though. He had to do something.

He'd been thinking of giving up photography, full time anyway, to take a job with Dad's building company, before. Because of Ginny, but it was different now. He wasn't giving anything up. Everything had been taken away.

"Take a look in the pantry," Edie urged. "We can fix the things I set up wrong, and order anything that's missing. I'm glad you're here. Especially now."

She sighed, and her voice came out in a faltering whisper, the same voice she'd used to confess the mistake she'd made in marrying Jack. "I think I'm in trouble, Peter."

He drew in a breath, ready to argue, but there was no time to say anything. The doorbell rang.

Edie flinched.

It wasn't even seven o'clock yet. This could only be the police.

As they looked at each other, startled into silence, there was another ring and a carrying voice. "Mrs. Gainsford? It's Sergeant Forbes."

Peter felt his brow crease. "Again?" But what he really meant was *so soon?* Because he'd known, hearing Edie's account last night, that they'd be back. He just hadn't imagined it would be this early.

Edie looked ready to faint. "I'm...I'm not ready."

"Let me. Go put some lipstick on." His sister's latest burgundy hue wouldn't fix anything, but a glance in the mirror might pull her together. "I can get you a couple of minutes."

She nodded once, then vanished downstairs.

Luckily, he had a good excuse to move slowly. Peter began making his way down the hall. He had two types of crutches, and was fastest with these forearm ones, but the police didn't know that. Painstakingly, he hopped to the doorway. *Thump, swing, thump, swing.*

The bell rang again.

"Coming," Peter called. He opened the door. "Morning."

"Good morning." One man answered, but there were four on the porch, wearing the brown belted everyday uniforms of the RCMP.

"Can I help you?" Peter asked, carefully bland, though his fingers twitched, wanting to shut the door in their faces. "Awfully early, isn't it?"

These guys had kept Edie all day yesterday. Couldn't they leave her alone?

"We've a warrant to search this property," one of the men said. He had three stripes and a crown badge stitched onto his right arm and was presumably the officer in charge.

"Now?" Peter blinked, pretending surprise. He might not be able to keep them out, but he wouldn't make this easy.

"Yes. If you could step aside, Mr...."

"Simmons. Peter Simmons. I'm Ms. Simmons's brother."

The nearest man shuffled a half step forward, telling Peter to hoof it without stooping to words.

"Give me a moment. I'm not too steady with these," Peter said, taking an ungainly hop backward and almost pitching to the floor. "Sorry. Need more practice."

"Be careful, Mr. Simmons. We don't want you hurt."

"Yeah. I'm just used to more space. There's so many of you." He paused. "Maybe we could just have two of you? The halls aren't wide, you see, and usually I get around in my wheelchair. Though I guess if you won't be long—"

"We're required to conduct a thorough search, Mr. Simmons."

"Of course. Well—oh, I suppose I should ask to see the warrant." He planted the crutches and held out a hand. "If we're being thorough and all, I suppose I should be too."

The first man reached into his breast pocket for a folded paper. "Here."

Peter read it through twice. "So, you're looking for..."

"Items connected to Jack Gainsford."

"Hmm. Well, Edie and he were married for several years. I imagine some of his things might be kicking around. Can I see your badges?"

He studied them too, one at a time. "Sergeant Forbes. Corporal Labelle. Constable Lefthand." Forbes had a nose so thin and high bridged, it almost deserved its own introduction. Different from Labelle's face, which was pink and puffy. Lefthand's features were obscured by the wide brim of his brown Mounties hat, but his height—a good six inches taller than Labelle—made him appear stern. "And Constable McSorely."

"That's me," said the youngest one, unnecessarily. His cheeks were smooth, and he looked like he should be in high school.

"Thanks. Good to have names for you all. This way."

If anything, his courtesy was only impeding their progress around the arch in the hallway into the living room. "Have a seat?" Peter offered.

"We really—"

"Coffee?"

"—should start our search."

"Edie?" Peter called, ignoring this. The house was small. It was unnecessary to shout, but when he'd gone to the door, he'd heard Edie turn on the water, and it hadn't shut off until he'd finished checking badges.

"Coming!" She breezed into the room, in a terry cloth robe and towel, looking like she'd just stepped out of the shower. From the basement, Peter heard the washing machine chugging.

"Sorry," Edie said, adjusting the towel on her head. "Wasn't expecting visitors."

"Good morning, Mrs. Gainsford," Forbes said.

"Yesterday I asked you to call me..." She paused, evidently deciding not to offer her first name again. "You know I go by my maiden name now."

"Good morning, Ms. Simmons." Corporal Labelle, maybe feeling that his colleague wasn't getting off on the right foot, stepped forward to offer his hand and a second series of introductions. Forbes shifted his weight impatiently.

"So, what's this about, then?" Edie asked. "I don't really think there's more to say, Sergeant Forbes. I was with you at the station forever yesterday."

"We're sorry to trouble you," Labelle said. "We've a search warrant to look over your property for items connected to your ex-husband."

"Can I see it?"

"Your brother—"

"He's a guest here. It's my house," Edie informed him.

"True," Peter inserted. "She's putting me up. Just got out of the hospital."

Forbes produced the warrant again.

"I suppose it looks in order," Edie said. She turned to Peter. "Did you think so?"

"Far as I can tell," he said with a shrug.

Forbes shuffled his feet again, edging closer, but Edie didn't surrender any ground.

"May I see your badges?"

It took another minute or so to get that settled. "Well, if we're done with preliminaries..."

"Yes, go ahead." Edie waved a casual hand. "I'm just going to get dressed. I'm already running late, so I can't stay. Peter can help if you need anything."

She vanished into her room. Peter smiled benignly, wondering where on earth she was going and how long she was counting on him to run interference with the police.

Well, he could do that. Between the two of them, they weren't doing so badly already.

"It wouldn't be too much, would it, to ask one of you to move my typewriter?" Peter glanced hopefully at Forbes, then at the rolltop writing desk. "It's a bit drafty, right by the window."

From the desk, he'd also have a better view of the search.

"Sure, that's no trouble," Constable McSorely answered, earning a dark look from his superior that landed unseen on the back of McSorely's head. The young man was very blond, and weedier than usual for a police officer. Together, it made him seem less substantial than his uniform.

"I'll just clear a space," Peter said and hopped over to the desk. Edie used it more as a repository for mail than anything else, so it was littered with papers.

Lefthand and Forbes set about dismantling the room, while the others took apart the kitchen. "Forbes?" Peter asked, and the man interrupted his inspection of the sofa.

"What?"

"Have you contacted Jack's firm? Or the mine? I believe he worked for them. His work brought him out here from time to time, so that's probably—"

"She said that, yes."

"And have you contacted them?"

"It's on my list." Forbes turned back to the sofa, just as Edie reemerged with a floral scarf tied around her head, and an expensive bag he hadn't seen in ages swinging from her gloved hand.

She blew Peter a kiss. "I'll be at Pinky's. Call me when they've finished."

"Uh, Ms. Simmons?" Lefthand straightened away from a box of Edie's LPs, exchanging a glance with Forbes.

"We'd prefer you remain here," Forbes said.

"Am I under arrest?" Edie asked.

Peter held his breath.

"Not presently," Forbes admitted.

"Then I'll proceed with my plans for the day," Edie told him. "Peter, anything you need from the city?"

He shook his head, hoping he'd concealed his surprise. These so-called plans were entirely new. Why on earth was Edie visiting her former mother-in-law? They'd never liked each other, and while Peter accepted the necessity of concealing some information from the police—in her situation, it was only prudent—he didn't like her keeping secrets from him.

"How are you getting there?" he asked.

"I'll call Dr. Irwin. Ask to borrow his car." Edie sent a swift frown at Constable Lefthand. "Any idea when I can have mine back?"

"Can't say just yet, ma'am. But we're working as quick as we can," Lefthand said, working his way through the bookshelf, cracking each volume and flipping through the pages without any pause.

"We'll have to search you," Forbes informed her. "Before you go anywhere."

Edie rolled her eyes but held out her handbag. Forbes took it.

"Would you like me to call to the station for one of the women?" Forbes asked.

"No, I just want to be on my way." Edie spread her arms. "This good enough, or should I strip?"

"This is just fine," Forbes said, and nodded at Lefthand, who advanced and patted her down gingerly.

"Nothing," he reported.

"Everything looks in order here," Forbes said, returning her purse.

"Thank you, detective." Edie vanished into the kitchen, re-emerging a few minutes later. "Couldn't reach Dr. Irwin, but Katya will lend me her car. I'll be back before dinner."

"Drive safely," Peter said, because that seemed the only acceptable caution he could offer, with the police listening to every word. He'd get answers later.

She kissed his cheek, whispering, "Remember what I said about trouble?"

He nodded, just a fraction of an inch.

"Gotta see what I can find out," she said, and Peter remembered the police wouldn't know Jack's mother as Pinky. To them, she was surely Mrs. Gregory Gainsford, and she probably answered their phone calls via her housekeeper. Edie had always gotten along with Mrs. Wilson.

"Don't be too long," Peter told her. "Be careful."

Behind them, something crashed in the kitchen.

"Dropped the utensil drawer, but everything's okay," McSorely called.

"Just put it back when you're done," Edie told him, but the look she gave Peter wasn't nearly so offhand. Under her breath, she whispered, "The whole town's gonna be talking about this." Then, hearing herself, she rolled her eyes. "Be sure to tune in to our next episode..."

Peter whispered back, in what he hoped sounded like a gangster voice, "No problem. I got your back."

Edie smirked. "You better." She tucked a loose strand of hair under her scarf with an unsteady hand.

CHAPTER SEVEN

Katya's car had a crack in the windshield and needed coaxing to go from first to second, but Edie was grateful for a set of wheels to take her out of town. She glanced left, saw empty highway, and stomped the accelerator. Spraying gravel, the car leapt forward, flying into the eastbound lane. Her heart thumped as speed pressed her against the seat, Clairbeck and the police disappearing as she raced downhill.

The windows were down, she had a full tank of gas, and the temptation to push the car even faster was almost irresistible, but the last thing she needed was to be pulled over for speeding. Also, Katya would kill her if she knew Edie was driving her car like this. Easing her foot off the gas, Edie reminded herself the feeling of outrunning her problems was illusive; no matter how fast or how far she drove, trouble was just a step or two behind.

It waited ahead too. Pinky had never liked her.

She might get some breathing room from the police though, if she could explain what Jack had been up to.

But that only reminded her of her biggest, most unnerving question. Jack was dead, the police were certain someone had killed him, and Peter had shared that, in unexplained deaths, the prime suspect was always the husband or wife.

Edie couldn't imagine any of Jack's family or friends as a killer. In Forbes's shoes, she'd think she was guilty too.

Unfolding her sunglasses with one hand, she slid them onto her face and adjusted the scarf tied around her hair, checking her face in the rearview mirror.

She'd learned to arm herself before confronting Pinky, but this was as ready as she'd ever be. Ignoring the yellow sign telling her to slow down for the upcoming curve, she whipped around the bend. The wind was cool in her face, and the lake on the side of the highway sparkled in the sunshine.

Jack's parents lived in Mount Royal, two blocks from the home of their only son. Edie pulled into the drive and checked the rearview mirror, smoothing windblown bangs and reapplying lipstick.

She locked the car, then advanced to the front step and rang the bell. The housekeeper, Mrs. Wilson, answered, starting with surprise. "Edie? What are you doing here?"

"Hiya, Ann." Edie smiled. "I'm here to see Pinky."

"You sure?" Ann's nearly invisible blond eyebrows rose even higher.

Hesitation wouldn't help; Edie nodded once, sharply, and strode past the other woman into the house, wearing all the confidence she could muster. She knew her way around these rooms, and the solid furniture and heavy draperies hadn't changed. Even so, the house felt colder—she was an interloper and Jack was gone.

Edie moistened her lips and peered into the living room. The curtains were drawn, the air sharp with the scent of lemon Pledge.

"Who's there?"

Edie changed direction for the music room, following the sound of her former mother-in-law's voice. "It's me. Edie," she called.

The door was ajar. She stepped inside and saw flowers everywhere:

on the tables, the grand piano, surrounding Pinky and the cream velvet sofa. Such a profusion might make another house look like a funeral parlor, but Pinky's home was too stylish for that, the lilies and white roses lending the room the glamour of a celebrated actress's dressing room. Almost.

Pinky had a wineglass at one elbow and Jack's fiancée, Jill, at the other. As usual, she wore her pearls and a full-skirted day dress. Too late, Edie realized she should have anticipated and matched the color. Both Pinky and Jill were dressed in unrelieved black.

"What are you doing here?" Pinky demanded, her crinolines rustling. Beneath the perfect makeup, she wore a ravaged face.

Strong tactics might still have worked. This was the time, if there ever was one, with Pinky small and shrunken on the couch, stocking feet tucked up beside her, high heels abandoned on the floor. There was, Edie noted, extra padding inside one shoe, and a painful-looking bunion on the corresponding foot, which she'd never seen before.

The fierceness Edie'd nurtured on the hour-long drive vanished. Jack was dead. She'd loved him badly for a time, and he was Pinky's only child. She'd gotten cancer when he was small, and treatment had made it impossible for her to have others.

Edie slumped against the doorframe, fighting down a lump in her throat. She motioned at the almost empty wine bottle. "Can I have some?"

At first, Pinky looked ready to throw the bottle at her, but then her face changed. "What the hell," she said. "Sit down, Edie. Jill, you do the honors. Actually, you may as well get us another bottle."

Dark-haired and pale, with bruise-like shadows beneath her eyes, Jill got off the couch.

"Hi, Jill," Edie said, as she passed. "I'm really sorry."

Jill left without a word, so Edie flopped onto the couch and kicked off her loafers.

"I can't believe he's gone," she said.

Pinky's hand tightened around her glass. "Don't say that. You have no right."

"Why not?" Ignoring the nettle-like sting, Edie returned the question with the skill she'd once poured into her backhand—necessary, as Pinky was also in top form today. Shouldn't have expected any different. The sympathetic lapse had been a mistake.

Edie fixed her eyes on the creases of her trousers. "You heard where he was found?"

"The police told us."

She'd figured as much. Didn't make things any easer, though. Every word she spoke felt heavy. "I was as shocked as you are."

Pinky just grunted.

"Jill thinks I did it, doesn't she?" It hadn't been hard to interpret her silence, or the hatred on her face as they'd passed each other on the thick wool carpet.

"She hasn't said that to me." Pinky sipped her wine.

"Do you?"

No answer.

"Well, I didn't." Edie reached across Pinky for the bottle. "I don't have any quarrel with him, not anymore."

"That's not what he said," Pinky murmured.

Edie smothered a sigh. Jack was always getting her in Pinky's bad books. It was entirely typical that, even in dying, he'd edged her into a corner.

"What *did* Jack say?" Edie asked, emptying the bottle into an unused glass.

"That you were meddling with him and Jill."

"I like her. She's a nice girl," Edie said evenly. Jack's hasty engagement was none of her business.

Pinky grunted. "He goes...he was going by John these last few months. Had too. Jack and Jill is ridiculous."

It was, but Edie had never said so and never would now. She cast a sideways glance at her former mother-in-law. "You're free to disbelieve me, but I'm...I'm torn up about this too." In truth, her feelings were foggy, but she'd never wanted Jack dead. Sitting here, he seemed more gone than ever, and the knowledge that he'd never stroll into this room again caught her by the throat. She blinked hard and stared into her wine.

"You have no right," Pinky said again.

"Maybe not," Edie conceded. "But I am sorry."

"Then why were you wrecking things for him?" The glaze in Pinky's eyes, Edie realized, wasn't just tears. They were there, sure enough, but Pinky was drunk, something Edie had never seen before.

"Is that what he said I was doing?" But of course, he had. Jack had accused her, to her face, of doing the same thing. And he'd tried his best to return the favor.

"Dragging him out to that town all the time. Helping you with this and that. Acting concerned for Jill the minute they got engaged. I'm not sure what kind of lies you fed her, but that's what they were. You should have kept him when you had the chance," Pinky said.

Edie bit her lip so she wouldn't say what she was thinking. Jack hadn't visited her as much as Pinky was implying, and every time he came to Clairbeck, he'd given some kind of excuse. Work. A fishing trip. His grandmother's missing brandy decanter.

Though Pinky was distressed, she wasn't nuts, so Jack, as usual, had been making shit up.

"I never asked him to come to Clairbeck," Edie said firmly. "Not ever. But I did meet with Jill. She's young, and Jack and I divorced for a reason. I wanted her to have a chance to hear things from me."

Pinky's eyes flashed. She'd strenuously opposed Edie's decision. But then, she'd always believed every word Jack said. Not much had changed. Never, not once, had she considered Edie's side, so she certainly wouldn't now.

"You know me," Edie said. "I wouldn't hurt Jack."

"Then why'd you leave him?" Pinky demanded. "He was devastated."

"Here's the wine." Jill stood framed in the doorway, bottle in hand. Edie bit her lip, and Pinky immediately transferred her attention to her glass.

Jill must have washed her face, because her make up wasn't smeared now, though her eyes remained red, and her voice was rough from previous crying. Edie couldn't tell if she'd just come back or if she'd been listening for a while.

"I didn't ask Jack to come to Clairbeck," Edie told her. "Not once. The few times I saw him, he told me he was out there for work."

Jill looked away.

"I have no idea how he died or what he was doing in my car," Edie said. "I hoped you might be able to tell me something that will help it make sense."

Jill strode into the room and set the bottle down hard on the coffee table. "I'm going outside. I need some fresh air."

A few seconds later, the back door slammed.

Pinky gave her a look. "What was he doing in Clairbeck?"

"I really don't know," Edie insisted.

"Well," Pinky said acidly, "According to him, once you had trouble with the local plumber. And then your taxes. And changing the insurance on your car."

Some of this was true. Not the taxes, but the rest of it. She'd handled the problems on her own though, and certainly never mentioned them to Jack. So, who'd told him about the plumber and the insurance?

Edie rubbed one forearm, wishing Pinky would turn up the heating.

Had to be a coincidence. Trouble with a plumber was easy to invent. There were so many jokes about hapless housewives negotiating with plumbers and auto mechanics and...anyone really. Jack was good at inventing excuses, especially ones that made her look bad.

"He'd been out to Clairbeck every two weeks for the last six months," Pinky informed her. "Sometimes overnight."

Edie's stomach tightened. "Jack hasn't been staying with me." She'd put up with the surprise visits and the late-night phone calls. But Jack hadn't stepped inside her house often. Not when she could help it.

Pinky refilled her glass. "Jill nearly called it off last week. After talking to you. She stopped by his house, found him gone. Waited all night and confronted him in the morning."

Smart girl, Edie thought. Unfortunately, she'd come here to get herself out of trouble, and this news wasn't helping. When Pinky and Jill told this to the police, they'd assume she and Jack were having an affair.

"Did the police say how he died?"

"No. We're waiting for the medical examiner's report."

Jack was healthy, golfing twice a week. A regular at the tennis club. He shouldn't have died, not at thirty-two.

"I didn't see him last week," Edie said.

Pinky's lips thinned. "Well, I make a point of walking past his house every morning. When I walk the dog. Been going that way all summer, and at least once a week, there's no one home."

Pinky was pretty smart too.

"He's probably overnighting with Jill. Or going to the office early," Edie said, but her answer was too quick to convince herself, let alone Pinky.

Sure enough, Pinky gave her a pitying look. "You know I play bridge with Marilyn."

Edie remembered Jack's secretary, and not with any fondness either. Not because Jack had cheated with her—well, who knew. He might have, but she wasn't nineteen anymore. Stepping out was something lots of men did, and she hadn't divorced Jack because she'd been unable to contemplate living with infidelity.

But it seemed Jack couldn't—not that infidelity was even the right word. They were divorced. She could date or remarry or do whatever she chose, in theory. But of course, Jack didn't like the idea of her having someone else.

She should have expected it, judging from the tight surveillance he'd maintained throughout their marriage. Even if she'd wanted to, infidelity would have been almost impossible; he knew if she forgot to pick up the dry cleaning, if she canceled lunch with her mom.

Marilyn, the secretary, had helped him with it.

Edie remembered the first time Jack had surprised her at her home, almost a year after the divorce. That evening when he'd spotted the hickey on her neck.

The other visits had come after, along with the news that "John" and Jill were dating, then engaged.

"I know he was going out to see you," Pinky said, swallowing a hiccup.

"I never asked him to come—or wanted him—in Clairbeck," Edie said. "I wanted a clean break. I don't know how this happened."

"Well, you ought to!" Pinky snapped. "My son is dead, and if you hadn't left him, he wouldn't have been out there. None of this would have happened. If you'd just—"

She choked, and Edie's hands tightened on her wineglass. Even in distress, Pinky wouldn't want Edie to touch her.

"Pinky..." she began instead.

"Don't! This is your fault. Even if I did believe you, it's still your doing. My Jack—John," she corrected, "is a good man. He deserved better than this. He deserved better than you."

A sob ripped her lips apart, and she buried her face in her hands.

Pinky didn't let Edie comfort her, but she did accept a tissue from her purse, dabbing it at her eyes with quick stabbing motions.

"I know. It's not right," Edie said over and over, wondering whether it was better to go, but not wanting to leave Pinky alone.

She hates me already. May as well stick around.

"I'm so sorry," she murmured.

Finally, Pinky subsided.

"How's Greg?" Edie asked, her voice almost a whisper. She didn't like to imagine how her former father-in-law was faring. Jack was everything to him, and Greg wasn't nearly as fierce as his wife.

Pinky blotted her eyes again. "I'm sure you can guess."

Edie sighed, and this time Pinky sighed with her.

"What did he say? When he saw you—the police said he went there two days ago." Pinky licked her lips. "Before..."

"Yeah. He came." Edie nodded.

"Well?"

"He was angry about me talking to Jill," Edie said heavily, then repeated the story she'd given to the police. "Did Jack tell you he was coming?"

Pinky didn't answer, just thinned her lips again, which meant that either he had or that she'd known. If Pinky was watching Jack's house and checking his movements with Marilyn, he couldn't have had many secrets.

But apparently, he'd had enough, because putting her story and Pinky's together didn't reveal anything useful. This was all still as confusing as ever—unless you were pointing fingers at her. That answer fit all too neatly.

"Jack showed up uninvited at my work at the end of the day," Edie said. "He insisted we go for a drink. He was angry, and I said I wouldn't talk to Jill again."

He'd said other things too, though. Edie swallowed.

Pinky said nothing.

"I have no idea how this happened to him," Edie said. There was one more thing, but she didn't add it aloud. *Jack told me you'd kill him if his wedding was called off.*

She hadn't believed him. Still didn't. It was the kind of thing people said, but never seriously. Except Jack was dead, and Pinky clearly knew where he'd been.

She's more likely to kill me than Jack though, Edie thought.

"So, what do *you* think happened?" Pinky asked.

"I don't know," Edie said. "I was hoping you had an idea."

"Not if it wasn't you." Pinky's voice was as sweet and poisonous as ethylene glycol. "If you really did take a tranquilizer..."

"I really did," Edie told her.

"Well then. I don't have any ideas either."

CHAPTER EIGHT

I TURN OFF THE SIDEWALK ONTO A DIRT TRAIL, HEADING FOR THE creek, creel slung over my shoulder, fishing rod in hand. I like the woods, and I like the water. Helps me think.

Yesterday, people were saying the dead man was Nurse Simmons's husband. Today, the story is she killed him. Why else was he in her car?

Why, indeed. Doesn't make sense, and I need to be careful, because—

A branch snaps, spinning my head around. I wait, heart pounding, but there's nobody in sight and the noise was too big for a little ground creature.

Nothing. No one. Just trees, creaking in the wind. After a while, my pulse steadies. I resume walking.

None of this makes sense, but the police were at her house this morning. That's something. And I don't have to work out everything if they do their jobs. Except they haven't arrested her yet. She went to Calgary this morning, driving a borrowed car.

I'd like to know why, and it's frustrating that today isn't the day to ask. Better to listen than come out with a bunch of questions. If I wait, someone else will ask them soon enough.

They ought to, at least. I'm worried I've placed too much confidence in the police.

I glance up and down the banks of the creek looking for a place to sit, but the sound of the water rattles between my ears. I can't sit here, waiting, even with the excuse of a fishing rod in my hands. Not today. My heart is loud and my fingers feel charged with trapped static—stinging power with no place to go. I'm so jumpy, the fish will sense it and stay away. It feels as if even the trees know, because after all their protesting moments ago, now they are much too still. The silence presses on me.

I remind myself that in the mountains, winds change suddenly.

Almost automatically, I reach into the creel hanging from my shoulder, for the bottle hidden beneath a wax-paper-wrapped sandwich. As my hand closes around the glass cylinder, my heart steadies, reassured by the presence of six small pills. They are packed in cotton wool so no matter how fast I walk or where I take them, they don't make a sound.

Simple, small, potent: The pills reassure me, like they always do.

The water turns quiet again. The trees sigh.

CHAPTER NINE

Writing in the middle of a police search was about as effective as cutting hair in an earthquake. The house was noisy, and the movements of four policemen unsettling. Worse yet, Peter kept having to hop out of the way.

After an hour, he gave up pretending to work and watched the officers, trying not to think about what they were looking for, and how long it would take them to give up.

The focus and intensity of their search wasn't encouraging. Forbes was clearly expecting to find something.

It was going to take forever to put everything back together.

"Please try not to make a mess," Peter said.

Nobody paused or even looked up. Peter shifted in his chair, rearranging his legs with his hands to take a little more space, as if that would remind them that he was there. He'd never been this invisible before, but back then, before his illness, he'd had the confidence and stature of an athlete, and an enviable career.

"Sorry. Just doing our job." Lefthand's voice carried to Peter, but not much farther. He emptied the basket of Edie's knitting, sending a ball of emerald-green yarn rolling across the room.

"No bloody knives there, I'm afraid," Peter said. "Maybe try under the couch?"

Lefthand didn't smile. "Yeah, I'll get there." In a few moments, he was tossing aside the cushions and sweeping a hand through the cracks.

"Here you go," he said, setting two dimes, a pencil stub, and a hair barrette onto the desk.

"Thanks," said Peter, resisting the temptation to ask if the RCMP vacuumed too.

He thought that would be it, so far as the couch went, but Lefthand moved it away from the wall and turned it onto its back, revealing the upholstery staples at the bottom and the dust bunnies on the floor.

"Anything suspicious?" Peter asked sarcastically, but then Lefthand bent forward, retrieving a crumpled green paper packet hiding beside the baseboards. Peter stiffened.

"Your sister smoked Camels yesterday at the station." Lefthand frowned at the packaging, which lacked the familiar logo and was an entirely different color. Even the quickest glance would detect the difference.

"Those are mine." Peter reached out a hand, forcing himself to relax.

Lefthand surrendered the pack. Peter closed his fingers around it, pinpricks of alarm tattooing the curses he couldn't say across his back.

Stay calm, Peter.

The paper wasn't coated in dust, so it couldn't have been beneath the couch for long. Inside the wrapping, he felt three cigarettes left. "Thanks for finding these," Peter said, as casually as he could. "Must have dropped them."

He'd quit smoking on the advice of his doctors while he was in hospital, but Newport menthols had never been his brand. He'd always smoked Camels, same as Edie, starting with ones they'd pirated from their father.

Jack smoked Newports, but it didn't look like Constable Lefthand knew that. Yet.

"Got a match?" Peter asked. "Left my lighter in my room." Hopefully he still had one somewhere, because Lefthand seemed like the type to check.

Lefthand offered his lighter, and an ashtray from the windowsill holding remnants of a lone cigarette. Edie must have smoked it during the night, because yesterday evening, the dish had been clean.

"I'll take it outside," Peter said. He had to get rid of these, before Lefthand and the rest of them realized Jack must have been here, sitting on the couch Lefthand was lifting back onto its' feet.

Peter rubbed at his hip, where the tops of the braces tended to pinch. What else wasn't Edie telling him?

"Let me carry those for you," Lefthand offered, reaching for the cigarettes and the ashtray, realizing the difficulties Peter had carrying anything on crutches.

"Thanks."

He lit up on the porch, watching Lefthand and the others searching through the window, trying not to think about the doctor who'd commanded him to quit for the sake of his recovering lungs.

Or when Jack had sat and smoked in this house.

Peter lit the second cigarette from the end of the first, and, as he consumed the last one, started a flame on the packet, burning it out of sight before one of the officers thought about testing it for prints.

Could you get fingerprints off paper? He didn't know. There was a shelf of tattered crime novels in the hospital. In the last one he'd read, the detective had found incriminating fingerprints on a pill bottle. And probably a window ledge? The details were escaping him, but it wasn't like the author had been an actual detective. The book had been a closed-room mystery, more puzzle than story. Certainly not a how-to manual for police work.

What would the police think, when they found Jack's fingerprints in this house? Labelle was still working with powders and brushes, moving from room to room. He'd taken dozens of prints already.

Peter felt sick.

Carefully, so the detectives wouldn't see, he rearranged his leg, flattening the ash of the burnt cigarette packet beneath his slippered foot.

Edie left Pinky in the music room. Their conversation had been disturbing and dissatisfying, but she was hoping for better outcomes with the others.

She peeked into the garden. No sign of Jill, though she smelled cigarettes.

"Jill?" she called.

No answer, and if Jill was determined to avoid her, there wasn't anything she could do. That only left Ann, but of the three women in the house, she was most likely to help.

Edie made her way to the kitchen, where Ann was assembling a rainbow of cut fruit in the base of a Pyrex dish. Behind her, a saucepan of gelatin was heating on the stove—lime, judging by the juiced peels resting on the counter, and the tart smell in the air.

Edie reached into her handbag and laid a box of Junior Mints beside the cutting board. "Brought these for you."

"My favorite." Ann glanced up from her work with a smile.

"I've missed you," Edie said.

Ann nodded without slowing her hands. "I wish I could give you a slice of this, but it won't set for hours yet and as much as I might like it, I'm guessing you aren't sticking around."

"Pinky didn't invite me for dinner," Edie admitted.

"Didn't figure she would," Ann said.

"It's okay," Edie said. "I like this salad, but the pistachio was always my favorite."

"I can write you out the recipe," Ann offered.

"That'd be nice," Edie said, though she doubted she'd ever make it. Wouldn't be the same.

"Give me a minute," Ann said, adding the last three strawberry slices to the dish. She poured in the gelatin, carried the dish to the refrigerator, and washed her hands, drying them on her ruffled blue apron.

"How are you doing?" Ann asked.

Edie shrugged, not quite sure how to explain. "It's just unbelievable. Shouldn't even be real." Quietly, embarrassed to admit it, she added, "The police are searching my house right now."

Ann frowned. "And you left them at it?"

"My brother's there. I wanted to find out if anyone knew Jack was going out to Clairbeck that night. Because I didn't."

"Not Mr. Gainsford. He wouldn't see anything if it was right under his nose," Ann sniffed. "But Mrs. Gainsford?"

They exchanged a look.

"She knew," Edie said.

"She doesn't miss much," Ann agreed. "And she's been unhappy about something." Ann reached into a cupboard for a mixing bowl and two measuring cups. "Thought maybe she wasn't really that keen about Jack's new girl."

"Jill? Why not? She's lovely."

Ann sent her a look. "She's got no starch."

"Jack would have supplied plenty," Edie said.

"Yes, that's the trouble," Ann said. "But I don't know much about her. Probably just imagining things. Mrs. Gainsford sure wasn't happy when she heard things might be called off. She was all about righting the ship then."

As she spoke, Ann took out canisters of sugar and flour, eggs, butter—everything necessary for tonight's cake. But the only recipe cards she took from the box was a blank one from the back and the one for pistachio pudding. The cake, she must have known by heart.

"Grab me a pencil?" Ann motioned with her eyes at the telephone desk.

"Sure. Do *you* like her?" Edie asked.

"Haven't seen enough of her to decide. She's quiet. Doesn't say much," Ann said.

"She's young," Edie said.

"Maybe, but you shouldn't have felt the need to look after her. She can look after herself."

Edie grimaced. "You heard about that?"

"Couldn't help it, not with Mr. Jack shouting."

"At Pinky?"

Ann shook her head, frowning as she copied ingredients onto the blank card. "Miss Evans. Jill." She paused, glancing up at Edie with a half-hearted smile. "You were never very good at staying out of trouble, huh?"

Edie leaned against the counter, sliding her hands in her pockets. "No, not really."

Ann scribbled down the last two steps of the recipe and held out the card. Edie tucked it in her purse. "What was everyone doing here? The day it happened?"

Ann didn't answer at once. Maybe she was preoccupied with measuring the cake ingredients. Edie bit her bottom lip, determined to wait.

At last Ann spoke.

"Mrs. Gainsford and Miss Evans were scheduled to go shopping. A dress to wear to next week's party at the Petroleum Club. Mrs. Gainsford already has hers, but she didn't like what Miss Evans was thinking of wearing. No money in that family, that's for sure."

Edie frowned. That kind of shopping expedition might have taken them all day, but it wouldn't have kept either woman busy in the evening. Not after the department stores closed.

"Except they didn't go. Mrs. Gainsford had a migraine. She had me phone Miss Evans to tell her to meet with her shopper instead."

"Miss Kemp? At the Bay?"

Ann nodded, retuning her attention to the cake, measuring out cups of sugar.

"Want me to cube the butter?" Edie asked.

"Not unless you're going to put on an apron," Ann said. "And you probably should get going, anyway. Mrs. Gainford won't like it if I'm talking to you."

True enough.

Edie combed a hand through her purse, looking for the car keys.

"Thanks for the candy." Ann unwrapped the butter and used the paper to grease the cake pans, her frown deepening. "Got a call from the store though."

"Oh?" Edie paused. She still hadn't unearthed the keys.

Ann lowered her voice. "Miss Evans never kept the appointment. Miss Kemp was expecting her at the store all afternoon, but she never showed. And she didn't come here for supper. Said she didn't want to trouble Mrs. Gainsford, not when she was unwell, but Mr. Gainsford was still expecting her. I cooked four pork chops and only needed one of them, because Mrs. Gainsford never left her room, and you know we didn't see Mr. Jack."

The formal moniker, John, clearly hadn't stuck with Ann. But—

"Jill usually eats here?" Edie asked. It hadn't been that way—not much, at least—when she was engaged to Jack.

"Most nights," Ann said. "Better than eating at the university dormitory."

Of course. Jill wasn't living at home. Her people lived outside Calgary somewhere. Farmers, Edie thought.

"Best get going now," Ann said. "Before one of them comes looking for more wine."

Edie nodded as her fingers closed around Katya's keys. "Found 'em." They jingled as she held up the ring. "On my way. Thanks for talking to me, Ann."

Ann dismissed the thanks with a wave of her whisk. "You worried about the police, Edie?"

"I didn't kill Jack."

Ann snorted. "I know that. Question is, do they?"

Forbes and his men finished turning the house upside down in the early afternoon, but they didn't leave. In spite of Peter's protests—he was tired; he needed to begin restoring the rooms to some kind of order—Forbes insisted on grilling him.

"I can't say that you or your sister have been very cooperative," Forbes said.

"Really? After all that we've let you get away with so far?"

Forbes looked surprised.

"You kept her all day yesterday, giving her no time to think or to grieve. You've done all this"—Peter waved a hand at the destruction—"and how am I supposed to fix it?"

Wordlessly, Forbes disappeared to the basement, returning with a basket of laundry. Silently, he held up each item: wet shirts, underclothes, linen.

"These are your sister's clothes."

"So?"

"They've been bleached," he said caustically.

"Naturally," Peter said. "Don't you?"

But Forbes wasn't interested in talking about housekeeping. Or in Peter's suggestion that, now that the laundry was out of the machine, the police could at least hang it on the line. "Not easy for me, you know."

Forbes grunted. "I'll need to talk to your sister about this."

"Last time I checked, laundry wasn't a crime." By now Peter was fairly certain that Forbes, besides suspecting Edie of murder, absolutely hated him.

"We'll talk again soon," Forbes threatened and left.

Leaning on his crutches, Peter surveyed the disorder—books stacked on the floor, cupboards hanging open, the contents of the house stirred up like someone had dropped the whole thing into a blender. The floor was littered with obstacles: a dangerous challenge with crutches and completely incompatible with his wheelchair.

Not long ago, he'd scaled vertical rock faces with speed and confidence. Now he was trapped in the living room, barred by a laundry basket, loose cushions, spilled knitting and piles of books.

Forbes had scored the last point. But he hadn't played fair.

Peter rubbed his fingers, the invisible residue of Jack's cigarettes lingering on his skin, reminding him that he was cheating too. More than that, really. He'd destroyed evidence.

Yet he didn't believe he'd made a mistake.

He reached down and began gathering up the loose yarn. He'd believed divorce would make things better for Edie, but now he wasn't so sure. Jack had made complete extrication impossible, got himself murdered, and planted Edie squarely in the role of prime suspect.

It took more than an hour, but Peter finally cleared a path to the telephone. By this time, he was frustrated enough to use it, though he'd been determined not to dial the number Edie'd scrawled at the top of the grocery list pinned to the corkboard. He hated calling for help.

"Hello?"

"Hi, Leo. It's Peter, from next door."

"How are you? I see the police have finally left."

Peter smiled. It was better than swearing. "Yeah, afraid that's why I'm calling. I'm in a bit of a fix. Feel like rescuing me again?" Painful as it was to ask, Peter figured Leo wouldn't mind helping a little, in exchange for some gossip. Maybe a bottle of beer. "I hate to bothe—"

"Don't be silly. I'm on my way."

"You aren't busy?"

"Nope."

"Thanks, Leo." Peter didn't want to say more on the phone. The police had searched the house, so they might also have tapped the line. And even if they hadn't, phone lines were shared here, with several houses assigned to each. Another neighbor might be listening.

"You don't need to come to the door," Leo added. "Edie gave me a key a long time ago."

Leo peered into the living room and whistled. "They weren't kidding, eh?"

"Nope."

"This still about her ex-husband?"

"I'm afraid so." Peter rubbed the back of his neck. "But listen, Edie didn't do anything wr—"

"I know that." Leo pushed away the assertion with a casual hand. "She's got a real kind heart. Picked up groceries for me when I had pneumonia last winter—kept my sidewalks clear for a whole month too—and that's a lot of work in January." He dropped his eyelids. "Been worried for her. How's she holding up?"

"She's pretty upset," Peter admitted, relieved to say it out loud.

"'Course she is." Leo glanced at the chaos again. "Looked like she'd had the stuffing knocked out of her last night, and this doesn't exactly make things easy for you either, does it?"

Peter shook his head. "If I can, I want things looking normal by the time Edie's back. She's got enough to handle as it is."

"She working today?" Leo frowned. "You'd think they'd give her a day off."

"No, she had to go into Calgary. See her ex-husband's family."

"Ah." Leo nodded. "This must be a terrible time for them."

"Yeah." Peter settled his eyes on a scratch in the floor planks, and reminded himself that Leo was harmless, a friendly neighbor with time on his hands, who liked keeping up with local news.

But yesterday, Leo said the police suspected Jack had been poisoned—information Peter hadn't been able to wrest from Forbes. Might be a rumor, but if Leo had information, Peter wanted it, true or not.

He frowned at the chaos in the living room, trying to think of an ordinary way to broach his questions, but how did anyone bring up stuff like this? He wasn't a cop. Murder wasn't in his conversational repertoire.

"Well, let's get to it," Leo said. "You tell me where things go, and I'll pick up and carry."

They worked a couple hours, returning jumbles of cutlery, canned food, LPs, and papers to their places. Leo lifted the mattresses back onto the beds, and made them too, after he saw Peter nearly topple over trying to tuck in the sheet.

"Did I do all right?" Leo asked, when he finished, critically surveying the covers. They were slightly askew, and he'd stuffed the sheets under the corners with nothing like Edie's crisp precision, but—

"It'll do," Peter said with a smile.

"Never married," Leo said with a shrug. He'd gone rather pale, hoisting Edie's mattress onto the bed frame, and twice, tucking in the sheets, he'd winced. Maybe he had some kind of back trouble.

Peter closed a dresser drawer, now refilled with shirts and sweaters, with more force than necessary. He hated taking this much help. Hated needing it.

"I suppose we should do something about all that?" Leo gestured at another pile of clutter the police had left on the floor of Edie's bedroom. "Unless you think she won't want us touching her things?"

This pile held contents from the top drawer: bangles, scarves, and things Leo probably called "unmentionables." The flush on his cheeks was a dead giveaway.

"If you pile it on the dresser, I can get started putting it away," Peter said. No way he'd be able to pick all that up off the floor. "Why don't you grab yourself a drink? There's beer and iced tea in the fridge."

Leo nodded, scooping up the detritus in large armfuls, which was probably more comfortable for him than extracting one piece at a time.

Edie might not care to have Leo handling her intimates either, but it seemed slightly better to put everything away, instead of leaving it until her return, hammering home the unavoidable certainty that Sergeant Forbes and his colleagues had poked through *everything*.

The last thing Edie would want to do a day after her ex-husband's death and directly after confronting Pinky Gainsford was pick through a mess, right?

"Lot of stuff, isn't it?" Leo snatched up a trailing scarf, and a glassine envelope tumbled free from the shambles in his arms. He transferred the lot to the dresser top, then bent to pick up the packet of photographs. "Shoot. Sorry, Peter. Looks like they're a little bent."

Without pausing, Leo slid them out and surveyed the damage, shuffling through the pictures. "Oh, it's just the top two. The rest are fine."

His features softened into a smile. "This Mount Robson?" He held out a picture of a lone snow-capped mountain peak.

Peter caught the inside of his lip between his teeth. Robson, the tallest mountain in the Canadian Rockies, was unmistakable. "Yeah. Sure is."

"Glad this wasn't bent."

"Me too." Peter settled more weight onto his crutches, countering the unsteadiness rising from his knees to his shoulders. "I took that one at Boy Scouts camp." It was one of his first good pictures, taken the summer he was thirteen.

He swallowed. Two summers later, when he was fifteen and had just started going steady with Sheila Armitage, his unenthusiastic parents packed him off to the mountains again—this time to work as a hotel bellboy in Lake Louise.

The job had its intended effect. Within two weeks, Sheila was going steady with someone else.

He'd felt pretty cut up—mad at his parents, at her, at Edie for being unsympathetic—but not for long. Because the hotel wasn't busy that summer—few could travel during the war years—and he'd started hanging out with the Swiss climbers working there. Normally they'd have been guiding parties of wealthy international guests, but they had time on their hands and were doing lots of trail building that summer. Peter was happy to help.

By the end of the season, he'd gone from gangly to muscled, and fallen in love with climbing. His parents hadn't expected that.

"Have you been to Berg Lake?" Peter slid the mountain photograph to the bottom of the pile. He liked seeing it, but it made his lungs feel tight and slow—like being back inside one of the ventilators.

"Yeah, I've been. A few times." Leo coughed, perhaps acknowledging that neither of them currently looked the part. "Tried Robson too. The Kain route, but we were turned back by weather at the Dome."

Peter's eyebrows lifted. Only serious climbers attempted to summit Robson. "I didn't make the summit until my third try," he admitted. "It was an incredible climb."

"One of the good ones," Leo agreed. "Wish I could have tried again but I never made it back—broke some ribs down in the mine the following spring, so I wasn't up for it when my friends tried again the next summer. After that..." He shrugged. "God decided I was done with climbing, I guess."

Peter grimaced. "Me too." Except he didn't think God had anything to do with it. Mom and Dad had done their best, but he wasn't much of a churchgoer.

"My friends gave me some pictures of their ascent though. I'll have to show you," Leo said.

"I'd like that," Peter said, before he thought better of it. He would like seeing Leo's pictures...kind of.

Grimacing, he started to stuff Edie's snapshots back into the envelope, but Leo stopped him with a grunt and a tilt of his head.

"Hey, let me see that one."

There was a different photo on top now, of Edie and Jack after their engagement.

"She looks happy," Leo said.

"She was." Then. Peter was surprised she'd kept this.

Leo leaned closer. "That her husband?"

"Ex-husband," Peter corrected automatically.

Leo reached for the photo, holding it up, then moving it slightly farther from his face.

"That's Jack," Peter added unnecessarily, and Leo's forehead creased into a frown.

"The dead guy?" Leo pressed.

Peter flinched. *Why'd he have to put it like that?* "Yeah," he admitted, aloud.

"I've seen him around here," Leo said, rubbing the back of his neck. He looked a little upset, even. "You're telling me she was married to"—he exhaled, lowering his shoulders—"to this guy?"

"Where'd you see him?" Ice congealed in Peter's stomach, and his mouth was once again full of the taste of Jack's cigarettes. Had Leo spotted Jack here? Or just in town?

Leo hesitated, moistening his lips.

"You sure you saw him?" Peter pressed.

Leo's eyes drifted to a point somewhere behind Peter's right shoulder. "Yeah. He bought the house behind mine a few months ago. Don't think he's living in it, though. Not there often enough. I figured—" He shook his head. "Shit. I didn't know he'd been married to Edie."

Peter rubbed his forehead with his thumb and two fingertips, smoothing out the frown. Jack had a house here? Near Edie's?

Leo huffed. "That's pretty messed up. She never saw him there?"

"Of course not. If she'd known—" Peter broke off, warned into silence by the sharpening interest in Leo's eyes.

If Jack hadn't wanted her to see him, it wouldn't have been that hard to hide. And if Edie had seen Jack, she would have said as much. Right? Except she'd only just admitted the frequency of his visits. And the phone calls. Jack wasn't an occasional headache to her. He was a chronic condition, who'd forgotten his cigarettes in her living room.

"Edie works pretty long days, you know," Peter offered.

"I took him for an investor," Leo said. "But a dumb one, cause if the company goes ahead with the layoffs they keep talking about, none of these houses will be worth anything." He shrugged. "Takes all kinds, you know, and I didn't want to pry."

Peter set down the pictures, thinking of Jack's late night phone calls, the unexpected visits to Edie's work. And now a house.

He cleared his throat, not wanting to give away his concern in the tone of his voice. "Can you point out the place?"

CHAPTER TEN

Peter stared through the kitchen window at a gray bungalow crouching behind a screen of emaciated spruces. He wished Edie's curtains weren't so thin. Other than the wooden blinds in the front room, all her window coverings were airy cotton in colorful prints that did little to guard her privacy.

"It's crazy," Leo said again. He was standing right at Peter's shoulder, just close enough to make him slightly uncomfortable. But a four-inch sidestep was tougher with crutches, and much more noticeable, so Peter stayed put.

"Why would *he* buy that place?" Leo wondered.

Peter pressed his lips into a thin line. He had an idea, and he didn't like it. "Let's take a look around."

"I don't think that's—"

"I want to know if Jack's been there," Peter said. Leo seemed confident with his identification, but Peter wanted to be sure.

Edie might keep some things from him, but she couldn't have known Jack was hiding out a stone's throw from her house.

"Breaking and entering is illegal." Leo's eyes were twice as wide as usual. "Your sister's already suspected by the police. If you get in trouble too, that's not going to help."

"Edie hasn't been anywhere near that place," Peter asserted. "You saw how surprised I was. This is news to both of us."

"Well, yeah, but—"

Peter shook his head. "She does not know." And if the house was Jack's, Peter definitely wanted a look before the police came hunting.

"We discovered this accidentally," Peter said, so they could get their story straight. "And we're leaving Edie out of this. She didn't know, and she's in enough trouble with the police already."

"Her car," Leo said, nodding. "And the morphine overdose."

"What?" Peter swiveled, looking at Leo head-on.

"Didn't you know?" Leo seemed surprised. "I heard that from Orvo. Buddy of mine."

"No, I didn't know that," Peter said.

"Well, they say that's what killed him. And Edie's a nurse, so it's possible for her to get the stuff. Not that I think she would," Leo added.

"No, she wouldn't." *Not without a good reason*, Peter added silently.

"We don't have to look," Leo said. "We don't have to say anything. Leave the job to the police."

"The police will find out about this place," Peter argued. "Probably soon. If Jack bought it, there will be records that come out in probate, or something like that."

Leo studied the front of his shirt. "Makes sense," he conceded.

"So, we'll tell the police," Peter said. "*After* I take a look. And then they'll find it that much sooner, right?"

Judging from Leo's lowered head, he didn't like the idea.

"Until we look inside, we don't really know it's his," Peter added. "Not for sure, anyway."

Leo nodded reluctantly. "It's…it's just odd."

It definitely was, but Peter kept his automatic rejoinder tight behind his teeth. "Mind grabbing my camera?" With police suspicion fastening firmly onto Edie, they'd have little reason to trust him. "I'll take some pictures. It might help. Should be on my desk."

"Ok." Leo jogged off.

Peter stared at the house. If there was evidence against Edie, he'd get rid of it. She'd never let him down, not when they were kids, not when he got sick and Ginny broke up with him, not in all his time in the hospital. He couldn't offer her any less.

She was his sister, and when it came to her and Jack...even if she'd done something impulsive, Peter was sure there was a reason for it. Edie wouldn't hurt anyone, not unless she was badly pressed.

And if that house was his, Jack had been applying a good amount of pressure.

Peter maneuvered out the back door and started down the steps. The backyard was mowed, the blooms of summer already gone, Edie's irises and peonies deadheaded and cut back. Only the poppies were still spindly, the browning pods ready to lose their seeds in the next strong wind.

"Sure about this?" Leo's breathing was unusually quick as he caught up and handed over the camera. Peter nodded and slowed down to accommodate him, a good idea anyway, over the uneven pavers that led to Edie's back gate.

"We aren't breaking and entering," Peter said. "We're being good neighbors. I've an idea."

The weight of his camera, hanging by the strap around his neck, imparted some much-needed confidence. Just as well, because Leo clearly wasn't over his misgivings.

Diagonally across the alley, the gray house waited behind a drunkenly leaning fence. One of the spruces had been cut back, improving the vantage point from the house's back windows. Peter's hands tightened on the grip of his crutches.

There were no chairs on the porch, no laundry on the line, no curtains in the vacant windows. But the car door on the garage had a shiny new lock.

"Let me get that," Leo said, scrambling ahead to open a loudly protesting gate. This backyard was overgrown, the fence surrendering to a tangle of raspberry bushes. A rabbit stared at them from beneath the bent canes, half hidden by the long grass.

"Check under the flowerpot," Peter suggested. There might have been a plant in it once, but all it held now was dirt, and Jack wasn't the kind to leave an empty thing on the back steps for no reason.

"Found it." Leo held up a brass key. "Do you think we should worry about fingerprints?"

"Nope." The police would know they'd been here anyway. Peter picked up a bit of loose brick from the steps, hopped a few steps back, and threw it at the window. The shattering glass echoed like a gunshot, but once the reverberations passed, the yard was as silent as before, the rabbit still watching warily from the bushes.

"I'm not sure that was a good idea," Leo said.

"Come on. It's the perfect excuse. You and I heard the noise, saw the broken pane, and came to look things over. Just being neighborly."

"Some neighbors," Leo grumbled.

"Jack was never good to my sister," Peter insisted. "If I don't do something, the police will have her up for his murder." She could go to prison for the rest of her life. If things went really bad, she could get the death penalty. His stomach roiled, rejecting the thought.

Leo chewed his lip. "What if I'm wrong? I think that picture was him, but...but what if the place isn't his?"

"You were pretty sure before," Peter said.

"Yeah, but—" Leo swallowed.

"I'm going." Peter tried a smile. "So, you gotta come too. I need you to tell the police I behaved. Don't want to be accused of tampering with anything."

Leo raised his eyebrows. Peter summoned his most sincere look. "Messing with evidence—if there is any—won't help my sister," he lied. "Come on. The place is empty. It won't take long."

Peter snapped a photo as soon as he was inside, with Leo crowding behind him. Then he paused at the threshold between the mudroom and the kitchen for more pictures before stepping in for a closer look.

"Smells funny," Leo said. "Like he never opens his windows."

The house *was* stuffy, the lino scuffed and old. It didn't look like a place belonging to Jack, who was aggressively fastidious. No visible dust, but there were dirty dishes in the sink, beer bottles on the counter—and a pair of binoculars on the windowsill.

Peter rubbed his palms against his trousers. The trimmed branches outside had warned him, but he hadn't wanted to be right.

"That's no good." Leo pointed at the binoculars. "What a creep."

Peter approached the sink and raised the glasses to his eyes, frowning at the clear view they provided of Edie's kitchen and bedroom windows. From here, Jack could have watched her wash up the dishes and undress before bed. He could have watched her in the garden, seen her get in her car to drive to work.

You don't know for sure it was Jack, he told himself. But honestly, who else would it be?

Leo pointed at the dirty dishes. "Looks like he ate here pretty recently."

Lips tight, Peter set down the binoculars and opened the fridge. There were three apples in the crisper and a half-empty takeout container of Chinese noodles. The thought of Jack, eating takeout in the dark, with the binoculars held to his face...

"Ooh, I like that stuff," Leo said.

Peter slammed the fridge door so hard the dishes rattled in the sink.

"You okay?" Leo looked startled.

"Yeah." But he wasn't. Not even close. He'd been angry with Jack plenty of times, but never this much, and never with such a strangling sense of helplessness. What if, this time, he couldn't help Edie out?

The pale-yellow telephone, mounted on the nearest wall, looked newly installed. Jack could have made those late-night calls from here. Peter could imagine him, waiting by the phone until Edie's lights went out.

"I'll check the living room," Leo offered.

Peter hesitated, not wanting Leo to find anything bad on his own. Too late to stop him, though. Leo was already gone.

"I'll search the rooms over there," Peter called, already regretting his show of temper. He needed to keep Leo on his—and Edie's—side. He needed to be a reasonable guy. Likeable. Not the type who broke windows and slammed things. Tempting as it was, smashing things wouldn't help.

He turned into the hall.

No furniture in the smaller bedroom, but he found a razor and toothbrush beside the bathroom sink. A single hair rested on the pink porcelain, but it was short, blond, a good match for Jack's.

Peter sniffed the shaving soap. He didn't know Jack's brand, but that ignorance didn't lighten his mood.

There was a bed in the next room, and a small suitcase sitting on a shabby chair. An expensive-looking tweed jacket was folded over the back. Peter picked it up and searched the pockets. No keys or wallet, and only a few coins in change, but the breast pocket held a silver card case, full of pristine cream rectangles, all inscribed with *John G. Gainsford, Esq.*

"Motherfucker." Saying it aloud made him feel a little better.

Peter glanced around, but there wasn't much else to see. Aside from the furniture, the room was bare. Except—

He leaned forward, frowning at the neatly folded blanket on the bed, and the perfect angle of the creased sheet corners.

He shook his head reflexively. *No. Edie wouldn't come here.*

But as he moved closer, he spied one of the black elastic hair ties she used, lying on the floor, pushed almost out of sight beneath the bed. He'd just put away a whole packet of these, tucking it next to her rolled-up nylons.

Bracing himself on the bed, he picked up the hair tie, carried it to the bathroom and flushed it down the toilet. By the time he finished, he was short of breath.

Better go back and take a picture.

Methodically, he photographed all the rooms. The police might not want these pictures but having them would prevent them from planting anything. After this morning, Peter didn't trust them, and he couldn't afford to be careless, especially since it seemed like Edie might have been.

Time you and I talked, he thought grimly, hurrying back to the kitchen, where Leo was methodically going through the drawers.

"Find anything?"

"Doesn't even have a can opener," Leo said. "You?"

Peter held out one of the expensive business cards. "This place is Jack's all right."

Leo made a face. "We should get out of here."

Peter glanced into the living room, but all he saw were scratches on the floor, an old sofa, and a stack of paperback novels.

"He reads sci-fi," Leo said in a bewildered tone, shaking his head.

Peter decided against admitting to cracking a couple. "Let me turn out my pockets before we go. Then you do the same. We'll vouch for each other. We came, looked around, but left the place undisturbed."

"Good idea." Leo pulled out his trouser pockets, then began to do the same with his coat. "Shoot. Forgot. Had this already. From home." He fished out a crumpled letter. "See? Got my name on it. Picked it up from the post office just this morning."

Peter nodded. *Leo Martin* was clearly typed across the envelope. His other pockets were empty.

"Let's get out of here," Leo said. "Feels strange. Too quiet."

CHAPTER ELEVEN

"GUESS WE SHOULD TELL THE POLICE NOW?" LEO SUGGESTED, pushing aside the raspberry canes so they could access the back gate.

Peter pushed out his breath, puffing out his lips. He didn't like the idea of whittling away further at Edie's innocence. But Leo was watching, and saying nothing to the police looked bad.

"You bet," he said.

Sergeant Forbes had left a card, which Peter had tucked between the telephone and the wall. Once inside, he dialed the station.

"RCMP, Clairbeck detachment," a female voice sang.

Miss Clark. Peter grimaced. "I'd like to speak to Sergeant Forbes."

"He's gone home for the day. Can I take a message?"

Peter suppressed a smile. *Perfect.* "It's Peter Simmons. I have some information—"

"I just need your name and your number," she said, voice clipped. "Sergeant Forbes will call you back when he's returned to the office."

Peter gave the number, then hung up, feeling better than he had all day. He'd gained some badly needed time, and Leo, leaning against the wall beside him, looked relieved, now that they'd done what good citizens should.

"What a weirdo," Leo said, glancing where the house would be, if it was possible to see through Edie's walls.

"Yeah, I didn't much like the guy," Peter said. "But I better get busy. It's getting late, and I ought to start some supper." Except to do that, he'd probably have to go to the store.

Leo chewed his lower lip. "You really feel like cooking?"

Peter huffed a laugh. "Not really."

"Let's go to the local for a bit," Leo suggested. "It's Friday and the guys will be there. Edie's not even back yet, so you've got time. It'll help you relax. She shouldn't come home to a worried face, not today."

"I don't know." Peter glanced in the direction of the gray house where Jack had hidden, binoculars in hand. Where Edie might have made the bed and dropped a hair tie. Penalties were different for manslaughter than for what newspapers termed "murder one." So far as Peter understood, manslaughter was when death was accidental or when someone had some slight justification for killing, like feeling threatened. But for manslaughter or murder one, you still were put away.

He swallowed hard. He wasn't losing Edie.

"You're worrying too much," Leo said. "She didn't do it. The police aren't fools. They'll find the truth."

Peter manufactured a smile, wishing he felt half Leo's confidence. But Leo hadn't watched Forbes and the others for hours, disposed of a suspicious hair tie or slowly smoked those incriminating cigarettes.

"It's poker night," Leo said. "I'll introduce you. You can have a drink, then pick up take-out Chinese for dinner. Save you from cooking."

Peter started to shake his head, then stopped, realizing Chinese might not be a bad idea. And he could ask around some, see if anyone besides Leo had spotted Jack. "Sure. I'll leave her a note." If Edie arrived home while he was out, she could call him at the local. "But I can't stay long."

To keep ahead of the police, he needed answers, fast.

The union hall was a white clapboard cube with a carved wooden sign identifying it as Local 1387 of the United Mine Workers. The building looked old as the town and occupied a corner just two streets away from Edie's and Leo's houses. Peter, who'd suggested they drive, realized he'd have to recalibrate his ideas of distance to fit Clairbeck.

"Didn't know the local was this close," he said, as Leo braked and pulled into the side of the street.

"Doesn't take long to get anywhere here." Leo shrugged. "I don't mind taking the car."

"I'm not bad with these," Peter protested, tapping his right crutch.

"I know. But I might need to give someone else a ride home," Leo said. "The guys will stay late, and some of them also have trouble getting around."

"Don't worry about me," Peter said. "From this close, I can make my own way back."

"Don't make so much of it. We're neighbors." Leo exited the car and waited for Peter to lift his legs to the sidewalk, then arrange his crutches to one side so he could push onto his feet using the car doorframe. Leo didn't hover in the way, trying to help.

"Thanks," Peter said again, this time with a smile.

"There's a side door just there." Leo pointed to a shallow ramp on the long side of the hall.

"Sure." May as well make it easy on himself.

Inside, they passed a row of offices, currently closed, and a board covered in a patchwork of notices: items for sale, illustrated admonitions from Workman's Compensation, and a poster advertising the town production of *Kiss Me Kate*, which would be held next week.

"This way." Leo led him into the hall. It was a big room, with a scattering of people gathered around temporary tables, and a bar built against the far wall. More corkboards with notices adorned the walls.

Peter followed Leo to the bar, smiling at the men who greeted Leo on the way, and the volunteer bartender, whose grade school son sat on a nearby stool, doing his math homework.

"You Nurse Simmons's brother?" he asked.

"That's right. How'd you know?" Peter asked.

The man shrugged and gestured at Peter's crutches. "Heard you were getting out of hospital. Polio, that's a tough one. Jimmy, give Mr. Simmons some more space."

The boy looked up, catching the sound of his name, but maybe not much else. Surprise showed on his face, and in the sudden slide of his heavy textbook. It crashed to the ground, striking the top of Peter's foot.

"Da...arn!" Peter said, changing tack last minute, earning an approving look from the boy's dad. "Whoo, that hurt."

"You felt it?" The boy looked puzzled. "But I heard you were paralyzed."

"Jimmy, don't bother Mr. Simmons with questions. Do your math and mind your own business." The bartender turned to Peter, smiling apologetically. "People are always interested when someone new moves into town," he explained. "Most folk know your details by now, I'm afraid."

"It's all right," Peter said. It was easier to be polite now that the pain was fading.

And he was used, now, to fielding what some might consider prying questions.

Jimmy, the boy, scrambled off the stool and retrieved his book. "Sorry, sir. I didn't mean to hurt you."

"It was an accident." Peter moved out of the way. "Polio only affects the nerves that look after movement. So, I feel everything just fine. But the walking is tough." If the kid was curious, better for him to know.

"What can I get you?" The barman asked, seeming eager to change the subject.

Peter looked to the wall behind him. There were cupboards, a few bottles on a long shelf, and a whole lot of glasses, but nothing like a price list. "Can I get two beers?"

"Nah, don't worry about me," Leo said. "I'll buy my own."

"Not a chance," Peter said. "I owe you."

Leo tried protesting but was soon overruled. He left, promising to find them seats at the poker table.

"So, what kind?" the barman asked. "I've got Budweiser, Stag's Head, Cincinnati Cream, and Molson."

Peter hesitated, not knowing Leo's preference. "Two Molsons, I guess."

"Sure thing." The barman reached into the refrigerator. "How's your sister doing? Tough news for her, I imagine."

Peter nodded, not sure what to say.

The man opened the bottles and glanced at his son. "Jimmy, you wanna carry these for Mr. Simmons?"

The boy hurried to comply, giving Peter a wide berth.

So much for trying to be friendly.

Leo had joined a table where four other men sat playing with a smudged deck of cards. Only one of them looked fit enough for mining—one, Peter saw, was a double amputee and used a wheelchair. A lone woman sat near the table as well, but she was occupied with a stack of papers, not part of the game.

Peter steered toward the empty seat.

"That's Mel's place," a man across the table said, when Peter went to sit down.

"He's not using it," Leo said. "Sit down, Peter."

In spite of the urging, Peter hesitated. If Mel came back…

"Mel's an old friend of ours," Leo explained. "Died years ago in a mine accident, but we still miss him at our games."

"Ah." Peter felt more uncomfortable than ever. If this chair was left to remember their friend, then he didn't want to—

"Mel was a good guy. He'd be happy to share his place—just wouldn't want us to forget who sat there first," the man in the wheelchair put in. "Go on. Sit down."

Peter obeyed, reluctantly. The boy, Jimmy, had already left the bottles on the table, so excusing himself wasn't exactly an option.

"This is Peter Simmons," Leo told the others. "Just moved in next door."

The man in the wheelchair stretched out his hand. "I'm Orvo. This here's Mike, Steve, and Garrett. And that's my daughter."

He indicated the woman, sitting off to the side. She was blond and wore her hair in a braid that ended between her shoulder blades.

She looked up from her papers and offered a small smile. "Hi, Peter. I work with your sister."

"Brenda?" he hazarded, plucking out the name of the receptionist, who Edie had mentioned before.

"No, I'm—"

"Katya," Peter filled in, with a snap of his fingers. She'd lent Edie her car. "You're the other district nurse."

"Only one for a long time," Orvo said. "Until your sister came to town."

"Must have been busy," Peter said.

"Still is," she agreed, tapping her ballpoint against her clipboard. "But I don't mind. This is home." Her eyes shifted, passing appraisingly over Leo. "How are you doing today?"

"Same, same," he said, avoiding her eyes.

"How's the lawsuit coming?" One of the men asked. Peter thought this one was Mike.

"Still working on it. Information's harder to come by this time," Leo said, and Peter remembered the stacks of files spread over the backseat of Leo's car. Before he could ask, Leo turned to the man in the wheelchair. "Deal me in, Orvo?"

Katya's father riffled the cards, then thumbed them off in rapid succession to Leo, Garrett, Mike, Steve...and Peter.

"Oh, I don't know if I should play," he said quickly. "I haven't much time. My sister's coming back soon and—"

Katya leaned toward him. "It's low stakes," she murmured.

Peter swept his eyes across the table. Along with the worn cards, they were using a jumble of odds and ends instead of chips: paper clips, washers, scraps of paper. An odd collection of counters, but even if they had a low exchange rate, there was still an awful lot of them, gathered in piles of various sizes around the table.

"These guys don't have any money—" Katya's face changed. She started forward. "Where'd you get that?"

One of the men—Mike, if Peter was remembering right—looked up. "Oh, this is—"

"No, that." She left her seat, circled the table, pointed at a button that had rolled away from the small hoard piled in front of him.

Mike picked up the button. It was blue, with a white rim. "Won it last week, I think."

Katya turned to Orvo. Her face was stern. "That's mine. You didn't take it, did you?"

Orvo shifted in his wheelchair. "Might have found it somewhere—"

"That was Mom's." Her throat seemed to tighten, and her cheeks were pale. "From her favorite sweater. Don't you remember it, Dad?"

From his confused expression, it was clear that Orvo didn't.

"Don't worry, Kittycat," Mike pressed the button quickly into her hand. "Just a mistake."

She calmed, coloring as she noticed all the eyes on her. "Sorry. I—"

"Don't be sorry," Leo said. "We wouldn't have used it if we'd known. You took such good care of your mom."

"I'm sorry, Kittycat," Orvo mumbled. "Didn't realize. You know my how my memory..."

"It's okay, Dad." She tucked the button into her shirt pocket and picked up her clipboard again. "Go back to your game."

Head down, shoulders hunched, knees together, as if embarrassed for speaking up, she perched on the edge of her chair, looking a bit like Peter's eleventh grade lab partner. The back of her neck was bright red. Maybe not only embarrassed—was Katya upset?

Had Orvo's wife died recently? Peter rubbed the edge of the photo sitting in his pocket, wondering if it might be an acceptable distraction. The mood around the table had changed, and no one seemed ready, yet, to follow Katya's advice and resume the game. The players—so free with the nickname Kittycat—looked stricken by Katya's distress.

"Maybe I can trouble you for a minute." Peter drew out the photograph, the one of Jack and Edie after their engagement, which had remained inexplicably with the others in Edie's top drawer.

He set it on the table. "Any of you seen this guy?"

"That's your sister, isn't it?" the one in the chair next to Mike's, Garrett, asked. He was leather cheeked, with basset hound eyes.

"Yeah."

"And that's—"

Peter nodded.

Katya leaned forward. "Can I see?"

Peter nodded, glad she was availing herself of the distraction. She carried the photo a step away from the table, angling it in the light.

"I'm just trying to help my sister," Peter explained, since the looks from the men at the table seemed to ask for something. "The police have been asking her a lot of questions."

Garrett grunted. "Probably better to leave this to them."

"They know their job." This from the guy so pink, he looked

permanently sunburned: nose, cheeks, and shiny pate. Peter reviewed his memory of the introductions and pulled up a name. Steve.

"Peter's just worried for her," Leo put in. "Any brother would be."

Garrett tapped his cards on the table and sent Peter a sideways glance. "I heard the police searched your house. That true?"

Peter glanced to Katya, hoping she'd say something in his sister's defense. She worked with her, after all. From what Edie said, they were friends. But Katya was studying the photo, holding it in the same hand as her clipboard.

"They searched the house," Peter admitted. "Didn't find anything."

"We aren't used to this kind of thing." Orvo folded his arms. "And we don't know your sister. Not well."

Muscles stiffening, Peter scrambled for a reply but was spared the necessity by Katya saying, without looking up, "Don't be silly, Dad. You like Nurse Simmons."

Peter's chest loosened until Orvo retorted, "Yeah, but she's divorced."

"So?" Katya's eyes flicked up. Her cheeks were reddening again. "You were glad enough when she chose to move here. So, all of you are going to look at this picture. You're all going to help."

She folded the clipboard to her chest, not looking like that shy lab partner of his anymore. If Peter hadn't already known, he could have guessed that she worked as a nurse. Her tone was a dead giveaway: firm, fairly friendly, but absolutely implacable. Clearly, this wasn't the first time she'd kept these guys in line.

She motioned to Peter, who extricated himself from his chair and hopped the few steps to stand beside her. She edged another foot away from the table. "Sorry about them," she whispered. "They have good hearts, even if it doesn't seem like it."

Peter nodded.

"Even my dad," she added, dropping her eyes to the clipboard again.

"He's just testier than usual. He's in a lot of pain, and he's been out too long today. Must be overdue for his medicine."

Peter's shoulders loosened. "I'm sorry your dad isn't well."

"Yeah, well most of them have a few problems. Miners, you know."

He didn't, but he nodded anyway. Not hard to imagine, really.

Her eyes fell on the chair he'd left, the space they kept for Mel. "They stick together. And some of the people in town—well, this is the most excitement they've seen in a while. Gets their imaginations going. Please don't hold it against them. And tell Edie—"

"You going to bring over that photo yet?" Garrett called.

Katya's jaw tightened. "Edie couldn't have killed him. So, whenever I hear some idiot saying differently, I'll tell them so."

"Thanks," Peter said, meaning it.

She nodded, stepped back to the table and set the picture down in front of Leo, who was nearest. Her presence also seemed to tell him she was quite aware of the way he was covertly studying Garrett's cards.

Leo coughed and turned his attention to the photo. Walking past Steve and Mike, who were arguing about who was going to look next, Katya took hold of her father's wheelchair and murmured something to him in a language Peter didn't understand.

Orvo grumbled halfheartedly but didn't resist as Katya wheeled him toward the door.

Looking after Orvo couldn't be easy, Peter thought, then cringed. People probably thought that about him too.

"You guys take a good look at that picture," Katya said. "Edie and her brother deserve your help."

Abandoning the game, Leo and his friends passed the picture around amid squints, speculation, and more swallows of beer.

"City guy, for sure."

"Haven't seen *him* around."

"I did see an unfamiliar blue car parked downtown a couple times. Didn't see anyone in it though."

Peter bit the inside of his cheek, trying to hide his frustration. He'd had a house here, for God's sake. "I'm thinking Jack may have spent a good deal of time in town. Sure you haven't seen him?"

Leo would have piped up, but Peter sent him a look: *not you.*

"It's important," he said. "Jack was killed here. In this town. And it wasn't my sister." In spite of the cigarettes, the crisply turned sheet corners, and the hair tie he'd flushed down the toilet, he had to believe this was true. Or at least convince everyone else of it.

Garrett shifted in his seat and picked up his cards. "I believe you, Peter. But you gotta understand. No one in Clairbeck would do anything like that. This town's a small place. Mining's hard. We've learned to look after one another. No one here would do a thing like that. Not to anyone we know. Not to a stranger."

Steve nodded. "You're looking in the wrong place. You gotta show that picture around Calgary. Talk to people from *his* life. People that knew him."

More nods. Peter felt them drawing together, closing ranks. He glanced at Leo, who looked torn, but had picked up his hand of cards again.

"Thanks for the advice." Peter forced a smile he didn't feel, aware he couldn't afford to make enemies. "Guess I'm just concerned, is all."

"Course you are," Mike said.

"Must be upsetting," Garrett added.

"Yeah." Peter tried not to let his suppressed feelings sink into that lone word. Better get out now, while he could manage it politely. He wasn't in the mood for cards. "I better head home. See you another time?"

"Sure thing, Peter." Leo's voice was louder than necessary, and the others followed suit.

"Come again. Anytime."

"You'll join the game next time, right?"

"See you soon!"

Peter nodded, raised a hand in farewell, and escaped with as much speed as he could.

CHAPTER TWELVE

Peter closed his magazine as Edie came in the back door, still untying the scarf from her hair. Dusk hung outside the windows. It had darkened the house without him noticing, stranding him at the kitchen table in the small circle of light from the ceiling lamp.

He glanced at the cartons of Chinese takeout he was keeping warm in the oven, wishing this could be an ordinary evening. He was starting to fear they might not have one ever again. Surrounded by suspicion and watchful shadows, you couldn't just sit down and eat like nothing was the matter.

"Hiya, Peter." Edie flicked on the rest of the lights with one hand and used the other to tuck her scarf into her purse. Her eyes looked puffy, and her lipstick had worn off.

"Tough day?" Peter asked.

"Yeah." She set her purse on the table and sagged into a chair, then glanced around, her brow creasing. "When did the police leave? Figured there'd be plenty for me to do still, putting this place back together. You didn't do it all, did you?"

Peter shook his head. "Police left just after one. I called Leo and he helped. You're right. He's a nice guy. Introduced me to some of his buddies. They're a tight bunch."

She nodded. "They take that union brotherhood stuff way too literally. Kind of cute, I guess. How long did it take to clean things up?"

"Not totally finished yet. Leo and I stopped around five."

Edie grimaced. "Jeez, I'm sorry."

Peter shrugged. "It's all right."

Of course it wasn't, but not for the reasons she was thinking. Instead of retrieving the takeout cartons from the warm oven, Peter crossed to the counter and uncapped a bottle a beer.

He hated doing this. "Looks like you need it," Peter said, and passed it to her extended hand.

"I don't really. I've had plenty today already." She rolled her eyes. "Two glasses of wine with Pinky."

"Hey, it's been a tough day."

"One for the books." She stared at the oilcloth covering the table, tracing a finger over a circle in the pattern. "I didn't mean to be gone so long, but I had to stop at Mom and Dad's."

Peter took a sip from his own half-empty bottle. "What'd they say?"

"It was hard news. They always liked him, and it came as a shock. Dad's lawyer came to talk to me." She pressed her lips together. "Doesn't do criminal defense work. But he recommended someone. Also, they're hurt you didn't let them bring you out here. But they're glad I'm not alone."

"Yeah." Should he tell her about Jack's house? It was probably their biggest problem, but—

He gauged the exhaustion in her eyes. No, not yet. "Were Mom and Dad still in touch with Jack?"

Edie sighed. "I didn't ask. Wasn't thinking great by then."

Peter got up and went to the oven. "I thought you might like Chinese."

He watched her as he set the cardboard cartons onto the table, heart quickening as her face turned apprehensive.

"Chinese? I..."

"Noodles," Peter cracked open a carton and pushed it toward her, releasing a puff of anise- and pepper-scented steam.

"Are these spicy?" Edie glanced in and grimaced. "They're just so thick. Reminds me of worms. Don't think I can. Sorry, I've never really liked Chinese food."

Peter reached for his bottle, tense shoulders softening.

Don't make too much of it.

Disliking Chinese food didn't prove anything and was no real indicator of whether or not Edie was guilty of murder. But it made it far less likely—in his mind—that she'd been in that house, talking and sharing Szechuan noodles with Jack.

"I'll make you an omelette," he said.

Edie shook her head. "I'm fine with toast."

"You're not fine," he told her. A smile tugged at the corners of his mouth, just because she'd called the noodles "wormy." "Let me cook you some eggs." He opened the fridge and set the carton on the counter. "Cheese and mushrooms?"

She relaxed into a smile, the first he'd seen tonight. "You're the best."

Not quite, he thought guiltily, setting a heavy frying pan onto the range and turning on the gas. He still wanted an explanation for those cigarettes. "Mind dishing me up some noodles?" he asked.

Edie scooped some onto a plate. "Ick. You want a fork?"

"I know how to use chopsticks," he said. "There should be some in the bag on the table."

"Show-off."

His back was to her, his attention on the frying pan, but he knew she was rolling her eyes.

"I should have been here to help you clean up."

She'd passed the takeout test. Now she'd given him an opening. He'd be stupid not to use it. "About that," he began.

"Yeah?"

"I found something." He poured the bowl of whisked eggs into the pan. If she spoke, the words were lost under the sizzling. He dropped grated cheese and sliced mushrooms on top, then made himself turn around.

Edie was leaning on the table, hands still. "You found something?"

"One of the constables spotted it, actually," Peter amended. "Under the couch in the living room. A pack of Newports."

Her face blanched.

"I said they were mine. Smoked them on the porch before anyone questioned me and asked for them."

Some of her color came back as she gulped her beer. "You know you shouldn't smoke."

"It seemed the safest alternative."

"I'm sorry, Peter. I didn't—if I'd known—"

Peter turned back to the pan, folded the omelette, and flipped it. "Pepper?"

"Yes, please." Her voice was quieter now.

He reached for the grinder and scattered some around the pan. A moment later he transferred the omelette to a plate.

"I've got it." Edie reached past him and carried it to the table.

They sat down. Peter took a bite of noodles, chewing longer than strictly necessary, hoping the lull would goad his sister into speaking, knowing how much she hated silences.

"All right. Jack was here." She drained her bottle.

"Yes, I gathered that." He'd known it had to be so, but hearing her say it made him stab his chopsticks into the heap of noodles then jam his mouth with a too-large bite.

"Why'd you let him in here?" Peter mumbled around his noodles.

Edie laid down her fork. "He doesn't—didn't just surprise me at the office, you know."

He set the chopsticks down. The bamboo felt too frail to remain in his fingers.

"Sometimes he comes here," Edie admitted. "I told you when it first happened, months ago."

"You didn't tell me he'd come back here," Peter said. "Appearances at the clinic, yes."

"You had enough to worry about. Last time he was here must have been two weeks ago. He smoked that time, I remember it."

"Why'd you let him in?" Peter demanded.

Edie rolled her eyes. "What was I supposed to do? Let him shout at me through the door and disturb all the neighbors?"

"He wouldn't have done that." Jack Gainsford was too conscious of appearances.

"You don't know that. You weren't here," Edie snapped. "And I was pretty sure he would've."

"I'd rather he was on your step, even if he was shouting, than here in your house."

"Yeah, well, I didn't want a scene."

You aren't mad at her, Peter reminded himself. *Not really.*

She jabbed at the omelette with her fork. "It was upsetting. I debated for a couple of days, but the way he acted—that was why I decided to talk to Jill."

"What was he so mad about?"

Edie shrugged. "He has moods. You know that."

"I do. But this sounds like more. Jack was murdered," Peter reminded her. "The police think it was you. I can't help if I don't know what happened."

Edie licked her lips "I—"

Peter's jaw tensed.

"I might have started seeing someone."

"Like going on dates?"

She chewed her lip. "Not dates exactly. I didn't want the whole town to know, obviously. Nathan comes here."

Shit. Peter drummed his fingers on the tabletop, thinking of the house across the alley, and the view it had into these rooms.

"Does he stay overnight?"

"That's none of your business," Edie said.

"It's not," Peter said quietly. "Except I found something today. Something important." He leaned onto the table. "You aren't going to like it."

"I don't like any of this." She drew back, squaring her shoulders against the back of her chair. "So. What happened?"

"Leo's seen Jack around. He..." Peter licked his lips, wishing for another swallow of beer to ease the words through his dry throat. "Leo saw him in that gray house across the alley."

She tensed. "The run-down one? With the neglected yard? I thought it was vacant."

"Nope. But it seems he did his best to make it still look that way." Peter rubbed his hands over the tops of his thighs, trying to relieve his tired muscles. "I went inside for a look. Found a jacket with a pocket full of Jack's business cards."

"Why would he—"

"He was using the house to watch you. I'm guessing that's how he knew about you and—and Nathan."

"Watching m-m-me?" She'd stammered most of the way through elementary school. Suppressing the hitches in her words had taken years of practice. Peter remembered how, a year after her marriage, he'd noticed her hiding slips again. Drawing out words, avoiding p's and t's. Becoming so quiet, she was described as shy, and an "excellent listener."

Edie wasn't shy. But she did stutter when she was scared, which made his next words a struggle too. "Yeah. There's a pair of binoculars by one of the windows."

Her hands closed into fists. She gulped and looked with wide eyes at the kitchen window. "Staying there? W-watching?" Then she crumpled, like a shirt tugged from the clothesline by the wind. Her head dropped onto her arms. A second later, she was sobbing.

"Edie." He'd seen her cry dozens of times. When she got stood up in tenth grade. When she'd broken her wrist falling off her bike. When she picked him up at the airport, because he'd come home to help her divorce her perfect husband. This was as bad as all of them.

"It's okay." He got up and filled a glass of water. He patted her back. He lumbered to the bathroom for tissues, and to her bedroom for the wool blanket that she kept at the end of the bed.

Edie took it and wrapped it around her shoulders, disappearing behind thick folds of blue and green Welsh-patterned wool. She gulped, eventually steadying her breath. "C-close the curtains."

Cursing himself for not having done it sooner, Peter tugged them shut.

"D-do you know for how long?"

He shook his head. "But the police will be able to find out when he got the place. I left a message at the station. I've got to tell them about it. They'll find out anyway, and Leo knows. He searched the place with me."

Edie nodded, pulling the blanket closer and wiping at her eyes. "There's no way we can hide that." She shut her eyes and let out a trembling breath.

He'd crouch down beside her, if his legs worked. Instead, he put a hand on her shoulder, urging her to lean close. She sagged against him. Hiccupped, which eased his heart a little. If she was hiccupping, she was pulling herself together.

"Damn. I hate these. They hurt." She hiccupped again and reached for the water glass. "Police will really think I killed him now," she said, between swallows.

"Yeah." Peter sighed. "But you didn't, so we can fix this. We just need to figure out who did."

Edie looked up at him, puffy-eyed, with tear-spiked lashes, and such a defeated expression he had to hold her a little closer. "I'll make some coffee," he said. "C'mon. You didn't let him win before. We aren't gonna let that change."

"You're an idiot. This isn't a game," Edie said. But she stood up. "Let me do it. You make horrible coffee."

CHAPTER THIRTEEN

"Here you go, hon."

I smile up at the waitress as she sets down my plate of pie. Apple, no ice cream, but with a slice of cheddar cheese.

"More coffee?" she asks.

"Please."

As she pours, I note the skin sagging from her elbows. Dolores is aging. Doesn't move as quickly as she used to. As the years pass, more and more abilities will fall away. One day she won't be able to wash her feet or trim her toenails. Her joints, degrading already, will grate when she moves, and her heart will flutter. She'll get light-headed. Maybe fall. Every year, her bones get more brittle. She'll forget things. Shaking hands will spill food from her wavering spoon.

For now though, it only shows in her skin, and the favoring of her right knee.

The pie is excellent. It must show on my face, because Dolores leans against the counter and gives me a smile. "Good, huh?"

I nod, and when she carries the coffeepot away to the kitchen, I take out the notes tucked beneath my half-finished crossword. A half sheet of paper, jotted with things I've heard in the last two days. Still plenty of ideas circulating about this murder, but nothing about anything the victim might have found here.

I mean, Jack found out a few things, but what matters is that he found out about me.

But I've heard nothing about that. Just speculation about him and his ex-wife. Not that I can afford to be complacent. Someone else is hiding things, and although I have a good idea who, I can't be certain, not without revealing my own hand. That would be fatal.

My mind keeps coming back to the car. Ida McSorely says Jack had Nurse Simmons's extra keys, and her son would know. Edie must have given them to him, or else he took them from the house.

That fact stings. I didn't know he'd visited her there, but he must have.

Shouldn't surprise me. He watched the place often enough.

I tap my pencil against the page and lift my eyes to follow Dolores bringing out another order. She doesn't glance my way.

As often as I've wondered if Edie still loved him, I've never wondered much about him. I knew the first time I spotted him here, standing in the rain. That's love, all right, even if it's ugly.

I fold up the notes and slip them into my jacket pocket. Jack should have stepped back and left things alone.

Most people don't have difficulties with that. They just want to be comfortable. It makes them profligate with their trust, and happy to swallow whatever story you give them, so long as they don't have to think too hard.

I take another forkful of pie, with just enough of the cheese that I'll have some for every bite. It's tart and flaky. Dolores gives generous slices. After the last swallow, I dab at my mouth with a paper napkin, to brush away any crumbs.

I push away my plate, stand up, and walk silently past the other diners.

If Edie's extra keys were in the car with Jack, that's convincing enough for most people. She looks guilty.

Unfortunately, someone besides me knows that she isn't, and secrets like this aren't meant for sharing. This kind, you keep to yourself.

CHAPTER FOURTEEN

Edie left early for work the next morning, hurrying away from the house on foot. She'd returned Katya's car late last evening.

She walked most mornings anyway, unless she had to visit patients in their homes or travel to nearby towns. But it irked her this morning, walking away from her empty garage.

How had Jack gotten her keys?

She glanced over her shoulder, telling herself the feeling of being watched was just her imagination. Yes, she had been, but Jack couldn't spy on her now.

As reassurances went, this didn't help much, so she sped out of sight of the darkened windows, shoulders tight, fists jammed into her pockets.

Don't think about it now. You can feel outraged tonight, after Peter tells the police.

Besides, she had another reason to hurry. Katya took care of the morning home visits on Fridays, which meant Nathan would be alone in the clinic until nine, when the receptionist, Brenda, arrived.

If she walked quickly, she and Nathan would have a few moments alone.

There was fog in the valley this morning. Her head was down, her eyes on the sidewalk, so when a magpie swooped from the spruce at the end of Leo's front yard, she started. Cawing angrily, the bird flapped away down the street.

Edie shut her eyes, steadied her breath, and reminded herself she had reasons for being so jumpy. This would pass.

She hurried past the school and the local, purse swinging from her arm. Although the walk was short, the police hadn't said anything about returning her car. Luckily, during her visit yesterday, Mom and Dad had promised to drive out Peter's old car from the storage garage in Calgary in time for her afternoon house calls.

She suspected they wanted to question Peter. They'd have more questions for her too—was she cooperating with the police? Had she called that lawyer?—and though the prospect was unsettling, Edie hadn't been able to think of any other way to get herself a car today, and she needed one, because she was scheduled to give immunizations in Hillview this afternoon, since the Nakoda reservation had no clinic. It wasn't fair to ask Katya to cover for her; she'd done both their work Wednesday, when Edie was at the station, as well as Thursday, besides lending her the car.

The clinic was locked when Edie arrived, which was strange, because Nathan's car was parked outside, and he usually left the door open. Edie unlocked the door and let herself in.

"Dr. Irwin?" she called, in case anyone else was around.

"In my office."

She followed his voice to the back of the clinic and pushed open the frosted glass door.

"Nathan."

"Good morning." When it was just the two of them, he used her first name, but he looked tense this morning, besieged behind his desk. It didn't make him less attractive. Even harried like this, his wide mouth, thick hair, and deep-set eyes would have made her look twice.

"Hi." Edie offered a faltering smile.

He studied her for a long moment, braced behind his desk, then, as tears welled in her eyes, he shook himself loose. "To hell with it," he mumbled, and came to her in long strides, folding her in his arms.

"I missed you," she mumbled into his shirt.

His heart was pounding, and his grip was tight. He seemed as scared as she was, but as she settled in his arms, she felt him relax too.

"How are you?" he asked quietly.

The question felt entirely inadequate for the happenings of the last few days. What she really wanted was quiet, surrounded by strong arms and a steady heartbeat. "Pretty terrible, actually."

"I can only imagine. This has got to be hard for you."

"I didn't k-kill him. No matter what the police say." Among other things, this thought had sped her steps this morning, because Nathan must have been called to examine Jack's body. So he'd already spoken to the police.

His arms squeezed a little tighter. She lifted her face, but he kissed her before she could speak, pulling her closer. "You don't have to explain anything."

The feel of his slowly traveling lips was better comfort than words, and much more reassuring.

Too soon, he pulled back.

He was even paler than before, as if he might be on the verge of tears too, and his hand shook as he pushed it through his untidy hair. Edie glanced at his desk, but the bottle of Scotch that sometimes appeared at the end of a long day was nowhere in sight.

"Edie."

His heavy tone made her stomach drop several inches.

"If people know about us, that will change how the police view my testimony. You know, when I was called to..."

He floundered for words, rubbing the back of his neck.

"The scene," Edie filled in. "Yeah. I thought of that too."

She stepped away and hunted in her purse for a handkerchief. "Here." She passed it to Nathan, and he wordlessly wiped away the traces of her lipstick.

"My brother heard from some folks in town that Jack died of a morphine overdose."

Nathan looked pained. "You know I can't tell you anything."

"But you can," Edie begged. "My brother didn't even hear it firsthand. Everyone else knows. Please, Nathan."

He hooded his eyes. "Looked like it. I don't know if they'll show me the autopsy report. They're sending to Calgary for it."

"I figured."

Another lull. This time, Nathan ended it. "Could it've been self-administered?"

"An overdose?" Edie shook her head. "I don't think so. Jack didn't use drugs when I knew him. He didn't even like me smoking. Said it was unfeminine."

Nathan leaned against the edge of his desk, inadvertently pushing a stray pencil to the floor. The clatter made him jump, and he bent to retrieve it. "I was thinking on purpose," he said, still facing the floor. "The dose must have been big. Too big for"—he cleared his throat—"casual use."

Edie bit her lip.

"He might not have seemed suicidal to you, but it's possible he regrets your divorce. I suggested that to the police."

He straightened, meeting her eyes at last.

"I never thought of that. Thanks."

He smiled sadly. "Maybe the reality of losing you was too much."

Edie shook her head. "I don't think—"

"That could explain why he was in your car," Nathan said. "To make it more of a message for you."

"It's possible," she said reluctantly. Jack hadn't been the easiest person to know, and they'd gotten married relatively quickly, but then, most of her friends had too. It was what you did, before you finished college if possible. If not, you definitely married as soon as you could afterward. Edie hadn't felt the rush immediately, but after working for a year, dating had started to feel like a game of musical chairs. And Jack—well, when she'd started dating him, he'd been easy to fall in love with.

She forced herself out the past, asking, "Did you find the tablets with him?" Unlikely as it seemed, suicide was a better conclusion than murder.

Nathan shook his head. "Wasn't tablets. Police spotted a syringe."

Some of her dismay must have shown.

"What's wrong?" Nathan asked.

"Nothing." Edie swallowed. "It's just...it's just really upsetting."

And Jack had a phobia of needles. He'd faint or hyperventilate every time he had to get blood drawn, and it had taken an absurd amount of persuasion to convince him to get his last tetanus shot. He'd never have chosen to kill himself with a morphine injection.

"Of course it's upsetting," Nathan said, brushing her cheek and offering his arms again.

She went blindly, sinking her face against his chest. "When I imagine what people are thinking—" Edie stopped. There was nothing to be gained feeding this particular worry—that amid so much talk, Nathan would distrust and avoid her.

He was just upset, like she was, but they were going to be okay.

Nathan shifted his hold, and she opened her eyes in time to see his throat bob nervously, destabilizing her just-mustered assurance. Nathan did not look okay, no matter how much she wanted him to.

"The police will want to find out where the morphine came from," he said.

Edie nodded, feeling his tension seep into her where they touched.

"It's only going to make things worse if people think you and I are together," Nathan mumbled.

She nodded again, bracing herself.

Do it. Just tear off the Band-Aid.

She couldn't. So, she offered another complication, another excuse. Another reason why, as a sensible man, he should drop her. "The morphine could have been stolen from here." Her voice sounded rough, like she'd talked for hours instead of this handful of pathetic sentences.

Their liquid morphine was ordered by the bottle and stored in a locked cabinet. Whenever they used some, they made a note in the patient's chart. They stocked a generous amount, too, in case of emergencies like fractures or minor surgeries. One of the reasons Edie had been offered this job was her experience in a city hospital as a nurse anesthetist.

It wouldn't be impossible for a motivated patient to find the morphine and take some—but Jack? She couldn't see it.

"You said he didn't take drugs."

"Not so far as I know," Edie put in. "Doesn't mean he didn't. He could have started the stuff after we divorced, and an accidental overdose seems more likely, in his case, than suicide."

If not for the needle, she added silently.

"Could he have stolen it from you?" Nathan asked. "I mean from your bag. In your house?"

Edie swallowed. Ordinarily, she'd bristle at an implication of carelessness. But Nathan's careful tone wasn't—she was certain—because of that. Somehow, he suspected that Jack had visited her. How?

She hadn't said anything. It was awkward enough when Jack showed up at the clinic. She always tried to pass his visits off lightly, but Nathan had a habit of bringing them up when they were alone. Even days later.

"I don't think so," she said. "But I'll check my supplies."

Nathan nodded. "Good. If we can establish, clearly, that the morphine didn't come from you, there's nothing the police can add to their case."

He didn't say them, but she heard the extra words.

Against you.

Her heart thumped. She'd already concluded that anyone sufficiently motivated could have found a way to siphon some morphine from the supply cupboard. They weren't *that* diligent with the log or the key.

"It wouldn't hurt if we were more careful around here," Edie said. "With narcotics. And with records."

He stiffened slightly. "I hardly think... Well, it certainly won't hurt."

Edie licked her lips. She understood why they needed to keep their relationship hidden, but wasn't sure if secrecy helped her as much as it helped Nathan.

She smoothed her white cotton uniform and reluctantly produced another problem for consideration. Might as well tackle them all, since she sensed, after this, that she and Nathan might not speak again for a while.

"You probably shouldn't telephone me," she said, as calmly as she could. "The police searched my house. Peter said they might also have tapped the line."

It shouldn't have been possible for Nathan to look more somber, but he did. "All right."

It felt like they were breaking up.

Edie wondered, if it came to it, how loudly Nathan would speak up for her. When she told him she hadn't killed Jack, he'd just held her. He hadn't said—with words—that he believed her.

Maybe he didn't.

"I should go," Edie said quickly, not waiting for him to agree before starting for the door. But she paused at the threshold, hoping he'd stop her. He didn't.

You're a murder suspect, she reminded herself, blinking through the blind hurry that carried her down the hall. Brenda would be here any minute.

She needed a drink of water. She needed to touch up her lipstick and tidy her face. Mostly, she needed to be realistic. Why would Nathan—or any man—stick with a relationship this risky, in such a small town?

After Edie left for work, Peter asked Leo to drive him and his wheelchair to the police station. The last two days had left him tired, and his legs ached. Also, it would look better if they went together, with Leo backing him up.

Leo wheeled him inside, and Peter nodded to the receptionist. She was wearing different glasses today. Green frames.

"Good morning, Miss Clark."

She smiled at Leo, then looked at him over the desk. "Mr. Simmons? What are you doing here?"

"Thought I'd come by and see Sergeant Forbes. He hasn't returned my call."

"He's busy right now. On the phone with the pathologist."

It took an effort, but he maintained a bland expression. "Really? About the Gainsford case?"

She glared at him, then transferred her attention to Leo.

"Are you here for a reason, Mr. Martin?"

"Same as him," Leo said. "We found something. Sergeant Forbes will want to know."

She looked unconvinced, but—probably because she couldn't force them out—permitted them to find places in the waiting room. Grudgingly, she offered them coffee.

Peter accepted, and asked for two creams and two sugars, just to make it more trouble.

Leo, after filling Peter in on the woes of the local hockey club, progressed to a detailed recap of a recent competition for the town's mining rescue team. "You'll be interested in this, Peter, because there's rope work involved. And climbing."

Peter smiled thinly. He'd never heard of this kind of contest.

"Our crew is the best, hands down," Leo said. "Lots of folk here thank them for their lives, you know."

Peter nodded. It was easy to forget, as Leo described simulated rescue challenges, that the team's real missions were much more serious. "Must be brave guys."

"Some women on the team too," Leo said. "Back in the day, I used to train them on rope work. Next competition, you should come watch."

"Sure," Peter said.

"Mr. Martin?" Miss Clark was trying to get their attention.

"Yes?" Leo asked.

"Sergeant Forbes will see you now."

Naturally, Sergeant Forbes was not pleased to hear that Peter had been inside the house.

"I took photos," Peter told him again. "You'll be able to see that everything's undisturbed." *Mostly.*

"I watched him go in and come out," Leo added. "Didn't take anything. We didn't bring anything in either, except his camera."

"May I have your film?" Forbes held out his hand.

"Of course." Peter held out a small cylinder. "I took them on a new roll, so it's only pictures of the house. We haven't seen any records to show ownership, but Leo saw him coming and going, and like I showed you, we found Jack's business cards."

"Yes, yes," Forbes said impatiently. "We'll look into it."

"I want you to know," Peter said, not for the first time, "that my sister is innocent. She and I intend to co-operate—"

Forbes cut him off. "Yes, you said. Is that everything?"

"That's everything," Peter said, folding his temper back, tucking it out of sight. Felt like taking down a tent in a windstorm.

"Course that's it, Mark," Leo said, more cheerfully. "What else could there be?"

Forbes didn't bother to show them out. Walking past an open door, they heard Miss Clark talking.

"—as soon as I finish typing the witness statements."

"Don't know why Forbes is making you bother," a man said. It sounded like Constable McSorely. Peter raised his hand, and Leo stopped pushing the chair. They stopped, just out of sight of the open door. Peter barely breathed.

"It's an open-and-shut case," McSorely said, like he'd been solving crimes for decades, instead of being the town's newest recruit. "Gotta be Nurse Simmons. How could it be anyone else?"

Peter didn't hear Miss Clark reply. His pulse was pounding in his ears, like he'd just sprinted a mile.

"Come on, Peter." Leo didn't wait. He just started pushing. If Peter spoke, he'd alert Miss Clark and Constable McSorely to their eavesdropping.

"That kid's an idiot. Don't listen to him," Leo muttered. "Let's get out of here."

Fortunately or unfortunately, there wasn't time to stew about what he'd overheard at the police station. At noon, Peter moved himself and his crutches to the front porch, to present as good a picture as he could to his mom and dad, who were coming from Calgary to drop off his car.

They arrived promptly, like always, and though Edie had warned him, it turned out she hadn't warned him enough. Of course, when she'd asked them to bring out his car, she probably hadn't known about this.

"So, what do you think?" Peter's dad said, beaming at him from the driver's seat. An array of ugly levers now shared space on the dashboard. Hand controls. Peter had heard about these, but installing them was so expensive...

"It will take practice, of course," his mother said. "We've been waiting to show you. If you hadn't run away—"

"Edie needed someone here," Peter said, throat tight, as he imagined the freedom of driving somewhere, anywhere alone. He blinked furiously. "You really shouldn't have."

"Why not?" his mother asked. "We want to help you, Peter. We know it's hard."

Peter smiled, anticipating a gentle barb. He knew his mother. He wasn't disappointed.

"This will make it easier, once you're ready to think about finding work."

He couldn't really fault her for this one. It was true. And even though he was unemployed, the prospect of driving again made him feel taller than he had in years.

He swallowed, failing to dislodge the lump in his throat. "I don't know what to say."

"Thank you?" Dad suggested.

"Thanks. Really. I can't—"

"You can," Dad said. "Get in. You too, Agnes. I'll show Peter how the controls work. Then he can give them a try."

Peter hesitated on the sidewalk, scratching the back of his neck. "It might take a while for me to get the hang of this."

"So? I taught you to drive once already. Can't be any worse this time around."

Peter thought back to a sunlit country road, and a perilous swerve into the ditch the first time he'd been behind the wheel. He chuckled. "I hope not. Mom, you'll definitely want to put on your safety belt."

CHAPTER FIFTEEN

EDIE WORKED THROUGH THE MORNING ON AUTOPILOT, SETTING UP exam rooms, taking temperatures, weighing babies, and tending diabetic wounds. Shortly before lunch, she retrieved the key for the white metal drug cupboard. It was always locked, but the key wasn't secured, just stored out of sight with the tea and coffee supplies in the staff lunchroom.

Someone off the street wouldn't know where to find it, but locating it wouldn't be impossible for anyone with sufficient time and determination. Nathan had his own key too.

The bottle was half full, and to the best of Edie's recollection, it had been two weeks or more since she'd used any. There was a box on the bottom shelf, filled with smaller bottles they could carry on calls or emergency visits, but this was still sealed. The bottle currently in her bag was full and in its usual place.

She couldn't believe that anyone here—Brenda or Katya or Nathan—would agree to give Jack drugs. They didn't know him. Wouldn't risk their jobs, even if, weirdly enough, he'd asked.

Not that she believed he'd taken them. Not with a needle.

She suppressed a shiver. Someone really had killed him.

Just after twelve, Edie ushered the last morning patient, a thirty-year-old woman with rheumatoid arthritis, from the clinic.

"Lock up after I'm gone, will you Nurse Simmons?" Nathan bestowed a polite smile as he passed. "I can let myself in with my own key after lunch."

Edie nodded. "Of course, Doctor." They didn't usually lock the clinic at lunch, but it was a good idea. Especially now.

In the reception room, Brenda was tidying her desk, slipping the cover on top of her typewriter. Brenda *was* graceful, but she always moved like she was performing. As if everyone was watching her. It irked Edie like an itchy sweater.

"Are you staying here for lunch, Edie?" Brenda asked.

Edie smoothed her uniform. "Be right with you."

You don't dislike her. It's anthropological, she insisted to herself. *Female competition.*

Because it *had* grated on her, moving here, just divorced and starting a new job, listening to Brenda going on about her perfect husband. As further proof, Edie had clicked right away with Katya, but *she* was single.

Today especially, Edie was not looking forward to eating lunch with Brenda, who was practically simmering with curiosity. But as she turned reluctantly to make her way to the staff room, someone banged on the clinic door.

"Um, Brenda? I'm locked out," Katya called.

Thank God.

Edie hastened over to unlock the door.

"Thanks." Katya squeezed past, arms full of charts and her heavily laden bag. "Didn't expect I'd have to dig out my key."

"Dr. Irwin wants the clinic locked now. If no one's in the reception room," Edie explained.

Katya's eyes widened.

"Just for our safety," Edie said.

"Did Brenda complain?" Katya asked in a whisper. "I know she said they do that at the pharmacy."

"No, no." Edie said. "I think...I think everyone's just a little tense. Thanks again for lending me your car."

The staff room was tiny and crowded with three. Edie took her usual chair and unfolded the top of her lunch bag.

"Coffee?" Katya asked, pushing a cup at her.

Edie didn't love Katya's coffee. Depending on the day, there was quite a bit of variety in the quality of her brew, but... "Thanks," Edie said, and picked up the cup.

They were acting like this was any other lunch, and it felt sickeningly unreal. Making matters worse, Brenda set down her bran muffin and cleared her throat.

Oh no. Edie braced for a pronouncement.

"We understand." Brenda stretched out a hand and put it on Edie's arm. "We know you're having a difficult day."

"I'd rather not talk about it," Edie said stiffly.

Katya stared at her sandwich. "I met your brother, Edie," she said quietly. "You never told us he was handsome."

"Is he?" Brenda turned her head, and Edie nearly sagged with relief.

Thank you, Katya, she thought.

"Where'd you see him?" Brenda asked.

"Yesterday. At the local. I was there with my dad, as usual."

"Oh, right. Poker night," Brenda nodded knowingly.

"Yes. Peter came in with Leo Martin."

"Yeah, Peter told me." Edie had been so distracted she hadn't realized that Katya would have been there. Her dad didn't get out, unless he had someone to help.

"He didn't stay long," Katya said, her cheeks taking on just a hint of a blush. Before Brenda announced this to the room, Edie picked up a carrot stick and launched a counteroffensive.

"Any plans for your anniversary, Brenda?" she asked and bit down with a crunch.

Brenda nodded, ducking her head in that way she had. Most people probably thought it was cute.

"Mitch is coming home tonight. Should be here by seven. We'll have dinner in Banff tomorrow. I can't wait. He's been gone three whole weeks."

"Are you having dinner at the hotel?" Edie asked.

Brenda nodded. Nearby Banff was busy with tourists, even this late in the season, and though there were plenty of places to stay, "the hotel" always meant the palatial Banff Springs. "We've only eaten there once before."

"Will you stay overnight?" Edie asked, only a shade maliciously. She and Jack had honeymooned there, and Brenda knew it. Edie suspected a night's accommodation would be too expensive for a medical student like Mitch.

Brenda's smile slipped. "No, it's way too expensive for us to stay there. At least until he finishes university."

"Next year." Katya said. *Her* comment was genuine.

Edie set down her carrot stick, slightly ashamed. Yes, she was tired, yes, she'd just had the worst few days imaginable, but she didn't need to be a bitch. Brenda didn't appear to notice, but that didn't excuse anything.

It had to be hard for Brenda, Mitch being away so much. That's probably why she talked about him all the time.

"But what about you, Edie? Aren't you going to ask us about the police?" Brenda asked. "You know they came by the clinic yesterday. They were here for ages."

Edie swallowed, immediately regretting her better intentions. Friendliness was wasted on Brenda.

"I'm not sure I'm allowed to ask you about it," Edie said crisply. "But if you're sharing..."

"Well, you're right. We aren't supposed to discuss it, are we, Brenda?" Katya said quietly. "Sorry, Edie. But of course, we said you had nothing to do with it."

Brenda got up, looked a moment at the coffeepot, then poured herself a cup. Maybe she didn't enjoy Katya's efforts either. "I don't think the police can reasonably expect us not to say anything. We work together every day, and the news is all over town."

Edie rewrapped her tuna sandwich. Maybe she was hungry, but in this room, in this company, there was no way she'd be able to eat. She turned to Katya. "Anyone to add to the afternoon home visit list?"

If she left now, she could avoid seeing Nathan when he came back from lunch at the diner.

"How were your afternoon visits?" Peter asked.

Edie shrugged, not wanting to answer. They'd made dinner, washed up, talked about Mom and Dad until there was nothing more to say. Now they were in the living room, on opposite sides of the coffee table. The blinds were firmly closed.

She'd picked up her knitting, hoping for a distraction. Peter was scribbling in a notebook. Something for his book, she hoped.

"How was it really today? You've been awfully quiet," Peter said.

Edie finished counting her row, but when she was done, he was still watching her expectantly.

"One of the patients wouldn't see me," she admitted. "Doesn't matter. I'll ask Katya to look in tomorrow."

"Did they say why?"

Edie purled two, knit one, and increased, pressing the tip of her tongue between her lips. "I didn't ask. What are you writing?"

She glanced up and saw that Peter had *guilt* spelled across his forehead.

"Well?" she prompted.

He stalled, struggling to his feet and hobbling across the room to switch the record on the player. The needle coughed twice before settling into the LP's grooves. A new song started, something twangy and country, and Peter hopped back to the couch.

He couldn't dance, not like before, and that made her sad. He probably didn't miss it, not like climbing, but she often thought about the things he wouldn't ever do again: sledding, skating, canoeing, riding a bike.

She'd never forgive Ginny for dropping him, for not even waiting to see if he'd recover from the paralysis. She'd jilted him almost the moment he got out of the ventilator.

Edie frowned at her knitting. Those had been terrible days, but not the only ones, not by a long shot. She made herself picture them anyway, and once more held up the painful thought that if she hadn't asked him to come home, her brother might not have contracted polio.

Maybe she shouldn't have asked about the book. He hadn't liked her setting up the dark room.

"You can look if you want."

Edie glanced up, saw that Peter was holding out the notebook, and smiled because he'd decided to let her see.

"These are my notes," he said. "On Jack's murder."

She flinched, then tried to turn away the discomfort with a joke. "Okay, Poirot."

He shook his head. "Poirot doesn't make notes. You mean Hastings."

"Whatever." She glanced at the page he'd been writing. It showed a timeline of Jack's known movements on Tuesday, according to what she'd gleaned from Pinky and Ann.

The next page was titled *Theories*. It was blank. But her throat tightened, because he was here, helping her instead of the other way around, trying to get her out of trouble. Again.

"I heard a theory today," she said. "At work, someone suggested to me that Jack might have committed suicide."

Peter made a face. "That's cheerful."

"Isn't it? Would make things easier for me though."

Peter's brows drew together. "Do you think he might have?"

Edie slumped deeper into the couch. "No. Jack hates needles. He wouldn't have taken morphine that way, whether he was trying to kill himself or not."

Peter flipped to another page and started scribbling. "I didn't know the morphine was injected."

"We probably aren't supposed to," Edie admitted. "But I heard it, so it can't be helped."

Peter shook his head. "This place is something else."

Edie, about to agree, turned instead to the sound of footsteps climbing onto the porch.

She must have tensed, because Peter levered himself up and hopped close to the blinds. "Can't see who it is. It's too dark outside."

"Who's there?" Edie called, climbing off the couch.

"Forbes."

Breath left her in a hiss. She looked at Peter. "Did you know he was coming?" Over dinner, he'd shared details of his and Leo's trip to the station. But he hadn't hinted at this.

"Nope." Peter jammed the notebook behind the couch cushions. "He won't like it."

Edie nodded. She wasn't keen either, but this was no time to tell him so. "Sit on top of it," she said. Of the two of them, Forbes was less likely to make him move. "Ready? I'll let him in."

"You must really hate using the telephone," Edie said as she opened the door. "You couldn't have called first?"

Forbes's uniform was wrinkled and, when he took off his hat, his hair appeared tired and dull. "Too busy? You sending me away?"

"Am I allowed to?"

He adjusted his grip on his hat. "You always have the right to request the presence of an attorney."

So. It was going to be like that.

"My brother's here. Come on in."

He stepped inside, banishing the coziness from her living room, in spite of the music, fire, and her partially worked knitting. With a nod to Peter, he dropped into an empty armchair, as rumpled as a pile of laundry.

"I suppose you can guess why I'm here."

"I'm afraid not." She assumed, if Forbes were here to arrest her, he wouldn't have come alone.

"It's about your ex-husband occupying the house across the way."

"Yes, my brother told me about that."

"Were you aware that he was observing your movements?"

"I was not."

"Can you think of any reason why he did this?"

"I cannot." She sounded like a legal transcript, but she was telling the truth. Forbes looked unconvinced.

"Did he ever threaten you with violence?"

She swallowed. "Not violence. Not explicitly."

Beside her, Peter shifted on the sofa cushions. She flashed him a look, ordering him to be still.

"Do you consider his behavior threatening?"

"Now that I know about it, yes."

Forbes looked unsatisfied.

"Your behavior isn't exactly friendly, either," Edie added.

Peter was so still now he might have been taxidermized, but his fixed expression practically shouted at her. *Shut up, shut up!*

"It isn't my job to make friends," Forbes said quietly.

"No, I suppose it isn't. Do you have any more questions?" Edie asked. She needed to step away, slow down, get Forbes out before things got even worse.

"I—"

"Because I think they can wait," she said. "You've covered the important ones. We can talk next week, after the funeral. I prefer to continue our discussion with a lawyer present."

The tension in Peter's shoulders softened a little.

Forbes nodded. He stood up and put on his hat. "Sure thing, Ms. Simmons. We can do that."

She closed the door behind him, locking the handle and the dead bolt.

"You did the right thing," Peter said.

Maybe, but Edie wasn't sure if having a lawyer would help.

CHAPTER SIXTEEN

Saturday morning, Peter struggled into a suit he hadn't worn since getting sick. It fit oddly over his leg braces, but that would be less noticeable in his chair. Edie's only black dress was more suited for cocktails, so she'd borrowed one from their mother, who owned two for funerals, both kept in paper in her guest bedroom closet. She'd brought one out yesterday, along with the car.

"You look nice," Peter said, when Edie came out of her room. He held out a plate. "I made pancakes."

"The dress isn't bad. I look like a mess." Edie carried the plate to the table and sat down. "Thanks for breakfast."

She looked tired this morning, but that made sense considering the upcoming funeral—and last night's unexpected visit from Sergeant Forbes, who seemed uninterested in lengthening his list of suspects.

"You look fine," Peter said.

Edie snorted and ladled a spoonful of sliced bananas onto her pancakes, then poured on a generous pool of syrup. As she lifted her first bite, a glance at the window arrested her hand. She set down her fork.

"It feels like he's still watching," she said, and got up to tug the curtains shut.

"No one's there anymore." He'd only opened them to keep an eye on the weather, but that was clearly a mistake.

"Doesn't make the ick go away." She swallowed, though she still hadn't tried a bite. "I can't believe I didn't know. I should have—"

"You aren't to blame," Peter said. "Eat."

She obeyed with a sigh, picking at her food fretfully. Edie loved pancakes.

"How's your head?"

"Not bad. Took an aspirin this morning."

After Forbes left, Edie'd brought out more bottles of beer. She drank two, enough to make her slightly sloppy. Peter brought out his notebook again—but she had no new ideas to help pinpoint a time or method for the theft of her car. So, he'd asked her about Jack's crisply made bed.

She caught his implication at once. "You know I wasn't sleeping with him," she said, adding a torrent of profanity and pointed information, much more than he'd ever wanted to know about Jack and her and sex.

"Did Jack make his bed that way?" Peter asked, hoping to make her stop. "Because if he didn't, someone else made it for him, and it would be excellent if we could find out who."

Edie snorted. "How should I know? Making the bed was always my job."

She'd certainly taken care of hers this morning, snapping the sheets so aggressively, Peter was worried anew. It was like Jack was still here, needling her about nothings, making her wary of walking in front of the windows. "Can I have the syrup?" he asked.

Edie pushed it across the table. "Do you think Jack did this to get to me?"

"Don't be an egomaniac," Peter said, intentionally light. This would be a hard day, and Edie looked beaten. "Jack liked himself too much to suffer a paper cut on someone else's account, never mind dying in some kind of complicated revenge."

She nodded reluctantly. "Feels like him, though." She circled her fork in the air. "My car. That house. This whole setup."

"It's someone else. *If* it's a setup," Peter said. "Probably just bad luck you're caught up in it."

"That fits. For me." Edie took another bite, chewing glumly.

"Or Jack. He deserved some bad luck, that's for sure." Peter cut a bite from his three-high stack, trying for more levity. "My money's on that fiancée of his. Jill. We could sneak into her dorm. See how she makes her bed."

Edie rolled her eyes. "She's training to be a kindergarten teacher."

"You think that precludes her from murder? I'd say that makes her an even better candidate. Seriously. Who wants to work in a kindergarten?"

"Not you, definitely," Edie said. "But some of us never got sent to the corner for eating plasticine."

He laughed, pleased to see some humor from her, but the relief was short-lived. Edie sobered on her next breath.

"The thing is, Pinky knew Jack was spending nights away from home. She thought he was seeing me. Maybe Jill did too." Edie licked her lips. "When I saw her at Pinky's house—just in passing, mind you—she looked pretty wrecked."

"Let's just get through today," Peter said. "We can figure this out later." While they had time.

At least he could drive.

They'd timed their arrival at the church early, but a highway accident at Blunt Creek turnoff put them ten minutes behind. Then Peter took a wrong turn, so it was nearly ten when they pulled into the parking lot. As he swore and sweated over the hand controls, trying to park between a gray coupe and a shiny blue Buick, Edie folded her arms, her silence practically shouting that it would have been better if he'd agreed to let her drive.

Then they had to find a way to get Peter's wheelchair into the building. Two of the ushers eventually carried him over the stairs and parked him at the back of the chapel, behind the pews, attracting Pinky and at least three other anxious onlookers.

"I'll bring a chair here," Edie told the shorter usher. "My brother shouldn't have to sit alone."

"I'm fine," Peter said, anxious to shed the weight of so many eyes. He hated being such a sideshow, but most places he went, things turned complicated just getting inside.

"No, Edie, there's a place for you with the family," Pinky announced. "Your parents are already there."

For half a second, Edie failed to hide her dismay, then it was gone, masked by a tight smile and a quick nod. "Coming." She flashed Peter an apologetic look.

"Don't worry about me," he said. Sergeant Forbes was sitting in the back row of the chapel, and it wouldn't hurt for him to see Edie sitting with Jack's family. She walked down the aisle, heels loud against the floor, and Peter had the uncomfortable recollection of her wedding, years before. She'd been smiling then, a little teary, but her back had been just as straight.

At least that hadn't changed.

"Sorry, sir." The usher, moving to close the chapel doors, inadvertently bumped Peter's chair.

"Not a problem." Peter set the brakes and rested his hands on the armrests. The organ swelled louder, and everyone's attention turned to the front of the chapel and the flower-heaped casket. It was closed, which seemed about right.

No answers forthcoming from Jack.

Edie sat through the service, eyes straight ahead, not wanting to be caught looking at Jill, at her former in-laws, at anything really, except the minister. His steep nose and balding forehead were preferable to the box holding Jack.

The speeches and songs concluded, and with a quick shake of her head, Edie avoided being swept along with the Gainsfords to stand at the door of the church. Just the thought of receiving condolences with them as Jack's penitent, grieving ex-wife made her cheeks burn.

As quick as she could, Edie found her way to Peter. "That was awful," she whispered, and held out a hand for the flask she knew would be in his pocket. Peter always brought one to funerals.

Her brother glanced sideways, confirming they were unobserved. Not much chance of being seen—in an effort to clear the way for the exiting crowd, he'd rolled right against the wall, practically inside a wide display of flowers.

"Thanks," Edie said, as he passed her the whiskey.

"Try not to get spotted with it. Forbes and McSorely are here."

A scowl tightened her face. Much as she'd like to say she didn't care what people or the police would think—it couldn't be worse than what they were saying already—she understood his caution.

"Be right back," she said, and slipped the flask into her purse.

The crowd was thick in the foyer, with people milling on the steps outside. Edie darted for the restroom and found Jill inside clutching a tuft of Kleenex.

"I thought you were with Pinky," Edie said, and Jill shook her head, choking on a sob.

"I can't face all those people. All that pity." Her voice broke.

"Want some?" Edie held out the flask.

Jill grabbed it like it was a lifeline, so Edie turned around and bolted the washroom door. "You need a break. If anyone has to go, they can use the men's."

Halfway through a nod, Jill dissolved into tears.

It took all the Kleenex in Edie's purse plus two handfuls of toilet tissue before Jill subsided enough to gasp, "I just can't get over it."

"No one's expecting you to," Edie murmured, moved by the girl's sobs. This had to be hell for her.

But part of Edie—not her better self—couldn't help thinking that at least Jill had a clear job description today. No one was looking at her sideways, trying to read her thoughts.

"We had dinner plans that night." Jill's voice was as wobbly as a toddler's first steps. "I hadn't seen him all week. I even bought a new dress."

"Want a glass of water?" Edie asked, thinking of what Ann had told her about the missed shopping appointment. Jill's "new" dress could have been purchased on any day at all, but where had she been the day Jack was murdered?

Jill tipped back the flask again. It must have been empty, because she gave up and screwed on the cap. The thing had been full five minutes ago, and Jill couldn't weigh much more than a hundred pounds. Soon, she would need help just getting out of here, but it was hard to tell, with her tear-blotched face and puffy eyes, how much effect the whiskey was having already.

As far as questioning opportunities went, Edie couldn't have dreamt up anything better, but she felt a little guilty as Jill fumbled with the clasp of her prim black clutch and extracted a comb to tidy her hair.

You better get on with it.

"What was the dress like?" A stupid question, but she had to start somewhere, and clothes were a safe topic.

"Pink. His favorite." Jill sniffed.

Edie turned away, reaching into her purse for a roll of mint Lifesavers. She still had one pink dress Jack had bought for her, packed away with her winter coat.

"I bet you look lovely in pink," Edie said, and Jill didn't seem to notice the hollowness in her voice. "Did you wear the dress? Or did he call to cancel?"

Jack had liked that dress of hers. She used to wear it a lot, but in the end, the neat waist, collared neckline, and crinoline skirt hadn't fixed anything. The right clothes, the right weight, the right hairdo weren't going to make him like her, even though they did help him act nice.

And now her heart was pounding, like it did back when she was married, and she realized she'd forgotten to schedule her tennis game or change the dining room flowers. It was the feeling of playing an unwinnable game, because there were just too many unpredictable rules.

"John didn't call at all," Jill said, and Edie reminded herself that with Jill he'd started going by his proper name.

"That's odd."

"I thought it was odd too." Jill looked at her so levelly, Edie took a step back.

"Breath mint?"

"Thank you." Jill accepted the roll of candy in exchange for the empty flask.

"I didn't know you were expecting him that night," Edie said, tucking the flask out of sight in her purse. "I didn't ask him to come to Clairbeck. And when I saw him, I told him to leave."

"Did you?" Jill's voice seemed to have taken some sweetness from the mint. It was just as cloying, not hiding the astringency underneath.

"Of course I did," Edie answered.

"Well, he didn't listen," Jill said. "But maybe you didn't want him to." She slipped the roll of Lifesavers into her clutch and crossed to the middle sink, turned on the tap, and splashed a handful of water on her face.

"I didn't believe he was dead when they told me." Edie didn't want her Lifesavers back as much as she wanted to get this conversation on better footing. Jill could have them. "I thought it was some sick joke."

"It is a sick joke." Jill splashed her face again. "All of this."

Quashing her misgivings—she had no reason to be afraid of Jill—Edie carried her compact to the nearest empty sink.

"More a tragedy than a joke I think," she said coolly. Raising her hand to powder her cheeks, she met Jill's eyes though the age-speckled glass of the church bathroom mirror. Jill let out a laugh, harsh as the smell of lingering disinfectant.

"You know, I actually believed you, when you said you were worried about me marrying him. I confronted John. I said I wasn't going to let him terrorize me, like he'd done to you."

Edie dabbed at her cheeks, paling under the vigorous application of powder. "Good. I'm glad. That's all I wanted. I know it must be hard to understand, but I had to tell you. You deserve to know what my marriage was like. I wasn't trying to make trouble."

Jill laughed again, and the sound was even more stinging than before. "You're such an awful liar." She placed another mint between her teeth, pulverizing it with a spine-grating crunch. "John told me about you. And your problems. And how you wanted him back."

Edie snorted. "I didn't want anything from Jack. I had more than enough."

"Oh yeah? It's interesting, you know, that tranquilizers are your only alibi. How many are you taking these days?" Jill's eyes, though glassy, carried a truckload of condemnation. "Because I saw the articles he was reading. Nurses can get pills so easily."

"I don't..." Edie was almost too stunned for speech, but Jill wasn't finished.

"You never deserved him, but he couldn't stop worrying and checking on you."

None of her denials would work, because Jill believed what he'd told her. She should have expected he'd concoct some story like this. It was almost like being married to him again.

"I knew John was visiting you that night."

"You knew he was in Clairbeck?" Edie closed her compact with a snap that rang loud against the bathroom tiles.

"Where else would he be?" Jill jabbed the comb back into her clutch. "And he was right. You do have problems. I went looking for him, you see. It took me forever to drive out there, because I had to wait until my roommate finished her evening shift so I could borrow her car."

Edie's skin went cold, but her lungs filled with the first hopeful breath she'd taken in days. "You came to Clairbeck? Looking for Jack?"

Jill smiled, the gleam of her teeth freezing the skin on Edie's arms. "I came to your house. He wasn't there. It was past midnight. You were sleeping. Alone."

Edie gripped the side of the sink. "How do you know?" She'd locked her doors, made sure the house was shut tight—unusual for her, but it had felt necessary, after sneaking away from the clinic to avoid Jack.

"I knocked. No one answered, but it wasn't hard to get inside."

"You came into my house? You saw me there?" Her breath was too fast, too shallow.

Jill shrugged. "I unlocked the back door through the milk chute. It's not hard. Used a stick I picked up in your yard. You were so sound asleep you didn't hear a thing."

Edie pushed a shudder down from her shoulders, compressing it into a roiling ball of nausea deep in her stomach.

"John wasn't there." Jill leaned forward to apply a layer of pale pink lipstick. "But you were. And your bottle of tranquilizers. You left them by the bathroom sink."

As soon as she got home, she was throwing away that bottle and anything else Jill might have touched. "Why didn't you tell this to the police?"

"Why would I tell them?" Jill's voice was scornful. "They don't need to know about me. By the time I left, it was early morning. You had time to kill him, all those hours when he and I were supposed to be together. It was dark by the time I reached Clairbeck. No one saw me, and no one knows that I wasn't home that night. My roommate isn't going to tell."

"But I didn't kill him." Her voice, frayed with panic, sunk to a whisper. "You have to tell them I was at home."

Maybe it was the whiskey stiffening Jill's spine. Maybe she'd always had steel inside her and been sneaky about it. You didn't learn to break into other people's houses without at least a little practice. As Edie stared, Jill extracted a compact and powdered away the evidence of her angry tears. "I don't *have* to do anything. And I think I'll like seeing you go to prison. Seems fair, and it only makes sense."

"It makes no sense," Edie retorted.

"That's just because you don't know. Pinky didn't want to tell you yet."

Edie's pulse slowed, her blood thick and sluggish. "Tell me what?"

Jill fumbled again with the clasp of her clutch. "John never—" She drew a long breath and closed the bag. "John never updated his will." A throbbing vibrato swelled her voice, and Edie knew this was how hate sounded. She took another step back.

"You're getting everything."

"I didn't know. How would I kn-now that?" Edie stuttered.

Jill lifted one shoulder in a careless shrug. "Maybe he told you on one of his trips to Clairbeck. I certainly couldn't say. But I know the police find it very interesting."

She turned, presenting a wan, frail face anyone would fall for. Jack had probably fallen for this act too.

"Thanks for the whiskey," Jill said, then unlocked the door, leaving Edie alone by the sinks.

CHAPTER SEVENTEEN

Edie returned, pale behind her lipstick. Peter watched as she hugged their parents and responded with brave smiles and colorless words to the few others who offered condolences.

"Will you stay for the lunch?" Mom murmured in a low aside to Peter.

He glanced at Edie, who was once again biting her lip, and shook his head.

"Good. Then we can get out of here too." Mom's smile was sturdier than Edie's, so the relief in her voice surprised him.

"Will you come by the house?" Dad asked.

"No, I think we should go home," Peter said, and Mom squeezed Edie's hand instead of trying to dissuade them.

"Call us once you get back," she said.

"Let me drive. Please, Peter."

Her face was so stricken, he didn't have the heart to argue—until they were closed in the car and she slipped him his flask, empty, by the feel of it. Peter raised his eyebrows.

"Wasn't me. I can still drive," Edie told him. "Jill drank it all."

"Jill? The kindergarten teacher?"

"I found her in the washroom." She laughed bitterly. "You might be right about her." Her eyes were on the rearview mirror, pulling the car out of the parking spot, so he couldn't interpret her expression.

He went for a joke. "And? Did she do it?"

Edie's hands tightened on the steering wheel. "I think she's capable of it. But I don't see exactly how. She told me she came to Clairbeck on Tuesday night. She told me—" Edie broke off, giving her head a shake. "I gotta get out of here."

Peter reached for his safety belt. "Please don't floor it until we're out of sight of the church. There's police here, remember?"

She cursed under her breath but drove as mildly as a nun—at least until they turned the second corner.

Minutes ticked by in silence, Edie's mouth an angry line. His parents must have had the car serviced before bringing it out, because there were no squeals or protests as Edie accelerated into the turns of a back road that would take them to the highway.

At last, they were on open road heading west. "Well?" Peter prompted.

As she told him, he felt paralysis overtaking him again, stealing the life from his legs, arms, and lungs.

"What am I going to do?" Edie said, and he didn't need to see the tears streaking her cheeks to know she felt desperate. She'd been driving ten under for the last five miles.

"It's bad," he admitted, because he knew from lying helpless in the hospital how important it was to know what you were up against.

"I know that." Edie banged one hand against the steering wheel. "I—"

"But remember, you didn't do it," Peter said. "So that means it was someone else. And that there will be evidence. Real evidence, not just circumstances that make things look bad for you. We just have to find who it really was."

"I don't think we can. Not fast enough. I'm inheriting Jack's money, and I'm his ex-wife. He was about to marry a girl I was stupid enough to warn off. Even I would suspect me."

Peter swallowed. They'd worried about privacy from the windows, all without knowing that Jill had been in the house. But she hadn't hurt Edie—though she could have stolen a knife from the kitchen or held a pillow over her face.

"Is there any way Jill could've gotten that morphine?"

"Not that I can see," Edie said. "So as far as the police are concerned, I'm it."

"Could she have stolen it from you?"

She turned wide eyes to him.

"From your nurse's bag. You bring it home with you."

She frowned. "Mine is still there. I already checked. Besides, by the time Jill came to my house, I think it would have been too late. And I bet if I tell the police she was there, they won't believe me."

Peter shook his head. "They'll have to. You didn't do it."

She didn't agree, but she didn't contradict him either. And honestly, he didn't need her to say anything. She wasn't a killer. So, he kept talking.

"Doesn't matter what the police think. It's not what happened. It's not the truth. What really happened is something different. We'll find it."

She let out a long breath. "I'm scared, Peter."

He reached across and took her hand, resting their joined fingers on the seat between them. "It's going to be all right," he said.

But he was scared too.

"I'm not leaving the car on the street," Edie said, when they got home. "Look what happened to me last time. It's got to be locked in the garage."

"Good idea," Peter said.

She got out to unlock and raise the garage door. "Why don't you go ahead," she told him. "I'll bring in the wheelchair."

Peter nodded. By the time he'd arranged his crutches and levered out of the car, she was ready to pull into the garage. "I'll go in front," he said. "Thought I saw something on the porch."

Looked like flowers, but it was hard to tell in the quick glance he'd taken as they drove past.

He rounded the side of the house and started up the steps. Yep. It was flowers all right, a jug of dahlias that must have come from someone's greenhouse, because the nights were too cold for outdoor flowers now. A card had been taped to the jug—

Thinking of you, from Brenda and Mr. and Mrs. K.

Such a tangible kindness, after everything else today, felt unexpectedly good. And the flowers weren't alone. A potted fern (and another taped note, this one from Katya) stood next to them, and there was a loaf of bread and a jar of homemade jam. A plate of cookies rested on a foil-covered casserole dish, stacked between the screen door and the door of the house.

Peter unlocked the door and stepped inside, then realized someone had come and gone in their absence, because more gifts were stacked on the coffee table.

Just Leo, Peter told himself, forcing his breath to slow. *Remember? He has a key. It's normal for neighbors to bring things like food in here, so rabbits and deer, or bears, can't get them.*

Besides, people with malicious intent did not come bearing cookies.

"We're not going to have to cook for a while," Peter called, when he heard Edie coming up the porch steps.

"Those flowers are beautiful," she said, coming in with her arms laden. "I hope these are Mrs. Rupert's scalloped potatoes. Hers are the best, and she won't share the recipe with anyone."

"There's more," he said, pointing at the table. This was just what his sister needed, after all the suspicion and talk.

"Let me put these down." She crossed the room and set everything on the coffee table.

Peter hopped over for a better look.

"We've got some scalloped potatoes here," he said. "You'll have to tell me whose they are though. Don't see a card."

"We'll find out. Whoever made them will want their dish back." Edie hung up her coat and slipped off her shoes.

"What's in that one?" She pointed at the foil-covered Pyrex under the plate of cookies.

"Haven't looked yet." Peter reached for the bright blue dish. Unlike the others, it wasn't warm.

He peeled back the foil and stilled, breath catching in his throat. Not potatoes. Not cookies. The dish held a single human ear, gray green at the edges, black and crusty on the cut edge.

He recoiled like he'd been stung, swaying on his feet, his right crutch falling to the floor.

"Peter!" Before he toppled, Edie flew to his side, steadying him on his feet.

"Don't look," he said, but it was too late. She was staring into the dish, completely rigid.

Finally, with a voice that cracked, she said, "Why didn't you want me to see?"

Peter bit his lip. There was no real reason, other than instinct. Though it was too late now, he still wished he could get rid of this, before she knew what someone had done to her. All the bouquets and jam in the world couldn't counterbalance this.

"Don't touch it," he said, suppressing a shudder.

"No. Not without gloves," Edie said.

Peter stared at the ear, nestled on a bed of crumpled newspaper. It made him think of dead snails. "Is it Jack's?"

She nodded. "I'm calling the police." She seemed to be speaking from far away.

"Peter."

He started as she laid a hand on his arm.

"Pull yourself together. I'll put it in the fridge."

This threat jolted him to life again. "Not there!"

"It's not going to touch anything," she said, walking away with the dish. "And it's covered in foil."

He tried to explain why that was entirely insufficient, but words deserted him. "Edie—"

"I don't like this any more than you do," she retorted. "But it's not all bad. Even the police won't think I delivered this to myself."

Peter wasn't sure they deserved that much credit.

Sergeant Forbes and Constable Lefthand arrived with a camera and evidence containers, but it took over two hours.

"On the slow train today?" Edie asked, standing in the doorway again. Honestly, by now she felt they almost had a routine going.

"We were still in Calgary, interviewing members of Mr. Gainsford's family," he said woodenly.

"Did you talk to Jill?"

Forbes's gaze sharpened. The bile brewing in her stomach must've singed the words of that question.

"She was too impaired to give a statement," he answered levelly. "So, we'll see her tomorrow. Her family live fairly close by, as it happens. Blunt Creek."

Edie's brows drew together. Blunt Creek was a thirty-minute drive from here, halfway between Clairbeck and Calgary. So, when Jill had come to Clairbeck the night Jack died, when she'd broken into this house, she was almost on home turf.

She glanced at her brother. Peter's forceful look wasn't hard to interpret. If she didn't tell Forbes what Jill had done, he was going to.

"You know, I spoke with her after the funeral," Edie began.

"I heard," Forbes said.

Edie's heart quickened. If he knew they'd talked, knew Jill lived nearby, maybe he'd at least consider her story. "Jill Evans admitted driving to Clairbeck late that night, looking for Jack. She said she came to my house. Used the milk door to come in the back." No response. Edie swallowed. "To see if Jack was here."

"That's an interesting claim." Forbes folded his arms. "But what I'm told—by her, by her mother, by Mrs. Gainsford—is that you plied her with a full flask of whiskey today. By the time I talked with her, the poor girl could hardly keep her eyes open."

Forbes' smile was anything but friendly, and his eyes were full of distrust and dislike.

"I offered her a sip. She wouldn't stop taking them," Edie countered, then pinched her mouth shut. What was the point in saying more? Forbes didn't believe her. He didn't believe anything she'd told him.

"The whiskey was mine, actually," Peter inserted, calling from the living room. "You need to consider Miss Evans as a suspect. She's admitted to being here—"

"She's drunk," Forbes said. "As it happens, I have a statement of her movements already, taken by the Calgary police, that includes nothing about coming here. Miss Evans was in Calgary the night of the murder, and two witnesses back that up."

Edie sent Peter a look. *Told you.*

"So, what's this emergency you called about?" Forbes asked, shifting impatiently, sounding just as skeptical as before. "You wanted us here, so why keep us on the doormat?"

Edie exhaled slowly, bottling the heat building in her middle. "Found something in my house after the funeral. Come take a look."

She stalked to the kitchen. Let him try and dismiss *this*.

She opened the fridge. Pointed at the dish on a shelf by itself.

Forbes swaggered in. "Ah. Leftovers."

"No," Edie said stiffly. "Look."

He took his time peeling back the foil...then froze. "Well." He straightened, nodding slowly, talking to the ear and ignoring the rest of them. "So, there you are."

"Aren't you going to use a light meter?"

"No." Constable Lefthand, clearly tired of questions, pressed the camera shutter, nearly blinding Peter with the flash.

Edie huffed. She was leaning against the refrigerator, still fuming, but unlike him, probably not at Lefthand's shoddy technique.

Lefthand pressed the shutter again.

Peter winced. "You could cover that with a handkerchief," he said. "Too much flash will wash out the image."

"The coroner will take pictures too," Forbes said. "But if you want to take over—"

He should, but clearly that wasn't what Forbes had in mind.

"Peter." Edie jerked her head, signaling him to step back. Reluctantly, he followed her to the kitchen table.

Too quickly—Peter would have taken twice as many photos—Lefthand departed for the station, carrying their statements, and a taped and labeled box.

"Well." Forbes sat down, uninvited, across from them. "Shall we talk about this?"

Peter glanced at his sister, rigid in the adjacent chair. "I don't see a lawyer here."

"I've got a question," she spat, unbothered for now by the lack of attorney. "When were you going to tell me my ex-husband was missing an ear?" Red patches burned high on her cheeks. She looked like she was running a fever.

"We thought it better to keep that discovery private."

Edie gaped at him. "You thought it better? Fuck you, Forbes."

He stared at his hands. "I understand this is disturbing—"

"It sure as hell is! You should have told me!"

No stammering, so she wasn't afraid, at least. Peter wasn't sure he'd ever seen her this angry. She looked ready to spontaneously combust.

"Do you know what it's like to come home from his funeral," Edie demanded, "find this thing on my doorstep, and recognize it by a stray freckle?"

Forbes took a breath and let it out slow. "I'm afraid I don't know. I'm sorry, Ms. Simmons."

"It isn't nice."

"I wouldn't imagine so."

"For the record, you've got a terrible imagination."

"Maybe so." The detective folded his arms. "But I'm more interested in how it got here, not what your feelings are. Did you ever consider, Ms. Simmons, that given your circumstances, it might be a bad idea to share your house key?"

A fact they'd covered in their statement.

"Leo?" Peter scoffed. "He didn't do this."

"He's my neighbor," Edie answered at almost the same time. "I've got *his* key."

"I did some looking," Forbes said. "When you suggested your husband had work contacts in town."

"*Ex*-husband. Does...did he?" Edie asked.

Forbes nodded. "There was a lawsuit a few years ago regarding injuries Mr. Martin accumulated during his work in the mine. The suit was dismissed in court. Mr. Martin would have seen your husband there."

"Ex-husband," Edie corrected again.

"Yes, well, he's on record, representing the Clairbeck Coal Company on that occasion. Four years ago, but I expect the circumstance was memorable to Mr. Martin."

Peter leaned forward, resting his elbows on the table and narrowing the distance between him and Forbes. "You can't seriously think—"

"When I want you to know what I'm thinking, I'll tell you," Forbes said. He turned to Edie. "So. You recognize the ear. You claim you didn't know it was missing."

"Claim?" Edie repeated, spreading her hands wide in disbelief. "Do you think I'm faking this?"

"Any idea who could have done it?" Forbes said, finishing as if she hadn't spoken.

"His fiancée says she was here. In town. The night he died," Peter snapped, goaded into speaking.

Forbes rolled his eyes. "Try again. I'm asking about your parcel."

"We don't know," Edie snapped. "We were at the funeral, if you happened to notice."

"I did." Forbes stood up. "Guess I'll have to ask Mr. Martin."

CHAPTER EIGHTEEN

The front door bolt snicked shut, and Edie stomped down the hall to the kitchen.

"Well?" Peter asked. He didn't think things had gone as well as she'd hoped.

"Honestly." She took a glass from the cabinet and slammed it shut. "That was fucking awful."

She filled the glass at the tap and swallowed down three aspirin tablets.

"Isn't that too many?" Peter asked.

"It'll be fine," she snapped. "I need them."

He didn't argue. "You didn't tell him the rest about Jill," he said, to change the subject.

She set down the glass, hard enough that it landed on the counter with a sharp smack. "I told him she broke into my house. He thinks I got her drunk. Why would I say anything more?"

"Because she saw you, sleeping here in your own bed, sound enough that you didn't hear her come inside. Which fits your story of taking a tranquilizer. Also, it tells them that she was here, at—"

"At the scene of the crime? Jeez, Peter! What is it with you? You are not a detective!"

"Well, the guy that just left isn't a very good one! Did you see the way his constable photographed that ear?"

"Forbes probably thinks I planted it. Telling him about Jill did not help. She must have planned for me to spill her story, so I'd look like a pathetic liar. She even made it seem like I got her drunk on purpose."

"We have to—"

"Just what are you trying to do here, Peter?"

He shifted his weight, easing the pressure on his hands from the crutches. "For starters, I'd like to keep you out of jail."

She poured out the rest of the water and turned the glass upside down in the sink. "I don't think you'll be able to stop that."

He shuffled a half step closer. This was not the time for staring at Jack's house through the curtains. "That's why we're going to keep trying. We've got to—"

She spun around. "In case you forgot, this is my problem, not yours. You aren't a police officer. You aren't even a photographer anymore. What do you really think you'll accomplish?"

His braces jammed, making it impossible to step back. Eyes burning, he turned his face away.

Who was he kidding? He wasn't going to fix this. He didn't know anything about interrogation, and anyone who wanted to hide something from him, including his sister, only had to put it on a high shelf.

Wincing—the braces pinched as he shifted, fighting to unlock the hinge—he unstuck himself, and hobbled to the counter. "Pass me the aspirin."

She slid the bottle across the counter. He shook out two tablets and swallowed them dry.

"I should just take the bottle," he muttered.

Her head snapped toward him. "Peter—"

"Forget it," he snapped and started limping away. A bottle of aspirin wouldn't kill him, so far as he knew. The least horrible way seemed to be poisoning yourself from the exhaust of your car. Though he'd considered ending things at low points in the hospital, actually taking steps had seemed as difficult as anything else. So he'd stuck with the rehabilitation program. Right now, that felt more like a draw than a win.

"Peter, I'm sorry. Don't listen to me. I shouldn't have—"

He stopped her with a lifted hand. "Not now. I need a minute." Then he gripped his crutches, walked to his room and shut the door.

Peter's reproach—quiet, eerily contained—chased Edie down the sidewalk. He needed space, and she needed company, hopefully to halt her transformation into a heartless bitch. What kind of person said these things to their crippled brother?

She hated that word. She didn't use it in front of patients, would never speak it aloud to Peter, but what she had said was probably worse. No matter how frayed she felt, ripping at his confidence was inexcusable.

Peter had always been more level-headed. It had made him a good climber and a safe one: methodical, calm, but quick thinking in emergencies. And he was her loyal little brother, so easy to lean on when she'd needed help.

Just look what that had done to him.

She needed to make this right, but what she really wanted to mend was past fixing. Her lungs hurt and the houses she passed were nothing but a hot blur.

By the time she reached Katya Virtanen's, her breath had eased and she could see again. It wasn't far, just a twenty-minute walk along Sunday afternoon streets. Most Finns in town lived mine-side, across the highway and closer to the active mines, but Katya and her dad had moved when he was injured in an accident, not long after her mother died.

The house was tiny, half hidden by shaggy trees, within hearing distance of the meandering waters of Policeman's Creek. The fading paint and untrimmed grass gave it a rustic look that suited the mountain backdrop. The doorbell didn't work, so Edie rapped on the window. "Katya?"

The bolt slid back, squealing so loud, Edie flinched. The door opened, revealing Katya in trousers and a loose pullover. Her hair was in its usual braid.

Edie smiled weakly. "I'm so glad you're home."

"What are you doing here? Isn't the funeral today?"

"Already went. It was this morning. I… Well it was rough."

She should have phoned ahead. Katya had lots to do, caring for her dad. Especially after covering Edie's absences at work earlier this week. Katya had also stuck up for her and let Edie borrow her car.

"Sorry. I don't mean to bother you," Edie said, ready to retreat.

Katya's face colored. "Don't be silly. You aren't a bother."

"I can go if you're busy," Edie said.

Katya shook her head. "You don't look so good. How about a walk? Dinner's in the oven and my dad's asleep. We can talk."

Without warning, Edie's eyes were stinging again. "Thanks. I'd love that."

"Do you have decent shoes?"

"I'll be fine," Edie said. Her loafers were sturdy enough.

Katya joined her on the porch. She laced up a pair of worn boots, locked her front door, and they set out, following a trail that skirted the houses, leading to the river.

In very little time, Edie lost sight of the houses and streets. The woods around Clairbeck were thick and filled with winding paths. It was cool under the trees, the air flavored by a rich blend of spruce, damp earth, and moss.

"We can cross at the rail bridge," Katya said. "Go along to the sulfur spring. It smells funny, but the water's warm. You can soak your feet. Be good for you."

Edie had heard of the place. It was supposed to be about an hour's walk. "Sounds perfect." She needed to get out of her own head for a while.

"So, what happened?" Katya asked, stepping over a thick root crossing the trail.

"I got—" Edie stopped. Edited. "I got an earful from a few people today." And she had, from Forbes and Jill. It seemed best not to say anything about the actual ear. "Then—maybe because I'm tired—I gave one to Peter and he deserves better. I said things I shouldn't have."

"Funerals can be hard," Katya said, pushing aside a branch.

"Yeah."

They came to the river and started across the bridge. Here, in the open, the peaks looked sublime in the sun. Edie's throat tightened.

"What's wrong?" Katya asked.

"My brother loves mountains." Edie shook her head. "I thought this would be a good place for both of us. A safe one." Not a place where she'd be watched unawares, where people thought the worst of her and a killer hid among seemingly friendly faces.

"I think I know what you mean." Katya shaded her eyes, studying the mountains. "It must be hard for him to see them and remember all he used to be able to do."

"Yes." It wasn't what she'd been thinking, exactly, but it was part of it.

Katya dropped her hand and started forward again. "I'm sure Peter misses many things." She smiled lopsidedly. "It's how life is for him now. You're a good sister."

Edie shook her head. "I'm really not."

"Nothing is all one way or another," Katya said. "That mountain. You could go anywhere in the world, I think, and not find a lovelier one. It's beautiful and dangerous. People die on it every year."

"Climbers?" Edie asked, suppressing a shiver. She'd often worried about Peter in the gaps between letters and postcards. But climbing was the life he'd wanted, and she hadn't worried then nearly as much as she had when he was in the hospital. She was worried for both of them now.

"Sometimes climbers," Katya admitted. "But not always. The mountains, they catch people unawares."

They sounded alive, the way she talked about them. Peter and some of his friends had talked that way too.

"There was a doctor, Lorna Lewis, who came here before Dr. Irwin," Katya went on. "She was meant to take over when Dr. Williams retired but didn't make it through her first winter."

Edie pushed her hands into her pockets. Though the day was warm, the infrequent breeze carried a chill. "What happened?"

"Went walking, like we are."

"I'm sure it was a little more than that," Edie said sharply.

Katya smiled apologetically. "Well, yes, but that's the danger, isn't it? You think you are going for a walk, but you don't really know. There's bears. Rock falls. Dangers you forget to prepare for. Dr. Lewis went on a hike. Later in the year than this. Toward the end of October. The weather was fine when she started. Somehow, she wandered off the trail. She might have been all right, even then, but there was an early snow, and she hadn't brought any matches to build a fire."

Edie bit her lip. Her pockets were empty. She had no matches. No pocketknife. She'd been in such a hurry to leave, she hadn't even taken her key. "Hypothermia?" she asked quietly.

"Yes. I was with the search party that found her the next afternoon, but it was too late."

"That's awful." Edie curled her fingers into her palms.

"Don't worry about us," Katya patted the pockets of her trousers. "I always bring the basics. Even at the spring, we're still in easy distance of the town."

But if all it took was wandering off a trail...

Edie shook her head. Katya must know this route well. "You must think I'm silly. Or stupid."

"Not at all," Katya said. "I wouldn't expect you to consider those things. You're still pretty new here. And you've had a hard day. I'm sorry if people were unkind. I assume it must have been your ex-husband's family?"

Edie nodded, not wanting to get into it. "Divorce is, in my case, a necessary nightmare, and funerals—well, you know. But there are compensations," she added, trying to lighten the mood. "I think Mrs. Rupert left me scalloped potatoes."

Katya laughed. "My father says those are almost worth the funeral. He'll be jealous."

She must have been given flowers and full Pyrex pans after her mother died, and again, following her father's accident, but without any hidden horrors.

"Bring your dad over for some," Edie suggested. She needed to think of other things. Calming ones. "Peter and I can share."

Katya shook her head. "It's pretty hard to take my dad out. I'd love to, but I better not."

Edie's heart twisted. This particular organ of hers had been aching all day, but this time, the pang wasn't for her or Peter or Jack. Katya was always looking after someone: her father, their patients.

And now me, she thought.

"I'll bring some over for him then," Edie promised.

Katya started to protest.

"No, there's plenty," Edie insisted. "Not just scalloped potatoes. People in town have been very kind."

Katya dropped her eyes, choosing her footing on the uneven trail. "They are, you know. Think about their gifts today, and don't let other people's sharp words bother you."

Edie let out a breath. She wished it were that simple.

CHAPTER NINETEEN

Half an hour after Edie left, the doorbell rang, and if Peter hadn't been precariously lurching down the hallway, balancing himself, his crutches, and a thermos full of coffee in full view of the front door, he would have ignored it. But he could see whoever it was on the doorstep, peering through the cut class, and knew they'd be able to see him too.

"Give me a minute!"

The person pulled away, doubtless due to the exasperation lacing his voice. "Edie?" they called.

"No. She's out."

Peter set down the thermos, hopped to the door, and wiggled the dead bolt (it tended to stick) until it retracted grudgingly. In a similar frame of mind, Peter swung open the door.

"You must be Peter."

Long-lashed eyes. Smooth black hair.

The woman on the doorstep was horribly pretty.

And he'd just yelled at her.

"I brought pie." She held out a pan. Her hands were in oven mitts, so it must be warm. "For you and your sister?" She looked nervous.

Because she expected Edie, not some angry asshole.

"Edie's gone out." Peter brushed the hair from his forehead. He felt sweaty, haphazard, and stuck. "I—" He reached for the pie, then paused, remembering how impossible that would be. "I'm afraid carrying isn't so easy for—"

"No," she said, forehead wrinkling. "I see that." She looked wary, like he might growl or swipe out at her, like a wounded bear.

Well, his greeting hadn't been that far off.

"Sorry if I sounded snappy," Peter said. Why had he been so brusque? And why was he so sweaty? Yes, it was awkward, brewing coffee for himself, lurching about the kitchen, capping the brew in a thermos so he could carry it to a chair instead of drinking it at the kitchen counter. But those challenges weren't like running a marathon, not anymore.

"I was having a tough time getting to the door." He swiped at his hair again, trying to surreptitiously wipe the shine from his forehead. "It can be frustrating, getting around."

He felt like a jerk. Even on crutches, he loomed over her. She looked ready to fling aside the pie dish and run away. "If you just set it on the step," he suggested.

She stiffened. "No, that's okay," she said. "I can bring it in."

"That's awfully good of you," Peter said. "Edie will..." He trailed off. He didn't know when she'd be back. "I'm sorry, but I didn't catch your name?"

"Oh." She blinked. "I'm Brenda."

Already flustered, Peter struggled to contain his surprise. This was the receptionist who worked with Edie. He'd heard her name at least a dozen times, but he'd assumed she was white. Brenda Leigh, not Brenda Li.

He should have realized, since this wasn't Katya, and Edie knew her coworkers the best out of anyone in town.

"Mrs. Li." Peter smiled for all he was worth, about ready to melt into the floor. "I'm sorry. I didn't realize it was you. You caught me in a tough spot, and I'm not thinking great today."

Her mouth tightened briefly, but she too managed a smile. "Well, that's why I thought you might like this." She raised the pie an inch, like she was offering it for inspection.

It looked perfect and smelled like apples and cinnamon.

"Wow." He stepped back, so she could come through the door. "Kitchen's this way."

As she drew closer, he noticed a heavy layer of powder around her eyes. As if she might have been crying before.

She set the dish onto the countertop. "Hope you enjoy it." As she turned to go, Peter stopped her.

"Will you have some with me?" he asked. "You see what I wreck I am on my own."

God, what was he saying? She'd never agree, and why would he want this excruciating awkwardness to continue? But he wanted to redeem himself. He wanted a better look at her face, just to know if she really had been crying.

"Please," he said. "I'd love some company."

She let out a breath, but his was stoppered inside his lungs. He couldn't push any air out.

She blinked. "Okay. Sure."

He wasn't sure why this felt like such a relief and told himself not to think about it.

"Ugh." Edie smelled the spring before she saw it. Grimacing, she searched for a handhold to brace her descent. The trail down to the river was steep. "Smells like bad eggs."

"Give it a minute and you won't notice. The soak is worth it, especially in winter." Katya was several paces ahead, almost to the spot where the spring fed into the river. They'd conversed easily—on pleasanter things—the rest of the way here, and Edie was realizing how much more talkative her friend was outdoors, walking, not face-to-face.

"The best way is switching between steaming water from the spring and the river water." Katya smiled back at her. "In winter, it's so freezing when you go in that it's hard to breathe. Your skin burns and prickles and goes numb, and when you can't stand it any longer—"

Edie shuddered. "I'll stick with the hot water, thanks."

Katya smirked. "You don't know what you're missing."

Along the river's edge, rocks placed at the outlet of the spring dammed up the flow of hot water into three shallow pools.

"This one's hottest." Katya pointed. "The last one is only comfortably warm. Of course, the river's cold, even in the summer. You haven't come here, yet?"

Edie shook her head. "I've heard about this place. Just haven't made the time." She wobbled, catching herself as she moved from one boulder to the next.

Edie was no mountaineer. She enjoyed Clairbeck's mountain setting, but she'd chosen it for Peter. By the time she moved here, she knew that even if he made a full recovery, it would take years. She was divorced, alone, and a nurse, so it made sense to be ready to offer her brother a home, one he'd be happy in.

All she'd wanted was a decent job and a place away from Jack. Sounded simple enough, but she'd definitely failed with that last one. Now, with things so uneasy with Nathan, the job wasn't great either.

"I should have made time," Edie said, taking in the view. Since moving out here, she'd never visited this spring or hiked Ha Ling Peak. She'd never even skated at the pond just a few blocks off Main Street. So much of her free time had been spent visiting Peter in the hospital.

But he was here now, and that changed things for her too, something she'd overlooked with everything else that had happened. Edie wasn't sure now if this was the right place for either of them. The mountains seemed to haunt Peter as much as help him, and—she grimaced—events here would haunt her forever too.

"Come in," Katya urged. "You'll feel better in the water." She'd already taken off her boots, and in spite of the smell, the prospect was tempting. Steam lifted from the water, and the sound of the river was already eroding the fatigue weighing on Edie's joints, and the views—well, surrounded by mountain and forest, any way you looked—the prospect was pristine. Stunning, even.

Maybe it would be worth trying to get over some things. Assuming she didn't end up in jail, why couldn't she make this town hers too?

She looked at Katya, then the nearest pool, recalling that Finns like the Virtanens probably didn't just dip in their feet.

"Are you going in?" Edie asked, and Katya, usually so contained, grinned sheepishly, revealing the truth. She went in the water, swimsuit or no.

"I won't if it bothers you," Katya said. "You'll feel better, even just soaking your feet."

Edie compressed her lips. *You aren't a prude.*

She'd already stored her ex-husband's ear in the refrigerator today, so why balk at a little skinny dipping? Edie shrugged and untucked her blouse. "We came all this way."

"You won't be sorry," Katya told her.

Soaking in the smelly, steaming water really did feel amazing. The water came into the pool almost scalding, turning both of them red as lobsters, and the sulfur—or something—made it feel slippery, almost soapy against your skin. Edie'd been to the hot spring pools in Banff half a dozen times, but now she could see why Katya scoffed at that for not being the "real thing."

"Feeling better?" Katya asked.

Edie nodded and stretched out her toes. "You're right. This is the perfect cure for a rotten day."

From now on, she'd do better. She'd be kinder to Peter. She'd cooperate with the police, even if they were rude and didn't believe her. She'd sew up some thicker curtains and grow a thicker skin and make a real home here. She'd forget about...about a lot of things.

"Time for the river?"

"Not a chance," Edie said. "I like it right here."

"Well, I'm going." Katya stood up. Edie tried not to look, but before her eyes swerved to the trees, she glimpsed a series of thin white lines drawn onto Katya's sides, so faint they were all but invisible.

Stretch marks?

Plenty of women have them, Edie reminded herself. But when they fanned like that, over the sides of the abdomen...

"You really should try it," Katya called, and raced for the cold water, shrieking as she confronted the cold.

"You're crazy!" Edie shouted. It did look fun though.

In a minute or so, Katya had had enough and sprinted back to the hot water. "Ah," she sighed, leaning back, sinking down to her chin. "So what else is troubling you? Were you sad today? Because he's gone?"

Like other Finns that Edie had met, Katya could be blunt.

"I didn't love him anymore," Edie said. "If that's what you're worried about." There was no good way to explain Jack, not without going into things she'd already hashed out with Peter and the police. She picked up a rock from the bottom of the pool and dropped it back into the water, watching it sink.

"I worry about how this happened to him," she admitted. "Mostly because it doesn't make any sense. And of course, I'm upset that he died."

"Of course," Katya nodded.

"I loved Jack for a while," Edie said. "But the idea of him was so much better than the real thing, and for years I couldn't give that idea up. And then I did." She shrugged. "I'm sad for him. And sad for the life I thought I had but never did, even though I've given up on it."

She scooped up a palmful of water and let it trickle through her fingers. "You ever loved anybody?"

Katya sat up.

"Sorry," Edie said. "I saw"—she gestured under the water at her own side—"the marks."

Katya frowned.

"It's none of my business," Edie said. "But you know. We're here, talking." She shifted on the stones. Once in a while, Katya would mention going on a date, but she'd never admitted anything serious. And Edie hadn't wondered—much—because with most of Katya's free time spent caring for her dad, a social life couldn't be easy.

But maybe there was more to it than that.

"It was a long time ago," Katya said. "I was sixteen."

"Oh." That was young, if you wanted to solve the problem by getting married. At that age, most girls were sent away. "What happened?"

Katya turned her face away.

"Sorry. I shouldn't have asked," Edie said.

"No, it's fine." Katya faced her again, forehead smooth, eyes clear and untroubled, but Edie found this absolute calm even more disconcerting, and wished she'd bitten her tongue.

"It was nothing special," Katya said. "I spent six months at a maternity home. My parents told everyone I was visiting an aunt."

Edie nodded slowly. "And your baby?" She was afraid to ask, but it seemed necessary, now that they'd started.

"Adopted. I held him once. Came home a week later." Katya's cheeks contracted in a mirthless smile. "Made the honor roll in school again that fall. My mother said after going away I had to be extra careful. So, I was."

A drop of sweat slid away from Edie's hairline, rolling down the back of her neck. She was overheating, but this was no time to dive for the colder water, even if she wanted to.

Some of Edie's classmates had trained in maternity homes. They weren't easy places to work, and being a patient in one wasn't something you'd wish for a friend.

"It sounds hard. I'm very sorry," Edie said.

Did people in town know? And just not say? There must have been talk at the time. And what about the guy who'd left her to manage alone?

"I'm ready for the cold again," Katya said. "You coming?"

"Sure. I'll try it."

It seemed wrong not to go, after a confidence like this. No backing out now. Muscles tight, Edie marched into the water. No stopping, because the only way out of this was through.

Her heart nearly stopped from the cold. Her lungs seized, but from the first skin-burning second, Edie understood why Katya loved this. The paralyzing cold was real and immediate, and it would be deadly, given enough time. But as her lungs heaved against the icy weight, and her heart screamed at her blood to invigorate her stinging skin, Edie realized she couldn't worry about anything.

It felt incredible.

"Run!" Katya said, and Edie laughed and raced back to the warm water at the river's edge.

"Thanks for the pie," Peter said. His plate was empty, twice over, and Brenda, who ate slower, was nearing her last bite. "It's the best I've had in ages."

Brenda blushed. "Glad you like it."

"More coffee?" Peter offered the thermos, then realized it was empty. "I can brew more if you—"

"I can make it." She'd also dished up the pie, saving him from having to hop about in front of her. "Do you want some?"

Not really, but… "Sure." He'd drink more coffee if it let him keep her. Brenda's company was much better than his own today.

She got up. "Would you mind if I made tea for myself instead? I like it better than coffee."

"Go ahead. Sorry, I should have offered."

"It's all right."

"If you're making it, I'll have some too," he said, and pointed her to the tea, teapot, and fresh cups. As she bent to retrieve the seldom-used tea tin from a drawer below the counter, he averted his eyes, afraid to be caught staring.

He shouldn't be staring.

"Sorry for keeping you so long." He fixed his gaze on the patterned tablecloth. She'd been here at least an hour, and they'd talked a lot. About the funeral, but about easier things too, like Clairbeck, the peculiarities of miners, and Brenda's work at the clinic. "If you need to go—"

"I don't need to be anywhere."

Had she sighed? He couldn't see her face. Filling the kettle, setting it on the stove, her movements were efficient, unhesitating. She didn't seem sad, but if she was, there was one easy guess. He tried it.

"Edie told me your husband is in Edmonton for university." It was a four-hour drive from here, not an easy distance.

"Yes, Mitch is in medical school. Both our parents are here, though, so one of us has to stay and help," she explained. "And I make better money here than I would in Edmonton."

"Must be tough. Bet he really misses you."

"Yeah." This time, she definitely sighed. "Mitch was going to come home this weekend, but—" She stopped, dropping her eyelids. "He phoned last night. Couldn't make it. Midterms."

Peter thought it might be a tad early for them but didn't want to say so.

"Anyway, we talked for a bit. Not too long of course. Long distance."

"You guys must spend a fortune," Peter said.

"Yep." Brenda leaned against the counter. "It's only for another year. Then he'll move back. It will be good for the town. It's hard when there's only one doctor."

"I bet," Peter said.

The kettle whistled. She reached for it and poured steaming water into the teapot. "I'm just glad to be out of the house. Sometimes I feel like I'm rattling around there, on my own. Thanks for inviting me in. You're a good listener."

Peter spread his hands. "That, I can do."

She rolled her eyes. "At this rate, you'll let me run on forever."

She set the tea things on the table and poured out two cups, offering his with two hands, not bothering with milk or sugar. The way she held the tea nudged Peter into murmuring *"Mh goi"* as he took the cup from her fingers and let the steam float over his face.

"Where did you—" Brenda colored. "I hate to disappoint you, but I don't speak very good Chinese."

"Oh?" Peter felt his eyebrows climb.

She shifted in her seat. "My grandparents spoke Cantonese. My dad can, but my mom's is shaky. Mine's worse. I can speak some, but I'm slow and—" She shrugged. "Granddad, my *yeh yeh,* always said I spoke funny."

He'd put her on the spot, made her uncomfortable. By the sounds of it, her family had been in Canada longer than his. "Sorry. I'm an idiot. I only know a few words. I shouldn't have..."

"Where did you learn *mh goi*?" she asked.

His cheeks flamed with embarrassment, not because of the tea in front of his face. "I went to Hong Kong," he muttered. "Few years ago."

He'd been on his way to India but came back to Alberta instead. Where would he be now, if he'd kept on going?

Not here, that's for sure.

He might as well have mentioned Hong Kong to Leo, though, because Brenda had clearly never been. Which he should have guessed, speaking to her. She made apple pie, spoke without an accent, and had talked about attending high school here in Clairbeck. "I'm an idiot," he repeated.

"Forget about it," she told him.

"You grew up in town then?"

She nodded. "My parents too."

Responding to her unspoken reproof, he lowered his head to his cup and changed the subject. "Clairbeck's a beautiful place. I'd have loved being a kid here." Recalling his years as a Boy Scout, before he started climbing, he asked, "Do you hike?"

Brenda smiled. "Not like you. I mean, Edie showed us some of the pictures you've taken. I don't—" She blushed. "Well, actually, I was knock-kneed as a kid, so I never participated in PE classes until high school. I always had to do remedial running during that block instead."

Peter made a face. "Is that as fun as it sounds?"

"Pretty much." The smile she gave him was lopsided, just a little. "So, I never went much, when I was young. Kind of a waste, I guess, living here. But my dad and I always liked fishing."

This surprised him, because Brenda looked too perfectly groomed to enjoy an uphill scramble, let alone baiting a hook.

Her eyes roved to the line of covered dishes on the counter. "Looks like you're set for a while."

"Yeah," Peter said, and his lack of enthusiasm must have shown, because her eyebrows drew together.

"Most people have been really kind," he said quickly.

She studied him, chin propped on her elbow. "Most people?"

Peter shrugged. "We had to speak to the police again today and see them at the funeral. People in town are saying things too."

And not saying things, he thought, remembering what Forbes had told them about Leo's court case. Had he really not recognized Jack from the trial years before?

"People always talk," Brenda said. "I've heard what they're saying, but they don't mean it, Peter. People like your sister."

"They should. She's a good person. And she's not a murderer."

"Of course she isn't!"

Peter forced a tight smile. "I think you're the first person I've heard say that."

"I'm not the only one."

She was right. Katya had too. Peter loosened his shoulders. "I should just enjoy the flowers and the scalloped potatoes." He smiled at her. "And the pie."

"Well," Brenda hesitated. "Since we're being honest, I'm afraid I didn't bake it for you."

It took him a moment to catch on. "Oh, right. Because your husband, Mitch, was supposed to come home."

She nodded, tilting her head in the direction of the counter. "I brought the dahlias over with my parents this morning, while you were at the service. But then I was going a bit crazy on my own. It's harder, I guess, because I was expecting Mitch, and instead he's there and I'm here. Again."

Peter nodded. He felt bad for her. Mitch seemed like a bit of a heel. *But he'll be Dr. Li soon enough,* Peter reminded himself.

Brenda shrugged. "I decided to go out. Went to Katya's, she's the other girl in our office."

"I've met her," Peter said.

"Oh, right. Well, she wasn't home. So, after a quick visit with Mr. Virtanen, I warmed up the pie and came here." She shrugged apologetically. "I didn't mean to barge in on you, but I'd kind of hoped—" Her face colored.

"I needed help, remember? And it's nice for me, talking to someone." He stared into his cup, almost empty now, though he couldn't recall drinking it. "I worry about Edie, for obvious reasons."

Wanting to help, not feeling able to. Edie not thinking he could, which was as bad as the rest of them.

He sighed and leaned back in his chair. "What's on your mind? Just Mitch?"

She hesitated.

Peter turned his empty hands toward her. "I'm just trying to be fair. I've said lots. If you want a turn—"

She flushed. "I'd hoped to talk to Edie, but—" She bit her lip. "In some ways, maybe it's easier talking to you."

Peter kept his face smooth. In the hospital, some of the nurses had said similar things, and he didn't take it as a compliment. To them, he was safe because he was broken. Not another woman, but not a whole man. Like he was everyone's kid brother.

"It's not the easiest thing to bring up with her either," Brenda went on. "I probably shouldn't say anything."

Peter mustered a smile. If listening to her helped, he should offer, if only because she'd done the same for him. Until a minute ago, he'd felt better than he had in days. "Don't tell me if you don't want to," he said. "But if it helps…remember, I have an older sister. I've heard just about everything."

Brenda stared at her hands, rubbing her polished nails with one thumb. They were tidy hands, pretty ones, and he really shouldn't be admiring them.

"I tried to ask Edie a long time ago," Brenda began. "When she first started working at the clinic. But I think I came across as nosy."

"She can be prickly," Peter admitted.

"Then things were better for a while, so there was no point in bringing it up. But this weekend, it's our wedding anniversary—" Her chin dropped even more, and she blinked twice. "Anyway, I…I think when it comes down to it, I'd rather ask you. Edie knows more people here and—"

"What do you want to know?" Peter asked quietly.

She tucked her hair behind her ear. "Is it terribly hard to get a divorce?"

Peter leaned back in his chair again. He hadn't noticed shifting forward.

"I'm not…I'm just wondering," Brenda said miserably. "Having information isn't the same as doing anything with it."

Peter nodded. He understood, in a different way. Hadn't he found out the relative painlessness of carbon monoxide poisoning compared to other methods?

"It wasn't easy," he said.

Brenda nodded. "When I asked Edie about her divorce, she said the first lawyer she spoke to said it would be easier to murder him if she could get away with it." She bit her lip. "Not that I ever thought for a moment—"

"No." Peter said, more firmly than he intended. He remembered his sister telling him that too, years ago. Stupid, throwaway words, meant in jest, but now, if they were passed on to the police… "It was difficult," he said. "And expensive. But she had my help, and eventually my parents' too."

Brenda nodded.

"It can be easier, if you have a reason," Peter began, unsure how much to say. "If, say, your husband is in the habit of hitting you." But even then…

"No, no," Brenda said quickly. "There's nothing like that. It's just—" She swallowed. "It's hard, you know. So many years of him living away."

"I'm sure it is," Peter said. He shifted in his chair. "I can tell you the name of the lawyer Edie used."

"I'll probably never use it," Brenda said in a rush. "It's just, sometimes, when I'm particularly angry, I get to thinking and realize how little I know, and that makes it worse."

Yes, he understood that too. His notebook, perfectly proving the point, was on the table beside him. Peter opened it and flipped past his useless notes to the first empty sheet, tore it out, and scribbled down a name with a too-dull pencil. He wasn't angry. Not at Brenda.

"Mind, this guy doesn't come cheap."

"I doubt I'll ever call," Brenda said. "But at least I have it."

Peter smiled wanly. "Need some more tea?"

She looked smaller in her chair since confiding in him.

She regrets telling me, Peter thought. She'd probably avoid him after this.

"No, I'm fine." Brenda glanced about, like she was looking for a clock or a darkening window, some cue that could push her out of the room. "I should get going," she said lamely, folding up the torn sheet, and tucking it into the sleeve of her cardigan. "Thanks, Peter. You…you won't tell anyone?"

"Not a soul," he assured her.

CHAPTER TWENTY

Ha Ling Peak sits behind the town, a sharp summit rising from a curved ridge high above the tree line. If you drive out of town, along a gravel highway, passing the dam and the reservoir to the other side of the mountain, it's possible to hike to the top. Once you reach the ridge—folks usually call it the saddle—you can see all of Clairbeck, spread out on the valley below. The town hugs the highway and the rail line, and there's fewer mines open now than there were twenty years ago.

I can see my own roof amid the clusters of houses. There's a ball diamond, a track, and a football field in the wide green space surrounding the middle school. I can name all the shops and businesses on the three-block length of Main Street. There's a car, pulling out of the parking stalls on the side of the police station.

Pretty sure they've never had to take a severed ear in for analysis before.

Don't know why I took it, really, but maybe it's because I knew this one wasn't going to look like an accident. Lopping the ears off is what they do with pigs, so it had felt fitting. Took some of the tension off.

The police car moves along Main Street, then turns west by the railway, disappearing behind the warehouses built along that side of Policeman's Creek.

I can't know for sure what they make of this, but I'm pretty sure that ear will keep them guessing, looking in all the wrong directions.

Just like Jack. He'd come so close to finding me but missed what was right in front of him because he was focused on evening their score.

Well, he lost.

Not that she's won, either, but people like them tend to think they're the only ones in the game.

I scoot around on my rock, a skinny perch high on the razor's edge of the saddle. Up here, it's only wide enough for one. A false step—but a lucky one—would send me tumbling down the steep scree I climbed to get here. A fall in the other direction, a difference of inches up here, means a deadly plummet off the sheer cliffs that make such a stunning backdrop for the town.

I understand dying better than most, but I square my back to the edge, turning away from the drop. This view, the one away from town, is better—rank upon rank of mountain peaks, as far as the eye can see.

I drink some more water from my canteen and toss away my unfinished sandwich. A raven flutters down from the rocks higher on the saddle. He's hungry, and he's learned people like me tend to carry our lunch. This guy's picked up some other things too.

"Hi," I say.

"Hi," he echoes back.

I cough, and he mimics me perfectly.

I've seen ravens imitating car engines and the calls of other birds. They're clever creatures.

He picks up my crusts and flies away. I watch him disappear, then dust off my clothes and start down the mountain.

CHAPTER TWENTY-ONE

WHEN PETER EMERGED FROM HIS ROOM THE NEXT MORNING, EDIE was waiting in the kitchen, apron on, spatula in hand. "I made pancakes," she said apologetically. She opened the oven and lifted out a warm plate.

"Two days in a row?" Peter asked.

She shrugged.

"Mine looked better," Peter said, but in truth, yesterday's batch before the funeral felt like a decade ago. What idiots they were, thinking pancakes could fix anything.

"I'm sorry," Edie said.

"Think I missed that," Peter said, not quite ready to forgive.

"I was wrong. I shouldn't have said those things. You've worked so hard at starting over, and if you want to help me out of this mess—"

"No pep talks today, please." His mood had worsened after Brenda left, and though he'd heard Edie come home, he hadn't come out of his room. After sleeping poorly, again, he was not in the mood for "attaboys" or positive thinking.

But he was hungry, and Edie had gone all out: bananas, syrup, and whipped cream.

She didn't speak again until he reached for a second helping. "Can I just—"

"Okay. Go ahead."

She took a deep breath. "I'm an idiot. I'm sorry. It was wrong to let my frustrations goad me into being cruel to you."

He rolled his eyes. Couldn't help it. Couldn't help grinning either. "Sheesh. How long did you practice that one?"

"You really want to know?"

"Yup." He helped himself to a spoonful of sliced bananas.

"I've been trying out apologies since the minute after I said it."

That helped too.

"This is good," he said.

"It better be. Was so worried you'd never forgive me, I burnt the first one."

"You know what they say about the first pancake."

She sent him a look. Their parents had always called her their first pancake—a roundabout apology for their parenting mistakes—"because you can't expect much from first timers, right?"

It always annoyed her, which Peter knew perfectly well.

"Peter, if I know anything, you'll find a way to show me up, prove me wrong, and win every game of Clue. So if you want to keep playing Nancy Drew—"

"I actually have some more thoughts about the police. And their camera work." He straightened in his chair, daring her to shoot him down again.

She didn't. "I'm just glad you care enough to help, Peter. Thanks. Really."

He raised his eyebrows. "You're still in the soup. Don't thank me yet."

"Okay." She winked and reached for the coffeepot. "Let's give it another week."

A week was optimistic, but Peter didn't intend to waste time. He spent Sunday scribbling into his notebook, rearranging the dark room, testing camera equipment, and listening to Edie call the lawyer their dad had recommended.

Monday afternoon, while Edie was at work, he took himself to the town library. It was surprisingly busy, with a clutch of children gathered for story time, patrons browsing the shelves and—Peter stepped around a magazine rack for a better look—his next-door neighbor, busy at a microfiche machine.

"Leo?"

He pulled his face away from the viewer and blinked a couple of times. "Oh, hi, Peter. What are you doing here?"

"Came to see if they have any books about photography."

Forensic photography, but he wasn't going to admit that.

"Aren't you writing one of those?"

Peter nodded, though this wasn't strictly true. He hadn't worked on the project in ages. "What are you doing?"

Leo shifted in his chair. "Oh, you know..." The folders that had been in the backseat of Leo's car were splayed across the desk. Peter leaned closer to the magnifier, scanning the slightly out of focus magnification of an old newspaper. He adjusted the dial, sharpening the edges. "What are you looking for?"

Leo shrugged. He didn't say anything, but Peter could see the obituaries filling the column that was positioned in the middle of the magnifier.

"Anyone you know?" he asked.

"It's to do with a project of mine," Leo said.

"So, I see." Peter glanced at the folders and the pages of notes again. The sheet nearest Leo was a handwritten list, names scribbled in blue pen or smudged pencil.

"All these people died from accidents?" Peter's stomach plunged. There were well over a dozen names on Leo's paper.

Leo shook his head. "Occupational illness, not accidents. Lung cancer. Chronic pneumonia. That kind of thing. Clairbeck Coal Company needs to take responsibility."

"These can't all be miners, though," Peter pointed at a name near the top of the list. "Sally Jackson?"

Leo grunted. "Same illness, though. And she's from here, so it's possible—"

Peter reached for a nearby chair, and tugged it closer to Leo's desk, worried now. "You're not sick, are you?"

"No," Leo said. "Or maybe I should say not yet. Had a bad bout over the winter, though." His lips thinned. "And I've lost too many friends."

"I heard you lost one lawsuit already," Peter said quietly.

"Where'd you hear that?" Leo's chin lifted a little, and Peter rethought admitting this tidbit came from the police.

"People here talk," he said. "I heard it was dismissed in court. No settlement, then?"

Leo shook his head. "They offered me a pittance. Before the court date. I refused. Probably should have taken it."

"I also heard who the lawyer was. You said you didn't recognize Jack Gainsford."

"I didn't," Leo snapped. "One guy in a suit looks just like another to me. And there wasn't just one lawyer. The company sent three of them."

Peter wasn't sure he had the heart to disbelieve him. How many faces had Leo seen in the intervening years before spotting Jack again in the house across the alley? More tellingly, Peter just couldn't picture Leo leaving Jack's severed ear for Edie to find, even if he had her house key. Leo wasn't that cruel. He wasn't mean.

Peter shifted more weight onto his crutches. "I'm sorry your case went badly."

"Won't happen this time," Leo said. "I'm making sure of it. Not my claim this time. It's for my friends. Won't go to court until I'm ready. Not until I have proof. And there's plenty. I started with Howard, friend of mine. Died of lung cancer last year."

Peter nodded, remembering that Leo used to come to Calgary with Edie, to visit someone in the hospital.

"When I look at the number of deaths here compared to Banff, say, or Blunt Creek, there's far too many." Leo shook his head. "I should get to it. Lots to be done." He turned in his chair, ready to reacquaint himself with the magnifier. "Hope you find some decent photography books."

Perhaps not surprisingly, the library had only a few slim volumes about photography in general, nothing about forensic techniques. But the librarian unearthed a book catalogue, and she and Peter pored over available titles. If Peter was willing to pay for them, the library would order as many titles as he liked.

"Not cheap, though." She frowned at the catalogue.

"I wouldn't mind a look at these two," Peter said.

She took the pencil from behind her ear and added check marks next to the titles. "Want to think it over? You can call if you want me to place the order."

"Thanks. I'll let you know."

He worried what Edie would say when she saw them—she'd laid off the teasing, but he didn't feel up to her Poirot bit again. It was easy, after she'd doubted him, with the police trusting Jill's story over theirs, and Brenda treating him like a kid brother, to wonder if anything he tried would even matter.

Even without a forensics background, he'd take better evidence pictures than Lefthand, but looking at him, who'd believe it? He sighed and turned away from the circulation desk.

Leo was standing by the door, folders tucked under his arm.

Peter swallowed. "Hey. You walking home now?"

"Thought I'd look in at the local. You want to come?"

Peter didn't, but he wasn't in a great mood to go straight back home either. On his own, he'd brood and decide the photography books were a waste of money, and he didn't want to believe that. Not yet.

Leo's friends were at the same table as last time, playing with the same cards. Steve even wore the same shirt. Orvo and Katya were missing, though, leaving more vacant seats.

"How was the funeral?" Garrett asked.

Peter shrugged.

"You saw the stuff people brought Edie?" Leo asked. "I put it inside for her when I saw it piling up on the porch."

Peter licked his lips. "Yeah, we found it."

"Told you we take care of each other out here." Leo pulled two chairs up to the table. He seemed sincere. Friendly. But Peter wasn't sure it was just the remembered horror of seeing that ear that underlined Leo's words with the hint of a threat. He took his chair carefully, wondering now if he was trusting Leo too much, too quickly.

"We'll deal you in on the next hand," Garrett offered. "Grab yourself a beer while you wait."

Peter winced. He'd left his overcoat and his wallet back at the house. He stuffed a hand into his trouser pocket, experiencing a wildly disproportionate rush of relief when his fingers closed on a crumpled bill. "All I've got is a couple bucks," he admitted shamefacedly. "What are the stakes?"

Leo snorted and gestured at the debris spread over the table. "We aren't playing for money. None of us can afford to do that. This is all exactly what it is. We don't trade it in for anything."

Peter took in the scattered piles. There were a few dimes in the mix, but like the other day, most of it looked like rubbish—a tattered coupon for five cents off cans of Bush's Best and some Calgary transit tokens. Garrett's pile held nothing but an old hockey card and a package of peanuts, and right now Steve appeared to be wagering a cellophane-wrapped fortune cookie and two sticks of gum.

"It's just about the game," Leo informed him, reaching into his jacket pocket, pulling out a small drawstring bag that made Peter think of the fiercely competitive marble tournaments from his grade school recesses.

These guys. He almost shook his head.

"What have you got?" Mike asked.

Peter rubbed the two-dollar bill between his fingers. "After I buy a beer, I'll have some change..."

"I can stake you." Leo winked and spilled the contents of his bag onto the table: paper clips, rubber bands, old nuts, and washers. "Just once though. Next time, you gotta come prepared."

There was, Peter discovered, an incredibly intricate economy underpinning Leo's friends' poker game. Washers, remarkably, seemed worth more than his nickels and dimes, and nothing on the table outvalued the coupon for baked beans, which was worn at the edges and had expired some four years before. But Leo hooted with triumph when he won it from Steve, and the others cheered and banged the table.

"I'll get you for this," Steve warned Leo. "Won't stand for it. Don't you dare think of leaving without giving me a chance to win that back."

Leo drained the last of his beer and cleared his throat. "Told you I could only play until four. It's already twenty past."

"One more hand," Peter coaxed. He'd nearly taken the thing himself, two hands ago, and figured there was a decent chance of succeeding if he tried again.

"Look what's happened to you." Leo shook his head. "One game, and already a hopeless gambler."

"I blame you," Peter said.

"Nope. This is your fault," Steve said. "And if this is the most fun you can get into after that long in a hospital, you have a very sad lack of imagination."

Steve dealt out the cards again, taking Leo's agreement for granted. And Leo did pick them up, so it seemed to work.

"Last hand," Leo said. "And let's not take all day about it." He glanced at his cards and pushed two bus tokens and a button to the center of the table, before succumbing to a cough that seemed to scour the sides of his chest.

"You sick again?" Garrett asked.

"Just my asthma," Leo returned shortly. "Your cigarettes don't help."

Garrett stubbed it out. "All right. Can't have you saying I won the beans from you by unfair means."

Leo snorted. "You're not getting the beans back, Garrett. Neither is Steve. Not today."

Peter hid a smile. Certainly not with his cards.

"Thanks for walking with me," Peter said, when they reached the front walk of Edie's house.

"I'm going the same way," Leo said with a shrug. "It's no trouble, and I don't trust Steve not to jump you on the way back."

Peter laughed. He'd won the beans. Probably would lose them immediately in the next game, but for now, he really enjoyed the feeling of carrying that old coupon in his pocket.

It was easy to see why Leo's case was important to him. He cared about his town and his friends.

Leo's friends might be a little odd—most probably had thirty years on him—but they didn't spend their time thinking about what they'd been able to do last year or ten years before. They made the best of things without being sanctimonious about it. Adjustments were necessary, that's all.

He understood a little now, why they kept a chair for Mel. He liked them better for it.

"We were talking about my picture of Robson the other day," Leo said, interrupting Peter's thoughts. "Want to take a look?"

Peter hesitated. He'd believed Leo when he said he hadn't recognized Jack from the courthouse. But with the sun dipping lower in the sky, hiding half his friend's face in shadow, trusting Leo's word felt riskier. If he were climbing, Peter would have searched out a firmer-looking handhold.

You're being ridiculous, Peter told himself. "Why not?" he said aloud.

Leo's house was practically identical to Edie's, built on a similar plan but flipped, so everything was in the opposite direction than it was next door.

"Don't trip," Leo warned, as Peter approached the hall runner. "The one of Robson's right there." He pointed to a frame, at least three feet wide, occupying the place of pride over the fireplace.

Peter stopped. The shot was a masterpiece: three climbers poised on a face, one turned to the camera, her grin capturing all the joy of their adventure. The immaculate white glacier and a thousand contrasting textures were beautifully captured in black and white. The photographer had been incredibly lucky with his lighting, even catching the distant, sought-for peak, which was nearly always obscured by clouds.

Peter let out a breath, his chest so tight he might as well have been starting breathing exercises again.

"Lovely, isn't it?" Leo said beside him.

It wasn't a good enough word. Peter nodded anyway.

"I'd have liked to make that climb," Leo said. "But some things aren't to be, and I can enjoy the view every day like this."

Peter wasn't sure he'd have the strength to keep this picture in his living room, now that his climbing days were done. "You didn't tell me you climbed with Bruno Engler," he said. "This has to be his shot." Especially since the grinning climber was Georgia Englehard, Engler's famous American friend.

"Oh, well—" Leo shrugged, clearly not the type to brag.

Or maybe he was simply the kind who kept things to himself—like the details of the accident that stopped him from climbing and the lawsuit he'd lost.

"You've got to tell me about climbing with them." Peter motioned at the photograph. He'd idolized guides like Engler and Conrad Kain since he was fifteen, working his first summer at Lake Louise.

Leo gave a sideways smile. "You might not have that much time."

"I've got time," Peter said.

Leo was more of a climber than he'd let on. Most of his life, he'd been inside or on top of some mountain. His skill with ropes and the strength in his shoulders had made him good in both places, but then asthma started giving him trouble in the mines and the thin, cold air of the high altitudes, and then he severed a tendon in his left little finger, never recovering all his grip.

"People don't notice," he said, showing Peter how he used his ring finger to curl in his little finger, so it didn't stick out when he grasped his coffee mug. "But of course it made a difference at work. And every finger counts for climbing."

Then, a fractured femur, cracked ribs, a couple months in traction, and double pneumonia. "Went back to the mine after, but I knew and they knew I wasn't fit for it. Can't be down there like that. You're too much of a risk to others. But I'd worked long enough to have a pension. Hoped for more but—" Another shrug.

Peter thought for a half second, then dismissed his qualms. Wasn't any of his business, but sometimes you just had to reach. Leo would understand. He was a climber. "I have a question about that," Peter said. "Your lawsuit."

"My first lawsuit," Leo corrected. He wilted a little. "The failed one."

"Yeah." Peter swallowed. "You said you didn't recognize Jack from the courthouse...at first. But what about the next time? Or the time after that?"

Leo pressed his lips together. "Does it matter?"

"It might," Peter countered. There was a big difference between a whole truth and a half one. "Edie's in a bad spot."

Leo nodded slowly, not meeting Peter's eyes.

"So did you recognize him?"

Leo rubbed his shoulder. "Yeah. Eventually."

Peter let out a breath he hadn't realized he'd been holding. "Did he recognize you?"

"Doubt it." Leo sighed. "Barely bothered to answer when I said hello the first time. Trying to be neighborly. But I knew him by then, and I was suspicious of why he was here."

A chill tiptoed up Peter's spine, pausing between his shoulder blades.

"Forbes asked me the same things." Leo's low voice, and the gentle ticking of the clock, were the only sounds. They hummed in the air, like the crunch of booted feet in heavy snow.

"What did you tell him?"

Leo hesitated. "The truth. I recognized him." He snorted. "'Course I did. First couple of times, I knew he was familiar, but I didn't place him until I saw him in a suit, carrying a briefcase."

His jaw tightened. "He was the lawyer who convinced that judge to throw out my claim. Said that, with the number of my injuries, it was impossible to conclude they were solely from mining and not from my amateur climbing, so I shouldn't be eligible for a larger pension. Slick reasoning. The company must have been plenty pleased with him."

Peter licked his lips. "Sounds unfair."

"I think it was. Judge didn't. Couldn't afford to appeal though, and the union didn't want to take it higher."

"I'm sorry."

Leo shrugged, but the looseness of his shoulders didn't match the nervous playing of his hand, twisting frayed threads on the arm of his chair. "When I saw Gainsford lurking about, I figured he was here on the company's behalf. Thought they'd heard I was preparing another lawsuit, and that worried me. A lot, so I kept an eye out."

"That all?"

Leo raised his eyebrows. "Peter, I'm not a bad guy."

Probably not, if he'd climbed with Bruno Engler.

"If I was, I could have lied to Forbes," Leo added. "But I didn't. Because that's not who I am, and because it wouldn't be fair to your sister. I know she didn't kill him, but I didn't either."

Fair enough. Peter's hands loosened around his mug, and he took a sip of the coffee Leo'd brewed about an hour ago. Cold, but it didn't taste too bad.

He wasn't any closer to clearing his sister, though. Forbes might have found another suspect after talking to Leo, but Peter couldn't afford to count on it.

"I never connected Gainsford to Edie." Leo leaned forward, resting his elbows on his knees. "Not until you showed me that old engagement photo, and by then he was already dead. She introduces herself as Simmons, remember? And I'd have asked, if she'd used the Gainsford name, because I remember it." His expression darkened. "You know—"

Not wanting to distract him, Peter kept still, though he'd have liked to rub some warmth into his arms.

"—I was so worried the police would find something in that house about me." Leo shook his head. "So, when you insisted on going to look, I had to go along."

"The letter in your pocket," Peter said, half-formed suspicions connecting, snug as the pieces of jigsaw puzzle. "You said it was from the post office."

"I lied," Leo said. "I took it from Jack's house. Found it between the pages of his book, so he did still work for the company. They know about my case. Somebody must have told them I've been poking around the records. So, Jack could have come here to get in my way, but I don't think so. We never spoke, except in passing."

He rubbed his hands together. "It might affect my case, but I gave the letter to Forbes."

Cynically, Peter wondered if that had made Forbes less suspicious of him. Too bad Edie didn't have anything she could pass along to buy some credibility.

Well, there had been the cigarettes. And the hair elastic. But Peter didn't regret hiding those. Wouldn't have had the same effect.

"I never thought Gainsford might have come here for her." Leo huffed, then took a second breath, more of a wheeze. "Feel bad for her. That guy was a real shit, huh?"

Peter grunted. Leo wasn't going to get any argument out of him.

The older man shook his head. "Drove me nuts seeing him creep around in his fancy jackets and expensive shoes. Less work for miners these days, but lawyers always do all right, don't they?"

"Not always," Peter said, thinking of Jack, dead on a mountain road.

Leo laughed roughly. "Yeah, I guess not." He reached for his coffee cup, swallowing quickly, but it didn't soothe his throat. He succumbed to another fit of coughing, painful hacks from deep in his chest.

"Leo, are you getting sick?" Peter asked.

"No, it's just—" Leo curled forward, coughing into a crumpled handkerchief. "Bit"—*hack*—"worse today"—*hack*—"than normal."

He straightened, wiping his streaming eyes. "Sorry. All that coughing makes me teary."

"I'll get you some water." Peter pushed off the sofa, not waiting for permission, heading for the kitchen. "You don't sound good. Probably should get checked."

Leo coughed again. "Probably."

Peter filled a glass of water and watched Leo drink half of it in the kitchen. "You all right?"

"I'm fine."

Leo'd stopped coughing, but his eyes were still streaming. "Just a dry throat," he insisted. "I'll go to the clinic tomorrow."

CHAPTER TWENTY-TWO

The good thing about work, Edie thought, was that it kept her busy. It was three days since the funeral—and the ear—and she hadn't thought about either until now.

Peering through an otoscope tended to make you think of ears though. But as this one was clearly infected, she didn't have much opportunity to brood about Jack's severed one.

She straightened and turned off the otoscope's light, returning it to the mount on the wall. "I'm afraid you'll have to see the doctor, Frankie. Stay here." She smiled at the ten-year-old boy, dangling his legs over the examining table, and his mother, perched in the nearby chair.

"Dr. Irwin won't be long."

She picked up the clipboard with Frankie's chart and shut the door behind her, intending to finish her notes in the hall.

Katya passed, buttoning her coat one-handed and carrying her bag. "Leo Martin just came in. No appointment. Said he's been coughing more than usual. I'd look at him myself, but I'm already running late."

They had a lengthy list of patients expecting house calls today, including a number of diabetics with persistent wounds. Dressing those took time.

"I'll see Leo," Edie said. Hopefully it was nothing. Nathan wouldn't enjoy it if she had to ask him to make room for yet another appointment.

She wouldn't enjoy asking either. All week, he'd been prickly, avoiding her presence, not meeting her eyes. Hiding their relationship made sense, given the current police investigation, but the way he was acting...

He hadn't even asked about the funeral, or how she was, rudimentary, courteous questions you'd extend to any coworker. His omissions stung like a slap.

Edie smoothed her white dress, told herself to ignore the lingering smart, and hurried into Leo's exam room. He was sitting on the table, feet dangling, not so different from Frankie, except for the stack of papers beside him.

"What are those? Anything medical?" Maybe she could help.

"Nothing to do with me," he said. "I'll ask Dr. Irwin about them, if he has time. You guys are sure busy today."

Edie nodded. "I hear you aren't doing so well?"

"Just my asthma acting up again," Leo explained.

Edie listened for a long time at his chest. It didn't sound good. He tried to hide it, but he winced with every deep breath.

"We'll need some X-rays," Edie said. "Come with me down the hall."

Normally, they sent patients home, instead of having them wait for Dr. Irwin to read the films. Today, the way Leo's chest was sounding, she told him to stay in the waiting room. Just in case.

"Does Mr. Martin need a cough drop?" Brenda asked.

Edie jerked away from the illuminator, where she'd pinned up Leo's chest X-rays.

"Sorry," Brenda said. "Didn't mean to startle you."

"I was just putting these up for Dr. Irwin," Edie explained. She glanced at the images again. Frowned. "Leo's gonna need more than a cough drop. Codeine syrup for sure."

Strictly speaking, she had no business forming opinions from Leo's

X-rays, but when something looked like a duck, walked like a duck, and talked like a duck, generally speaking, it was a duck, and this particular duck was called pneumonia.

"Brenda, Mrs. Polson just arrived." Katya breezed into the room. "You need to check her in."

"On it," Brenda said and vanished like Katya had brandished a magic wand at her.

"Back already?" Edie frowned. She'd seen the list. No way was Katya finished.

Katya huffed. "Forgot to stock up on gauze."

That wasn't like her, but Edie knew she wasn't the only one feeling stretched thin today. She turned back to the X-rays. "Oooh," Katya said, peering over her shoulder. "Who's are those?"

"Leo Martin's." Edie picked up her pen and tucked it in her pocket. "I'll ask Dr. Irwin to look at them straight away. Leo will need testing. Probably antibiotics."

She hurried out of the supply room, almost colliding with Brenda, who was conducting the next patient, Mrs. Polson, along the hall. Honestly. Everywhere she turned, someone was underfoot.

"Where's the doctor?" Edie asked. If he wasn't even finished with Frankie's ear infection yet...

"Just saw him go into his office," Brenda said.

Normally, this was a sign he didn't wish to be disturbed, but Edie wasn't inclined just now to show him any special consideration. She rapped on the door.

"Enter."

She allowed herself an eye roll, then turned the handle. "Leo Martin came in. I don't like the sound of his cough. Took some films. You'll want to take a look."

Two weeks ago, this wouldn't have raised Nathan's eyebrows. She'd liked working for him, then. He was a competent doctor and considerate of his staff—not one to raise eyebrows any time one of his nurses made a suggestion. But this wasn't even the first time he'd done it today.

"I only just sat down," Nathan said. "I've heaps of paperwork." He gestured at his desk.

"Leo had pneumonia last winter," Edie reminded him.

"Fine. I'll take a look when I'm finished with that ear infection," he told her. "In the meantime, I want you to check the supply room."

"Every dose of morphine is accounted for," Edie reported. "I told you so yesterday."

"Check again." He frowned at the papers in front of him. "What about syringes?"

"All the instruments in the supply room have been wrapped, autoclaved, and marked on the sheet. We might have lost a syringe or two, but I can't tell if that happened last week or six months ago."

"And samples of Obetrol? We should have almost a full box. One arrived from the distributor last month, and it's not something I've tried with many patients yet."

Edie pressed her hands against the sides of her legs. It curbed the impulses of her tongue, stopping her from snapping at him for fretting over samples of diet pills.

"I'll take a look," she promised. "You'll make time for Leo? I really don't think he should wait until tomorrow."

"I said I would, didn't I?"

Edie stepped into the hall and shut the door.

By the time she'd counted the drug samples (there were twelve remaining, so Nathan must have given away more than he'd supposed), measured their remaining morphine, counted the unopened bottles, and verified amounts against the balance in the ledger, Leo was gone.

"Don't worry, though," Brenda told her. "Dr. Irwin saw him. Mr. Martin left after, straight away. I think he had to stop at the pharmacy."

That was reassuring. The sooner Leo got proper medicine into him, the better.

"You know I tidy up the supply room every evening," Brenda said. "There's no need for you to do it as well, especially when we're so busy. Mrs. Polson's been waiting twenty minutes."

"Dr. Irwin's asked me to keep a close eye on our drug stores," Edie said.

Brenda's eyes narrowed. "Why?"

All day, Edie had kept a tight hold on her temper. Now, it slipped. "Gee, I don't know. Maybe because my ex-husband died of a morphine overdose, and he wants his clinic to stay clear of trouble?"

Brenda retreated half a step. "I didn't mean—"

Whatever Brenda was about to say, Edie didn't want to hear it. "I've got to clean the exam rooms," she said and practically dove for the nearest door.

Alone, she snatched a tissue, dabbed at her eyes, then disinfected the sink, counter, and examination table like her life depended on it. But working through the afternoon was even worse than before, with constraint between her and Brenda piled atop the existing pressure with Nathan. By the end of the day, when Edie carried her stack of clipboards into the file room, it was a relief to find Katya there, studying an open chart.

Katya looked up and closed the file, tucking away the notes and X-ray films.

"I was afraid all those visits would have you working late," Edie said.

"Me too. Lucked out. Things went quickly today."

"Is that Leo's?" Edie glanced at the closed file.

Katya nodded and bit her lip.

"Everything all right?" Edie asked, worried by Katya's expression.

"Not really." Katya turned the clipboard toward her. "Dr. Irwin's prescribed him morphine."

"No, he has pneumonia—" Edie snatched the chart, turning it so she could read Nathan's writing.

Numerous diffuse growths, right and left lungs.

No way. But below that...

Diagnosis: Cancer. Inoperable. Patient declined referral to the Calgary Cancer Clinic.

"It's a mistake." Edie pointed to the illuminator. "I saw his films."

She was no doctor, but she knew her ducks. They saw lung cancer often enough. Charlie Mikkenen had been diagnosed just last year. He'd only lasted a couple of months.

"Edie." Katya put a hand on her arm. "I don't think it's a mistake. You know how prone—"

"No. There's a mistake," Edie said. "I'll talk to Dr. Irwin about it."

Katya moistened her lips. "It might be better to put him on the home visit list. Dr. Irwin didn't ask for it, but—"

"I'll talk to him."

Katya shook her head. "Edie, you can't just—"

"I'll talk to Leo too," she said. Tell him to go the cancer clinic. Peter could drive him, and they'd find the mistake.

Nathan was still with a patient, as the clock wound past five. He emerged from the exam room, only to disappear into another, so it was a good half hour before Edie caught him alone in his office.

"Does Leo Martin really have cancer?"

Her question surprised him. He also didn't seem to like it. He set down his pen. "Nurse Simmons..."

"You're sure?" Edie prodded.

"I'm sure."

She licked her lips, trying to re-envision the X-rays. "I took his films," she told him. "They looked all right to me. Pneumonia."

"If I had any doubt, I would have ordered a second opinion. Telling a man he has cancer and being wrong is not a mistake I ever want to make."

Edie took a step toward the desk. "Leo lives next door to me. He's a nice man. Can you look again?"

"Believe me, I looked long enough. The metastases are diffuse, so I could see how, to an untrained eye, they might appear as pneumonia. No chest X-rays were taken last winter. The cancer was almost certainly giving him trouble back then. But the medications he had for pneumonia and asthma could have—"

"That's not what I saw," Edie said. "I know what diffuse metastases look like."

His expression shifted, telling her at once that she'd made a mistake.

"Oh? You learned that in medical school?"

She flushed. "Nathan..."

"No. This isn't—" He shook his head. "You're under a lot of pressure. I know that. But I'm sure of his diagnosis. You need to be professional, Nurse Simmons. And I need to go home."

He walked past her and out of the room without a glance, his strides brutally efficient.

Slow breaths, she told herself. *Don't cry. Don't cry.*

Edie grabbed her coat and flew out the door without looking at Brenda, who was still tidying her desk. If Brenda saw her face, she'd know she'd been crying.

She should have kept her mouth shut. This job was difficult enough. She'd just given Nathan an excellent excuse to be angry. He might even fire her, and she needed the job. She'd been so committed to starting over that she'd bought the house here, instead of renting a place.

If she went home now, Peter would know something was wrong, but maybe he'd think it was just leftover angst from everything else. Either way, it was too much. She couldn't go home yet.

Turning around in the middle of the block, Edie retraced her steps, stalked past the clinic all the way to the end of Main, to a trail that wound to the river and the railway bridge. Walking would pull her together again. Now, at the golden hour, with the sun glowing over the mountains and pulling impossibly vibrant colors from the water and the trees, she'd think her way out.

She could handle the tension with Brenda by being less touchy. And she could handle the tension with Nathan, though that was less simple. *Just pretend like nothing happened.* It would work. It had to, because this evening, watching Nathan's face change as he prepared to walk past her, she realized she'd pushed her luck way too far.

But she could fix this. Somehow, from this mire of hurt, anger, distaste, and dying attraction, she'd salvage a working relationship with Nathan. It wouldn't be easy, but she could do it. And as soon as she could, she'd talk to Leo.

That problem was going to be harder.

CHAPTER TWENTY-THREE

Edie didn't get a chance to talk to Leo until the following evening, and after that, she needed another walk because he refused to consult a different doctor. She tried talking to him again at the end of the week, but to no avail. Leo said it couldn't be helped, that he'd seen enough cancer to know. He just wanted to get his things in order and pass all his work off to one of his friends.

She wasn't sure what he meant—he'd just pointed at his worn folders and changed the subject. Later, at home, Peter explained them to her. It made her sick to her stomach, that Leo'd rather spend his efforts on another hopeless lawsuit, instead of fighting for his life.

She couldn't stop thinking about his X-rays, unable to believe any doctor would give such a dire prognosis, based on what she thought she'd seen. It was easy, though, to doubt her memories. She was anxious and worn down—and no, Nathan, she hadn't been to medical school—but she wasn't incompetent.

And, for whatever reason, she hadn't been arrested yet. If she was going to do something about Leo, she'd better act quick, while they both had time.

So tonight, instead of going home after yet another walk filled with agonizing internal debate, Edie scuffed her muddy loafers clean on the grass, turned her back on the gray mountains and fading pastel sunset, and returned to the clinic.

No lights on, and Nathan's car was gone.

Digging into her purse, she retrieved her key and let herself inside, flicking on the lights. Tonight, it was strange to be alone here. Though the low hum of the bulbs made the place more ordinary, it was still too quiet, like the night she'd hid here, alone, waiting to sneak away from Jack. She didn't know what had happened afterward, and that was more unsettling than ever, just now.

Her steps echoed, racing ahead of her through the waiting room and down the hall. She reached the record room, but when she tried this light switch, nothing happened. Even when she toggled it, the room stayed dark.

"Stupid bulb." She'd noticed it flickering earlier in the day, but she'd been too preoccupied to bother changing it. No way was she going to hunt around for a bulb to change it now.

She could come back and check Leo's X-ray films tomorrow. But then Nathan might notice, and she was in enough trouble already.

If I thought I had cancer, and someone thought maybe I didn't, I'd want to know right away.

Sighing, Edie retreated to the waiting room. Maybe Brenda had a flashlight.

There was something off-putting about the rigid order inside Brenda's desk drawers. Everything had a place, everything was organized, tucked in small boxes or tiny porcelain dishes. Hand cream. Aspirin. A tin of breath mints and a half-eaten Dairy Milk bar, the wrapper pulled around the open end and secured with an elastic hair tie. Bobby pins, all facing the same way, rested in a blue and white china dish, half the size of Edie's palm, and three pairs of clip-on earrings, arranged in order of increasing size, were tucked in a velvet-lined box next to the pencil tray.

"C'mon," Edie muttered. There had to be a flashlight somewhere. She lifted the box of earrings and froze. Three packets of Obetrol were hidden in the space beneath.

Edie's eyes narrowed. What was Brenda doing with these?

Without thinking, Edie pushed the packets into her coat pocket. She'd confront Brenda about these herself. A face-to-face inquiry was better than showing them to Nathan, because Brenda might just deny taking them.

Right now, Edie couldn't count on Nathan to take her word over Brenda's. He might, in frustration, just decide to fire them both, and they both needed the work. They were each supporting someone.

Shit. What was Brenda thinking?

Edie opened the next drawer and found a flashlight, next to the typewriter ribbons and a bottle of clear nail polish. Thank God.

Back in the record room, she waved the light around until she found Leo's file.

It couldn't be cancer.

Biting her lip, she flipped open the manila cover. Leo's chart held decades of notes: every check-up and antibiotic prescription, every cough, cold, and broken bone. Over the years, he must've had several, because a stack of films filled the pocket in the back.

Yesterday's films were on top. Edie took them out laid them onto the illuminator, but when she flicked the switch, nothing happened. She tried again. Maybe a blown fuse? Had to be, if this and the overhead light weren't working.

Swearing under her breath, she carried the films into the hall, heading for the illuminator in Nathan's office.

She tried the handle, but Nathan had locked his door, another change from before. The light in the hall wasn't nearly good enough for a thorough inspection of the films, so Edie returned to the dark file room and switched on the flashlight, moving it behind the film in slow, methodical rows, like mowing a lawn. On the third pass, she found some light gray welling in the dark recess that was Leo's lower right lung. For a minute, she stared, then started her scan again. She couldn't have missed this earlier. Yes, the branching, threadlike tumors were faint, not so obvious as a solid mass, but when you compared this side to the left lung, away from the mass of the heart, the cancer was clear, spreading outward like fluffy gray mold.

The way she remembered it, the cloudiness had been more symmetrical, as well as more indicative of pneumonia.

She swallowed and ran the flashlight under the film again. Nothing changed, and she couldn't blink it away.

Maybe she should take some time off. Work was going to be awful, at least for a while, and the pressure of everything was clearly getting to her. Looking at this, she could see why Nathan had been so annoyed by her questioning this diagnosis. She'd made a colossal mistake.

Edie set down the film and the flashlight and palmed her eyes.

Poor Leo.

She returned the film to his chart, feeling tired and cold. But as she shone the flashlight over the file drawers, looking for the right place for Leo's chart, her fingers tightened on the folder.

Peter had an illuminator at home, even though it was a small one. She could look there—during the day, she could even try holding the film up to the living room window. She would take a long, thorough look, because she resented this X-ray for proving her mistake, for killing hopes she didn't want to relinquish.

Another look in better light wouldn't hurt.

CHAPTER TWENTY-FOUR

There's a wind tonight, prying cold fingers between the buttons of my coat, infiltrating my shirt's heavy flannel and raising goose bumps on my skin. Should have worn a scarf.

Edie Simmons is a block ahead of me, hurrying down the sidewalk. It's late for her to be returning from work, and she has a large envelope tucked under one arm.

She's up to something.

At the corner, I hang back. Her brother is waiting for her on the front porch. She's preoccupied, but he might notice me, so I sidle behind a tree.

I'm too far away to read his face, but he greets her with a hug. A bracing, comforting one, which proves I'm right. Something is bothering her. Her dead ex-husband, probably, though the envelope she carries makes me wonder, just a touch uneasily, if it might be something new.

I shrug inside my coat, drawing my face deeper inside the collar. It's too cold to stay and watch their windows tonight. And I have a problem, so I don't have time to consider Edie's.

Tomorrow, maybe. By then, I'll be finished with this one.

CHAPTER TWENTY-FIVE

"It's pretty obvious." Peter moved a magnifier slowly across the cloudy masses that Edie said were tumors. His illuminator wasn't as large as the wall units in the clinic, but it was already set up in the darkroom/pantry and could hold several strips of negatives at a time. The films didn't quite fit, but he didn't need to see the margins, just the lungs.

"You wouldn't have missed this." He set aside the magnifier.

Edie shook her head. "Except I did. Must have seen what I wanted or been tricked by bad lighting or glare."

Peter rubbed the back of his neck. That made some sense. He didn't want to believe this either. The shadowy cancer encroaching on Leo's lungs made him uneasily aware of his own organs filtering, breathing, pulsing inside his belly and chest.

He didn't want to ask how much time Leo had left, because Edie had already said the dreadful word: inoperable.

Peter turned off the illuminator and picked up the film, angling it this way and that under the overhead light. "See? I can't erase them, no matter how I hold the film or how the light reflects off it. The shape's wrong, and there's too many separate bits. So you couldn't have been thrown off by glare."

"So how do you explain it?"

"Film doesn't change once it develops. The picture stays the same. Unless the film gets damaged, but this one is fine."

That was the magic of photography: You could filter or frame, but you couldn't capture anything that wasn't there. Your picture captured truth, replicating it and saving it forever.

He set the picture back on the illuminator. "This isn't the same film."

Edie opened her mouth to argue, but sat down on the single stool instead, resting her chin in her hands. "Okay. I guess that's possible, but I only took one set of chest X-rays that day."

"Did anyone else?"

"I don't think so. The chances of mixing them up are practically nonexistent."

Peter opened the chart, propping it on an empty shelf.

"What are you doing? That's confidential." Edie made a grab for it, but Peter pulled it out of her reach. She might be more mobile, but he had longer arms, and the space wasn't big enough for her to move around him. "I already saw the X-rays," he reminded her.

Her face twisted, then relaxed. "Fine. But you can't tell anyone."

He returned the file to the shelf, and his attention to the first page. Immediately, his eyebrows shot up. "Wow. How's anyone supposed to read this?"

She shrugged. "That's Irwin's writing."

Irwin, not Nathan. Peter glanced at her sideways, from the corner of his eye. He'd have to ask her about this name change...later.

He flipped back a few pages. The handwriting in this section of the chart was different, but not much better.

"Dr. Williams worked here then," Edie explained. "He's retired now. There was a Dr. Lewis for a few months in between, but she—"

"Does Dr. Williams still live in town?"

"Think he moved to Vancouver Island when he retired."

Peter pushed the file to his sister. He couldn't read the scrawls or understand the hieroglyphic abbreviations: *Dx, Rx, Hx, PRN*. He wasn't even sure what to look for.

"Leo was a climber," he said, gesturing helplessly at papers. "Like me. Said he missed a second chance at the summit of Mount Robson because he cracked his ribs."

As confusion cleared from Edie's face, Peter's heart sped, propelling his next words out in a nervous rush. "It would have been years ago, but old breaks should show on X-rays, right?"

"Yeah." Edie picked up the magnifier and bent over the X-rays. "Check the chart," she ordered. "Use the dates to go back a few years, then look for any entries with a number sign. That's the symbol for fractures."

Nodding, Peter flipped back several pages more.

"I don't see any breaks here. On the right or the left." Edie's face was inches from the film, her features distorted by the sharp contrast between the illuminator's bright light and the shadow of the closely held magnifying glass.

Peter scanned another page. And another. "Here!" He stabbed a finger at a lightly penned entry in the middle of the page.

Edie read over his shoulder. "Left side. Broke ribs eight to ten." She glanced again at the film, her face softening into a smile. "These are definitely not Leo's X-rays."

She slumped, covering her eyes with her hand. "Thank God. He might be all right."

The slackening tension in Peter's chest allowed him to reach out an arm. He looped it around her shoulders, pulling her close. "You were right."

"Yeah." Her voice was strained.

He waited until she sniffed, then pulled herself upright. "So how did this X-ray get into his chart?" Peter asked.

Edie chewed the side of her fingernail. "I don't know. I mean, it happens, but it's hard to imagine how it would here, where we take so few X-rays. We're a rural clinic, not a big hospital." She shook her head. "We can sort it out later. We gotta call Leo. Right now."

"It's really late," Peter said, glancing at his watch.

"It's never too late for good news," Edie said.

"Good point."

They nearly crashed trying to get through the door of the makeshift dark room—too much excitement, too small a space, too many arms and legs and crutches.

"Careful!" Edie shrieked, grabbing for his arm.

Peter adjusted his stance, and the left brace locked and steadied him. "Yeah. I don't want to break anything. Go ahead. You call."

He went to the sink and filled a glass with water.

Edie's brow creased. "Leo's not answering."

Peter pulled back the window curtain. "He's got a light on. Probably working on his lawsuit. Try again."

Edie redialed. Shook her head.

Peter shut the curtains. "Let's go over."

Edie nodded. "I'll grab beer. We should celebrate." She shucked off her house slippers and jammed her feet into her old loafers. "First thing tomorrow, I'm telling Nathan about the mistake."

"Not your mistake," Peter inserted.

"Nope." Edie reached into the fridge and collected three bottles. "Let's go."

Peter leaned on his crutches as Edie rang Leo's doorbell. After a minute, she tried again, but Leo didn't answer.

"I can hear his radio," Peter said. "He's definitely home."

"I'm going to try the door." Edie opened the screen door and tried the handle. "It's open. Maybe he just couldn't hear the bell?"

It was also possible that he didn't want to be bothered, but he'd forgive them, Peter was sure, once he heard their news. Edie wasn't about to be put off, either.

"Leo? It's Edie and Peter," she called, stepping into the hall. "Guess what?"

Peter negotiated the swinging screen door and the high threshold, following Edie and the sound of the radio into the house.

"Leo?" She paused outside the living room. Leo lay stretched out on the sofa, his back to the room, a plaid blanket draped across his legs.

"Asleep?" Peter said.

"You'd think he'd have heard us," Edie whispered, "We weren't trying to be quiet."

She crossed to the sofa, putting the beer bottles onto the coffee table. Her expression changed as she put a hand on his shoulder. "Oh no."

"What's wrong?" Peter stopped halfway across the room, balancing in the middle of the rug. Leo should have stirred by now, but he and the house were far too still.

Edie choked, raising a hand to her mouth. "I need my bag." She rushed past him, shouting over her shoulder. "Call an ambulance!" The door banged behind her.

Move, Peter, he ordered, but the action of his braces and the coordinating swing of his crutches were excruciatingly slow—like a difficult climb, assessing each hand and toehold. His fingers were numb on the crutch grips.

He found the phone and dialed the operator. "I need an ambulance," he said, stumbling over the subsequent questions. He couldn't remember Leo's house number, so he gave Edie's.

"But not that house. It's the one next door. Blue."

"Dispatching them now. Stay there. Stay calm." The operator disconnected.

Edie wasn't back yet. He hopped back to the living room, trying to remember his Boy Scout first aid.

He made it as far as the coffee table, when he realized that it didn't matter that he'd never earned the badge for correctly demonstrating artificial respiration. Leo was on the couch, and there was no way, not with his legs and his braces, that he would ever be able to kneel on the floor to reach him.

Peter swore, squeezed his eyes shut, and bit his lip.

"I'm back! Move!" Edie dashed past the screen door, bag in hand, and when Peter couldn't hop aside fast enough, she hurdled over the coffee table. Next instant, she was kneeling beside the couch, holding a stethoscope to Leo's chest, and listening with fierce intensity. Shaky with relief, Peter stepped back even farther.

"Where's his morphine?" Edie demanded.

The word made Peter's heart thud sluggishly, but he searched the room, lifting cushions, peering, as best he could, under the furniture.

"I'll check the bathroom."

"He has it. I know he does. Nathan prescribed it. It's written in the chart." Panicked now, she rifled through her bag, tossing out bandages and bottles of disinfectant onto the rug.

"I don't even know if he took it! If I don't have the bottle, I can't tell if this is an overdose or something else—" She squeezed her hands into fists, closed her eyes, and let out a breath like a tidal wave.

"Okay. Just gotta do what I can." She launched into action like an old-fashioned newsreel—jerky, everything happening at double time—whipping a syringe from her bag, filling it from a bottle of liquid, and jamming the needle into Leo's neck.

Peter found himself swaying and steadied his crutches, planting them more firmly on the floor. "What can I...?"

"Shhh! It might not be too late," she muttered, reaching for the stethoscope again.

Peter stood helplessly, ears ringing—no, that was the whine of a siren from far away.

Edie was working again, pinching Leo's fingertips and shining a light into his eyes. "I'll give him another dose." She filled the syringe again.

"What are you giving him?" Peter asked as her thumb pressed down the syringe again.

"Nalline. It'll counteract the morphine and strengthen his breathing."

Peter hoped so. From here, it didn't look like Leo was breathing at all.

Edie pressed her lips together. "It's new, but we carry it because there's a higher number of suicides in our county."

"Leo wouldn't—"

"Dr. Irwin just told him he has lung cancer," she snapped. "One of his friends died of it just last year. If he hasn't taken morphine, then the Nalline won't hurt him. Much." She pushed the stethoscope under Leo's shirt again and shut her eyes.

Peter knew it wouldn't help, letting shock push him into the nearest chair. Not that standing here was doing anything either.

Edie moved the stethoscope. In her hurry, she must have torn off the top button of Leo's shirt. He'd worn this one to the poker game just yesterday, but his face—Peter swallowed. Leo hardly looked the same at all. His face was like putty.

"I think the Nalline's helping," Edie said.

"I'll watch for the ambulance." Feeling old and stiff, Peter moved to the front door, trying to judge if the siren was any nearer.

At last the ambulance arrived, braking hard in front of the house and backing onto the lawn, disgorging three men with bags and a stretcher.

Peter opened the door.

"Excuse me." The doctor pushed past him with barely a glance. "Nurse Simmons, what's your assessment?"

Peter never heard her answer, because an ambulance attendant nearly knocked him over with an oxygen canister. "Clear the way, sir. We'll need to bring in the stretcher."

Peter flattened himself against the wall. "How close is the nearest hospital?"

He got no answer. Irwin barked orders, and the others gathered so close around Leo there was no room to move.

Peter drew back, into the darkened guest bedroom. Best if he just got out of the way.

CHAPTER TWENTY-SIX

Neither of them was up to making pancakes the next morning, even if they'd felt like eating them. Peter brewed coffee and set a brimming cup in front of his sister. She barely noticed, only glancing up briefly before dropping her forehead into her hands again.

Edie had gone to the hospital in the ambulance and returned only a few hours later. The hospital staff had done nothing but paperwork. By the time they'd arrived, Leo was dead.

"You did everything you could," Peter offered, because the coffee wasn't helping. Leo's death felt completely unreal. He wished it were.

A tear, then another, splattered onto the tablecloth below his sister's face.

Shit. Crying again. Well, she didn't want words or hugs, so Peter wheeled his chair beside her and waited.

"I could have done more," Edie told the coffee mug.

More? There'd been no time to do anything. Leo had been given his tragically incorrect diagnosis days before. Peter wasn't even sure, given the panic and distress of the failed efforts to save Leo, if she'd managed to make the mistake clear to Irwin yet.

There'd been no time for anything. Last time Peter had talked to Leo, they'd still been on for poker, with Leo vowing to win back the beans.

Edie rubbed her eyes dry. "I should have tried harder. When I spoke to Nath...Dr. Irwin, he almost snapped my nose off. Said the diagnosis was obvious. But I'd taken Leo's X-rays. And you and I know...if I'd stood my ground, maybe—"

"This isn't your fault." She'd argued with Irwin. She'd broken rules and brought the X-rays home to study them. After seeing her in action, fighting to save Leo, he wouldn't let her blame herself. "You did everything you could."

"Didn't matter, though, did it?" She wiped at her eyes again. "I just—"

"I know." Sometimes, you tried and you couldn't. He knew the feeling better than most, but this failure was especially hard. Leo was gone, and they never should have lost him.

"Hey." Peter reached for her hand. "Hey." Dumb words, but he didn't have any good ones, and his eyes were brimming now, tears rolling unchecked down his cheeks. "I wish—" He swallowed hard. "I wish we could have done more too."

"At least it's Saturday," Edie said, after they'd drunk their cold coffee and washed the empty cups. "It would kill me to go into work today."

Peter nodded. Doing things helped though, even just washing dirty dishes. "I'll fold the laundry. You saw your telephone messages, right?"

"Sure did."

"From the lawyer?" She'd ignored two calls from the guy already, and that worried Peter, a little.

Edie looked confused. "Talked to him just the other day. He's all set to come for my next interview with Forbes." Her face darkened and Peter cursed internally. If he'd been thinking, he wouldn't have mentioned anything to bring that to her mind. Another inquisition, the chance of arrest...

"That's not who I meant. This is a different lawyer, Bradley Kulak? He's called twice." He hesitated. "He said it was about Jack's will. I wrote it all on the message board."

Edie made a face. "Kulak can wait. I'd rather do laundry."

"Of course," Peter said, eager to abandon the topic. "I just wanted you to know he'd called." Best if he just kept them moving today, doing things that offered some distraction.

They were matching socks when the telephone rang. Edie answered it, and her face went so still that Peter stopped moving too.

Luckily the call was short. Edie made a couple noncommittal noises, and finished with, "That will be fine. See you soon."

"Who was that?" Peter asked.

Edie folded her arms, pressing them tight against her stomach. "Pinky. She's on her way over."

Of course Peter had questions, but Edie was uncommunicative. "She just said she needed to speak to me."

Maybe, but Peter wasn't sure if agreeing to a meeting was wise today. Unfortunately, with Pinky already on her way, there was nothing he could do, except help Edie tidy up the living room and watch her madly sweeping off the porch.

When she suggested it, he tucked in his shirt.

Pinky pulled up in front of the house right at the appointed time, in a green late-model Cadillac. Sitting on the living room couch, Peter watched her exit the car and march up the front walk, tugging off a pair of black gloves that matched her dress, hat, bag, and heels. The hat had a veil of net sweeping over the top half of her face.

"Here goes," Edie said and walked to the door.

It opened with a groan, saying some of what Peter felt. This was not going to be good.

"Hello, Pinky," Edie said. "Will you have coffee?"

"No, thank you," Pinky said. "We can sit on the porch."

This was going to be worse that he thought. At least Edie's effort sweeping was paying off.

He got up and followed his sister outside.

"Well?" Edie said. "You have something for me?"

Pinky nodded, mouth pinching like it held something bitter. "I'm not sure—" She broke off. Started again. "I got these from Marilyn."

The name meant something to Edie. Peter could tell by the twitch of her right eyelid, though nothing else moved.

Pinky reached into her purse and pulled out a thick, full-sized envelope, stamped with the name of Jack's law firm. "I think Jack found something that got him in trouble. Someone's secret. It's all here."

Edie's eyebrows lifted fractionally, unimpressed.

"Just look at it, will you?" Pinky said.

Edie unwound the string fastener and dumped the contents in her lap: typed pages, clipped newspaper articles, a packet of photos, and film negatives still in the developer's packaging. A drugstore's logo was partially visible on front.

"I went through it all," Pinky informed them. "I saw the pictures of you and your boyfriend."

Edie's cheeks flushed. "Jack took pictures?"

"Oh yes." Pinky smiled unpleasantly.

"Why bring them to me?" Edie asked. "Why not the police?"

"Because I want you to see them."

"Pinky..." Peter tried, but she gave him no chance to finish.

"He wasn't perfect." Pinky's voice wavered beneath her rigid musculature. "Of course he wasn't. But he loved you. He was never the same after you left. I thought he would be all right, but he kept coming here. And after he died, when I saw all that"—she waved helplessly at the pile filling Edie's lap—"he just couldn't let you go.

He had to try and—I don't know. But he must have been planning something."

Edie picked up a newspaper article and frowned skeptically.

Pinky bristled. "I may not know who killed him, but I'm sure that it wasn't you."

"Thank you," Edie said dryly.

Pinky glared back. "It's still your fault. My son died because you chose to leave him and come to this place. It killed him, seeing you with somebody else. Without that, he never would have—" She turned her face away from Edie and the jumble on her lap.

"Take a good long look," Pinky said. "See what you've done. And then you can take it to Sergeant Forbes."

She closed her handbag with a snap, pushing to her feet like the seat was burning her. "Jill is urging us to contest Jack's will," she said.

Edie shrugged. "Fine with me. I don't want his money."

Pinky snorted. "Call Brad Kulak then and tell him so."

Edie drew a breath—it looked like a fighting one—so Peter touched a hand to her arm. Pinky was on her way. Why do anything to stop her?

Edie swallowed and said nothing.

They watched Pinky drive away in a spray of gravel.

"You think this will help me?" Edie asked, after they carried Pinky's envelope inside.

"Won't know until we take a look."

Edie shook her head. "Pinky's losing it."

"Lost it a long time ago, I'd say."

They laughed—giddily, excessively—and Peter wondered if they were losing it too. Acute strain, confusion, grief: He and his sister could put up strong fronts, so long as you didn't look close, but he felt tense as a fraying rope.

"Pass me the photographs." Peter reached for the packet.

"Nuh-uh," Edie held it away. "Not until I look first. I don't know what Jack might have seen, peeking through my windows."

"Good idea." Peter leaned back.

She shuffled quickly through the pictures, grunting once or twice. "Here."

"Nothing dirty?" Peter asked.

She rolled her eyes.

It seemed Jack hadn't tried his hand at bedroom photography, though there was a picture of Edie wrapped in a man's arms taken through the bedroom window. Peter couldn't see the man's face, but there was a better shot of him leaving through the back door. It still wasn't a particularly good image, with the features obscured by glasses and a low sitting hat.

"That's Irwin?" Peter asked, recognizing the doctor from the ambulance last night.

"Yeah."

"You don't call him Nathan anymore," he observed.

"No, I do not."

"You done with him? Or is it the other way around?"

Edie shrugged.

"You okay?"

She nodded, telling him without words to leave it at that.

"Okay." Peter returned to the photographs. Edie's house, Edie climbing in or out of her car, Edie walking into the clinic. The man, Dr. Irwin, walking down Main Street, a paper-wrapped sandwich in one hand.

Peter frowned. "I don't know that it will help, showing these to the police. At this point, if they learn about your relationship with Irwin, it only makes you look worse."

"Makes him look pretty shifty too. He'll fire me if we give these up. Pinky will love that." Edie set aside a newspaper clipping. "Otherwise, her big plan is a failure. I feel no guilt whatsoever. Jack was totally unhinged."

"Do you know where this is?" Peter held out a picture of a handsome old brick building: steep roofed, ornamented with tall windows at precise intervals, three stories high. "It's not in town."

Edie frowned. "I don't recognize it. There's a sign by the door, but it's too small to read."

Peter squinted at the partially obscured plaque mounted beside the front door. "We have the negatives. I could enlarge it." He flipped through the stack of photos. "And we're missing a print. There should be twenty-four photos, but we've only got twenty-three."

"You could make another copy though, right?"

Peter nodded. The negatives were all here. He started up from the couch, but Edie stopped him. "Later. Let's finish this."

She picked up a collection of pages, torn from a book and held together with a paper clip. She spread them out on the coffee table, frowning at an array of columns and tables. "What on earth did Jack want with these?"

Peter leaned closer. "Look." He pointed at the header on the nearest sheet.

Annual Report: Alberta Department of Public Health 1952

"These are death rates. Rocky View County. Blunt Creek. And here's Clairbeck."

Edie picked up the newspaper clipping she'd set aside. An obituary. "You said Leo was collecting information for his case from local obituaries. Linking those deaths to industrial illness. Maybe Jack showed these to Leo?"

Peter shook his head. Jack had no reason to help Leo or harm him. He was fixated on Edie—his photos and the purchase of the old house proved that. "Wouldn't Jack get in trouble, for giving up information that hurt one of his clients?"

Edie chewed her thumbnail. "Yes, but we don't know what all this means yet. Maybe it hurts Leo's case."

"Higher death rates don't look good for the company," Peter pointed out.

"But they aren't necessarily the company's fault. Take out Hillview and the recent spike in suicides, and the numbers in our district should be pretty similar to Rocky View."

"But they're not. Still higher."

She chewed her lip, clearly troubled. "If Leo killed Jack, maybe that was another reason why he—" She broke off. "If Leo's conscience was getting to him, and he thought that he was terminally ill, wouldn't that explain it?"

"His suicide?" Peter couldn't say it without flinching.

Edie dropped her eyes. "That's what the doctors called it."

"The doctors at the hospital?" Peter asked. "Or Irwin?"

"All of them."

Peter frowned. "You said there are more suicides in this county. It's why you carry that stuff."

"Nalline." Edie nodded and picked up the pages of the health report again. "Yeah. No one likes to talk about it, but there have been a few. Old people, and ill ones."

Like Leo.

Peter compared the figures, looking back and forth between the different tables until his head hurt. "This is crazy," he said, leaning back in his chair.

His eyes fell on the picture of Irwin striding down Main Street. He swallowed.

"What if Jack and Leo were finding the same problem but seeing a different answer?"

Edie didn't look up, still intent on the numbers. "I don't get what you mean."

"Leo saw a higher number of deaths, and he blamed it on mining because he had a grudge against the company."

"Don't know that I blame him," Edie said. "It's—"

"Yes, yes," Peter said impatiently. "But if Jack saw the same thing, and..." He broke off, still trying to fit his ideas together.

"What?"

"Irwin made a mistake with Leo's diagnosis," Peter ticked off one finger. "Leo's X-rays were misfiled. When we found him, Irwin was second on the scene. He tended Leo in the ambulance."

"What are you saying?" She didn't wait for an answer. "I'd already given Leo Nalline. It was too late." But she looked worried.

"If Irwin wanted Leo dead, and the morphine wasn't going to do it anymore, couldn't he have done something on the way to the hospital?"

No answer.

"A spate of local suicides has the district nurses carrying Nalline," Peter added. "What if they aren't suicides, Edie? What if Irwin's behind this?"

Her thumbnail was back between her teeth. "Jack was getting back at me by exposing Dr. Irwin?"

"By ruining your new boyfriend." Peter liked his phrasing better.

"If Dr. Irwin was that bad, I'd have noticed. I'd have—"

"You didn't question why you needed to carry Nalline all of a sudden."

"It wasn't all of a sudden." Edie bit her lip. "Almost as soon as I came here, there was a death on a ranch outside the town. And Hillview's so far from here and from the hospital already." She shut her eyes. "Mistakes this big—even one or two—that level of incompetence is tough to credit. They'd have to be intentional."

"Murders," Peter said.

"Yes, and you'd need some kind of terrible luck to keep anyone from noticing."

She looked sick.

"I'm not so sure," Peter said quietly. "How hard would it be, if nobody's looking?"

Nobody but Leo and Jack, and both of them were dead.

Edie rubbed her forehead. "There was a case in England. I read about it a few years ago in one of Jack's law magazines. This doctor... dozens of his patients died in comas before he was investigated. He wasn't actually even convicted, but they did take him off the register."

Peter winced. "But he killed them?"

"They certainly died. But murder? That was never proved." Another bite at her thumb. At this rate, she'd have no fingers by tomorrow.

"The thing is, we don't dispense drugs at our clinic. We have plenty, but just for use in the clinic or on home visits. Leo and everyone else in town gets their prescriptions from the pharmacy, so chances are—"

She broke off and began rummaging through the pile of photos and papers. "Where is it?"

"What?" Peter asked.

"The package from the photos. It was here—"

Peter leant over and picked up the wrapping from where it had fallen to the floor. "This?"

Edie took it and smoothed it out onto the table. "This is the only pharmacy in town," she said quietly. "Brenda's father owns it."

CHAPTER TWENTY-SEVEN

"Brenda is not a secret killer," Peter scoffed.

Edie leaned forward, adamant at the other end of the sofa. "Peter, she worked at that pharmacy all through high school. Still keeps shop for her dad some evenings. The place is right here." She jabbed a finger at the snapshot of Dr. Irwin walking down Main.

"In the background," Peter countered. "Brenda is a receptionist. She brought us pie."

"Yeah, well, there were probably people who liked that British doctor I told you about. Brenda's—"

"What? Guilty of being nice?" He wished he hadn't told her about Brenda's visit.

Edie huffed. "I know why you like her. She's cute."

"That's not why," Peter said, ignoring the heat flooding his cheeks.

"She's also married." Edie's voice softened. "Look. I get it." She waved her hands, searching for words. "Brenda's...bubbly. A little flirty, even. But if you had to hear about her perfect husband as much as I do, you'd know her smiles and her pie don't mean anything."

"Jeez, Edie!" Peter picked up the photo and scowled at the shop-front in the background. "I'm not an idiot." Brenda wasn't *interested* in him, even if her marriage wasn't what Edie thought it was.

"I never said you were." Edie sighed. "But I can always tell when you like someone. You blink when you hear their name. Did it back in grade school."

This was about as uncomfortable as ants crawling over his skin. They, at least, were easier to brush off. "I don't like her," he said, quietly. "Even if I did, it wouldn't matter. The idea that Brenda's behind whatever Jack may have uncovered is—"

"She's stealing drugs from the clinic," Edie said.

Peter looked up.

"I've been watching the morphine supply since…since you know. I don't think any's missing. Unless someone is skimping on doses and saving the extra, it's all accounted for," Edie said quickly.

"Brenda isn't giving any doses," Peter pointed out. "She's not trained like you and—"

"It's not morphine that's missing," Edie said impatiently. "Na…Dr. Irwin asked me to check other stores as well. Which, you have to admit, is a stupid thing to do if he's trying to hide things."

Peter nodded reluctantly. "Okay."

"Last time I checked, we were short on samples of a diet drug, Obetrol. The night I took Leo's X-rays, I found some in Brenda's desk."

Peter chewed the inside of his cheek. Working at the clinic and in her dad's pharmacy, it was possible Brenda could have acquired the know-how to—to what? His mind halted. Did he really think Brenda was capable of quietly killing people?

"Someone could have put them there," Peter argued. "Good way to dodge blame, especially since he was the one who put it in your mind to check."

Edie thought about this. "Maybe, but he wouldn't have known I would look through her desk."

"Might have stashed samples in a few places if he was trying to implicate her. Did you check Katya's coat pockets? Your purse?"

Edie's shoulders squeezed in a shudder. "That's possible," she conceded. "But the way Brenda keeps her things—Mom's silverware drawer is nothing compared to it. Brenda's desk is so organized it's scary."

Peter lifted his eyebrows, until Edie flushed. "Okay. Maybe not scary, but it was a little weird, you know? Brenda seems easygoing, but when I looked in those drawers, it was like finding this whole hidden side to her."

"I think you're making too much of it."

She flopped back against the coach. "Probably. It's hard to keep perspective. All of this." She flung a hand at the mess littering the coffee table. "And next week I gotta meet with the police again."

"We still have a few days," Peter reminded her. So far, the criminal lawyer representing her was good at stalling.

"Hopefully," Edie said, in a beleaguered voice. "But then I'll have to give them this. They'll find out about Irwin and me, and they'll know I'm a liar."

"Him more than you," Peter insisted. "They never asked you about him, did they? It's different with him. When he was called to the scene, he should have disclosed—"

She palmed her eyes. "I don't know what to do anymore. There's just so much of it."

"We have a few days," Peter said. "If Jack figured this out, we can too."

Edie lifted her face. Her eyes were huge, surrounded by years of worry shadows. "What if it's not safe?"

He wanted to squeeze her hand, but feared that might start her crying, so instead he started stacking the photographs and returning them to the envelope.

They weren't safe now. Not with bodies left in her car, ears dropped on their doorstep, and the police assembling their case. But Peter didn't want to remind her of that.

"We'll be just fine," he told her, because although he didn't know that, he did know what he had to do.

CHAPTER TWENTY-EIGHT

It's pretty here, up by the reservoir, especially at night. As daylight fades overhead and in the reflection on the water, the mountain's shadow stretches over me, past the road, onto the town. Most of the birds go still, the water is as smooth as glass, and it's quiet, because the night fliers, owls and bats, can't hunt if they make any sound.

I tug a jacket over my sweater and set to work gathering bits of kindling into a pile. Matches are quick, but growing up I learned to use a flint to strike sparks. They fly from my knife and flare in the nest I've built of twigs and dry grass. The little blaze is hungry, so I feed it with sticks, until it can clutch the larger branches I've broken and carefully placed on top.

At last, I sit back, warm, with smoke smell clinging to my clothes. I like sitting here, my only light from this fire and the first stars.

Leo's thick folder of notes peers out from my knapsack. I wiggle it free and begin feeding pages of his painstakingly collected information to the fire. The pages blacken and curl, distorting, then destroying every word, every letter.

I didn't realize the danger here, until it was almost too late.

Should have noticed sooner, but I was caught off guard, distracted by the problem with Jack. First time I've stuck my nose out that far, stringing him along, letting him think that he was stringing me along. A little like fishing, which, turns out, Jack wasn't very good at.

He was, I think, rather broken, which distorted his thinking. He wrenched things up so much, trying to make them into what he wanted.

Leo did too, just in a different way. They both saw the answer they wanted and set out looking until they found it, and overlooked...well, me.

I don't look for things. I am the answer.

Real answers are hard. Nobody wants them, but they are as true and certain as fire is hot. They are always beside you, even if you keep your eyes shut.

Fairness is make-believe, and death waits to catch you. Endings cannot be prayed or pretended away.

Of course, people want to look for something better. Look hard enough, and most will find something resembling that thing that they want. Even if they have to invent it.

They don't understand that wanting means choosing a bad hand. Deciding to nod at people waiting to trick you. It's turning off half your mind, so that you can better trick yourself.

Like Jack. Like Leo. Like the police, who want to find Jack's killer, and want it to be his ex-wife.

It's simple that way. Easy to understand. I smile at the flames and feed in the last few written pages.

Safe, again. No one will know.

CHAPTER TWENTY-NINE

THE BELL OVER THE DOOR RANG AS PETER STEPPED INSIDE THE drugstore. Brenda, busy behind the counter, looked up and smiled. "Hiya, Peter."

He almost stumbled, trying to hop over the threshold. *Damn.*

"You okay?"

"Fine." He forced a smile.

"I was surprised you called." But pleased, judging by her expression. "So, what did you want to talk to me about?"

Peter laughed uncomfortably. "It's a bit of a long story."

Against Edie's objections, he'd walked by Brenda's house Sunday night but found no one home. Earlier today, when he'd called the clinic, Brenda had told him she'd be working the drugstore counter after work, and that Peter was welcome to talk to her there. It was more conventional, more distant, than sitting in the kitchen, eating pie.

At least she seemed happy to see him, though he doubted it would last.

"Your dad enjoying his new TV?" Peter asked. Brenda had told him about it on the phone, since it was, ostensibly, the reason she was working this evening.

She laughed. "Mom says he's addicted. Doesn't hear a word from him all evening."

"Edie and I don't have one," Peter said. "Though there was one in the hospital. I don't miss it."

She reached to straighten a counter display of chewing gum. "That makes sense."

Peter adjusted his feet, floundering as they plunged into uncomfortable silence.

"So, I have a question."

"Yes, you said."

He nearly shut his eyes. It sounded like he was working up the nerve to ask her out, not question her about a murder.

He should have left this to Edie. He should have stayed away. With a sigh, he reached into his pocket and laid the packets of Obetrol on the counter.

They could work up to murder. May as well tackle drug theft first.

Brenda froze. "Where'd you get those?"

"At the clinic. Edie found them in your desk."

"What was she doing there?"

Peter shook his head. "It was late. The light went out. She was looking for a flashlight—"

"She shouldn't have—"

"I know," Peter said. "I told her." He hadn't, but it seemed like the right thing to say. "She's worried about you. Doesn't want to get you in trouble."

Brenda was expressionless.

"I thought you probably had an explanation," Peter said. "Possibly to do with Mitch?"

Her eyes welled, and she caught her bottom lip with her teeth.

"These are diet pills, right?"

She nodded.

Yeah. He'd thought so.

"You want to tell me about it?"

Brenda shook her head. She didn't seem able to speak.

"I think you look fantastic," Peter said, then swallowed, because his voice had sounded much too fervent.

Idiot. He stuffed his hands in his pockets.

Brenda sniffed. "I'll put them back," she said. "I couldn't ask the doctor for them, because I'd have to fill the prescription here, and my dad would see it. You can't take this stuff if you're trying to get pregnant, so if I went on it, Dad would know Mitch and I aren't—"

Aren't having sex? Or aren't wanting kids yet? Peter watched her fingers curl defensively, like a bug turned onto its' back. Wasn't his business.

"I've gained a few pounds. I wanted them gone for our anniversary. It was stupid," Brenda said.

"Must be hard, when your dad is the only pharmacist," Peter said.

"Yeah." Brenda wiped her eyes. "You've no idea. It's better now, but I started working the counter here when I was thirteen. The boys from school were always coming in and asking to buy condoms."

Peter's eyebrows shot up. Even now, if he was to ever need one, he'd wait for Brenda's dad, Mr. Kwan. "Bold of them," he said.

"They were awful." She dabbed at the corners of her eyes but only succeeded in smudging her eyeliner.

"I'm afraid that's not helping," Peter said.

Brenda laughed shakily. "You mind watching the place for a minute? There's a mirror in the back."

Peter nodded, and she vanished, only to reappear a moment later, smudges and tear streaks gone. Her eyes immediately fastened on the envelope he'd placed on the counter—the photos they'd received from Pinky.

"Is that—"

"These were in Jack Gainsford's things," Peter said. "I think he had them developed here."

She nodded. "Dad's the only photo outfit in town. Closest competition is in Banff."

"Did you see Jack, when he brought these in?"

Brenda shook her head. "I'm only here once or twice a week."

"Do you know if he brought any others in?" People didn't always pick up their pictures, once they were developed. Jack could have left more here, before he was killed.

"I can check."

Brenda reached below the counter and brought out a wooden box partially filled with similar envelopes. "Don't see his name," she said, flipping through them. "Nope, don't have any."

"It was just a thought," Peter said.

"You going to give those to the police?" Brenda asked.

"Probably should. See if they can make anything of them. Most of the pictures were taken here in town."

He pulled out one—Edie, leaving her house. Brenda flinched a little. "He doesn't seem like a very nice guy."

"He wasn't." Peter tucked them away. *Is Mitch?*

He remembered, when he first came back home, how Edie had also worn heavy powder around her eyes. How tired and thin she'd been.

He glanced behind him, through the storefront, to the street. Empty.

"Can I buy you a pop?" Unlike bigger drugstores, this one didn't have a counter with a soda fountain, just a machine dispensing Pepsi-Cola and different flavors of Pop Shoppe at a nickel a bottle. The squat, round-edged machine sat at the end of a shelf stocked with Band-Aids and aspirin, but there was a small table nearby, four chairs, and a metal dispenser of straws and paper napkins.

"Why not?" Brenda smiled. "It's close enough to closing anyway." She left the sales counter, flipped the sign on the door, and turned out most of the lights.

Peter reached into his pocket.

"No, let me get them," Brenda said, in a tone that didn't allow argument. He took the nearest chair and asked for a bottle of cola.

The bottles were cold, chilling his hands, dripping condensation onto the table. She'd turned quiet again, fiddling with her straw between sips of cherry pop.

"Are you okay, Brenda?" Peter asked.

She nodded, a little too quickly. "How's Edie?"

Peter hesitated. He had, unfortunately, one more difficult question, and if he didn't broach it soon, their drinks would be gone.

"She and I are really broken up about Leo," Peter said, because it was true, and it brought them closer to what he needed to ask. He was starting to feel tired, but was that any wonder, with worries chasing suspicions through his brain, around and around, over and over?

"It's so sad," Brenda said. "I've known him forever."

Peter fixed his eyes on a scuff on the floor. "Edie and I found him."

"I heard."

This was it. Peter moistened his lips. "She said he'd been prescribed the morphine from Dr. Irwin. But I just can't believe Leo would kill himself."

Brenda set down her bottle. "He'd just been diagnosed with terminal cancer, Peter. That hits people hard."

"Yes, but—" Peter wiped the damp in his palms onto his trousers—condensation from his pop bottle, not sweat. His heart was racing. "Leo was working on a lawsuit against the company. It was really important to him."

Brenda's eyes didn't flicker. If this was news to her, it didn't show.

"I asked around the local, to see if Leo gave anyone his papers. But nobody's got them." Peter took another sip of cola, to moisten his mouth. "Which makes me think the morphine was a mistake."

Brenda leaned back in her chair. "My dad's really careful with narcotics. He doesn't give patients more than a week's worth at a time."

Was a week's worth enough? Peter didn't know. Did Brenda?

He tried again. "What if he thought he was doing Leo a kindness? What if Leo asked for them?"

Her mouth hardened. "If Dad knew about Leo's cancer—not that Dr. Irwin would have told him, but Leo might've—Dad would have been extra careful. He can't afford what you call 'a kindness.'"

Her eyes were fixed on the tabletop, her hands tense around the bottle in her lap.

"You need to know that even thinking this aloud is really dangerous," she added.

"Dangerous how?" After he said it, he regretted the challenge. Her eyes flashed to his, and they were hot with anger.

Edie knelt on the kitchen floor, scouring out the oven.

She hated this job.

She also hated knowing that Peter might be able to charm some answers out of Brenda. Peter's warmth, whether friendly or romantic, was always genuine. Mom called it his golden retriever quality. But it tended to cost him, because he could never charm without being at least a little charmed himself, and he was fragile right now, after polio and his broken engagement.

Edie straightened, eased her sore back, and reached for another wad of steel wool. Her gloves were covered in swirls of suds and brown gunk, and the cleaned, enameled surfaces of the oven should have provided more satisfaction.

Alone in the house, it was easy to fret: About Brenda and whether it was safe for Peter to meet her alone. About her upcoming interview with the police.

All of a sudden, her heart was racing. Edie sat on the floor, leaning against the cupboards. She put a hand to her chest and breathed deeply, trying to make her heart slow. Bits of conversation and shards of memories rose up and engulfed her, filling her ears, obliterating her hammering pulse.

She squeezed her eyes shut, until her head cleared and she could pry open her fingers. The rubber gloves stuck together, releasing with a smack.

Unsteadily, she climbed to her feet and hurried to the sink to strip the gloves from her clammy hands. Freed, she ran them under the tap. The cold water reminded her of that plunge in the river and helped bring her back.

She was going to have to give everything from Pinky to Sergeant Forbes. She was going to have to tell him, again, about Jill breaking into her house. She was going to have to tell him about Leo—if he would listen.

Her hands were so fall of sharp-edged facts, she was bleeding, trying to piece them together.

She dried her hands on the dish towel and went for the phone. No answer at Mom and Dad's, and she had no stomach to call the after-hours number of her lawyer. Hands shaking, she dialed a different number, one she knew by heart.

The ringing stopped.

"Gainsford residence."

Edie leaned against the wall, relieved to hear the housekeeper's voice instead of her ex-mother-in-law. "Ann? This is Edie. Are you alone?"

"Mm-hmm. How are you? I've been thinking about you."

Somehow, hearing that was such a relief.

"I'm scared," Edie said, wishing she could fly through the phone wires into Ann's kitchen. "Pinky surprised me the other day. Gave me some things of Jack's."

"She's having a terrible time, you know."

"I know. I'm kind of a mess myself. Cleaning the oven hasn't helped."

Ann laughed. She was the one who'd taught Edie that oven cleaning was a great minimizer of impossible feelings.

"Did you clean the grout?"

"No," Edie admitted.

"Where's that brother of yours?"

"Out."

"Listen, Edie." Ann's voice grew stern. "You are a strong woman. For a while, maybe, I had some doubts, but I haven't had any in a while. You will get through this. No matter what Mrs. Gainsford or anybody else does."

"Okay." When Ann said it, she could believe it. "I've got starch?" she asked, wanting to hear Ann say that too.

"Buckets full."

As Edie laughed shakily, Ann's characteristic term for strength and spine jogged something in Edie's memory.

Starch. Ann had said Jill hadn't any. Well, she'd been way off there.

"Did you know Jill came out to Clairbeck that night?" Edie asked.

"What?"

She imagined Ann, stopping in the middle of wiping the counter.

"Remember you told me that Jill missed her shopping appointment? Well, at the funeral, she said she borrowed her roommate's car and came out here looking for Jack."

"Edie, that girl couldn't have—"

"She broke into my house, Ann. She watched me sleeping. She told me she wants me arrested for this."

A long pause traveled down the line. Edie imagined it weighing down the wires, like when they sagged in the heat of summer.

"In your house?" Ann's voice was quiet now.

"Yep. Came in through the milk door."

Edie had done that herself, but not since she was twelve, sneaking home in the middle of the day to skip school. After twelve, she'd never have fit—the double-sided cupboards built into the back wall of most houses were never big enough for a grown up to squeeze through. Milk doors were made small, just big enough to hold a couple bottles of milk, maybe some eggs, depending on your dairy order.

With just her and Peter, she'd never bothered to sign up for milk delivery. Not here.

"How'd she fit?" Ann asked. "She's small, but that must have been quite the trick."

"Used a stick to release the dead bolt. She was here, Ann," Edie said. "She hates me. She wanted me to know the truth. I told the police, but they don't believe me."

"It sounds nuts," Ann said. "But I guess she's tricky to know."

"She's from Blunt Creek. That isn't far from here."

"No, it isn't."

"Could she get morphine?" Edie asked, feeling all the stupidity of her question. There was so much about Jill that Ann wouldn't know, but Ann was the best chance she had right now. "Friends in medical or nursing school? Maybe a—"

"Edie." The housekeeper stopped her. "I think—"

Ann sounded afraid.

"What is it?" Edie prompted.

"Jill's uncle is a vet," Ann said. "She's worked for him at least one summer, between college terms. She's put down dogs and cats. But bigger animals too."

Edie heard Ann draw a shaky breath.

"Do they use morphine for that?"

CHAPTER THIRTY

PETER BRACED HIMSELF, SO BRENDA'S GLARE DIDN'T SHOVE HIM OFF his chair, onto the floor. "Pharmacists are *always* first to be blamed," she snapped. "Dad has to be extra careful, because we're Chinese. You don't get it." She stood, crumpled her napkin and tossed it and her bottle into the trash.

Peter turned in his chair, trying to make sense of her anger, but all he got was a view of her back. "Brenda? I'm sorry. I don't get it."

"Of course not."

"Can you explain?" When she didn't respond, he added. "You can trust me."

She had to, as far as the Obetrol went. Maybe she was remembering that, because she turned around again.

"Fine. We'll see how far you get." She folded her arms and returned to her chair. "To you, running a drugstore seems pretty straight forward. But the drug laws are anti-Chinese, or at least, that's what they were meant to be."

"Anti-Chinese?" Some skepticism must have crept into his voice.

Her shoulders tightened.

"I'm listening," he added quickly.

She held off though, long enough that he thought she'd changed her mind.

"My grandfather and my great-uncle came to work on the railroad," Brenda said finally. "Worked twice as hard as white workers for less than half the pay. Bosses gave them numbers, because it was too hard to try and learn their names. Chinese workers got hurt all the time. Killed too, because they were always given the most dangerous work. Granddad and his friends often worked injured, and they'd use opium to cope with the pain because they couldn't stay here without money and a job.

But other people used opium too. Morphine, laudanum...all of it. And when they became addicted, when addictions caused trouble or crime, they blamed it all on us. We were easy targets. The crazy thing—bet you don't know this either—is that opium was never a big problem in China until the British started pushing it on us."

The cola he'd swallowed felt extra cold in Peter's middle. "That isn't right."

"You think?" She glared at him. "Granddad said back then journalists were always cooking up stories about innocents being lured into addiction by scheming Chinamen wearing pajamas and pigtails. People tried to stop more Chinese from entering the country. They told panicked stories of Chinese trying to marry white women—and do you know how much it cost for my grandfather to bring my grandmother over, with the extra tax? And what his wage was?"

Peter hadn't known any of this, or that she'd been keeping so much anger folded tidily inside.

"Granddad was allowed in to build the railroad, and if he was still alive when the tracks were done, he was expected to just work until he died, single and alone. And take all the blame for problems you people started on top of it."

Brenda flattened her palms on the table. "Do you know how careful my parents are? They need to have nice storefronts, but not the nicest ones, because people like Mrs. Sorenson don't like it. My dad won't ever buy a new car, though he can. Instead, he buys secondhand ones, always overpriced, from his neighbors. It's a strategy."

She shook her head. "The details of living haven't ever been strategy for you."

"Not before," Peter admitted. "It takes a fair bit of thinking now though, just getting around."

Her fingers tensed.

"I'm not saying what's tough for me is anything like the way things are for your family," he added. "But life's definitely changed for me, so I think I can see, a little, what it might be like. I wish things weren't this way. For your granddad, and your family. For you."

All these accumulated injuries, and he hadn't known. Hadn't thought to ask, even.

"Yeah, well, if I say my dad is careful, I mean that he's careful. In a way you probably wouldn't think of or ever expect to be."

"I see that now." Peter nodded.

"You cared about Leo. You care about your sister. I like that, and for what it's worth, you seem really nice." Brenda swallowed. "But you need to be careful what questions you ask. My family will suffer if you start saying things about Leo's medicines."

Peter nodded. His head felt heavier than it had just a minute ago, and the air was still crackling with Brenda's charged anger. "I wouldn't have asked if it wasn't important, and it is, because something—" Peter swallowed. Edie wouldn't like it, but shouldn't Brenda know? Especially if it might hurt her family?

"Something went really wrong with Leo," Peter said.

Brenda's eyebrows knitted together.

He leaned closer. "Leo probably didn't have cancer." Quietly, he told her about Edie's surprise over the diagnosis. The record of fractures in Leo's chart, and their absence in his X-rays.

Brenda's hand crept up to her mouth.

"Peter—"

"I know. It's awful thinking of it. But you can see why—"

"Yes, I see. What are you going to do?"

He paused, nonplussed. "Well, this. Ask questions. Ask you."

Her face took on a pained expression. "I just told you that you have to be careful. It will be so easy for my dad to take the blame."

"Can you ask him?" Peter asked.

He could tell she was struggling. "If there's a problem, it's not him," she said. "But I can ask. I won't do anything that might hurt my family. Just so you know."

"I'm not asking you to," Peter promised. "Don't worry."

"I've got to lock up."

Peter tested his legs and rose from the chair. "It's pretty dark. Do you want me to walk you home?"

He was unlikely to be of any use, in the event of trouble, and Brenda knew this town better than him. But Peter was no longer convinced that this supposedly friendly town was a safe one.

Brenda shook her head. "I'm fine on my own, Peter. You'd better go. Edie will be wondering what's keeping you."

CHAPTER THIRTY-ONE

Edie ran herself a bath. She was struggling through the first chapter of a novel, deciding whether or not to add more hot water when the doorbell rang.

Nope. Definitely not. She was home alone. Glancing out of the tub, she realized she hadn't locked the bathroom door.

And she was naked. Suddenly, Edie wanted clothes. And a large dog, to scare off whoever was standing on her front porch.

She hopped out the water, hastily toweling off.

The bell rang again, and she cursed. Peter must have left a light on. If she was quiet, the person on the doorstep would probably go away.

Leaving the water in the tub (the noise of the drain might carry), she coiled a towel around her head and slipped into her robe. She opened the bathroom door slowly (it creaked), tiptoed into the hall—

"Holy shit!"

Edie leaped back, slipping on the waxed wood floor, arms wheeling. A gasp, another curse, and she righted herself—enough to push back the towel that had fallen over her face and glare at the window set in the front door.

A man's face was pressed against the glass. He could see her.

"I'm calling the cops!" she shouted, heart thudding.

"It's just me, Mrs. Gainsford! Brad Kulak."

He moved back from the window, but not before she recognized his pale brows and long face.

"You haven't returned any of my calls," he pleaded.

Edie shut her eyes and took three deep breaths. She did not want to talk with Bradley Kulak, but he must have driven all the way from Calgary, and she didn't want to drive there next week or next month or whenever she couldn't postpone this any longer.

"Gimme five minutes." She spun on her heel and marched into her room.

"Take your time," he hollered.

"Damn right I will."

She did not want to put on a bra—not when she'd planned on spending the rest of the evening soaking, reading, wearing flannels, and worrying herself to death—but she wasn't talking to Jack's estate lawyer without one. Also, panties, trousers, sweater, slippers. Hair tugged back in a ponytail. Robe on the hook. Towel on the rack in the bathroom. *Okay.*

At least her hands had stopped shaking.

When she opened the front door, Brad flinched like she'd bared her teeth at him.

"Good evening, Mr. Kulak."

He swallowed. "Mrs.... Ms. Simmons?"

Her jaw relaxed slightly. "You can come in."

"Sorry for the trouble. I know you weren't expecting visitors."

"Yeah, the bathrobe's a dead giveaway." She sank into her favorite chair and waved him in the direction of the sofa. The tips of his ears were pink.

Face smooth, Edie tucked her feet up in the chair. The room felt cold. After finding out Jack had been watching her, the whole house felt different. Without knowing, she'd been living behind one-way glass, and the walls she thought had been sheltering her were feeble protection. Now she had Jack's lawyer sitting in her living room.

"I've been anxious to speak with you." He perched on the edge of the sofa, balancing his hat on his knees. "As Jack's legatee—"

"What do you know about the house?" she interrupted. "The one he bought behind mine?"

"There is a record of it in his papers," Brad Kulak admitted.

How nice.

"Do you know when he bought it?"

He cleared his throat. "The transaction was completed in April."

Not long after she'd started seeing Nathan. And not long after he'd come here and touched that hickey on her neck.

"Where'd he get the money?"

"Houses in Clairbeck are not expensive."

Maybe not, but Edie hadn't been able to buy this one on her own. No bank would let her, not on a nurse's salary. She'd had to ask her father to cosign, and even though she'd never missed a payment, it was impossible to forget that without his help, she'd be renting, probably paying more for less.

"He must have paid five thousand for it."

"Four," Brad corrected her. "He leveraged the Calgary home."

Two thousand square feet with an attached garage on a street with a view of the river. Pile carpeting and a bedroom that could have been a nursery, but they'd never ended up redecorating. Probably her fault, according to the doctor, but after a couple years she'd secretly decided it was just as well. Three years later, she had her divorce.

"Ms. Simmons?"

Edie refocused on his face. "I'm sorry. Come again?" She must have missed his question.

"The Calgary property is why I'm here. It needs your attention, with some urgency."

"Well, I don't want it. Even if I did, Jack's parents and Jill Evans are absolutely going to challenge this will."

"They can try," he said. "But I doubt it would be effective. I wrote the will, and it's a valid one. I think the Gainsfords are wiser than that."

Edie huffed. She wasn't going to try and explain Pinky. "Just sell it then."

"I can, if you wish it, once we are granted probate, but there's something to take care of first." Clearly, he had an objective and wasn't willing to lose sight of it.

"What's that?" The sooner she let him tell her, the sooner he'd go.

"Jill Evans is staying there."

Edie resisted the urge to rub her forearms. "Was she staying there before"—she licked her lips—"his murder?"

Jack cared about what his neighbors thought, and Pinky...

"I don't know. I didn't ask. But she's there now, and when I asked her to leave, she refused. It's important to inventory the household contents."

Edie grunted and leaned back in her chair, tuning out Brad's talk of probate applications and household furnishings, thinking about Jill and if she'd acquired a syringe of morphine. No way to know if Forbes had overheard her phone call to Ann. But she hoped so.

"Ms. Simmons?"

Edie stopped biting her thumbnail. "Sorry. It's a lot to think about."

"I understand. But you're the rightful owner of the house and contents—"

"I don't want them." Unless Jack had redecorated, she'd picked most things in that house, but she didn't want any of it here. The furniture wouldn't fit, and even though it might be nice to upgrade her secondhand pots or the cheap Woolco sheets and towels, the thought of bringing tangible pieces of her marriage—of him—to this house tightened her shoulders in a shudder. Especially now that Jill was hiding out there.

They'd both trespassed in her new home enough already.

"Are you certain?" the lawyer was looking at her like she was crazy.

"I don't care about the contents," Edie said, rearranging her hands because it forced them to relax. "Please tell Miss Evans to take anything she likes."

Brad stared at her, a half-finished word dangling from his lips. "We don't know the value—"

"Anything she likes," Edie repeated. "But I want her out of there by Friday. I'll see the place myself on Saturday." But she sure as hell wasn't going to see Jill.

"I'm not sure I'm available—"

"I work," Edie informed him. "So, Saturday's the only day that works for me. All I need is the key." If she remembered right, Brad was a golfer.

"I'll present your offer to Miss Evans," he told her. "It's very generous, and I expect it will solve the problem of her squatting in the house."

"I expect so," Edie said.

"You're certain? Under those terms, she could take everything that's not nailed down."

Edie nodded. "I'm sure." The police had searched the place already, and Wednesday afternoon, when she had to talk to Forbes, she'd tell him again about Jill, who'd killed enough dogs and sheep to know how to handle a human...and maybe a troublesome fiancé.

She'd tell him about Leo too, and Brenda, and all the rest of it. He was the detective. Let him put all this together. As for Jill...

"You know what?"

The lawyer stopped talking, surprised by her interruption.

"Give Miss Evans until tomorrow night. I'll see the house Wednesday morning."

Might as well take the whole day off. Her job was probably done for, and she had no reason to be nice to Jill. If she wanted Jack's stuff, let her sweat a little.

"Good. Well, I'm happy to be moving forward. As for your visit…I think Wednesday morning will be fine."

"Thank you, Mr. Kulak. I think so too." She stayed in her chair, listening to the lawyer let himself out.

CHAPTER THIRTY-TWO

"SEE? I GOT US HERE," PETER SAID, WEDNESDAY MORNING, PULLING into the driveway of Jack's house.

Edie grunted and screwed on the lid of the coffee thermos. She had a splash on the front of her coat, from Peter inadvertently pressing the brake lever when he'd meant to signal.

"Sorry about your coat," he said, but she didn't seem to hear, preoccupied with frowning at the house through the windshield.

"Looks like she's gone," Peter said.

"She better be."

They'd stopped at the offices of Jones, Wilcox, and Gainsford promptly at eight o' clock, for Bradley Kulak to give them the key. He said he hadn't been by the house yet, but that when he'd telephoned early this morning, Miss Evans was just leaving.

"Should we take a look?" Peter suggested.

Edie extracted the key from her purse, got out, and slammed the car door. "She could have at least mowed the lawn."

The grass was lank and overgrown, covered with dead leaves from the bare trees, and it looked even worse next to the neat grid lines mowed into the lawn of the house next door. "I'll have to call Bobby down the street. See if I can pay him to do it," Edie grumbled.

If Bobby's family still lived here—but then, people didn't buy houses on this crescent just to move. Edie leaving had probably been the biggest change this street had ever seen.

"Smile," Edie told him. "Mrs. Stewart is watching." She waved across the street, where a woman in a crinoline housedress was filling a bird feeder.

Peter offered the neighbor a half-hearted wave and turned away. "Let's get inside."

Edie halted the moment she stepped in the house, leaving him to balance awkwardly on the threshold. He glanced over her shoulder at the stripped walls of the bare living room and let out a whistle.

"Must have needed a pretty big truck."

Everything—the Hi-Fi, the television, the brown leather sofa and matching brass lamps—was gone.

Edie grimaced. "I didn't think she'd be this efficient, but it makes my life easier."

Walking through naked rooms, the reality of Jack's death was inescapable, even heavier than it had felt at his funeral.

"Huh." Edie turned around, her face cracking into a smile. "Did you know Jill lives in a sorority house? Where do you think she put it all?"

Peter shook his head. Storage wasn't an insurmountable problem, but the dedication necessary to pack and clear this place in so short a time was a little frightening. But then, Jill was crazy enough to break into Edie's house.

He'd changed the locks for her since and plastered the milk door shut.

"Wow. Look at this place." Edie walked toward the kitchen, trailing a hand along the patterned wallpaper. "You don't know how much I was dreading coming here, seeing things the same. But she's kind of done me a favor, without even knowing."

Peter produced a smile. It felt a bit lopsided, but his tension ratcheted down a little. "Think she took his clothes too?"

"Only one way to find out."

The bedroom was stripped bare, except for some haphazard piles on the floor. Half-used toiletries, socks and underwear, shirts, ties. "She took his watches." Edie knelt, picking through things abstractedly. "And his cuff links."

She dropped a shirt back onto the pile. "Smells like his aftershave. Let's get out of here."

Back in the kitchen, she ran the taps and splashed water on her cheeks.

"You all right?" Peter asked.

Edie straightened. "Yeah." Her eyes fixed on something behind him, widening like a cat's.

"What's wrong?" He had to repeat himself before she pointed.

"Look."

He turned and spotted a corkboard mounted on the wall beside the phone. Snapshots, a typed-out list of emergency numbers, and a pizza menu jostled for space with a notepad for taking messages. A torn sheet fluttered from it, with half of the page, and part of a penciled message, remaining. "That's Jack's writing." Edie swallowed. "And Nathan's phone number at the clinic."

She ripped off the sheet, examining it closely. Peter's eyes went back to the corkboard—and a photograph of the unidentified brick building he'd seen among Jack's pictures. The missing one, if Jack had taken a second shot of it.

Peter had forgotten to check the negatives.

This was a better shot, too, the lettering on the plaque clearly visible.

"What's the Keeley Center?" he asked.

"Treatment home. For inebriates and—why?" Edie asked.

Peter pointed at the photograph. "That's it. Why would Jack go there? Take pictures?"

"They help narcotic addicts too," Edie said slowly.

Drugs again. Another find uncomfortably adjacent to their questions. He couldn't help feeling like the right lines might join these seemingly disparate points into a constellation, pointing them the right way.

Peter reached for the notepad and the nearby pencil hanging from a string. Quickly shading over the next page of the notebook, he began revealing the letters that had been written on the leaf above: including the torn-off portion, below Nathan Irwin's telephone number.

"Look," he said. "Someone took down a message."

Dr. Belmead. Replying to John re: complaint against Dr. N. Irwin.

"His parents call him John now," Edie said. "So does Jill. And that's not Jack's handwriting, so I think she must have written this. Is there a date?"

Peter kept shading, revealing numbers—

"No," he said, disappointed. "She could have taken this message yesterday or weeks ago."

More letters followed the numbers. *Spray Lake Road.*

"That's where my car was found," Edie said. Her face was tense. Peter shaded faster, revealing a time: 10:00.

"Is that when he was killed?" Edie's voice rose.

Peter bit his inner lip. "I don't think this message is about that," he said slowly. "It if had been written before he died, this would have been taken by the police."

"I guess you're right." She sounded disappointed.

Peter glanced at his watch: 8:47. "It's possible, maybe, that this meeting hasn't happened yet. Could be today, even." He tapped above the message at Nathan's number, which also seemed to be in Jill's handwriting. "Because every other morning at ten, he's been in the clinic, right?"

"Not last weekend," Edie said.

"Yes. The meeting could have happened then," Peter admitted. "But I doubt he'd have gone on Saturday, after spending most of the night taking Leo to the hospital. You weren't back until three or four. He'd have wanted to sleep. And the Saturday before that was the funeral, so Jill wouldn't have agreed to meet anyone all the way in Clairbeck. There's always Sunday, but—"

"I'm calling the clinic." Edie picked up the telephone, chewing her nails until the line answered. "Brenda? Is Dr. Irwin there?"

A pause.

"Oh, hi, Katya. Oh. I see. Thanks."

"Is he there?" Peter asked, the instant she hung up.

Edie shook her head. "Canceled all his patients. Went home an hour ago. Said he wasn't feeling well. Brenda's gone too. Katya's still there, but she's just locking up."

A drop of water fell from the tap into the sink, echoing in the otherwise silent room.

"We could drive out there," Edie said. "To Spray Lake Road. See if Jill and Nathan are there. If we leave now, we'd just make it."

He could almost feel the ticking of his watch. They'd have to hurry.

"Wait," he said. "Just a minute."

He studied the corkboard again, worried he was missing something. That photo. The notebook and shaded message. He scrutinized each letter, but nothing came to him. There was a claim tag for some dry cleaning and, centered above the notebook, an unused thumbtack.

It was positioned too precisely just to be there. It was for holding something, Peter realized, just like the tack they had in their board at home. Where he hung his keys.

Peter spun and hurried to the garage.

"What is it?" Edie asked, but he was breathing too hard to speak.

The door stuck, requiring a forceful push that tugged him off balance when the door finally gave and flew open, banging the knob against the garage wall.

"Where's his car?" Peter asked.

It was dark inside without the lights on. But besides the lawnmower, a bag of golf clubs and an old bicycle, there was nothing to see.

"It's not here," Edie said. Then, numbly, "If you were Jill, and you took a message from Dr. Belmead, who Jack might have contacted before he died with his suspicions, would you call Nathan? Would you drive out there?"

Peter thinned his lips. "If I were Jill, I might." He glanced at his watch. "It's almost nine. We'd better hurry."

Just in case.

CHAPTER THIRTY-THREE

They drove out of Calgary at sixty-five miles an hour, windows down, with Edie drumming her fingers on the steering wheel. The deciphered address lay on the seat between them.

Peter clutched his camera, taken from the trunk of the car. It wasn't his best one. It was a small thing, a pocket camera, a Minox II. He'd gotten it because it wasn't always handy, on the mountain, to carry hefty equipment.

Now, he held it because it made him feel better. And because they might want proof of this meeting, if there really was one, when Edie went to Forbes this afternoon.

"Jill talked to Kulak before leaving the house," Edie said. "She might already be there."

"Why Spray Lake Road? There's not much out there," Peter said, pulling his eyes away from the speedometer. With two hands, he lifted his right leg, taking some pressure off the upper straps of his brace. "Not until you get to the dam, and even then, you'd think the bad associations would—"

"We don't know anything," Edie said, not for the first time. The reminders were getting annoying. "This is just a guess."

A guess that chilled him through.

He nodded, as she added that there was every chance they'd drive up and find the place empty. But she didn't slow down.

"There's a couple houses up there," she said. "Some old mines too. Closed now, but some buildings are still standing." She overtook a gray coupe and slid back into the right-hand lane. "Maybe we should have called Forbes."

"And told him what?" Peter asked. "We don't know anything, remember?"

"There is that."

Watching her grip the steering wheel like a life ring, feeling the sway of the car as they took one of the highway's few curves, he wished again that he was driving.

He was thirsty, the coffee was gone, and the only food they had was a packet of Lifesavers in Edie's purse. Peter unwrapped one and put it in his mouth, just to work some moisture into it.

"Want one?" He held the roll out to Edie.

"I'm fine." Maybe she was too intent on the road to feel much else.

They drove past the turn for Blunt Creek, then Hillview, and rounded the perilous curve by the lake. Peter glanced again at the gas gauge. Only a quarter of a tank. They should stop and refuel, but he doubted Edie would.

There's enough to take us up the road, then get us back to town. Even the way she's driving.

They bypassed Clairbeck, turning off the main highway early and taking an old mine road that joined the Spray Highway just south of town. The beat of Edie's fingers on the steering wheel sped faster.

She signaled to turn left, slowed just enough to take the turn without skidding, and roared up the road, leaving a barrage of flying gravel. Jack had been found on this road, but Peter didn't know what stretch. Edie's mouth pinched tight.

They bounced over a bumpy bit of washboard, flying past the

reservoir and into a steep turn. "We don't need to hurry this much," Peter said, as Edie punched the gas to avoid losing speed. "It's just past ten. If we don't see her, it's because we guessed wrong." They wouldn't miss her, because the only way out was down this same road, and the air was clear in front and thick with dust behind them. They were the first—at least in a while—along this route.

"I'm nervous," Edie said. "Especially if she's meeting Nathan." Her hands tightened. "One of them's in danger, and I'm not sure who."

"I'm betting on Nathan."

"Why?"

"Because Jill gives me the creeps," Peter said, trying to lighten the mood.

Her answering glare told him he'd failed. Truth be told, he was nervous too.

"Address?" Edie asked.

He consulted the page and gave her the number.

"I think this is the turn." Edie slowed and turned down a rough track that branched from the road. "But I haven't been here before. Just a different house farther along."

This road was even rougher. Edie squinted, trying to see through the trees shielding a bend in the road.

"Peter."

A car was parked a hundred yards ahead, dust lying thick on the chrome bumper.

"Jack's car," Edie said.

"So, where's the girl?"

"Dunno. Where's Nathan?" There was only the one car.

Peter opened the door and levered himself out, surveying a tangle of wild grasses, low scrub, and deadfall that made this ground a perfect nightmare.

"Wait here." Edie set off for the tumbledown building next to Jack's car, a weathered shanty with holes where once there'd been windows and doors.

"Wait," he protested, not wanting her to venture off alone. But she didn't hear, racing ahead and calling.

"Jill? Jill!"

The mountains pushed her voice back, a mocking echo embellished by the squawks of a crow, and Peter's head turned reflexively, pursuing the sound.

He didn't find the bird. Instead, his eyes caught on something lying in the grass: black with an unnatural shine. He moved closer, picking his way over the uneven ground until it was in reach of his crutch. He prodded it out from the grass: a single woman's shoe, an expensive-looking black leather pump.

"Edie!" he called.

He scanned the trees, but nothing moved. He couldn't see any danger, but his breaths came short and fast as he pushed through the scrub until, about thirty paces away, he saw her.

"Edie!"

No response. The only movement was from the crow perched overhead in the trees, stalking along the branch, waggling his head arrogantly at Peter.

"She's here," Peter said, as Edie crashed to a halt alongside him.

She clapped a hand to her mouth. But when she started forward again, Peter planted a hand on her arm.

"Wait." He searched the trees again. "Let me. You keep watch. He might still be here."

Edie tugged free. "That doesn't matter. She might be alive!"

Peter didn't think so, judging from the bloodstained ground and the proximity of the swaggering crow. But he let her go, and turned left and right and behind, afraid to look away from any one place for more than a second.

"No pulse." Edie's voice was much too high.

With shaking hands, Peter reached into his pocket for the Minox.

"No breathing." Edie sat back on her heels, turning to him with desolate eyes. "And I still can't find a heartbeat."

She had streaks of blood on her hands and the front of her blouse.

"Then I should photograph the scene," he told her. Quickly, in case the person who did this came back.

"No way." Edie jumped to her feet. "The killer might still be here. We've got to get away. We've got to tell the police."

"It'll take me one minute," he said. "And we might need to. You've got her blood all over you."

Edie looked at her hands. "Because I was trying to help!"

"I know." But when the police came here, they might just decide to close both cases by planting some evidence. He and Edie needed a record that supported their story.

Edie swiped at her cheek.

"Keep a lookout," Peter said. "I won't take long." He hopped closer, scanning in all directions before raising his camera.

"Hold up," he told Edie, focusing the lens on the ground leading to Jill's crumpled form. "There's blood on these leaves." Dark smears and what looked like drops on the grass, between the marks of a single high-heeled shoe. "Stay there. Let me photograph the ground. We might get some footprints moving away."

He took a shot, shook his head in disgust, and wiped his hands on his trousers. His palms were slick with sweat, and his hands and arms were trembling.

He'd never been this frightened, looking through a lens. Not on cliff faces, not on glaciers, not—

"Focus," he whispered.

"Please hurry," Edie urged, fidgeting with impatience.

"I only get one shot at this," Peter said levelly. "If you don't see anyone coming to kill us, I need you to go to the car. See if I have a light meter in the trunk. And extra film."

If he had the film, he could bracket his shots, taking three different exposures of each image—a safety net, in case he didn't get it right. The light was uneven, with shadows falling from the surrounding trees and a sky of shifting clouds. Limited to single shots, he wouldn't get the best images. Some would be obscured by shadows, some overexposed.

He'd need lots of pictures: close-ups of the ground and the victim—he tripped on the word, though it had come naturally into his thoughts.

Not now. He'd examine that later, after making a record.

"No one's here," Edie muttered a minute later. "Not that I can see." She passed him the light meter and film. "But hurry."

He'd planned his shots while he waited, and plotted a path to Jill's body, one he could manage on crutches without obscuring her own footsteps.

"I need you to walk around a bit and tell me the light readings," Peter said. "But be careful where you step. Watch the ground. We don't want to miss anything. And keep a lookout. If anything moves—"

"We're done for."

Probably. But they'd have some great pictures.

Edie picked her way through the grass, calling out when something that caught her attention was just a rock, and spitting out numbers. He pulled out a handkerchief, unfolded it, and wrapped it around the Minox's flash as a makeshift diffuser.

"Wait there," he called, and leaned over his crutches to photograph the ground.

"Do you need me to do it?" Edie said, as he struggled, unable to kneel down.

Edie'd never been great at keeping her hands steady, but really, he was kidding himself, attempting this now.

"I can do it," he said. "If you help me down and hoist me up again."

She rolled her eyes.

"These have to be good shots." He wasn't just trying to keep Edie out of jail. He was trying to catch whoever did this, because next time, it might be Edie lying dead in the grass. It might be him.

Together, they captured the broken branches, bent grass, and the blood on the ground, the prints left by Jill's lone black leather pump, and the thick marks of a pair of boots.

"I'm not sure how well they'll show on film," Peter said, trying a shot with the diffusing handkerchief off. He glanced at his sister. "Now let's look at Jill."

The crow, who'd flown off as they combed the ground, was back, watching them.

"It's such a lot of blood," Edie said quietly.

Jill lay crumpled on her side, one hand tucked by her middle, her plaid wool skirt tangled around her legs, one foot clad only in a muddy, torn stocking. There were cuts on her hands, shallow haphazard ones, with dried blood at the edges, not like the syrupy stickiness of the blood everywhere else. After photographing the surrounding grass, Peter lowered himself stiffly to the ground, avoiding the spilt blood, and leaning on Edie for support. The braces creaked, and one knee hinge needed extra persuasion.

He was short of breath and sweating. "Don't overdo it," Edie warned. "I can't carry you out of here. You've got to be able to make it back to the car."

Peter shook his head. His heart was pumping so fast that he wasn't feeling much of anything, but experience told him he should be feeling fatigue. "I'll make it." He positioned his camera, inventorying the wounds on Jill's hands and arms. The big one, the one that had killed her, was concealed behind her bloodstained blouse.

Edie picked up a stick, pushing back the blood-soaked fabric.

"Don't tear it," Peter said. He'd snapped a couple pictures already but wanted to keep the body undisturbed.

"I won't," Edie said. "It's ripped already. Look." She gave a light nudge, and the torn closure fell apart, offering a partial view of waxy, blood-smeared skin and a stained bra. "Two wounds that I can see," Edie said. "Just below the xiphoid."

"That doesn't mean anything to me," Peter said.

"Injury to the major blood vessels. Or the heart," she told him. "Probably both. No chance of saving her. Not up here."

She moistened her lips and stared into the trees. "Done with the pictures yet?"

"Nearly." He was almost out of film.

"Good." She hurled her stick away. "We've got to hurry and tell the police." She glanced at the car. "Whoever did this is out there."

The crow hopped closer and started cawing again.

CHAPTER THIRTY-FOUR

THREE. I'VE NEVER TAKEN THIS MANY, THIS CLOSE TOGETHER, AND the number feels significant, like a curse.

I have to stay calm. Hurry home, clean up, and act like I haven't just had another close call. Above all, I can't be seen with this blood on me.

But I know the paths in these woods, the weave of deer and rabbit tracks that tangle between town and the reservoir. I know the ways to come and go from the high quiet places along this road. Soon, I'll reach the water, and that will take care of the worst of this mess.

But I'm not home yet, and I'm hearing echoes. Someone's shouting. I swear under my breath. They aren't supposed to find the girl—maybe not ever and definitely not yet.

I don't need time, exactly, but I like to have it. I do things slowly, with deliberation. At least, I used to. There're too many surprises these days, and they're coming too close. I've had to adapt, be quick, but I also must keep low, stay hidden.

Jack and Leo caught me off guard, but not as much as this girl's phone call. And her demands. After all she said, I'm surprised she agreed to drive out for a meeting. Why not be more careful? I would have been.

Turns out, this one wasn't very smart.

CHAPTER THIRTY-FIVE

EDIE DROVE THEM BACK TO TOWN, BLANKETED IN A SILENT, HEAVY focus. Peter didn't mind. His thoughts were running in so many directions, trying to talk felt impossible. But when she drove past Main, instead of turning toward the police station, he twisted sideways, reaching out a hand for her arm. "Where are you going?"

"We'll go to the police. Soon." She shrugged free. "I want to talk to Nathan first."

She turned sedately around a corner, in a style completely opposite to the intensity of her voice and the tightness of her hands.

"It's too dangerous," he said quietly. "We can't go there. Not without the police."

"They won't listen, Peter!" Edie snapped, slamming a hand onto the steering wheel. "And even if we do, by the time we talk them into it, he'll be all cleaned up. We have to confront him now, while there's still blood and—"

"He killed her, Edie. If we go to his house—"

"There's two of us. We can do it." She pulled to the side of the road. "This is it."

Peter peered through the window at a wide two-story house with great views. Nathan Irwin, in baggy khakis and a sweat dampened camp shirt, was pushing a rotary mower across his lawn. He stopped and swiped an arm across his forehead. The lawn was nearly done. At the side of the house, a fire smoked within a circle of carefully placed bricks, probably consuming, bit by bit, the large pile of raked leaves.

Peter frowned and looked at his sister. His tension evaporated, leaving him feeling empty and sick. "What were you saying about blood?"

"Dammit." Her hand banged the steering wheel again.

"Let's go to the station," Peter said.

But Nathan had stopped mowing and was walking toward their car.

"Your blouse," Peter whispered, in a strangled voice, and Edie clutched the fabric with one hand, fumbling with the other in the backseat for something: a jacket or sweater.

"Nurse Simmons? What—" His eyes widened. He'd seen the blood.

Peter opened the car door. "Sick, huh?"

Nathan flushed.

"We gotta talk to you," Peter said. "About a call made to the clinic. Yesterday, maybe, or this morning—"

"I was barely there today," Nathan said. "I think the milk in the fridge must have been off. Soon as I had my first cup of coffee, I was dying."

"Really?" Peter leaned against the car.

"Well, I felt better, after I came home and threw up. I don't remember taking any calls yesterday." He turned to Edie. "The clinic was pretty quiet, remember?"

Sick or no, from the look of things, he'd been working in his yard for a while.

"It was quiet," Edie said, but the look on her face wasn't friendly. "But you haven't been great at telling me things. Like the threats you got from Jack, maybe?"

He winced.

"So, you're going to be honest with me. Starting now. Because I need to know the truth before I talk to Sergeant Forbes today."

"I don't—you can see I'm busy and—"

"Not too busy," Edie said.

"I can't—"

"You better. And it better be quick," Peter said. "We're just about to go to the police."

For a split second, utter horror filled his face. But he mastered himself and mumbled a sulky reply. "Gainsford warned me off. Jealous bastard. He couldn't—"

Edie snorted. "He didn't just warn you away from me. What did he know?"

"He was jealous, that's all. I swear," Irwin sputtered.

"I don't think so," Peter said.

"And I think someone else asked you about this. Or tried to," Edie said. "But she was killed this morning."

Irwin's mouth fell open. "Killed?" He swiped his hands on his trousers, leaving streaks of sweat.

Peter sent Edie a warning look. Irwin didn't need to know details. But Edie stuck her hands on her hips and launched another question. "What happened between you and Jack?"

Irwin glanced up and down the street. "You can't just come here asking questions!" he hissed.

"I can come back later with the police," she told him. "That's your other option. I'll tell them I was seeing you and how recently. That you came to my house often. That you had access to my extra car keys."

His shoulders folded together, like the walls of an abandoned barn. "Edie, I swear—"

"Nurse Simmons, please. Since you prefer formality."

"Can we talk inside?" he asked, eyes pleading.

Peter made some quick calculations. Irwin might not have killed Jill, but he was hiding something, and the police ought to hear it firsthand.

"We'll talk inside," he said. "At the station."

Forbes was not happy to see them, especially when they told him there was a dead body lying off Spray Lake Road. After dispatching Lefthand and McSorely with a few barked commands, he invited—ordered—them into his office, with Miss Clark along to record the proceedings.

"These are official statements," he warned.

Nathan wiped his forehead with a shaky hand.

Edie sat back and let Peter tell the detective about going to Jack's house, finding the messages, and hurrying back to confront Jill.

"You did this after deducing she might have killed Gainsford?" Forbes asked.

"We figured out something," Edie snapped. "Have you?"

"All the time," he said, looking at her coolly. "Tell me what you found out there."

She let Peter relate that too. "And if your officers think they can pin this on either of us, you should know I took pictures of everything," he finished. "If anything is planted out there, I'll know."

"Helpful of you." Forbes compressed his lips. "And after that, instead of coming immediately to me or calling from the nearest phone, you went to see *him*?" He jerked a thumb at Nathan.

"We thought he'd killed her," Edie said.

Nathan let out a pained sound.

"Did you?" Forbes asked.

Miss Clark held up a hand. "Wait. I need to sharpen my pencil."

She got up and walked to the sharpener mounted on the wall. It growled like a wild animal; then Miss Clark extracted the pencil and tapped it twice to clear away the dust. Satisfied with the point, she returned to her chair.

"Proceed."

"Thanks, Miss Clark. You heard her, Dr. Irwin."

He rubbed his palms against his trousers. "I didn't kill her. Couldn't have. Been working on my yard most of the morning. My neighbors will tell you. She may have called the clinic, but I didn't talk to her."

"And so, you are here because..."

"There's something I haven't told you." Nathan stared at his shoes, in a way that gave Edie a rush of satisfaction.

"For a couple of months, I'd been getting phone calls," he said. "Anonymous ones. Hang ups late at night. Sometimes here, sometimes at the clinic. Then one afternoon—"

"Which afternoon?"

"The twenty-first of September."

"The day John Gainsford was murdered."

"Y-yes."

Forbes glanced at Miss Clark. "I've got that down," she said, not looking up from her stenography pad.

"Go on, Dr. Irwin."

"He spoke to me. Gainsford."

"Yes, I gathered that."

Nathan flushed. "I worked in Edmonton before this. At the Royal Alexandra Hospital. Mr. Gainsford knew about that. And he knew—" He swallowed. "I'd developed a bit of a habit."

Forbes leaned closer.

"I sometimes took morphine—"

"How much is sometimes?"

"Not much." Nathan wove his fingers together, twisting his hands until they had to hurt. "More often I took cocaine. I stole another doctor's prescription pad and—" He wiped his forehead.

Edie loosened her jaw before it seized shut. "Did you skim pills from patients?"

"That too. My attending found out. Told the medical association. I checked into a treatment center and they let me keep my license, but my old hospital wouldn't take me back. So, I moved up here. My grandparents had lived here, and the new doctor had just died in an accident, so it was easy to get a job."

No one spoke. The only sound was Miss Clark's pencil, and that stopped soon after. Edie felt sick. Hadn't she heard this before? Suicides and accidents that no one thought twice about. And on top of that…

"You never told me about your problem," she said to Nathan.

"Because I fixed it," he said. "I don't do that anymore."

Edie stared at her hands. She didn't want to look at him. "So why were you so panicked about the drugs we keep in the clinic?"

Nathan raked a hand through his hair. "Because your ex-husband died of a morphine overdose. And the reason he called me that day—" He exhaled, like the air here was killing him, stood up, and began pacing the room.

"My sister found mistakes in the clinic files," Peter put in. "Irwin diagnosed Leo Martin with cancer, but someone had swapped his X-rays." He looked hard at Irwin. "Maybe as a way to get more drugs."

"Thank you. That's one idea," Forbes said. "Please allow me to form my own."

"It wasn't me," Irwin retorted. "His death was a tragic mistake."

"I'm afraid not," Forbes said. "Because Mr. Martin never filled his morphine prescription." His eyes narrowed. "I'm guessing that's news to Ned and Nancy."

Her brother's mouth dropped for half a second, before he pulled it shut. Edie glared at Forbes, but the look didn't trouble him.

"You see, because we're not complete idiots, we checked with the pharmacist after the pathologist couldn't find Mr. Martin's cancer. I know that might surprise you, but—"

Edie turned to Nathan, angry heat flooding her cheeks. "I told you about his X-rays. You shut me down, but I was right. Those films weren't his. Leo broke his ribs years ago, and the ones in the film showed no old fractures."

"I didn't know. I just saw the ones that were in the file. And they showed cancer, clearly." His fingers were twisting again. She wanted to kick him.

"Let's get back to Mr. Gainsford, please," Forbes said.

Edie forced herself against the back of her chair. It wasn't easy.

Forbes glanced at Miss Clark, waited for her nod, then asked Irwin, "So Gainsford called you, and threatened to expose...what?"

"I thought he meant what I did in Edmonton," Irwin said, flushing. "But of course I couldn't let him go into details. Not on the phone. So, I told him I'd meet him later. After he finished with—with Nurse Simmons."

Her eyebrows launched upwards. "How much later? Where? Because I left—"

Forbes's hand smacked into the desk, silencing her. "You met with the victim, Irwin?"

"I didn't want to," Nathan said. "But he insisted. So, I said I'd meet him at nine. At the clinic."

"Why not sooner?"

Nathan's eyes flew to hers, guilt suffusing his face. "He said he had plans with Ms. Simmons first."

"This, I assume, refers to your story?" Forbes glanced at her. "A drink at the Duck and Drake? And then sneaking home from the clinic, leaving Gainsford waiting outside?"

Edie nodded.

"Irwin, what time did *you* arrive at the clinic?" Forbes asked.

Nathan cleared his throat. "I went early. I needed to—I thought if I brought some cash—"

"Jack wanted money?" Edie sounded shrill, but it was impossible to smooth her voice or uncurl her tight hands.

"No, but I thought it might persuade him to forget about me. So, I let myself in. It was unlocked, you know."

Edie sent him a sharp look. "I did not leave the doors unlocked. I know I didn't."

"Keep going, Irwin," Forbes said, ignoring her.

Nathan took a deep breath. "I took the money from the cash box. I had planned to wait for him in my office, but—" He pushed his hair back with an unsteady hand. "Gainsford was already there. Found him in the chair across from my desk."

Forbes folded his arms. "What'd he say?"

"Not much. He was dead." Nathan gulped and clamped his hands around his knees. "His ear was cut off."

He laughed, with a high ring of hysteria. "The syringe was laid out too, neat as anything on my desk. So, I knew at once he hadn't done it. I didn't know what to do, but I happened to look out the window, and...and I saw your car. Then I looked in your desk in the file room and discovered you'd forgotten your extra keys. You lent them to me, a month ago, and after I returned them, I guess you never took them back home." He dropped his eyes. "Actually, I was counting on finding them there. Noticed them in the drawer a few times, borrowing your stapler."

Buzzing filled her ears, obscuring his next words, but she didn't need to hear them to know. Nathan had loaded up Jack's body, minus an ear, with the incriminating syringe and driven it partway up the mountain. Then he'd taken the call the next morning and examined the body, pretending he knew nothing about it.

The lying, stinking, little weasel had set her up.

CHAPTER THIRTY-SIX

After that, Forbes had to shout at Nathan. This took considerable time. Eventually he must have remembered that others were present, because he told Peter and Edie to get out. He kept Miss Clark.

"Do you think she's taking this all down in shorthand?" Peter whispered, out in the hall.

Edie didn't answer. She still looked frozen.

Peter shook his head. "Always thought he was a real shit."

"Which one?"

"Both." He took his sister by the arm, steered her into the empty break room and fixed her some instant coffee.

"We shouldn't be here," Edie said.

"We can move to the waiting room. If you want to," Peter said.

She nodded, so they relocated to the waiting room, occupying a pair of uncomfortable chairs.

"How long do you think Forbes'll keep going?" Peter asked.

"Not as long as he deserves."

Peter didn't say anything. There wasn't really anything to say.

He didn't want coffee, and Edie was taking forever with hers, staring at the opposite wall, hands wrapped around the cooling mug. So, he paced, braces clicking as he moved back and forth.

The waiting room wasn't large. After ten minutes or so, Edie asked him to stop.

"Go out there. Pace if you must. But not where I can hear you," she ordered. "It's driving me nuts."

She looked at the point of breaking, and Forbes's voice, yelling again, was coming clear though the walls. "There's a real chance Gainsford's murderer will get away with it, Irwin, and all because you had to be a lying jackass!"

"I'm going home," Peter decided. "Want to come?"

"No! We can't go until they say we can leave," Edie hissed.

"Why not? Forbes knows where to find us."

"No," she said, even more firmly.

Peter went to the hall and walked the same three strides, back and forth, hopefully out of range of Edie's ears.

"This is stupid," he said, returning to the waiting room. "I'm going home. If Forbes doesn't like it, tell him I'm developing the photographs."

Minutes later, he was home, shut in the improvised dark room, with the telephone off the hook.

The pictures weren't bad. Some were better, of course, and it was good he'd chosen to frame his shots, covering his bases in the changing light.

He held up an enlarged black and white photograph of Jill and shivered. There was nothing like black and white for details. In some ways, looking at these pictures was more upsetting than taking them.

She looked so broken and very young. Not like a woman who'd been capable of stealing into this house and staring at his sister lying asleep.

She must have been good at piecing things together. Better than him and Edie. His arms prickled at the thought.

He'd done a good job with the photos, but so far, they hadn't told him anything.

Why would they? You saw this with your eyes. There's nothing new.

He grimaced and started looking through the pictures again. He didn't know enough. Nothing about the nature of her wounds, nothing about the type of struggle that had put them there. He moved on to the next shot, then set it aside and went back.

The picture was a close-up of the wound, framed by the blood-stained edges of Jill's blouse. The button nearest the wound had been torn off, but above and below it—both buttons were still there.

If the missing one had torn off in the struggle, wouldn't the one above it have come off too?

Peter turned the photo, trying to imagine if this was the kind of top a woman might wear with the highest button undone. The collared neckline would have lain better with the blouse fastened all the way up.

Maybe the button had been missing when she put it on? Except Jill, with her nylons and polished leather pumps, didn't seem like the type to put on a top that needed mending.

He carried the picture to the kitchen, returned the phone to the receiver, then set the picture and a bottle of beer on the table. Unfortunately, staring longer didn't help. The beer was good though.

He leaned back in his chair, his eyes drifting to the kitchen window.

Jack's house. And Leo's.

He frowned. Leo had been missing a button too.

Peter got up and went to the closet, searching behind raincoats and galoshes until he found what he wanted. A crumpled brown paper bag. Edie had stuffed it here, not knowing what else to do with it, but wanting it out of sight.

Pinching it gingerly, he maneuvered himself back to the kitchen table.

For a long moment, Peter just stared at the thing.

Stop stalling. Biting his bottom lip, he unrolled the edge of the bag and reached inside, drawing out the clothes Edie had brought home, along with the news that Leo had died on the way to the hospital.

Peter rubbed his hands against his sweater, then unfolded Leo's plaid flannel shirt. The scent of pipe tobacco enveloped him, and Peter shut his eyes, swallowing the burn in his throat.

A button on the front of the shirt was missing. Peter fingered the loose threads, frowning.

Leo had been collecting information for his lawsuit, combing through old obituaries. Peter wanted those notes.

He got up and opened the drawer nearest the telephone, the one where Edie kept scissors and unpaid bills, a tin of thumbtacks, pencils. Because there was a key here, almost the twin of the one that locked her garage and front and back doors.

There. Peter picked it out of a box of paper clips, string, and rubber bands. The keychain advertised one of the local service stations. Edie had marked the key with tape and penciled *Leo's* across it.

The house next door was dark and stuffy, the lights out and the curtains drawn. It didn't smell lived-in anymore. Peter wiped his feet on the mat and cautiously flicked on the light, then smiled to himself, because of course, nothing jumped out at him. The place was empty and ordinary, and it was so close to normal he felt uneasy, because he'd liked Leo a lot, and now Leo was dead, and Peter had been unfortunate enough to find him that way. Or nearly so.

Just find the files, then you can get out of here.

He checked the guest room, where Leo kept a desk. No stack of files. No notes. Nothing in the dresser drawers in his bedroom or the kitchen cupboards.

Maybe the living room shelves?

The folder of notes wasn't anywhere.

Frustrated, on his way out the door, Pete realized he'd forgotten to turn off the lights. He reversed direction. Lights out in Leo's bedroom.

Lights out in the hall. As Peter leaned into the living room to kill the last switch, he halted, hand poised in midair.

The framed picture of Mount Robson was gone. Nothing filled the place either, leaving an empty spot over the mantelpiece.

Must have been given away to one of Leo's friends. After all, it was a great photograph. And valuable.

Peter turned out the light and locked the door, but as he turned to go, his crutch caught on the doormat. As he righted himself, his eyes fell. Something shiny lay just under the edge of the mat.

He bent and retrieved a clip-on earring: bright green beads of all shapes and sizes, gathered in a cluster.

Brenda's.

When had he seen it last?

From the sidewalk, he heard his telephone.

That'd be the police, and unfortunately, Peter wasn't ready to talk to them just yet.

Ignoring the strident ring of the phone, he darted inside his house and loaded a new roll of film into the mini camera. Then, because he didn't like carrying things with crutches, he took out a worn canvas knapsack and put in an envelope with half the photographs, because he'd made duplicates. He wasn't going to trust all of them to the police.

If Edie were here, she'd tell him not to go, but he couldn't let that stop him.

Couldn't afford to be careless, either. Two men had died of morphine overdoses, and Jill, who'd called and talked to someone at the clinic, was dead too.

Peter chewed the inside of his lip, wasting time he didn't have. Then, with a huff, he went to the closet and took out Edie's bag, poking past the thermometer, wound dressings, and the tangled stethoscope. He needed something particular, because he was certain now, that this killer kept her own ready supply. Leo hadn't filled his prescription. The morphine that killed him hadn't been his own.

A syringe and a bottle of Nalline were tucked carefully into an inside pocket of Edie's kit. Peter wrapped them in his handkerchief and stuffed them into his shirt pocket, beneath his oversized sweater. A little bulky, but more secure than the pocket of his trousers.

Just in case.

He flinched, remembering the pictures of Jill's body. No matter how improbable, it was worth being careful. He scrawled a note and pinned it by the telephone. *Gone to Brenda's, will go next to the police. See you soon. P.*

CHAPTER THIRTY-SEVEN

Edie finally gave up, more than an hour after Peter left. If she didn't do something soon, no one was ever getting out of Forbes's office.

She opened the door and stuck her head into the room. "Sorry to interrupt. But last I heard, being a jackass wasn't included in the criminal code."

"Obstruction of justice is. Get out, Ms. Simmons. I don't need you here. And stop eavesdropping."

"Can I go home then?"

He scowled. "You know you can't. I've got to hear back from my team. Verify your stories."

She smiled. "I'm afraid Peter already left."

Nathan jumped in, continuing the defense she'd interrupted. "And you know Gainsford was dead before he was put in the car. The pattern of blood pooling had to be all wrong. The pathologist will have told you!"

Forbes scowled.

Edie absorbed this. *She* hadn't known. Forbes, apparently, liked to keep his cards close to his chest.

"Why don't we see Peter, then," Edie said. "The photos he took should be ready now, and I'd prefer not to be here all day. It certainly sounds like Nathan has told you everything." More than once.

"Don't know if I can believe him, though." Forbes drummed one hand on the table. "You were one of the first called to the scene, Irwin, and are privy to some select details."

Edie nodded. "Like the ear neither of you warned me about."

Forbes grunted. "Yes, like that. Will you please shut the door, Ms. Simmons?"

Edie complied, taking a seat at the table, which she was quite sure Forbes hadn't intended. But he didn't complain or order her out. He did, however, clutch his pencil like he was trying to snap it in half. "You're lucky I don't lock you up."

Miss Clark paused, then took that down.

"You can stop recording," Forbes told her.

"Can we go then?" Edie asked.

Forbes sighed and set down his pen. "Irwin, I'd like to believe you, but after what you've done, your testimony is about as good as McSorely's after he farts. You have to give me some kind of proof. Something *like* it, even."

Nathan swallowed, like he was forcing something with sharp edges down his throat. "You know the syringe was left in the car with Gainsford."

"Because you put it there?"

Nathan nodded. "Yeah. But you didn't find any bottles of morphine solution, right?"

Forbes's gaze sharpened. "We did not."

"Well, I was terrified," Nathan said. "Hardly thinking, so I forgot. Left the bottle in my coat pocket." His hands flailed nervously. "Maybe it was partly subconscious?"

Forbes leaned onto his elbows. He looked tired. "So, where's the bottle now?"

"I got rid of it," Nathan said.

"Yes, I bet you did. Where?"

"Pretended to go fishing," Nathan said. "Well, I did actually fish. Caught a trout. Dropped it in Policeman's Creek."

"The bottle, not the fish, right?"

Nathan nodded.

Forbes pushed away from the table, like it too had offended him. "Come on then. Both of you. Irwin, you better hope to God we can find this bottle, because until we do, I'm not letting you out of my sight."

There was nothing good, Edie decided, about riding in the back of a police car, especially with Nathan fidgeting beside her. Especially when he stared at her with woebegone eyes.

"I'm sorry, E," he whispered.

"Good. You should be."

He nodded once, subsiding into silence. Edie looked out the window and frowned at the passing houses. The wind was picking up, the sunshine retreating behind lumpy clouds. Nathan's abandoned lawn mower might just get doused by the rain.

Hopefully, it rusted fast.

"Here." Nathan's brown corduroy coat landed on her lap. "You're shivering," he said.

It was true she'd dressed for warmer weather, and in the rush back from Calgary, she'd forgotten her coffee-stained coat. Stifling her reluctance, Edie pushed her arms into Nathan's familiar-smelling jacket. The silk lining made her skin itch, but that had to be her imagination.

Sergeant Forbes parked his car just down from the Virtanens' house. No sign of Katya, but Mr. Virtanen sat in his wheelchair on the porch, an afghan draped over his stumps and a mug in his hands.

Edie waved, mustering a cheery expression. "Do you need help moving inside, Mr. Virtanen?" He might get chilled, sitting outside for much longer.

"I'm all right," he said. "Katya will be up any minute. She's just finishing the laundry."

"Say hello, won't you?" Edie said, and smirked at Nathan, who slumped in his seat, trying to make himself invisible, even as Mr. Virtanen called out greetings to him and Forbes.

"Couldn't we park elsewhere?" Nathan muttered.

"Quickest access is here," Forbes said. "If you really do remember where you were fishing."

Nathan peered into the trees. "Yeah, it was around here. But out of sight of the houses."

"Naturally," Forbes said, slamming his car door with extra force. Nathan hustled after him, head down, shoulders hunched.

Edie took time to retie the lace of her shoe, waved again to Katya's dad, then followed the two men into the woods.

She shouldn't be enjoying Nathan's discomfort so much, but it did feel good.

Forbes's pace had them puffing after a hundred yards. "Here?" he asked, pointing at a bend in the water.

Glacier-fed, the creek was as clear as glass at the shallow edges and the deeper pools where the current slowed. Every stone and stick was visible, right down to the bottom.

Nathan shook his head, pointing upstream. "A little farther."

The noise of the water, which usually filled your ears with a soothing chuckle, was all but lost in the wind's rushing. Edie tugged the coat closer and walked deeper into the swaying trees.

Forbes grunted. "C'mon. We don't have all day."

A bird cawed—crow or magpie, maybe—and Edie jumped.

She didn't like thinking of birds, not after scaring off that one by Jill. He'd have flown back the moment they left. Her mouth twisted, and she stooped for a rock and hurled it in the direction of the bird calls.

"You all right?" Nathan asked.

"We should be making more noise," Edie said. It was what you were supposed to do to warn off bears. She took her car keys from her pocket, and let them dangle, jingling from her hand.

"That doesn't really do anything," Forbes said, but she didn't stop.

A few minutes later, Nathan halted. "This is my spot." The water was wide here, fast and shallow, diverting on one side of the creek into a quiet pool.

"Start looking," Forbes ordered. He, at least, had donned a pair of rubber boots.

"It should be along here," Nathan pointed.

Edie picked her way along some rocks, just above the water's surface. Her shoes were old, but they weren't made for wading.

Nathan, perhaps feeling more urgency, strode right in and bent down, picking through stones.

Moving along one section of the bank, Edie searched for twenty yards, reaching into the water with a stick, turning over rocks every time she spotted something brown or with a bottle-like shape. At least the stones were mainly blue and gray. Every so often, she missed her footing, landing a shoe in the stinging cold water. It soon soaked through the leather, creeping up her socks.

"Water's fast." Nathan's expression said he was losing hope. "It might have been swept away."

Forbes didn't say anything.

"I dropped it right here," Nathan insisted.

Forbes moved a few yards downstream. Edie followed, but all she found was a cigarette packet and a beer bottle caught in some long grass.

"We're never going to find it," Nathan said. "Not without more eyes." Water had soaked up his trousers to his thighs. He had to be freezing, but Edie wasn't about to relinquish his coat.

"You're who I've got." Forbes didn't sound pleased. "My officers are busy."

Edie thought of Jill and the blood and the bird. She glanced over her shoulder. Nothing, not even any elk by the water today, but she shivered and pulled the jacket closer.

CHAPTER THIRTY-EIGHT

Peter swore under his breath. With his luck, it only made sense that he'd arrive at Brenda's and find nobody home. The doorbell's chirpy ping faded, once again, to silence, so Peter pressed his face to the glass, looking for movement through the blue and green stained-glass squares decorating the front door.

Nothing. No sounds of movement either.

He walked around the house, hoping in spite of the worsening weather that perhaps she'd be sitting out back.

Nothing to find there, other than the fact that Brenda wasn't much of a gardener. Returning to the porch (he'd set his knapsack down beside the door), Peter rang the bell one last time, then tried the handle, purely out of frustration, and discovered the door wasn't locked.

Leo's voice, cheerfully unconcerned, spoke at his shoulder. *Most people don't bother around here.*

Peter shook off the memory like an irritated terrier. So, what if it was open? He couldn't just go in.

He did anyway, the thud of his crutches uncomfortably loud against the floor. "Brenda?"

No answer, of course, and calling her name didn't make this any less intrusive. The hum of the refrigerator, the soft ticking of an unseen clock pressed against his ears. He'd worked up a sweat, hurrying here, and now it gathered, cold and clammy, in the small of his back.

Peter lingered on the mat, unsure if he should venture any farther. He was ill-suited for furtive reconnaissance, but...

More thuds, as he advanced into the house.

He stopped. Nothing out of the ordinary in the hall, but the living room, which he'd never seen, was unrecognizable. Ripped sheet music littered the piano, and the record player was open, empty turntable spinning, the needle poised uselessly in the air. At least one record was smashed on the floor in jagged shards. But what chilled him was the sight of a murdered violin, the body broken, neck smashed, only the slack strings holding the ruined pieces together.

Think, Peter told himself, hand going automatically for his camera. His heart buzzed, like the first frantic rush from an overworked windup toy. But as he snapped the room from different angles, his pulse slowed, and his hands steadied. He checked his exposure, opened the curtains to bring more light into the room, then took close-ups of the smashed record and the mangled violin with and without the flash.

Maybe Mitch had done this—or maybe this havoc was about him. He thought about her telling him about growing up here and being careful. Brenda could be angry about a whole lot of things.

The telephone rang, making him jump. Without thinking, Peter reached for the receiver. It was only two steps away, because Brenda and Mitch had an extension set, resting atop the desk by the fireplace.

"Brenda, this is Katya. Are you home?"

Peter bit down on his lip. How was he supposed to answer?

"Brenda? That you?"

He should never have picked up this phone.

"Who is this?" Katya demanded.

Peter hung up. Hurrying now, careless of noise, he stuffed his camera into the knapsack and left the house.

He could return to the police station, give Forbes the photos, and tell him that Brenda was gone, her home a wreck. But after listening to Brenda talk about strategy, he knew that the police wouldn't be fair, to her or her family.

And this phone call had reminded him of the third person who had access to clinic records, X-rays, and Dr. Irwin's office.

He couldn't give Brenda up to the police unless he was sure.

Luckily, Katya didn't live far away. Peter had driven with Leo past the Virtanens' house. If he cut across the creek, it wouldn't take long to get there. He wasn't going to learn anything else standing here.

CHAPTER THIRTY-NINE

There was no fence around the Virtanen place, so Peter approached through the backyard, straight from the creek, with splashed trousers and soaking shoes. The creek was shallow where he crossed, less than four inches deep, but he'd had to plant both feet square in the water...twice. The snow-fed stream had soaked up his trousers, and now the damp fabric, pressed against his calves by the wind, made him shiver as he rounded the corner of the house, rehearsing his approach.

"Peter? What are you doing here?"

So much for rehearsals. Mr. Virtanen had spied him from the porch. His voice sounded as thin as his spindly arms, and the blanket hanging from his truncated legs swayed in the breeze. There was an empty plate on the deck beside him, and a partially drunk mug of coffee that looked dead cold, judging from the scummy film floating on top.

"Hi Orvo. What are you doing outside? It's getting chilly," Peter said.

"Just waiting for Katya," Orvo said. "You looking for your sister?"

Peter's eyebrows jumped. "Was she here?"

"Went into the woods a little while ago with Dr. Irwin and one of the cops." He tilted his head, studying Peter closely, as if he might know something about it.

"Huh. Afraid I've no idea what that's about," Peter said. "I actually came to see Katya. You expecting her soon?"

Orvo nodded. “She just went to the store.”

Gone. Well, maybe that was better. If he could convince Orvo to let him inside, he might be able to ask some more questions.

Orvo’s skin was too pale to show much cold, but he must be chilled if he’d been sitting here for any length of time. The sun had been gone at least an hour, and Orvo wasn’t wearing a hat over his wispy, wind-tossed hair. No coat either, just a gray Aran sweater.

“Let me get you inside,” Peter said. “And maybe a fresh cup of coffee?”

“That’d be nice.” Orvo grimaced. “I mean, if you can. Neither of us—you know.” His frustrated gesture took in his amputated limbs and Peter’s crutches.

Peter laughed. “We’ll find a way. Might take a minute though.”

Orvo nodded and unlocked the brakes on his wheelchair, while Peter contemplated just how he’d get them both inside.

“There’s a doorstop,” Orvo said, so Peter started with that, opening the door and nudging it into place.

“Okay.” He pushed his hair back from his forehead. “Got that done.” The door was open, and even if he hadn’t been able to position the door and the stop quite where they ought to be, he’d be able to navigate around it.

He positioned himself behind the wheelchair and passed his crutches to Orvo. “You can carry these for me? I’ll push you inside leaning on your chair. But you’ll have to set the brakes every time I step forward.” Otherwise, the chair would roll away from him whenever he put any weight on the handles.

Orvo nodded. “Yeah, that’ll work.”

It took some doing, but they made it. Orvo seemed glad to be out of the wind. “Thanks, Peter. I can take it from here,” he said, passing over the crutches. “I just have a hard time getting past the door and over the threshold.”

Peter nodded. He understood.

"Coffee things are in the kitchen," Orvo said. "Make yourself some too and cut yourself a slice of cake if you want one."

"Thanks."

Orvo turned his wheelchair into the living room, leaving Peter a clear path down the hall. This house was sparse with furniture, allowing space to maneuver a wheelchair.

In the living room, Orvo switched on the radio, thumbing the dial until he found a station broadcasting a baseball game.

Peter started for the kitchen, then stopped as his eyes fell on a familiar photograph, mounted on the wall opposite the telephone. He leaned closer, which wasn't necessary. He knew Mount Robson, and he knew this frame, and he knew that not many days ago, it had hung in Leo's living room.

Peter swallowed, working some moisture onto his tongue.

"This is a beautiful photo you've got here," he called. "Just by the phone. Mount Robson, isn't it?"

Leo and Orvo were friends, which might explain why this picture was here.

Orvo coughed, then cleared his throat, speaking over the radio. "Don't know. It's new. Katya bought it. She goes to all the rummage sales."

Rummage sales? Peter's eyes narrowed. "This one might be worth something," he called back, forcing lightness into his voice. "If it's what I think it is."

"Oh?" Orvo chuckled. "Won't Katya be surprised to hear that. I'll have to stop giving her a hard time about all her bargain hunting. That girl can't resist a flea market or a garage sale."

Peter rubbed the back of his neck, chasing away a prickling chill. "Give me a moment, Orvo. I'll get that coffee." Tearing his eyes away from the picture, he stumped into the kitchen. His hands shook as he measured out coffee grounds from the canister on the counter and filled the percolator with water. As he turned away from the sink, his eyes fell on a leather handbag resting on the kitchen table. The zipper was unfastened.

He plugged in the percolator and, with a guilty glance over his shoulder, went for a look.

Inside, he found a neatly folded rayon scarf in primary colors. Beneath that, a wide-toothed comb and a box of Kotex. No pocketbook, but it made sense for Katya to take that with her.

"Cake is in the tin," Orvo called. "Red velvet. Brenda brought it over it yesterday."

"Will you have a slice?" Peter called back, heart racing. Which was stupid. He hadn't found anything awful. Orvo was old enough to forget details about the photograph on his wall. It didn't mean anything.

Hard to believe, though, that Orvo would have forgotten the picture came from Leo.

"Sure, I'll take one. Why not?"

Abandoning a tube of cherry ChapStick and an Altoids tin, Peter plated a slice of cake and carried it to the living room with a fork, one-crutching it all the way, which made him excruciatingly slow. Carrying a mug of coffee was going to be awful. Orvo might have to wheel into the kitchen, but Peter didn't suggest it. Not yet. He glanced out the window, chest loosening with relief. No car. She wasn't back yet.

"You have a pretty wonderful daughter, Orvo."

Orvo picked up his fork. "Sure do."

"You two haven't had it easy," Peter said. "Losing your wife. That must be tough. Especially for Katya."

Orvo nodded. "Mary could be a difficult woman. She was real sick for a long time. Maybe took some of it out on Katya. Always getting after her to keep the house in order. Keep her hair neat. You know."

"Sounds like the things most moms do," Peter said.

"I guess that's so," Orvo said. "Katya hasn't let the hard things stop her, you know. She's a worker. She was with the rescue team who pulled me out of the mine, you know."

"Oh?"

"I thought I was dying for sure." Orvo shook his head. "It was a bad accident, that one. Took my friend Mel, and she tried so hard to get him out. He always had a soft spot for her. Gave her that silly nickname the guys all use. Kittycat."

It was an odd name, Peter thought, to give to your friend's daughter.

"Always a good friend to our family," Orvo went on. "Still miss him. Some broken timbers fell on him. Punctured his lung."

Peter winced. He knew what it was like when your body couldn't breathe. "Let me get that coffee."

Back in the kitchen, he dug his way to the bottom of the purse. Nothing, but what had he expected? A bloody knife?

Coffee bubbled in the percolator. Almost ready. He returned the ChapStick and comb to Katya's purse, then picked up the Altoids, inadvertently rattling the contents of the box.

He froze. That wasn't the right sound. He shook it again and flipped open the lid. No paper liner inside. No mints.

The tin was filled with buttons.

Peter stirred them with a cautious forefinger, remembering now, that first poker game he'd seen, before he understood their rules. Katya had been upset about her dad taking a button that had belonged to her mom.

Most of these were small shirt buttons, but there were some of every color, in all sizes: wide and worn, smooth and scallop edged, some spherical and painted to look like pearls in shades of white and iridescent blue.

Women keep buttons, he reminded himself. Edie had a collection: old ones and extra ones, stored in a jam jar inside her sewing basket.

This tin was full of them. No time to count, but if he brought the tin home and searched, would he find a match to the missing button on Leo's shirt? Or Jill's blouse?

His stomach slipped greasily inside him, relocating somewhere it didn't belong, revolting against the smells of coffee and cake that had changed, instantly, from pleasant to intolerable.

This collection might be innocuous. Still, he needed to check. Heart pounding, Peter snapped the lid closed and put it in his pocket, just in time to hear the swing of the front door.

"Hi, Dad." Katya was home.

Orvo said something, but in a language Peter didn't understand.

Katya laughed, replying in English. "Well, I'm glad you weren't left outside. My errand took longer than expected." She lifted her voice, so it carried easily to the kitchen. "How are you, Peter?"

Her footsteps moved down the hall. A door closed, and Peter leapt across the room to turn off the coffeepot. But she didn't join him immediately. For a few moments, all he heard was her moving around her room. Then she came into the kitchen, wearing trousers and a plaid flannel still bearing creases from sitting folded in a drawer. "Getting chilly out there," she said.

"I hope you don't mind me stopping by." He turned his eyes back to the percolator and poured out two mugs of coffee. Katya's face, in the stainless steel reflection, was flushed and windblown. Like she'd been out in the woods for a while.

"You mind taking this to Orvo?" He held out a mug. "Not the easiest thing for me, I'm afraid."

"You bet. Be right back."

"All right if I use your bathroom?"

"Of course."

She darted down the hall again, and Peter followed, veering into the pale green bathroom on the right. He locked the door, turned on the tap and set his crutches aside, then leaned over the scrupulously clean sink, his forehead damp with sweat, his breath coming like he'd just run a sprint.

He opened the medicine cabinet. Jars and jars of tablets lined the top two shelves, the labels all facing out: phenobarbital, Benzedrine, chloral hydrate, Tofranil. At least three bottles of morphine tablets and a small one of clear solution.

He fumbled in his pocket for the miniature camera and snapped two photographs. At the second click of the shutter, he heard Katya's voice through the door. "Trouble with the hot water?"

He'd let the taps run too long.

"No, just finishing." He shut off the water, and closed the cabinet, staring at the mirror and forcing some nonchalance onto his face. It wasn't working. He took the hand towel and dabbed at his forehead.

Now that the water was off, Katya and Orvo's voices reached him in indecipherable murmurs. Peter smoothed his hair, pasted on a smile, and turned the door handle. It moved fine, but the door didn't budge. Puzzled, Peter rattled the handle, leaning into the wood panels, but the door didn't give an inch.

"Katya? Orvo?"

"In a minute, Peter." Her voice was calm and cheerful. It should have been reassuring. She didn't sound like she thought anything was wrong.

Footsteps. The sound of the kitchen tap. "Just giving my dad his medicine," she said, walking past the door.

His heart seized, and he pushed the door again. It must be blocked. The doorstop from the porch? Or a kitchen chair beneath the handle? There was no way out—only a small frosted window, high in the wall above the pale green bathtub, far too high for him to haul himself out.

Her footsteps came down the hall again, each step raising the hair on the back of his neck.

"Peter?"

Pretend. For as long as you can. He cleared his throat. "Katya, I'm afraid something's wrong with the door."

"You know better than that, Peter." Her voice was perfectly friendly, but with a promise of menace firm enough to obliterate any doubt.

Peter closed his eyes and rested his forehead on the door, his gut hollow.

"I'm very sorry," Katya said. "But you'll have to wait until my dad's asleep before I can let you out."

He tried again, even though it was hopeless. "What's going—"

"Don't pretend. Something's missing from my purse, Peter. And Dad said you've been asking about my mom and Mel."

"Nothing important," he protested.

"They are important, Peter, given what you've taken from me."

"It's a box of buttons," he said helplessly.

"Yes, buttons," she said. "Mom's was first. Next, Mel's. I think, Peter, you have some inkling of what those buttons mean."

Panicked now, he spun away from the door and stumbled for the window, nearly falling headfirst into the tub.

"Help!" he shouted, struggling upright, his crutches clunking. He had to get close enough to bang on the glass.

"I recommend you stop that. That window faces the woods, you know," Katya informed him through the door. "None of the neighbors are close enough to hear. Please don't hurt yourself trying anything stupid. I won't be long."

He glanced at the window as her footsteps retreated, but it was still too high, too small. How long until she came back? He listened, but it was impossible to interpret the sound of her movements, and the creaks coming from the house.

Shit. Shit.

He could hold her off, swinging his crutches, but for how long? The room was too small to force his way past her and out the door. And she was faster. Even if he reached the phone, there wouldn't be time to call for help. Katya was strong, trained to lift patients and carry injured miners to safety, and he couldn't walk without crutches, let alone run.

He searched the cabinet again and the cupboard in the opposite wall, but found nothing but towels, more pills, and toilet paper. There wasn't even a bottle of bleach. Nothing he could use as a weapon. Impossible to win in a fight.

Stay alive then. Wait for another chance.

His braces locked, nearly toppling him as he sat down hard on the edge of the tub. His crippled legs stuck out like sticks.

Since contracting polio, he often felt helpless. Learning to dress himself again. To put on the heavy braces. Getting on and off the toilet, and in and out of the bath.

Peter blinked his burning eyes, fighting a manic laugh. He'd felt helpless then, struggling against petty frustrations and the whittling away of his dignity—stupid nothings, next to this. He'd die if he couldn't get out of here, and the only way out was letting her take him.

So, he shouldn't fight her, because then she'd resort to something like clubbing him with the iron doorstop or stabbing him with a knife. But if he seemed compliant, maybe she'd use her drugs instead.

Like with Leo. And probably Orvo too. His skeletal limbs, the sweats and trembling that occasionally overcame him, made another kind of sense, if Katya was manipulating him with narcotics.

Peter reached a hand into his shirt pocket, drawing out Edie's syringe and the bottle of Nalline. He'd never given himself a needle, and the bottle just bore a name label, with no suggested dose. This stuff might poison him just as easily as it might help him, but he didn't have any other plan, and if he left things to Katya, she might choose chloral hydrate or one of her other drugs. He needed her to select morphine. Or at least, to think she had.

If the Nalline killed him, at least he'd done it to himself.

Peter went to the sink, opened the medicine cabinet and cracked open a morphine bottle, shaking a handful of pills into his glistening palm. His eyes blurred. Impossible to count. Without turning on the water, he pushed half down the drain of the sink.

Then he sat down on the edge of the tub and set about filling the syringe. Though he'd seen it done a hundred times in the hospital, he struggled to uncap the needle, fit his fingers into the loops, and unscrew the antidote bottle.

I hope this works.

Twice, he drew, half filling the syringe with air, but his third try succeeded. Blocking his ears to the sounds outside the door—silencing the radio and walking back and forth—he raised the needle over his thigh, trying to remember what Edie had done.

As far as he remembered, she'd just stabbed Leo with it, not even bothering to peel back his clothes. Quick, then. Katya would be back soon.

Shutting his eyes, Peter jammed the point into the weakened muscle of his thigh and forced down the plunger. Too fast, he realized a half second too late, gasping with pain, his hands closing into fists.

His head swam as he lunged forward, depositing the bottle and syringe in the waste basket. Then he steadied himself, trying to see straight, gasping for breath.

If the buttons were any guide, she'd been killing a while. Leo. Jill. Mel and her mother. Which would she take from him?

"Peter."

He lifted his head. It felt like raising a boulder. "Why'd you kill Jack?"

Through his blurring eyes, he saw her again in the local, reclaiming her dead mother's button, tucking it into her pocket, then wheeling her father away, keeping him from laying eyes on the photo of Edie and

Jack. Orvo hadn't been allowed to see the picture, because he would have recognized him.

"I didn't want to." Katya's voice was muffled, barely audible above the blood rushing in his ears. She almost seemed to float in front of the open door. He couldn't hang on much longer.

"He found out that people were dying. Once he discovered it wasn't Dr. Irwin, it wouldn't take long for him to realize it was me. I'm sorry, Peter."

"I'm not letting you do it," he murmured. "My life is mine." Clumsily, he clapped his hand to his mouth. One tablet fell though his numb fingers, but his lips snatched the rest of them, forcing them back into his dry mouth. He gulped, once, twice, bitterness spreading over his tongue.

As the last tablet scraped down his throat, Katya caught him, prying the morphine bottle from his other hand. She tsked, gripping the back of his neck and tilting his face up. "Oh, Peter. I'm afraid you've taken far more than necessary. That's very wasteful. Careful now. You don't want to hit your head on the tub."

His breath slowed, no longer frantic and shallow. The walls turned sideways, clouding blue, then gray, then black.

CHAPTER FORTY

Edie had never seen Sergeant Forbes in a good mood, and he managed only a smile-like grimace when he, not her or Nathan, located the bottle beneath an overhanging tree by the edge of the creek.

"Believe me now?" Nathan asked. By this time, he had to be hypothermic, in wet shoes, with his trousers soaked.

"Maybe. Let's go." Forbes dropped the bottle into an evidence bag, and they hurried after him, past the Virtanens' house, and back to the car. This time, the porch was empty.

"Get in," Forbes barked.

"Nurse Simmons and I are cooperating," Nathan said. "There's no need to speak to us that way."

Forbes fixed Nathan with a stare that made him retreat a step. "You had better co-operate. You're still in serious trouble."

She thought he was referring exclusively to Nathan, but either way, better not to ask. Forbes was in a mood. Of course, his investigation wasn't going very well.

She slid into the backseat beside Nathan, wishing the action didn't feel portentous, like this was where she belonged. Where she'd be staying.

"Where are we going?" Nathan asked Forbes.

"Back to the station. In case you forgot, I have another murder to investigate." He started the engine and put the car in gear.

"Then where are we going? You said, once we found that bottle, that I could leave," Nathan whined.

"You probably can, for now, but I've got better things to do than drive you home," Forbes said.

"There's the pictures," Edie reminded him. "Peter will be finished developing them by now. You'll need them, for the investigation of—"

"That other murder, yes," Forbes interjected. At the corner, he swung the steering wheel left to her house, instead of the station. "I want to hear his version again, anyway."

"Do you want your jacket back?" Edie asked Irwin.

"I'm fine," he said, lips pressed together to prevent his teeth from chattering. He did not ask Forbes to turn up the heater in the car.

Forbes pulled to a stop in front of Edie's house. "Okay, let's see these photos." He sounded skeptical.

But when they let themselves inside, instead of Peter, all they found was a folder of pictures and a note.

Forbes read it before Edie could do more than steal a glance. He considered the scrawled message for an unusually long time.

"Well, Ms. Simmons." He tapped the scrap of notepaper against his chin in a way that wasn't encouraging.

"What?" Searching by the creek all that time had drawn most of the warmth from her. Her fingers were stiff with cold, but now her palms were leaking sweat. "What is it?"

Forbes held out the note. "You want to tell me why your brother's gone to Brenda Li's?"

CHAPTER FORTY-ONE

It's awkward moving a body in braces, especially when I'm so pressed for time. Instead of the carries I'm trained in, I roll Peter's body into a camping tarp and drag him to the car. His legs are stiff, and it takes forever to jam him into the backseat.

If I wasn't in such a rush, I'd strip him and take the damn braces off, but I'm running low on Thalidomide. I can't afford to give Dad another dose, and I need to be home before he wakes up. As long as I have something in the oven by then, he'll believe me when I tell him I never left. More importantly, that's what he'll tell everyone else.

Would be nice though, if I could give Dad just a little more. It would give me more time, but he's already pretty dependent on the morphine, and I can't give him too much of either, not together. I don't see Mrs. Taylor until next week—she often forgets her meds, so it's easy to replenish my supply of Thalidomide from her medicine cabinet. Until then, I need to ration it, especially since Edie and Dr. Irwin are keeping such a tight watch on the drugs in the clinic.

I lock up the house, then drive through town. At the crosswalk by the library, I come to a full and complete stop. The Li boy, Mitch's youngest brother, waves with his free arm, the one not laden with books.

I wave back. He's always so polite.

My smile falls away though, once I'm out of sight, because I do feel bad about taking that earring of Brenda's and leaving it on Leo's porch. But I had to kill him, and no one has noticed it yet, because it was still there after he died, when I went back for the picture from Leo's living room.

He can't use it anymore, so why shouldn't I have it—or the money it could bring?

Taking things helps me make ends meet, and though I can easily say that Leo gave it to my dad, with everything going on, I'm trying to think defensively.

Maybe I am cursed. Every time I think I'm clear, someone's at me again.

But the earring with throw them off, if anyone ever realizes the X-rays were swapped.

So will this, I think, turning west on the highway. Different direction. Different road. Better if Peter's body is never found. There's a lot of wilderness here.

Two miles along, I turn again, onto gravel. Dust flies behind me. Angling the rearview mirror, I glance at the pile of canvas in the backseat. Of course, the worn, dirty folds are inert.

He didn't need to take so many pills. Half would have been enough. When I kill, I'm not wasteful. Even when I had to hurry, like with Jack and with Leo, I used an appropriate dose.

Just enough to stop them, so they couldn't talk.

My mouth hitches up on one side.

Okay. I didn't *have* to cut off Jack's ear. That was probably excessive. Felt good though.

He thought he was so clever, confiding in me, telling me how hard it was to be abandoned. As if I didn't know about his fiancée the whole time. Did he think Edie and I never talked?

We work in the same office, but that didn't stop him from coming to my house with chocolates, and extracting bits of information, every question tantalizing me—*how much does he know?* Because almost right off, he asked me about my mom dying, and if she'd been prescribed morphine. He said he was afraid something was terribly wrong.

So, I cried a little and told Jack something to put him off track. Not the truth. Not about the pinches, every time I disobeyed. Not about her slapping me and calling me a liar, when I told her what Mel was doing to me, the touches, the groping that had gone on for years and years and years. And then, that big thing, that made her send me away.

Dad knew why I went. But he didn't know how. And when I came back, I took care of Mom. Took care of her so well that no one suspected a thing.

The accident at the mine was lucky. It was easy to rush back for Mel and stab him with that piece of wood. So much more satisfying than what I'd originally planned.

But I liked planning. I got so good at it, that when Jack kept coming to town with questions, I invited him to lunch and brought him fishing and went to his practically empty house. We talked so much, and I don't think he ever guessed I was playing him even more than he was playing me. I had to sleep with him to get him to tell me everything, but even then, he never suspected. He thought I was dumb and desperate and lonely, and he was fixated on 'the terrible truth about Dr. Nathan Irwin,' and how he was going to put a stop to it.

As if I didn't know it was all to spite his ex-wife.

Maybe some of that rubbed off on me, because, although I was astonished—afraid even—when his body wasn't found in Dr. Irwin's office, I liked seeing Edie confused. So edgy and exhausted. And it was easier for me if the police's attention didn't fasten too closely onto Irwin, so long as they still passed Jack's death off as a crime of passion.

I still think it was. None of this would have happened if he'd swallowed his pride and realized she was happier without him. But he just couldn't believe he was the bad guy. That he was wrong.

On at least two counts.

My hands ache. I'm gripping the steering wheel too tight. I let go and shake one hand at a time, bringing the feeling back. I tell myself to relax. Check my watch again. The drive's taking longer than I thought.

I'll relax later.

I adjust the rearview mirror again, and drive farther up the mountain.

CHAPTER FORTY-TWO

The first thing Peter noticed was the angle of his arm. It hurt, so he tried to move it, but only succeeded in a brief flop. Alarmed now, he opened his eyes and discovered that it was dark. And stuffy.

Heavy cloth covered his face, and his ears—yes, they were working too, apparently—filled with the rumble of tires on gravel, overlaying the hum of a car. One arm—the top one, not the one that hurt—fell over his chest as momentum swung him across the bench seat. He couldn't feel the upholstery, so she must have swaddled him in the thick canvas that brushed against his face, smelling of damp wax waterproofing and bug repellent.

She was driving him somewhere. *Better keep still.*

Of course, that idea made him even more aware of the rise and fall of his chest, and the dust-dry state of his mouth. Peter swept his tongue over his teeth and wondered just how long he'd been in this car. Beneath the canvas, he couldn't tell if it was light or dark out, but at least she couldn't look at him and notice the signs of him waking.

He hoped.

The tires wavered on the road, wobbling the car from side to side. Katya, presumably, slowed the vehicle, lifting her foot off the accelerator. They turned again and the canvas fell back. Peering out, he saw gray upholstery. The back of a car seat. A long swinging braid, bound with a black hair tie.

Peter swallowed—or tried too. His throat was so dry.

When Jack had threatened Irwin, Katya knew—and knew that Irwin wasn't to blame. She and Jack must have been close. Close enough that she could have forgotten a hair tie in his bedroom and helped change the sheets. Katya, also a nurse, would make up a bed with crisp hospital corners.

It must have grown easy, pilfering drugs from the clinic, stealing pills from patients, switching X-rays or other tests when she decided someone was ready—or needed—to die. Taking nice things when it suited her, like Leo's picture of Mount Robson. Maybe she'd taken his files too.

Yes, she must have taken those. Because if Leo had told her what he'd found—he might even have asked for her help—she'd probably had to.

One more button into the box. He fought down a shudder, and turned his attention to his side, pressed against the seat of the car. Nothing in that pocket. The tin was gone. Probably his camera too.

She'd make him disappear just as easily. His head ached, and his heart felt unbearably slow.

The car bounced again, heading uphill. The hum of the engine and the pop of gravel flying against the car weren't nearly loud enough to offset the silence from the front seat.

She hadn't taken off his braces, but he couldn't risk feeling about to find his crutches. Without them, there was no point trying to escape by opening the door and diving from the car. His hidden ace, that he was awake and alive, could only be played once. Wasting it, just to land helpless in a ditch, wouldn't help him see tomorrow morning.

His left arm, the one pinned beneath him, protested as they took another curve.

Don't move, he commanded himself.

She pressed the brakes, and Peter swayed forward as the car rolled to a stop. Keys jingled as she silenced the ignition. Some rummaging, then the car door opened and shut.

He had to keep still.

The door opened, dropping his head over the edge of the seat. Hopefully in a lifeless sort of way, because he wasn't ready yet, and couldn't see any point helping her drag him out of the car. He wasn't sure how she'd managed to pack him inside. He'd lost lots of weight in his illness, but he still weighed a hundred and fifty pounds.

The canvas closed around his face, and a second later he was being dragged from the car, landing hard on his shoulder, capturing a pained gasp just before it escaped his mouth.

That'll bruise, he thought, then reminded himself he'd had worse learning to climb and, more recently, learning to walk and move from a bed to a wheelchair.

At this point, a few bruises were immaterial. The way he hurt, she'd probably given him several already—the cost of getting him inside her car.

At least his sore arm had shifted. Blood rushed into his numb fingers, and he flexed them beneath the canvas as she dragged him over the ground, hoping she wouldn't see.

Yes, that was a rock. He shut his eyes and bit his lip, stifling the pain in his back. He was moving faster now, dragged downward over rustling grass. A sharp tug threw him to one side. Light knifed past the edge of the canvas and his fingers touched open air.

He kept his hand loose, trailing it over the ground, praying she wouldn't stop to investigate. After all that time in the hospital, he knew Katya would find a pulse at his wrist or at his thumb if she thought to check. But maybe just a touch of his skin would alert her. How long did it take for a body to turn cold?

Longer than this, he decided, peeking at the sky. Cloudy, but still light. It wasn't evening yet, though the way his body felt, a week—or a hundred years—could have passed.

She grunted, straining to tug him over a fallen tree that clawed through the canvas. It rasped against his spine like a grater over unwary knuckles. Then they were moving again, and his trailing hand brushed a rock.

His fingers closed instinctively, clutching like it was the handhold that could keep him from plunging off a cliff.

The stone fit well in his hand, sharp-edged, with a nice heft to it. When Katya stopped, he wouldn't face her with nothing, and that was some relief. Without moving his joints, he systematically tightened his muscles, making them ready, pumping his blood a little faster. She stopped tugging, walking a few paces away, too far for him to see through the gap in the canvas. A metal door screeched and clanged open.

The canvas rustled, falling open as she picked up the end by his feet.

Move! Now!

Down by his feet, she was too far away for him to strike. Peter rolled away, blinking against the assault of sudden daylight.

Katya cursed and lunged. Peter swung the rock with all his strength, catching her on the side of the head. She fell back, stunned, and he heaved onto his arms, then pinned her by flopping onto her chest. Without thought, he raised his rock again, smashing it against her forehead.

She let out a low moan as her eyes rolled back.

Panting, Peter sat up and rearranged his legs with his hands, then realized his dropped rock was rolling away. He lunged after it, but it was already beyond his grasp and Katya—he looked over. She was still, but he was afraid to think it would last.

What about the car? He glanced around, following their trail of flattened grass and broken twigs to a bit of red paint visible between the trees.

Katya groaned.

He couldn't run. If she regained her feet, she'd overtake him, even at a stagger. But just beyond her fallen body, lay a door in the ground. He'd heard her open it.

Peter dropped to his stomach and crawled closer on his elbows. The ground was scattered with black dust and bits of coal, though the path here was long overgrown. A rusty padlock and length of chain curled on the ground next to the open hatch. She must have removed it to pull the thing open. Peter grasped the entrance and pulled himself up for a look into the abandoned mine. A rickety ladder led to a tunnel, perhaps six feet or so below. A perfect place to hide a body. No one would have found him here.

Behind him, Katya stirred.

It would be easier just to bash her on the head again. Probably should, but unless she was questioned, how would they ever know? His camera was gone and so was the tin of buttons. Even if he escaped and showed Forbes her frighteningly well-stocked medicine cabinet, that didn't prove she'd killed anyone.

Peter grabbed the chain. If he bound her feet... But she'd have her hands. She'd work her way free. Hobbling her wouldn't be permanent, and without hand controls, her car was no good to him. What's more, he didn't know where he was, so the only way out was to follow the road home. Unless he killed her, there was no way to stop her from catching him.

He glanced at the pit again. The drop might kill her, but it was better than out and out murder or trusting the chain to hold her. But only if he got rid of the ladder.

He pushed against the rails; one side moved, but the other stuck fast, held in by a rusty nail. With a grunt, Peter tried again, and the nail bent and slid, but only by half an inch.

He scooted sideways over the ground and seized a broken branch to use as a lever. With that jammed between the pit and the aged gray wood, he pried the ladder free, glancing every second or so at the body lying behind him. Once he thought he saw her stir again.

With desperate haste, he hauled the ladder from the pit and tossed it aside. Then, armed with his stick, he scooted on arms and buttocks back to Katya. Definitely breathing, and now her eyes were closed. From a wary distance, he touched her arm with the stick. A twitch, but no movement. Unless she too was pretending.

Well, he'd decided to risk it. Better see the thing through.

Peter rammed her with both arms, rolling her onto the rumpled canvas and muffling her groans. With one hand, he grabbed the ends, then dragged it and himself inch by muscle-tearing inch across the ground, bracing himself with buttocks and feet, fighting for each forward jerk.

She stirred, mumbling sounds that might have been words. He switched hands, because the right was losing feeling, but switched back almost at once, unable to sustain the necessary grip on the bunched canvas with the other. Before, he could have held tight with one thumb and two fingernails.

Come on!

They reached the edge of the pit. Peter shoved, then yanked by turns at the canvas, maneuvering her up to the edge. Her hand fought free of the canvas and clamped hard on his arm.

"Stop!" she shouted.

He shoved harder, ignoring her, and this time, the force was enough. She toppled over, sliding from the canvas, which, caught on the edge of the pit, remained behind.

A thin wail, a thud—Peter dragged himself back, unwilling to hear more. Rolling to his stomach, he crawled to the discarded ladder and used it to pull himself upright. Then he looped his right arm over the rung closest to the height of his shoulder, and attempted a step, half as long as he was used to.

He didn't fall over, so he tried another.

Left leg, helped along with his free hand, then the right. Then lifting the makeshift crutch forward again. So many parts to each step, and so few inches forward.

Ten yards from the pit, he fell, the crash winding him, leaving him gasping with his face in the dirt.

His breath returned, with the sound of Katya screaming.

She might know these tunnels, from working with the rescue team. What if she knew a way out?

He rolled onto his back, looked at the ladder, and decided it wasn't worth using it the rest of the way up to the road. Except he'd need it then, to have any hope of getting far enough to find someone. So, he hooked one braced foot in the top rung, then scooted the rest of the way uphill to the car.

As soon as he made it, he slumped against the nearest tire, resting his back and arms. Katya was quiet now, but he wasn't sure if that should relieve him or make him more afraid. Either way, he couldn't afford to rest long. He might be miles from town, and he wasn't equipped to survive the night. He wasn't even carrying any matches, now that he'd given up smoking, and the temperature might drop to forty degrees.

If it came to it, though, hypothermia wasn't a bad way to go. At least, that's what climbers said to one another.

Didn't matter. He wasn't ready yet. He'd keep moving until he dropped. And then he'd get up again, until the ladder broke or he couldn't.

Peter stood up, supporting himself with the car, and got his first look through the windows. His crutches were propped on the front seat, tips resting in the footwell.

With crutches, he could move. He could move well.

Unable to breathe, Peter tried the door handle. Unlocked. He bit his knuckle and tried not to cry.

CHAPTER FORTY-THREE

There was no sign of Peter at Brenda's place. All they found was wreckage. The destruction was terrifying.

"He's on crutches," Nathan said. "He can't have gone far."

"But he's missing!" Edie bit her thumbnail, until she could speak without her voice breaking. "We have to find him."

"I called the station. Constable Lefthand and Constable McSorely are looking," Forbes said.

"We should too," Edie insisted. "We aren't accomplishing anything here." Peter should have gone to the station long before now, and more and more she feared he hadn't because he couldn't.

"All right." Maybe Forbes was thinking the same thing.

Nathan offered to get his car and search west of Main Street.

"Go ahead," Forbes said.

Edie didn't say anything. She just watched him leave, hoping he meant it.

"You can look with me," Forbes said.

"Guess I have to. Unless I go home for Peter's car. You still haven't given me mine back." She pushed a hand against her throat, because no matter what she said, just now, she wasn't really upset about her car. Words just flew from her mouth without her thinking.

"We'll find him," Forbes said. "Usually, these things are just miscommunications."

"Really?" Edie motioned around them at the wrecked room.

"You'd be surprised," Forbes said. "And for what it's worth, I'm sorry about your car. It takes a long time to get evidence back from Calgary."

"Doesn't look like you're trying to hurry things."

He threw her a wary, sideways glance. "And you've been so forthcoming?"

Tempted to retort that he'd given her little motivation to do so, Edie kept her face smooth.

"Come on," Forbes said. "We can hurry now. I'll even let you drive."

Edie smiled tightly. For the first time, he'd said something she wanted to hear. "All right then."

Abandoning the mess at Brenda's, they jumped in his car and tore down the street.

An hour later, after driving every street in town, talking to everyone they saw, they still hadn't found him.

"Where is he?" Forbes muttered, scanning the street.

Edie drummed her fingers on the steering wheel, wishing she knew. Peter wasn't at the local. He wasn't at the library. He wasn't at home. The only remarkable thing—

She stomped the brake, hard enough that Forbes lurched forward, hands flying up to brace himself against the front of the car.

"What the hell, Edie!"

"Ms. Simmons to you," she retorted, pointing to a car parked near the end of the street, near the Li house. "That's Brenda's car. She's back."

"Let's go," Forbes said.

She sped down the street, pulling in beside Brenda's car, even though it was the wrong side of the road. Forbes didn't say anything.

He was out of his seat before she put the car in park, and rapping at the front door by the time she joined him on the front step.

"Brenda?" she called. No answer.

"I know you're here, Mrs. Li," Forbes said. "I need to speak with you. It's urgent."

The door swung open. Brenda's hair was wild, her face tearstained and swollen. "This isn't a good time," she croaked.

"I'm sorry. If it were possible to come back later, I would." Forbes stepped past her into the hall. Brenda shuffled back.

"I'd rather speak on the porch."

"If it's any consolation, Brenda, we've already been here. You left your door unlocked."

Brenda bit her lip and turned away, like it hurt to have their eyes on her.

"My brother's missing," Edie explained. "We can't find him, and he left a note saying he was coming here. Have you seen him?"

Brenda shook her head. "I just got back. Where do you think—"

"I don't know." Edie swallowed and pointed to the living room. "But you can see why I'm worried. Not just for Peter. Did Mitch do this?"

Brenda shook her head, lips trembling. "No. No. This—" Her face crumpled, and she sobbed into her hands, choking gasps from the bottom corners of her lungs.

"Let's get you some water." Edie collected Brenda with an outstretched arm and led her to the kitchen. As Brenda caught her breath, Edie raided the freezer compartment for two cubes of ice. She dropped them in a glass, filled it at the tap, and pushed it into Brenda's hands. "Slowly."

Forbes cleared his throat. "We've been—"

Edie silenced him with a glance. "Why don't you call Mr. Kwan?"

"No." Brenda squeezed her eyes shut and downed another sip. "I don't want my dad here. Not today." She stared at the glass.

"All right," Edie said, hoping she didn't look as baffled as Forbes. "Do you want to tell us what happened? You don't have to."

"Actually—" Forbes cut in.

"I haven't seen Peter," Brenda repeated quietly, and Edie bit the inside of her lip. "I left Clairbeck last night."

She drew a long, shaky breath. "Had a phone call late in the evening from an acquaintance in Edmonton. About my...about Mitch."

Edie's stomach twisted. "Why don't you sit down? I take it none of this is a police matter?" She sent a pointed glance to Forbes.

"No, no. It's—" Brenda pressed a fist to her mouth. "A private problem."

"Then perhaps I can use your telephone?" Forbes suggested. "I can update the station."

He disappeared into the living room, and Edie reached for Brenda's hand. "I'm sorry," she murmured.

For a moment, Brenda just let herself be squeezed. Then she pulled her hand free, wiped her eyes and emptied her glass into the sink.

"Mitch is cheating," she said. "One of his classmates called me. Said I should ask Mitch who's been staying overnight. I..." She licked her lips. "It was hard news to hear. I lost my temper. Then I jumped in the car. Drove all the way to Edmonton and Mitch's apartment. Then I got scared, so I just sat there by the curb for the rest of the night."

Edie reached into the cupboard and filled another glass. She took a gulp of water big enough to make her choke.

"I thought maybe it might be better just to pretend not to know," Brenda said.

Edie nodded.

"But then Mitch came outside." Brenda's voice dropped. Even leaning closer, Edie couldn't hear her next words.

"Sorry?"

Brenda swallowed. "Mitch came out with another man."

Edie set her glass down on the counter. "Shit."

Brenda nodded. "I know him. Nick and Mitch were roommates before medical school."

"Did he see you?"

Brenda nodded.

"What will you do?"

"I don't know. Drink, probably. Avoid my mom."

"Not bad ideas," Edie conceded.

Brenda made a noise, part sob, part hiccup, part laugh. "So, Peter?"

Edie drew a long breath. "Yeah." Her missing brother. "I've got to go find him. Can't stay, but I hate leaving you alone."

Brenda shrugged. "I'll be fine."

Edie snorted.

"I could call Katya. Invite her over."

"Let's call her," Edie suggested. Brenda could use some company.

But there was no answer at the Virtanens'. Brenda called twice, letting each call go to ten rings. "Guess no one's home."

Forbes glanced at Edie, then shook his head.

"They should be," Edie said. "We talked to her dad not too long ago. Even if Katya isn't home, it's weird that Mr. Virtanen isn't answering."

Forbes folded his arms. "Do we know where she was this morning?"

Edie frowned. No, they didn't. Not after she'd left the clinic. And Nathan had said he felt sick after drinking his coffee.

Suppose Katya had answered the phone, when Jill called the clinic, then dosed Nathan to clear the place out? Katya wouldn't have needed to drive to the meeting place on the road, because she knew this area well enough to hike there—and that would have allowed her to travel there and back without being seen.

"I should go over," Forbes said. "Do you—"

Edie smoothed damp palms over her trousers. She didn't want to delay her search for Peter, but Katya had access to all the things she and Brenda and Nathan did.

Nathan, though, was sort of alibied by his lawnmower. Brenda had been in Edmonton this morning, watching her life fall apart.

"I'll come too," Edie said.

CHAPTER FORTY-FOUR

I'M NEVER GOING TO COMPLAIN ABOUT CRUTCHES AGAIN, PETER thought, untruthfully. But after crawling and being stuck, this felt like galloping. He must be two hundred yards from the car already, and if he kept this up...

Just keep going, he thought grimly. The braces would keep his legs from giving out. He just had to keep his arms working, a thought that slowed him some, and made him more cautious choosing where to plant his crutches on the road.

He'd tested his body more today than he ever had, even before leaving Katya's car. Eventually, fatigue would hit him, but it hadn't yet.

For now, he needed to get as far away as possible. Find someone who could help him get back to town.

Crutches. Legs. Crutches. Legs. When that got old, he switched to counting under his breath. *One. Two. One. Two.*

At least the road was downhill.

Back in the car, Forbes radioed the station and all his officers, but no one reported any leads.

"We'll keep looking," Constable Lefthand said and signed off.

"I'm sorry," Forbes said.

"It's all right. We'll find him." Edie said.

"Miss Clark's looking," Forbes said. "And she called out the rescue team."

Edie stared at her hands. This was good news, but it frightened her. "Thanks."

There was no car now at the Virtanens', and the lights were all out.

"Door's locked," Forbes informed her.

"Try the bell again," Edie said.

While he rang, she banged on the window. "Katya! Katya!" She pressed her face against the glass, trying to peer into the dark room. All she could make out was the bright yellow afghan Mr. Virtanen had covered his stumps with that afternoon. Maybe he was still with it? Lying on the couch?

"I can't break in," Forbes said. "Not without a reason, and—"

Edie swallowed, so she wouldn't snap at him. "Mr. Virtanen is a patient at the clinic. I'm a nurse. He's not answering. If he's home, he should have heard us. Or answered the phone. Break open the door."

Forbes shrugged. "Works for me, but you might end up paying to replace it."

"Just open it," she told him.

Forbes pulled back the storm door, then with disconcerting ease, kicked the front door in.

"After you," he said, stepping aside.

Edie rushed in, switching on the lights, heart stopping when she spied Mr. Virtanen beneath his afghan in the living room. He shouldn't have slept though this much noise.

He was still, one hand resting atop the blanket, looking eerily like Leo.

Edie swore and bent over him, pressing hard with both hands on his shoulders. "Mr. Virtanen!" She shouted in both ears.

His eyes squeezed tighter, and he mumbled, "What the hell?"

Edie slumped, covering her eyes with one hand. "I was worried. You weren't answering, and Katya's car is gone."

He blinked, focusing on her face, then glanced about the room. "No, Katya's here. She brought me my coffee. We were about to have cake with your brother."

Her hand tightened on his shoulders again, until he shrugged her off.

"Peter was here?"

"Still here, unless—" He swept a clumsy hand over his eyes. "You're saying he's gone? I guess I must have fallen asleep. Afraid I often do in the afternoons."

Forbes leaned in. "Was Mr. Simmons here with your daughter? Did they leave together?"

Mr. Virtanen plucked fretfully at the blanket, glancing between them. "No. Why would they do that?"

"It's important," Forbes said. "If you don't remember, I'd rather know."

Mr. Virtanen sat up, rubbing his forehead. "I'm not feeling well today. I…I'm pretty sure he left."

Forbes blew out a breath. He set the folder of Peter's pictures on the coffee table and paced to the window and back.

"What about your daughter? Would she leave a note?"

"Maybe. But not if she was just running out for a few minutes," Mr. Virtanen said.

"I'll take a look," Forbes said.

For a second, Mr. Virtanen looked ready to protest, but he must have thought better of it. He pushed himself partway up the cushions and watched from the couch as Forbes darted away to the telephone.

"We called you from the station," Edie said quietly. "That was a while ago."

"Didn't hear it."

Edie nodded, painfully aware of the near-empty cup of coffee, but not wanting to draw his attention to it. She crouched down and reached for his wrist. "You look a little worse for wear today. Can I take your pulse?"

Not that it would tell her much. What she wanted was a vial of blood, to test along with the coffee.

"I'm fine," he said.

"Do you want the bathroom?" Edie tried. "I can help."

"Sure. If you don't mind," he said, a little abashed.

"It's no problem." She slipped a hand to his waist, and he set one arm on her shoulder, to transfer back to his wheelchair. He swayed as he moved, sliding forward, as if his muscles weren't responding as expected. Edie just managed to keep him from falling, straining to help him shift to the wheelchair.

She wheeled him to the bathroom. "Want more help?"

"No, I'm steadier now."

Skeptical, Edie withdrew to the living room. "Okay, but call me if you change your mind."

She picked up the coffee cup, sniffed it, then dipped a finger in and brought it to her mouth. No good. The drink was brewed so strongly, you could have hidden anything in it, even before the heavy dose of sugar.

Abandoning the cup, she joined Forbes in the hall. He was still talking on the phone, listening and interjecting "uh-huh" at regular intervals. She caught him by the arm. "We've got to find Peter," she hissed under her breath.

He nodded, waving her away impatiently.

"Nurse Simmons?" Mr. Virtanen called.

Edie grimaced. "Coming."

She returned him to the living room, then went back to the bathroom to wash her hands, passing Forbes again. He was still muttering intently into the receiver.

Her stomach was discovering all kinds of new, elaborate knots. If anything happened to Peter...

There were scuff marks on the floor, just outside the bathroom door. On impulse, Edie leaned closer, tracing a finger over the scarred hardwood. She glanced ahead at the bathroom lino.

No scuffs once you passed the threshold.

Straightening, she turned on the taps and began scrubbing her hands. No scuffs and nothing out of place, not in here.

Nothing except the cabinet. It was slightly open, just a hair's breadth away from engaging the magnetic latch. And there were fingerprints on the side of the mirror. Everything else was wiped clean.

Edie pushed open the door to the medicine cabinet, and her thoughts dropped out of her head. She reached for the sink, steadying herself on numb hands.

"Sergeant Forbes?"

No answer. She tried again. This time, she heard him set the phone back on the receiver.

"What is it?" He sounded impatient.

"Can you come here?" She drew a long breath, staring at the shelves in front of her. "You should see this."

So many bottles.

CHAPTER FORTY-FIVE

His shoulders ached. The skin in his armpits burned. Peter chose a tree in the distance, close to the edge of the highway. He'd pause and rest his arms there.

Pain jolted him with every hop forward. Three yards from the tree, he shut his eyes and stopped, pushing his weight through his hands, shoulders sagging.

He didn't recognize this road, but with so much focus bent on mustering the necessary strength, he could be almost anywhere and not know it. This was worse than learning to breathe again on his own. Worse than fighting and failing to roll himself over in bed.

He shifted his weight into his shoulders again and let out a pained cry. But he'd hiked on blisters before, and this was the same. Sort of.

Lips ironed flat, he chose another landmark, a fallen tree about twenty yards off, and started moving again.

He made it half the distance this time, then tried again. His reserves were shrinking fast.

On his next break, he thought he heard something over the pulse in his ears. He lifted his head, breathing too hard to straighten all the way up.

A shout, and then the shrill of a whistle. It might have been coming from anywhere, an echo from miles away.

"Here!" he shouted, but his voice faded into silence. He tried again. "Over here!"

In all likelihood, the caller was Katya.

He started forward again, and this time made it about fifty yards.

Another whistle. Another shout.

"Help! I'm on the road!"

He waited for seconds that felt like lifetimes, then, faintly, caught the sound of the voice, calling words he couldn't understand. Then, louder, three blasts on a whistle, followed by shouted words again. He nearly stumbled at the last one—it sounded like "coming."

He stood by the side of the road, waiting as the shouts drew closer, answering each one, until at last he heard a car. When the police cruiser appeared, churning up clouds of dust, Peter raised a hand to his eyes, as if brushing away the sweat and the dust, and swallowed twice.

The car rolled to a stop, and the doors flew open, releasing Constable Lefthand and Brenda.

"Glad we found you," Lefthand said, jamming his hands in his back pockets. "Been looking a good while."

Peter nodded, unable to trust his voice.

"Got some water in the car," Lefthand said.

Brenda went for it, unscrewing the canteen before holding it out. Peter reached and nearly toppled, but Brenda darted to his side.

"Careful," she said, slipping a steadying arm around his waist.

Lefthand moved to his other shoulder. "You okay?"

No, not really. "I'll be fine," is what he said aloud.

He drank half the canteen, choking and spilling water from his mouth.

Brenda's grip tightened. "Let me help you to the car."

"Thanks." He needed it. Even with her help, there was a lot of wincing.

Lefthand busied himself with the radio, briskly sending out call signs. "Ten-twenty calling in from mine side road. We've found him. Repeat, we've found him."

"Any more water?" Peter asked, surprised to find the canteen empty.

"That's all of it," Brenda said apologetically. "But there'll be more soon."

In disjointed sentences, through cracked lips, he relayed the struggle between him and Katya. "She's hurt. Not sure how bad, but I had to get away. If she'd come after me—"

Lefthand cut him off with a nod. "We'll find her." He started the car, sending quick commands through the radio as he turned around on the road. A couple minutes later, another cruiser passed them, driving up the road, lights flashing. Some of the residual tension in Peter's chest slackened.

He must have looked as bad as he felt, because instead of driving to the station, Lefthand took him home. Brenda helped him into the house, and a minute later, Edie pulled up, tumbling from the car in her haste.

"Peter!" She burst into the house, smudge-cheeked, with bits of branch clinging to her trousers, and caught him in a hug so fierce he couldn't have escaped, even if he'd wanted to.

"Thank God," she said, the words almost lost in his chest.

"Tell me everything," Edie commanded, once he was lying on the couch, pajamas on, braces off, and legs elevated. "Half the town was looking for you."

"It was a close call," Peter admitted. He ran a hand through his wet hair.

"Where's Brenda?" Edie looked behind her. No Brenda in sight, but she'd left two glasses of ice water on the coffee table.

"Slipped out when that guy came in," Peter said, nodding at Forbes.

She'd left without a word, just a wave to him and a mouthed "See you later."

"I was so worried," Edie said. "I just about died a dozen times today."

"Me too," Peter said, with a half-hearted smile.

Her mouth pinched tight. "Tell me."

Peter glanced at Forbes. "You need to take this down?"

"Some," he said. "We'll get a detailed statement later, but I'm pretty sure I'll remember this."

The story was a long one, and twice they were interrupted by phone calls: from Nathan (a short call) and their parents (a much longer one). Edie was a thorough interrogator, grilling him even longer than Forbes, who took careful notes.

"We'll find her," he said, when Peter finished. "Orvo might say more, if he knows we can get him away from her, someplace safe." He shifted on his feet.

"It'll take a while, I'm afraid. We'll have to make a thorough search of the clinic records. But the picture in her house, the tin of buttons... it's all pretty suggestive."

"So is kidnapping me," Peter said.

"Yeah. Next time, see me first," Forbes said.

Peter thought of a sharp response, but he could tell that this time, Edie agreed with the detective. So, he kept his mouth shut.

"I've got to go. We'll call once we find her," Forbes said.

Edie walked him to the door. She returned by way of the kitchen, carrying a sandwich and a glass of iced tea.

"You should eat."

"Who's looking after Mr. Virtanen?"

Edie shrugged. "I'm sure someone's gone over. His friends will make sure he's not alone. Not that anyone knows what to think of this."

"I sure don't." Peter tugged the blanket higher, and reached for the sandwich.

"I don't either." Edie sat down across from him. "Finish that. Mom will kill me if you don't. She and Dad are coming out tomorrow."

Peter ate the sandwich.

"No, don't get up." Edie snatching the empty plate. She shivered. "I need a bath. But if you want to go first—"

He shook his head. He definitely needed one, not just a splash at the sink. Too tired to manage it now though. Maybe after a nap.

"Gonna sleep first. I can barely move."

"Let me help you."

He wanted to argue, but knew that right now, he probably couldn't do it without her.

She pushed his wheelchair to the bedroom and helped him into the bed.

"It'll take you a while to come back from this," she said. "You need to rest."

"Yeah."

But he couldn't think about that for long. He was asleep almost as soon as she turned on the water.

The phone rang, startling him awake. Peter sat up, listening to Edie stumbling down the hall to answer it. Though the curtains were closed, he could tell it was dark, but he didn't know if he'd slept for hours or days.

"Yes?" Edie said.

"Oh, hi. Yes...yes, I understand. Thanks for telling me."

The rain that had threatened in the evening was pelting the windows now, driven in violent gusts. He must have been sound asleep, not to wake in this storm.

Everything ached, but his own smell was bad enough to drive him out of bed. Time for that bath. Peter positioned his legs with his hands, ready to drag himself from mattress to wheelchair.

"Sergeant?" Edie's voice came again from the hall.

"Alley-oop," Peter whispered under his breath, and launched, landing hard in the chair.

"*Sergeant?*"

Frowning, Peter wheeled into the hall. "What's wrong?"

Edie frowned at the receiver. "I lost him," she said, pressing her finger on the hang-up button. "And there's no dial tone. I can't call him back."

"What did he want?" It was the middle of the night. Too late for ordinary phone calls.

"They haven't found Katya. Search teams went into the tunnels, but they couldn't find her. Forbes wanted us to know." She rubbed her arms, then marched past him and shut the living room window.

"Sorry. I'm being silly," she said when she turned around. "Forgot about that one. Good thing it's under the porch."

"After a day like today..." Peter shrugged. "Forgetting things makes sense to me."

She relaxed into a smile. "Yeah."

"I'll check the back door," Peter said. "Make sure it's locked."

She nodded, and he wheeled off, tires squeaking on the lino. "Everything's fine," he called. Even from across the kitchen, he could see the dead bolt, locked. He turned away, satisfied, and spotted a black smear on the edge of the countertop.

He wheeled closer. It had been a while since he or Edie had done the cleaning. But neither of their hands ever got as dirty as that.

He steered to the sink, still desperate for a drink. A used cup was in the bottom, and he didn't mind using that. His mouth tasted like death.

A drink of water, first. Then he'd brush his teeth and *then* take a bath. By the time he was out of the water, Edie could have a fire going in the living room. He was going to park himself on the couch and not move for a week.

He reached into the sink, then stopped. He looked back at the smudge. A hand wasn't that black unless it touched coal.

His skin went cold. "Edie?"

Something moved. Maybe she'd gone to check the window in her bedroom.

"Was that your door, Edie?" He wouldn't have seen her pass, not here at the sink.

No answer. His pulse jumped. "Edie?"

Silence, but then… "What is it, Peter?"

She was more upset by Forbes's phone call than he'd thought. Her voice was tight, strangled.

"Wanna put the radio on?" Some noise would lighten this atmosphere.

"Maybe later."

He frowned. She didn't sound right.

"I'll make some tea," he said and turned on the tap. With the noise covering the sound of his tires, he swung out of the kitchen, gathering momentum as he sped down the hall. Most of the nurses had looked the other way when he and a couple guys on the ward held races down the corridors. But some of the nurses joined in—timing them or setting up an obstacle course. Peter had learned speed, and to turn on a dime.

Yanking one wheel back, he lurched sideways, turning into the living room. Katya was pressing his sister back in her chair, hands tight on her throat.

No time to think. Pushing with all his might, he careened into her, momentum taking her out at the knees. She fell forward, grip loosening. Edie let out a gasp, thrashed her way free, and shoved Katya back into his lap.

"You're gonna—" That was as far as she got. Peter's arms flew around her, pinning her close, and Edie lunged, grabbing her by the throat.

"Gonna what?" Edie snarled, arms tightening. "Send you to prison?"

Katya kicked Peter's shins. Pain lanced up his leg, but it barely twitched. He clasped tighter, waiting for her struggles to lessen, but she squirmed and bucked with impossible energy, clawing at his arms.

"Don't let go!" Edie gasped.

"I won't," he muttered.

And he didn't, until she slumped in his lap.

"Is she dead?" he asked, when Edie let go and took a step back.

"I don't much care. See if you can find a pulse if you want." She pushed a hand through her hair. There was a rip in the shoulder of her pajamas, from sometime during the struggle, and bruises shadowing her neck.

"Don't let her move." She went to the front door, then returned with her bag. "What's her pulse?"

"I'm not sure." He was too rattled to detect anything.

"Well, I'm not risking her waking up." Edie pulled out a bottle and a syringe. Peter opened his mouth, then bit his lip.

Edie filled the syringe, flicked the glass twice, then jammed it in Katya's arm. "A tranquilizer. Just in case."

"Mind taking her off me?"

Edie raised her eyebrows. "I have to call the police."

She left the room, and Peter gave Katya a push, sending her falling to the floor.

"Dammit, Peter."

"What?"

"We've got a flood in the kitchen." The water switched off. Until now, he'd forgotten all about it, not even noticing the sound.

"Bad?" He backed away from Katya. With her body blocking the way in front of him, backward was the only way out.

"I got it. Watch her. Call if she twitches."

He didn't want to look at her. It made him feel light-headed again, like waking in her car and struggling down that interminable road.

Edie's footsteps came closer.

"Is the phone working?" he called.

"No. I think she must have done something to the line. She came for me as soon as you went to the kitchen. Caught me by surprise."

Peter's hands tightened on the rims of his wheels. It helped with the shaking. "That was a close one."

"Yeah."

She picked up his hand and held it for a long time. A hand squeeze was easier in a wheelchair than a hug. Peter concentrated on the warmth of her fingers. Right now, a hand squeeze was just fine.

"I think we should avoid the close calls for a while," she said.

"Definitely."

"How are we going to call the police?"

With Katya unconscious in the living room, they decided it was probably safe for Edie to use Leo's phone. Peter watched from the window as, armed with a flashlight and a dusty golf club, Edie sprinted across the yard there and back.

"They're coming," she said, between pants, upon her return.

Then they waited until police stormed the house and took Katya away. To the hospital, they said, but Peter wasn't sure it would help. His sister was tired and tense, and though she said the dose she'd administered would sedate Katya for several hours, he couldn't see that she felt any scruples over the drug doing anything worse.

Wasn't sure he felt any either. Mostly, he just felt sore.

But that, he knew from experience, would pass. Wearily, they both waded through another batch of questions.

"You want me to leave a constable here?" Forbes asked.

They glanced at each other.

"Edie's got her golf clubs," Peter said. "We'll be fine."

Forbes nodded. "Yeah, people will think twice now before trying to take either of you out."

"Hopefully," Edie said, with just a splash of vinegar.

Forbes grinned. "I sure would."

The front door clicked shut. Edie rose to lock and bolt it.

"Hey," Peter said.

Edie glanced at him.

He held out his hand. "We'll be okay."

She nodded. "Yeah. I might need to move though."

Neither of them said anything for a long time. "Houses aren't everything," she said at last.

CHAPTER FORTY-SIX

THREE MONTHS LATER

"Sure you don't want to come?" Edie paused at the front door, in the middle of buttoning her coat.

"Yup. Have fun." Peter had absolutely no interest in the mine rescue team and couldn't think he'd be any use at all to them, unless they wanted someone to record the meeting minutes. But Edie had taken an interest. She gone to their meetings for the last three weeks.

"Is Irwin going to be there?"

"He always is. He's the medical supervisor." Her voice was clipped, neutral.

Not him then. But Edie'd been careful with her lipstick tonight, so maybe there was someone else. Not a bad thing, really. He'd have to wait and see.

He studied the contact sheet of photos he'd taken: shots of Jill. According to Sergeant Forbes, they were instrumental to the prosecution's case. Katya had pulled through and was now in prison, awaiting trial.

"What are you thinking?"

Peter looked up and found that Edie had moved beside him.

"Do you think I could do this? Make a living at it?"

She put a hand on his shoulder. "You did a great job with them.

Forbes said so a few times. And you've been really busy with all those books."

She motioned at the stack of forensic photography texts piled beside him on the couch.

"I had a call today," Peter said slowly. "There was a fire yesterday, at a ranch near Cochrane. The insurance firm wants someone to take pictures for their investigation."

"Think Forbes passed on your name?"

"Must have."

"Well, then." She smiled. "Sounds like maybe you could."

"It's not the sa—"

"Peter." Her hand tightened briefly on his shoulder. "Nothing will be."

"I know. But I might like this. Is that weird?"

She shook her head. "Not at all. Well, maybe just a little. But I think you'd be brilliant at it. No one else noticed the buttons."

These were also key evidence in the case, and the multiple charges laid against Katya Virtanen. There'd been seventy-three buttons in that Altoids tin.

"No one else noticed the switched X-rays. You spotted that."

"Wish I'd seen it sooner." Edie chewed her bottom lip. "Leo noticed it. And Jack. They just looked the wrong way. I guess we did too, for a while."

Peter thought about asking her how Nathan was doing, then thought better of it. The police had charges pending against him too. Peter guessed he'd plead guilty. Garrett had mentioned yesterday that the town council was talking about recruiting a new doctor.

"I'm glad you're okay," Edie said.

"Of course I am," Peter said, then realized maybe she meant more than getting away from Katya. She was looking at the contact sheets, spread out on his lap. "I'll have to leave for Cochrane pretty early tomorrow."

To do the job well, he'd need an assistant. His mobility wasn't good enough to do everything on his own. But that wasn't an insurmountable problem. His mom had agreed to drive out from Calgary tomorrow to help, and if he found enough work, he'd eventually look at training someone.

There was even a course he could take, in Winnipeg, next fall. Though confident with his cameras, it wouldn't hurt to have specific training and extra credentials.

"See you later." Edie squeezed his shoulder. "Have fun planning."

He watched the car drive away—hers, finally—smiled briefly at the for-sale sign stuck in the front lawn, and picked up his notebook to go over his list of equipment again. With his legs the way they were, he needed to appear as knowledgeable and competent as he could.

It had been fun today, testing out his flashes, filters, and tripod. They'd been packed away for too long.

He was putting away the contact sheets when the doorbell rang.

Peter reached for his crutches. He couldn't just invite the caller in, because Edie would have locked the door. They were both pretty nervous about that, these days.

"Give me a minute." He hopped to the door and peered through the window.

It was Brenda. He opened the door.

"Hi, Peter." She had her hair in a ponytail, and wore a slim-fitting sweater, cropped trousers, and black ballet flats—one foot was hiding, rubbing the back of her other leg.

"Come in." He felt bad that she seemed nervous, but she probably suspected he knew about Mitch. And Edie *had* explained to him why Brenda had left town, after tearing apart the front room of her house.

He smiled, so it wouldn't look like he was uncomfortable or feeling sorry for her. "How are you, Brenda?"

"I've been taking some time off work," she said.

"Yeah, Edie told me. Want a beer? Tea?" He remembered that she preferred it to coffee.

"Tea would be great. But I can make it."

"My arms are fine now," he said.

"I'd feel better doing it," she said, looking down at her feet. "I'm here to ask a favor."

His eyebrows shot up. "Okay. We can both do it." Fixing a couple cups of tea wasn't exactly a job for two, but he understood that sometimes difficult words came easier when your hands were busy.

He brought her to the kitchen. "Tea's in there." He pointed to the canister and went to fill the kettle.

She didn't say anything though, until they both had full cups, and were seated at the table.

"There's milk in the fridge, if you want."

She shook her head. "I want a divorce," she said. "Edie told me it's not easy. I asked her a lot of questions, and it sounds like hell. Then I spoke to that lawyer, and he confirmed it. And I've talked to Mitch. Talked and talked to him. He just says no."

Her lips pressed together, disappearing. "He wants me, but just for appearances. I can't live like that."

Peter stared at his cup. "You shouldn't have to."

"I don't think so either. He disagrees. But I think if Mitch knows I can show proof of..." She faltered. "adultery..."

"You want photographs," Peter said.

Brenda nodded once. "I've thought it over. Not to show anyone—he should have his privacy. When he explained what his life has been like, I do feel bad for him. He hasn't liked lying to me."

She sighed and swiped hastily at one eye. "But I deserve some things too. And I need to convince him to give me what I want."

"What's that?" Peter asked.

Brenda drew a deep breath. "A fresh start. Some alimony. I've worked to put him through medical school, and I've tried to be a good wife. So, I shouldn't leave with nothing. I want what's fair."

Her shoulders were tight, just inches from her ears.

"I'll do it," Peter said. His pulse thumped, loud and fast in his neck.

Maybe this wasn't a good idea. Too much, too fast, but if this was an actual opportunity, he didn't want to let it pass.

Just say it. Take the jump.

"I want to try this type of work." He turned his cup in his hands, too nervous to look at her. "Forensic photography. Fire inspections. Crime scenes. Surveillance, like what you want on Mitch. But, well..." He gestured at his legs. "I can't do it on my own. I'll need an assistant."

He licked his lips and chanced a look up. Brenda frowned at him, thoughtful.

"Want to try it out?" *She won't*, he thought to himself. *Why would anyone?*

"I don't know if I'd be very helpful," she said.

"You could be. Don't know until you try." He took a swallow of tea, and winced, because it was still too hot.

A smile, slight at first, grew at the corners of her mouth. "Ok. Yeah. Sure."

"I'm actually photographing a fire scene tomorrow," Peter rubbed the back of his neck. Mom wouldn't mind if he canceled with her. "And you don't have to work. You want to come along? We could tackle Edmonton right after."

"I'm not going back to the clinic for another month," Brenda said. "Let's try it. Why not?"

Peter grinned and raised his cup for her to clink. He had a good feeling about this, and it was pretty great, just to be trying.

AUTHOR'S NOTE

Most of this book is based on true things, but some are made up, and when I write a book, disclosure feels almost as necessary as the final arrest. So, let's imagine we're in an Agatha Christie–esque library—I'm ready to confess.

Canadian readers (especially Alberta readers) will have gathered that Clairbeck is Canmore, a jewel of a town with a gritty, coal-mining past. In recent decades, it's become a bougie retreat full of resorts and weekenders, and if you ever get the chance to go, you must. It is a wonderful place. So many of my best memories are from here. I truly loved imagining it as the setting for this book. The Clairbeck I wrote is smaller than Canmore was in the 1950s, which is why I felt the name change was necessary. I also changed the proximity of some nearby towns, so they became Hillview and Blunt Creek. Other places, which stayed truer to their real size, appearance, and location, retain their actual names.

Ha Ling Peak is real, and it's named for the railway worker who summited it at incredible speed on a dare, but in the 1950s, this mountain would have been called another, less complimentary name. The official name change took place in the 1990s when community members advocated for more accurate and more equal naming of this beautiful mountain.

In the 1950s, Canmore was home to numerous immigrant

communities, some new, some generations old. The discriminatory policies described by Brenda Li are all real. And while it is only touched on elliptically in this book, so is the oppression of Indigenous people in nearby Mînî Thnî (Morley) and throughout Canada.

Unfortunately, there's ample history that served as inspiration for Katya Virtanen. If you've read my novel *The Specimen*, you're aware of my preoccupation with medical ethics and instances where they are ignored and unexercised. The vulnerabilities and power imbalance inherent in health care practice give rise to truly frightening scenarios. Some known serial killers who worked in health care and medicine include Dr. Thomas Neill Cream, Elizabeth Wettlaufer, Charles Cullen, Dr. Harold Shipman, and Dr. John Bodkin Adams, who Edie is supposed to have read about in Jack's legal journals. Except I cheated here, because Adams's trial for murder (and his acquittal) occurred in 1957, after the book takes place. But in the 1940s and '50s, over 150 of his patients died in comas, and many of these deceased patients left him financial legacies or valuable gifts in their wills. I also read testimony that he was sticky-fingered and known to lift things from patients: fountain pens, art, expensive wines.

More things I didn't make up: Divorce procedures in the 1950s in Alberta. Minox II mini cameras. Polio.

The most severe epidemic in Alberta was in 1953, the same year Jonas Salk began testing his vaccine on 1.6 million children in Canada, Finland, and the U.S. In the years that followed, widespread vaccination nearly eradicated the disease, and for many, the terrible consequences of polio infection were largely forgotten.

I didn't "know" polio, but growing up, my grandmother told me stories about driving to visit her young son, my uncle, in the polio ward at a Calgary hospital, several hours' drive from their home in southern Alberta. Even as a child, I could tell that had been hard. She showed me black-and-white pictures of visits they made at Christmases and birthdays, and portraits they had taken, when my preschool-aged uncle was allowed a visit home. My dad says some of his earliest memories are of that long stretch of straight Alberta highway and the hospital parking lot.

Back then, it was common for polio patients to spend years in the hospital. Paralyzed by the virus that destroyed their motor nerves, patients fought through years of rehabilitation. As nerve cells that were spared slowly grew new branches and reinnervated muscles, patients could recover their ability to breathe independently, sit, stand, and walk.

But dead neurons don't come back, so recovery was variable (and, as many young patients eventually learned, it couldn't always last).

As a practicing occupational therapist, I've met some wonderful people who use wheelchairs or other mobility aids. I am not a wheelchair user—yet—but I've learned that, in the natural course of things, I probably will be someday. Walkers, scooters, wheelchairs—at some point, if we are lucky enough to get that far, accessibility will matter to all of us, so it's something we all should think about now. Peter is made up, but I have seen his style of adaptability, courage, and persistence many, many times.

Back to the mountains. It's time to own up to my other lies.

First, the hot springs in this book are not in Canmore. The ones I've written about—Lussier Springs—are actually in the Kootenays in British Columbia. They are even better than I can write them and are worth seeking out. One nice thing about writing is you can just plunk two of your favorite places beside each other, as if they'd been together all along.

Also, I said that Peter is made up, but there is a real Peter, one who never got polio or worked as a climber-photographer or felt compelled to solve a crime. But he did grow up in Banff National Park, where his dad worked for the park service. And he hiked and skied and loved the mountains and taught his kids and his grandkids to do the same, including me.

So that part—a guy who loved his people enough to do just about anything and found happiness and peace hiking up trail and scree to find a perfect view—is definitely true.

READING GROUP GUIDE

1. Discuss the relationship and differences between Jill and Edie. Do you think Jill has a reason to dislike Edie or vice versa?

2. How does chronic illness and disability play a role in the novel?

3. Discuss the sibling relationship between Peter and Edie. How does it grow over time?

4. The community and friendships in this small town are vital. Discuss some of the relationships or friendships and how they interact with other characters.

5. Mountain towns and mining communities historically have had issues with substance abuse. Discuss what causes these issues and where we see them in the novel.

6. Being inside of the killer's head with their POV chapters allows us some insight into their thoughts. Discuss the motivations of the killer and if there were any identifying clues in their POV.

7. Do you think Jack was a bad person? Consider his dynamic between Edie and Jill and his investigation into Irwin.

8. No-fault divorce was especially hard to file for during this time period. Discuss the evolution of divorce and what rights women have now that they didn't in the 1950s.

A CONVERSATION WITH THE AUTHOR

You have a few books under your belt at this point. How is *Don't Look Close* different from what you've done previously, and which book would you say was hardest to write?

It's strange to think that, but yes, I guess I do! *Don't Look Close* is different to me because it draws more from my family than other books, being closer in time and place (and people). I'm not sure if this made it harder or easier. I cut more from this book than I have with other projects, probably because I was letting too many memories seep in—bits inspired by stories my grandmothers told me about going to university here in the late 1940s, things they'd eat and wear and buy, stuff that wasn't necessary to the story. I find that every book is exciting and difficult to write in its own way—*The Specimen* grew longer with each revision, and this book tightened up.

And of course, writing these solo novels is very different than co-writing as Audrey Blake. Some things are harder with solo writing, and some things are easier. I get to decide and write everything. And I *have* to decide and write everything.

Peter is an interesting character, with a rich background. Was it difficult to write a character with polio? Was there any research or resources you used to inform his illness?

I was careful with my research but probably not in the way you think. There's ample material online and in books about polio and people affected by it, and I used public sources extensively. The care came because, in writing a character for public consumption, I didn't want to impinge on my extended family's privacy. I purposely did not ask my uncle to tell me about his childhood in the hospital or his experiences as a polio survivor while writing this book. And because Peter contracted the disease as an adult, his experiences would have been significantly different.

What colored Peter for me were the stories I heard before I started writing the book—tender and painful reminiscences from my dad and my grandmother, which inspired me to go looking in the provincial archives and learn more about the polio epidemic here and the treatment, recovery, and lives of the people who were affected. While Peter came to me as a character because of things I knew growing up in the family that I did, I drew facts and details and images from other places as much as possible. Also, I've worked as an occupational therapist for a while now… That background helps.

When writing this novel, how different was it to have main characters that were siblings?

It was so different! Usually protagonist pairs are linked romantically, and though I enjoy a love story as much as anyone else, I was excited to try writing something different. I wonder if centering romantic storylines by default (especially in fiction for women) is a little unhealthy? People are so much more than their romantic relationships, and I know that my life is better because it has lots of kinds of love in it.

Losing romantic impetus as a plot device was a challenge, but it allowed me to draw instead from my wells of sibling experience: arguments, insane pettiness, incredible loyalty. Siblings have so much shared experience, and for many of us, our siblings are the people we will know the longest. I liked that Peter and Edie could have hang-ups and conflict and still be strong allies.

What do you hope readers will take away from this novel?

That they enjoy the read! Most of all, I hope readers are drawn in by the characters and the predicaments and feel things along with them. Writing and reading is sharing an imagination. I am always inspired by the magic of that partnership (and I think that's why I tend to be sparse with physical descriptions of my main characters—I have tried adding more, but I like letting readers color inside those lines better). I'm always grateful for the gift of readers' time and attention and hope they feel it has paid off.

Peter's hobby of photography is an interesting one in how it evolves over time, from nature to forensics. When creating your characters, how do you determine what hobbies or skills they have?

Shoot. This is a tough one. My own interests really come into play (looking at you, history and medical ethics). In writing *The Specimen*, the years I spent playing violin really helped me connect to a musician character like Isobel Tait. But sometimes I pick up a hobby because it seems appropriate for a character and it helps me write them better. For instance, I tried a couple of embroidery projects while writing *The Specimen*, and Edie is a knitter because that's what I was doing at the time. (Specifically, a thistle-patterned colorwork sweater that I was inspired to try because of the setting of *The Specimen*. Is the sweater finished yet? No, it is not.)

Also, knitting seemed like the perfect thing for Edie to do back when she was working nights as a student nurse.

Peter probably became a photographer because I was looking at so many stunning pictures. Mountain climbers were really pushing limits then and recording their achievements with incredible images. As a career, photography just made sense for Peter, given what he loved and where he was. The shift to forensic photography also made sense, because it suited his strengths and his changed physical abilities. Also, there were a lot of fascinating technological advances in forensic science throughout the twentieth century (I see that my own interests are coming into play again), and the field seemed like a good place for Peter to land. That mattered to me because I like him a lot.

There are POVs of the killer scattered throughout the novel. Was it hard to get into that headspace? How different was writing those scenes compared to Edie's or Peter's POV?

This killer is based on actual killers (see how careful I'm being to avoid spoilers? Just in case!), and there were lots of good sources about them. So I was able to pull characteristics to create a composite person I hope feels authentic. These scenes did take lots of revising because it was hard to say enough without giving away too much. The balance between dropping interesting breadcrumbs and obvious giveaways wasn't exactly easy for me.

This is the second book you've worked on that deals with ethics in medicine. What motivates you to write about these premises?

My own weirdness? I mean, at this point, I have to admit I've gone really far down the rabbit hole, and it still fascinates me. That said, I think health care ethics are an important subject. When our providers aren't trustworthy, we are so vulnerable. And when we don't (or won't) trust health care providers (or science), we lose too, especially in the area of public health.

Divorce was especially difficult for women to obtain during this time period, especially a no-fault divorce. Can you talk about what Edie and Brenda might have had to face in order to make this happen?

In fact, no-fault divorce wasn't available in Canada until 1986. Before that, divorce was only available on the basis of a "matrimonial offense." And until 1968, there was no federal divorce legislation at all. Divorce was under provincial jurisdiction, and in Alberta, it was only available by an act of legislation. It's exhausting even to think about.

To get a divorce in the 1950s, you had to enlist an elected official, who would have to agree to enter a petition that would have to be passed by the provincial legislature. To succeed, you needed connections, and a lot of money. It also helped if your hopefully-ex-spouse wasn't fighting the proceedings. Because most lawyers and legislators at the time were men, I imagine it must have been incredibly difficult just to recruit people willing to take on your case.

Another problem women faced was that their divorced husband typically remained financially responsible for them for the rest of their lives. So you can imagine how motivated they would be to make a split legal. I read so many cases where women were murdered by their husbands, who didn't want to have to pay for their upkeep. It's tragic.

When education and employment opportunities for women were so limited, it makes sense (kind of?) that government wouldn't want divorced women to be destitute. So this was a protection for women (sort of), but it played out in pretty ugly ways. Thankfully, as financial opportunities grew for women and divorce laws liberalized, this changed. But vigilance about our rights and ongoing advocacy remains important.

ACKNOWLEDGMENTS

This book owes much to many, and I'm bound to embarrass myself by forgetting to mention someone. Probably that person knows how scattered I tend to be and understands. Point it out to me, and I'll make it up to you with chocolate.

I am very grateful to my family, who inspires so much of this book: First, pancakes and hikes in the mountains and arguments at a tempo that outsiders can't follow (something I had to edit out in this book) but mostly the assurance that when push comes to shove, you are there with help and humor and comfort. I am absurdly fortunate to have you all, particularly such a supportive (and numerous!) band of siblings and siblings-in-law. I'm not going to name you because there are enough of you that it feels like bragging. But you are the best.

Oversized thanks are due, as ever, to my agent, Jennifer Weltz, who read my writing and liked it enough to make it better *and* finagle it onto bookshelves, which is much more complicated than it sounds. I am lucky enough to be supported by her and the team at JVNLA, including Ariana Philips and Cole Hildebrand. Thank you.

Somehow (and honestly, it's starting to feel ridiculous), I also get to work with a fantastic editor, Jenna Jankowski, and an incredible publishing team at Sourcebooks and Recorded Books, including Gretchen Stelter, Melissa Rechter, Annabelle Harsch, Ashley Burns,

Lynn Gonzales, Aimee Alker, and Sarah Brody. Jenna, thank you for the trust, encouragement, and confidence. And for finding my big and small mistakes.

Sarah Brinley of Wildflower and Main Editorial assisted me once again with insightful and timely developmental editing. She reads first, and so she probably suffers the most.

I was fortunate to receive grant funding from the Alberta Foundation for the Arts in writing this book, which allowed me to take extra time away from work to focus on drafting and conduct additional on-site research. And when I confused myself working on the grant application, I was ably and generously helped by the late Brenda Hennig. My interactions with Brenda were brief, but her support is remembered and appreciated by me and many others in the Alberta writing community.

Finally, there are not enough pages to express the gratitude I feel for readers and friends who pick up my books and enjoy them. But these thanks are ones that particularly matter, and I hope that in giving my best, I show sufficient gratitude for your time and trust and attention.

Many thanks. Happy reading.

Jaima

ABOUT THE AUTHOR

© Alexander Aulenbach

Jaima Fixsen is a *USA Today* and international bestselling author living and writing in Alberta, Canada. Her novel *The Specimen* was a finalist for the 2025 Crime Writers of Canada Best Novel Award. Jaima studied occupational therapy at the University of Alberta, spurring an interest in health care ethics, which often figures in her books, including the historical novels she cowrites under the pen name, Audrey Blake. Jaima loves reading, snow, mountains, snow, history, snow...and her dog.

MORE FROM JAIMA FIXSEN